THE STARTERS

ROBIN ALLEN

Book 1:
Unexpected

The following story is fictional.
It does not depict any actual person or event.

THE STARTERS
BY
ROBIN ALLEN

The Starters: Novel Series - Book 1: Unexpected
Copyright © 2012 - by Robin Hampton Allen
All rights reserved.
ISBN: 1468111485
ISBN-13: 9781468111484
CreateSpace, North Charleston, SC

ROBIN ALLEN
www.thestarterbooks.com

This book is dedicated to
Cara Diandra Allen and Cassidy Milan Allen
Be starters in everything you do.
I love you forever and ever.

Dear Reader:

Let me introduce you to some high school girls with extraordinary gifts and tremendous powers in my new teen book series: *The Starters*. A teen drama about a racially-diverse group of high school girls, the series follows the eventful lives of five high school athletes. They are starters for their high school varsity basketball team. They have super athletic skills, and unbelievable talent, strength and passion:

- Run down the court, almost as fast as a gazelle.
- Jump so high to block a shot or catch a ball, it looks like they can fly.
- Throw a ball to the other end of the court with the speed of bullet.
- Dribble a basketball while speeding down the court.
- Steal basketballs from opposing players.
- Score baskets while running, blocking or dodging another player's move.
- Score three-point baskets from 20 feet away.
- Shoot from the free throw line with crowd screaming and their heart beating.

That's just on the court. Their normal lives are filled with you-never-know-what's-going-to-happen-next: at home, in class, on the bus, at a game, in the locker room, at a party, on a date. They deal with high school issues and family drama, so you don't have to know about basketball to enjoy their stories.

The first book in this new series is: *The Starters: Book 1-Unexpected*. I love to hear from my readers: email me at robin@thestarterbooks.com or visit the website: www.thestarterbooks.com.

Check out the book's theme song: *We Run The Court*. Download from Amazon or iTunes.

Look for the next book in the series in 2013: *The Starters: Book 2-Unleashed*.

Happy Reading!

Robin Allen

STARTER

*A starting lineup in **sports** is an official list of the set of players who will actively participate in the event when the **game** begins. The players in the starting lineup are commonly referred to as starters, whereas the others are substitutes or bench players.*

THE STARTERS

Theme Song

Lyrics by Robin Allen and Cassidy Allen
Copyright © 2012 by Robin Allen and Cassidy Milan

Download **We Run the Court** by Cassidy Milan

We Run The Court – Amazon - by Cassidy Milan
We Run The Court – iTunes - by Cassidy Milan

CAST OF CHARACTERS

RIVERBROOK HIGH SCHOOL- GIRLS' VARSITY BASKETBALL TEAM

Chase Anderson
Freshman, 14
Black; lives with both parents and siblings;
Mother: Shellie Anderson
Father: Michael Anderson
Brother: Evan, 16
Sister: Blake, 12
Grandmother: Grammy

A perfectionist about everything she does, whether it's a basketball games or grades, Chase is a prankster and loves movies. She was shocked when she made the varsity team. High school is exciting sometimes, but her sheltered home life didn't exactly prepare her for the real sights and sounds of high school life.

THE STARTERS

Elise Peterson
Sophomore, 15
White; lives with both parents and siblings;
Mother: Stephanie Peterson
Father: Greg Peterson
Brother: Cole, 17
Brother: Darren, 10
Brother: David 10
Sister: Molly, 8

Elise's family expects her to be a starter. Her mother played basketball at Riverbrook High many years ago. But Elise knows the new coach is demanding; she's going to have to fight to be noticed, the way she has to at home with three brothers and a sister.

Marley Woods
Sophomore, 15
Black; parents divorced, lives with father, mother lives in Chicago;
Father: Cooper Woods
Mother: Franchesca DuBois
Cousin: Egypt Woods
Aunt: Lydia Woods
Uncle: Kenneth Woods

Sassy, spoiled and a wardrobe that Beyonce would admire, Marley loves basketball, makes all A's, adores her father, and has a difficult relationship with her career-driven mother who left her when she was 7-years-old.

Selena Sanchez
Junior, 16
Hispanic; lives with parents, siblings and relatives;
Father: Felipe
Mother: Rosa

Brother: Juan
Brother: Paco
Sister: Maria
Sister: Bella
Cousin: Eva
Uncle: Hector

Pretty, perky and popular, Selena juggles basketball, work and school. Her father came to America from Mexico many years ago. He disapproves of Selena playing basketball and worries that she is straying from her Mexican heritage. She falls in love with a popular baseball player at the school.

Rachel Whitfield
Sophomore, 15
Jewish; lives with parents, two older siblings away at college;
Mother: Mary
Father: Bernie
Sister: Maddie
Brother: Peter

Shy, smart and a loner, Rachel was an awkward basketball player until her father hired a personal trainer who taught her basketball moves and style. Now, she's just socially awkward and struggling to find her place on the basketball team and in high school.

The Starters

Ja-Nay-A Banks
Senior, 18
Black; lives with mother and stepfather;
Mother: Tanya
Stepfather: Kirk
Sister: Natalie

Tall, thin and funny, Ja-Nay-A often speaks without thinking, but she never stops thinking when she's on the court. Her sister got a basketball scholarship, and her mother is counting on Ja-Nay-A to get a basketball scholarship too.

Layne Evansville
Senior, 18
White; lives with both parents and siblings;
Mother: Judith
Father: Thomas
Brother: Justin, 17
Sister: Morgan, 13

Blonde, brown-eyed, medium-height, Layne went to a predominately-white private school until she attended racially diverse Riverbrook High. Afraid when she started Riverbrook, Layne discovered that she likes different people and cultures and loves her high school. Soccer is her main sport, and some of her soccer fierceness comes out on the basketball court.

Zoey Burkhart
Senior, 17
White; parents divorced, but live across the street from each other;
Mother: Alana
Father: Richard
Sister: Ashley, 13

Zoey and Layne have been best friends since pre-school and have done everything together. Petite, red-headed Zoey is wild and unpredictable. She stalks her stepmother and is obsessed about Layne's brother Justin. She's fast on the basketball court and loves fast cars and boys.

Tequila Paxton
Junior, 17
Black; lives with single mother and brother;
Mother: Rashonda
Brother: Tevon

Tequila lived in New York and wishes they never moved to Atlanta. She loves basketball, but hates school. She dreams of playing for the WNBA and becoming a fashion model. She struggles with her grades and worries about her family's survival now that it's just her mom and brother and no relatives living nearby.

Bailey White
Senior, 17
White; parents divorced, lives with mother and stepfather;
Mother: Jennifer Hayes
Father: Scott White
Stepfather: Robert Hayes
Brother: Bobby Hayes
Sister: Darby Hayes

Bailey thought her parent's divorce was the worst thing that could happen to her. Wrong! When her mother married a black man, she discovered that some people hate you just because of your skin color. She's quiet and doesn't like to be noticed, but her want-to-be-rock-star girlfriend supports her mission to find a boyfriend before she graduates from high school.

THE STARTERS

Kaylee Wang
Junior, 15
Asian; lives with parents and siblings;
Mother: Lucy
Father: Thomas
Sister: Beth
Kaylee is a great violinist and basketball player. She loves both, and may have to choose. For now, basketball is her focus and trying to find her place in a world that challenges her Asian roots.

Heaven Jackson
Junior, 16
Black; lives with grandmother;
Grandmother: Alma

Heaven doesn't see the pretty girl that stares back in the mirror. She lived with her alcoholic mother until moving in with her grandmother in middle school. Heaven feels free when playing basketball and hopes that becoming a star athlete will bring her mother home.

PREVIEW

"Today, you find out if you are a starter!" said Coach Olivia Remmington.

Coach Olivia Remmington stared at the twelve high school girls sitting on the bench, sweaty and exhausted from running laps around the gym. She slowly made eye contact with each girl: Marley, Bailey, Selena, Rachel, Kaylee, Ja-Nay-A, Heaven, Tequila, Zoey, Layne, Elise, and Chase.

"Today is the day you find out if you are a starter," said Coach Olivia.

"That's the first thing I thought about when I opened my eyes this morning," said Marley. "It was the last thing I thought about before going to sleep," said Tequila.

"I'm tired of waiting," said Heaven.

"I know I'm a starter," said Ja-Nay-A, giggling. "I just want to know for real, for real."

"You will know…at 7 o'clock tonight," said Coach Olivia. "That's when I will post the names online."

"Coach O! Why you playing us?" asked Tequila.

"Seven o'clock! That's too long," complained Layne.

"Please tell us now," pleaded Selena.

"You're tormenting us," complained Rachel.

Coach O laughed. "I never said I was going to tell you at practice."

"But you said today…" said Bailey, her voice above a whisper.

"Today, but not now," Coach O said. She looked at the clock on the gym wall. "Check the web site at 7. And … girls, expect the unexpected."

"You always say that," said Tequila. "What does that mean anyway?"

"She's unpredictable," said Marley.

"Expect the unexpected," Coach O said with a sly smile. "Names will be posted on the bulletin board by the locker room before school starts tomorrow morning."

"One more thing, young ladies," said Coach O. "Just because you make starter doesn't mean you are guaranteed to stay a starter." She paused. "You have to prove it every time your feet hit the court."

"And the starters are…."

Marley Woods

Marley Woods and her father Cooper Woods laughed at the advice a "teen relationship" expert was suggesting on the radio.

"That made no sense, Daddy," she said, sitting in the passenger seat of the Infiniti SUV.

"None," Cooper agreed. "I have something for you. It's in the gift bag in the backseat."

Marley reached for the bag. "For me? Not for girlfriend 505. Nicole, Nia, Kendra?"

"Be a smartass and I'll take it back."

"What is it?"

"Open it and you'll find out."

"Tell me," Marley said. "Please."

"It's just something to congratulate you for being a starter."

"I'm not opening it," Marley firmly said. "I don't know if I'm a starter yet."

"You have to believe you are a starter to be a starter. I've watched the practices and you're smarter and faster than some of the other girls."

"I'm just a sophomore."

"That's what I like about this coach," said Cooper. "She thinks outside the box. I don't think she's going to pick just juniors and seniors."

"Everybody thinks she's crazy."

Cooper pulled into the parking lot of his office building. "Crazy wins games." He opened Marley's car door. As she got out of the car, he reminded her that boys should open doors for girls.

"Daddy, that is so Cinderella," said Marley. "A thousand years ago."

"There weren't cars back then. I'm just trying to teach you how a boy should treat you," said Cooper. "One day you'll understand, hopefully."

"When I go back in time," said Marley.

"Marley, Marley, Marley…never mind rock head," he said, shaking his head. "I'm going to a meeting. I should be out by seven."

Marley followed her father up the stairs to his offices on the second floor. He turned left, she turned right. Marley entered his office and plopped down on the sofa. She dropped her book bag, purse and mysterious gift on the floor.

Suddenly, Marley was anxious to open the gift. She removed the decorative tissue paper and saw a beautiful jewelry box. Without further hesitation, she opened the box. Inside was a white platinum basketball charm hanging on a silver chain. There were diamonds on the basketball. She smiled. *It's beautiful. Daddy has exquisite taste.*

Marley opened her book bag and removed her laptop. She opened her MacBook, entered her wireless access code, and then logged on to the website for her chemistry textbook. She scanned the chapter that was required reading, but could not focus. She looked at her cell phone: there were several text messages with the same question: *are you a starter?* She didn't know, so she didn't reply.

She listened to a message from her grandmother. Marley smiled when she heard her grandmother's raspy voice: "I'm predicting your success."

Five minutes before seven, Cooper came into his office. Marley was so intently reading her chemistry book that she didn't realize he was even there. "I see you opened the gift."

"Oh, hey, Daddy," she said, looking up from the MacBook. "How was your meeting?"

"Outstanding." He sat in the chair behind his desk. "Did you open the gift because you wanted to know what was inside the bag or because you believe you are a starter?"

Marley curled her lips into a mischievous grin. Her father knew her well. She had to say it with conviction. "I'm a starter for Riverbrook High School!"

"Yeah, that's just what I want to hear. You were more curious than Curious George, weren't you?"

"Maybe," she said, half-admitting the truth.

"So what are we waiting for?" Cooper pressed some buttons on his computer's keyboard. A few seconds later, they were looking at the school's web page for the girls' varsity basketball team. He clicked on the starter list.

Marley covered her eyes with her hands.

Cooper slowly read the names. Marley was the first name on the list, but he read the other names before softly saying, "Marley Woods."

"Yes! Yes! I made it!" Marley screamed ecstatically. She ran over to the computer.

"Why are you so excited? I thought you already knew."

"I was 95 percent sure, Daddy!"

Cooper hugged his daughter and kissed her forehead. "I had your back, sweetie. I had your five percent."

"Thanks, Daddy. Would you put my necklace on?"

"Of course, sweetie." Cooper carefully removed the necklace from the box. "Move your hair."

Marley swept her long black hair up towards the middle of her head. Cooper draped the necklace around Marley's neck and closed the latch.

"It's beautiful, Daddy," she said, twisting the charm with her hand. "I love it. Thank you."

"You're welcome."

"I love you, Daddy."

"Me too."

"I'm going to call Franchesca and tell her the news."

"Okay," he said with an unreadable expression.

"You think she'll be able to come to more of my games this year?"

"I don't know, sweetie," Cooper said. "Your mother is…your mother."

"Such a dedicated mother," Marley sarcastically said.

Cooper ignored what Marley said. "Tell all the starters that I will take them out to dinner this Friday."

"Cool," she said.

Layne Evansville
Zoey Burkhart

Zoey Burkhart whipped her two-seater car through the narrow roads of Layne Evansville's neighborhood. Zoey's bright red hair—which almost matched the color of her car—blew wildly in the wind. Minutes later, Zoey pulled into Layne's driveway. She opened the car door and hopped out.

"Hey," said Layne while shooting baskets.

"You know I hate your neighborhood. Such an unnecessary display of wealth," Zoey said, referring to the houses in the expensive neighborhood with five bedrooms, three baths and full-length basements.

"Yeah, yeah, yeah," said Layne.

"Not that I hate you," said Zoey. "People who can afford to live like this are dysfunctional."

"You drive a freaking new car," said Layne.

"That's just my dad's guilt for leaving my mom for a child-woman," said Zoey.

"Your neighborhood is just like mine. And your divorced parents live across from each other," Layne said, looking at Zoey as if she just escaped from mental retard land. "That's rather dysfunctional."

"My country tis of thee. Land of dysfunction…al…i…ty," Zoey said, mocking the national anthem.

Justin, Layne's brother, opened the front door and stepped outside of the house. He walked around the corner to the large driveway area.

"Ooh, ooh, ooh your brother!" Zoey oozed, observing the tall, blonde-haired boy twirling a ball inside a lacrosse stick. "I would do anything to have him. Anything!"

"You're a freak," Layne said. "How many times do I have to tell you he has a girlfriend? She's in college."

"Duh! She's not here. I'll be his girlfriend while she's away."

Zoey ran over to Justin and gave him a big hug. Justin stood like a statute as Zoey awkwardly embraced him. "Hey, sexy Justin," she said, her hand traveling below his waist.

Justin grabbed Zoey's hands and stepped away from her. "So are you two starters?" Justin asked. "You should be. You start for soccer."

"To be or not be a starter," said Zoey. "That is the question."

"I have a shot," said Layne, sitting on the hood of Zoey's red two-seater car. "Coach O said "expect the unexpected."

"I expect my ass will be sitting on the bench." Zoey shrugged. "I love the bench. The bench is my best friend."

They all laughed.

"So, what's up?" asked Justin. "I thought you were going to find out today."

"Coach is posting the starter list online at 7 seven clock," said Layne. "Our mysterious and dramatic coach."

"Well, doo-doo heads, it's," he said, glancing at his sports watch, "7:15."

"I don't really care because I'm not trying to get a scholarship and I don't want the pressure of having to be perfect," said Zoey. "And I don't want Ja-Nay-A or Heaven harassing me."

"I'm not scared of them," said Layne.

"Yeah, right," said Zoey, her voice ripped sarcasm.

"I told you girls should have stuck with soccer," Justin said.

"If I were awful, I wouldn't be on varsity," said Layne. "I wanted to try something new and I'm pretty good. I'll play soccer in the spring."

"I like basketball. It's fun. The girls are really different," said Zoey. "Playing basketball irritates my parents, but their divorce irritates me like a UTI."

Justin scowled. "What's a UTI?"

"A urinary tract infection," explained Zoey.

"What?!"

"Justin, you don't need to know," said Layne. "TMI."

"Sounds like someone should see a shrink," said Justin.

"Doesn't everybody?" quipped Zoey.

"Not me, said Justin. "Let's just see if your names are on the list," he said, removing an iPhone from his pocket.

"I would love to see Mom and Dad's faces if I'm starter. They weren't exactly thrilled when I tried out for basketball," said Layne.

Justin shrugged. "You know how they are."

"What did Dad say? 'That's a black sport," said Layne. "You don't belong there."

"They'll come to your games," said Justin.

"That's their parental duty," said Layne. "They go by the 'I'm-a-good-parent' checklist. Like coming to my soccer games."

"And my lacrosse games," said Justin.

"You know I'm your biggest fan, Justin," said Zoey. "I'm so proud of your lacrosse scholarship."

Justin ignored Zoey. "You can still get a soccer scholarship."

"Maybe," shrugged Layne.

"It's now 7:20." said Justin.

"Let's get it over with out," said Layne.

"If I don't make it I will be scarred for life." Zoey leaned her head on Justin's shoulder. "Justin, you have to take me out to help me get over the pain of it all. Dejection, rejection, low self-esteem…"

"You're twisted Zoey." Justin scrolled through several screens on his iPhone, and then looked at his sister and her strange best friend.

"Well, to be a loser or not?" asked Zoey.

"You're not starters," Justin flatly said.

Layne stomped her foot on the pavement, her face full of disappointment. A moment later, she said with a crooked smile, "Oh F-ing well."

"Justin, ready for that date?" asked Zoey.

"No," Justin said, turning away.

"Hey Justin, you still owe me fifty dollars. You bet me that I wouldn't make varsity," said Layne. "And I did."

"Either pay her or screw me," said Zoey.

"Go home, Zoey," said Justin.

"You know I practically live here," said Zoey.

"Unfortunately."

Tequila Paxton

Tequila and Tevon ran to answer the house phone because the ringing sound was loud and annoying. "Got it," said Tequila. "Hello."

"Hi girl, are you a starter?" asked Rashonda Paxton, Tequila's mother.

"I don't know," said Tequila. "Coach O is posting it online at seven tonight."

"What? She should have told everyone straight up," Rashonda said. "If she was trying not to hurt someone's feelings she wasted her time, because they're going to find out."

"Coach O is crazy."

"I gotta get back to work. Watch your brother and call me when you find out," said Rashonda.

Tequila hung up the phone, walked down the hallway and went into her bedroom. She took off her clothes, piled them in a heap on the floor, put on a T-shirt, and slid under the covers. She set her alarm for 6:45 PM.

She drifted into a deep sleep, dreaming that she was a starter for the boys' varsity basketball team. And she was the only girl on the team. She was making a free throw, waiting for the ball to drop into the net when the alarm went off. Tequila opened her eyes and it felt like morning. She turned off the alarm clock. The dream still fresh in her mind, she imagined the ball dropping inside the net. Swish! She looked at the alarm clock.

It was seven o'clock.

She jumped out the bed and ran into the living room. Tevon was using the computer.

"Move, Tevon," she said, pushing her brother out of the chair. He landed on the floor.

"Oww," he said. "That hurt."

Tequila clicked on the Internet Explorer browser, but nothing happened. "What's wrong with this freaking computer?"

"It's slow…and it's old," said Tevon.

"Everything's old in this house!"

"You have to reboot," said Tevon.

A growl of frustration blew out of Tequila's mouth. "That takes forever."

"I'll do it," said Tevon.

Tequila got up and Tevon sat down in front of the computer. He pressed the restart button and waited. "It will come back to life in a few."

"Back to life? It's a computer." She shook her head, and impatiently waited for the desktop screen to appear. She watched as Tevon opened several web pages, and landed on Riverbrook's varsity girls' basketball page.

"There's your name," Tevon said, spotting his sister's name on the list of five starters.

When she saw her name—the last name on the list—Tequila jumped up and down as if she'd won the lottery. She screamed, "I made it! I made it! I'm a starter!"

Tevon pounced on the sofa. "I'm a starter!" he screamed. "I'm a starter!"

She laughed and hit him in the head with a pillow from the sofa. "You're not a starter, big head."

"I know," but he kept jumping up and down on the couch.

"Oh yeah! Oh yeah!" Tequila said, while scanning her text messages. She had a bunch of messages asking if she was a starter. She had an answer that made her happy. She smiled and called her mother.

Elise Peterson

Stephanie Peterson kissed her husband Greg Peterson when he came into the cluttered dining room. It was a long, tongue-exchanging kiss.

"Yuck," said Darren and David at the same time, Elise's twin brothers.

"Mom! Dad!" complained Elise's oldest brother, Cole, a senior at Riverbrook. "We're supposed to be having dinner here."

"My stomach is turning," said Elise.

"That's how you guys got here," Stephanie said, smiling at her children sitting around the table, amidst the scattered piles of mail, papers, magazines and newspapers.

"Gross!" said the twins.

The youngest, eight-year-old, Molly, was reading, and ignored the every-evening chatter. She thought the people in her books were more interesting.

"We were planning on having at least six kids," said Greg.

"Please no more little brothers or sisters," said Elise.

"You never know," said Stephanie. "Your father and I both went to Riverside…"

"We know," said Darren, one of the ten-years-old twins.

Stephanie said, "And we have known each other since…"

"Fifth grade," said David, the other twin.

"We've been together ever since then, started our family young…"

"We know Dad," said Cole. "You've told us a thousand times."

"Not like some of your friends whose parents are old enough to be grandparents," said Stephanie.

"Whatever Mom," said Elise. "I just want to eat and go out and shoot before it gets dark."

"I'm proud of you," said Stephanie, her eyes on Elise.

"Proud of what?" Elise blurted. "My name wasn't on the starter list." Her voice was filled with indignation and anger.

"Sorry, sis," said Cole.

"You said that already!" Elise said, irritated.

"Sorry sis," said the twins.

Her father kissed Elise on the forehead. "I haven't officially said I'm sorry."

"I'm proud of your attitude, pumpkin. You didn't collapse into a ball of tears. You just said: I'm going to be starter next year. That's the right spirit," her mother said.

"Your mom didn't make starter until she was a junior," said her father. "I was at all her games."

"I might not look like it now, but I was a darn good player back then," said Stephanie.

"Riverbrook had great sports teams back then. Everybody went to the football and basketball games," said Greg.

"We're losers Dad," reminded Cole. "Some sports we're good at and some we suck at."

"I think Riverbrook is about to have a comeback," said Greg. "Elise, you are going to be there when they starting winning basketball again and fans start coming to the girls' games."

"Can we eat so I can practice?" asked Elise.

"I'll shoot with you," said Cole.

"What if I shoot with you," suggested Stephanie.

"Mom!" whined Elise.

"I still got skills," said Stephanie.

Everyone laughed, except for Stephanie.

Kaylee Wang

Kaylee walked inside her parents' nail shop. It was near closing time and only two customers were in the shop. Kelly greeted both customers: "Hello." "Hi Kaylee," said the older customer. "Do you still play the violin?"

Kaylee wanted to say no, but that would be a lie. She slightly nodded her head.

"You usually come in with your violin case," said the customer who was in her early sixties. She was stylishly-dressed.

"It's in the back," said Kaylee. "I just came from basketball practice. I have a violin at school, home and here."

"The violin is your gift," said Lucy Wang, her mother.

"I want to be good at something else," explained Kaylee.

"Oh, would you play the violin for me?" asked the regular customer. "You play so beautifully." She turned to the only other customer in the store. "Do you mind?"

"Not at all," said the younger woman. "It would be a nice change from that crap they play on the radio."

"My mom is tired and ready to go home," said Kaylee, not interesting in playing the violin. Her mind was on basketball.

The Starters

"Play Kaylee," said her mother. "We like to make customers happy."

Kaylee went to the back area where there was a table for eating, small refrigerator, microwave and storage cabinet. A few Vietnamese newspapers were scattered on the table. She went into the closet and removed the violin case. She picked it up and placed in on the table, harder than she intended. As she opened the case and removed the violin a different feeling took over her. She really loved the instrument. Within seconds, she decided what to play and returned to the customer area.

She planted her feet, positioned her head and stood in the proper posture. She placed the violin on the left side of her neck. "First I have to warm up," she said.

After warming up the instrument, she started playing the violin version of Beethoven Symphony 5. While skillfully strumming the bow across the violin's strings, she forgot about basketball—at least for the next ten minutes.

The two customers and her parents clapped when she finished playing.

"Lovely, lovely," said the older customer.

"Beautiful and relaxing," said the younger customer. She removed her hands from the nail dryer and stood up. She carefully picked up her keys. "You keep playing. You are very talented, young lady."

Kaylee responded with a warm smile. "Thank you."

Looking out the window, the regular customer said, "My ride is here." She moved towards the door. "I will see you next week, Lucy."

"We might see you on TV one day playing the violin," said the other customer.

After the two customers left the store, her father Thomas Wang locked the door.

"I did not want to play," said Kaylee.

"You did," said her father. "You're a good daughter."

Kaylee peered at the clock on the wall. It was 7:20 PM.

"The coach posted the list of starters at 7," said Kaylee.

"I wonder why you didn't call me after practice," said her mother.

"She made us wait."

"She torment you," said her mother.

"I'll look on my laptop for you," said her father.

Kaylee heard her phone vibrating. She removed it from her purse and saw a bunch of messages. A text message from Elise listed the girls who were on the starter list.

"Never mind, Dad." She looked up from her phone. "I didn't make it. Elise just texted me."

"Maybe she wrong," her father said, pressing buttons on the computer.

"Mama tell him she not wrong," said Kaylee.

Her mother stood at the register counting money. "Can't think about it right now."

"Father, I have two other texts from other girls on my team," said Kaylee. "I didn't make it," she said exasperation in her voice.

"Your name is not on the list," said her father.

"I told you!" she said, stomping her feet.

"Kaylee," her father said in a firm, reprimanding tone.

"Sorry."

"Too bad for team," her father said.

"Coach O says she doesn't like to lose," said Kaylee. "I would help her win."

"You never know what's going to happen," said her mother. "Maybe you get chance later."

Ja-Nay-A Banks

The house was quiet when Ja-Nay-A got home. She hated the creepiness of a silent house, so she immediately turned on the television to hear voices. She hated darkness, so lights were blazing all over the house. She usually turned them off before her mother and stepfather got home from work—the sound of the garage door opening was her warning to turn off the lights. She frequently got caught with the lights on and the television blaring.

Ja-Nay-A heated up a slice of two-day old pizza, took two bites before throwing it in the trash. She plopped on the sofa, picked up the remote and scanned though the channels stopping at *Law and Order*, one of her favorite TV shows. She ignored the ringing telephone and focused on the television. But she kept hearing her sister's Natalie's ring tone: a snippet of song from rapper/singer Drake. She wanted to wait until seven o'clock so she could tell Natalie that she was a starter—just like Natalie had been when she was a student at Riverbrook High.

After the fifth time hearing the Drake ringtone, she answered the phone. "What? What?"

"What you mean what?" asked Natalie. "What happened at practice?"

"Nothing."

"Turn down the TV so you can hear me, and you better turn off those lights before mom and dad get home."

"Give me a minute."

"I was blowing up your phone because I want to know if you are a starter."

"I better be a starter."

"Why you sound worried?"

"I'm not worried." With a gush of fake confidence, Ja-Nay-A said, "I got this."

"I thought you were going to find out today."

"Coach is posting it online at 7."

"She's cruel," said Natalie.

"She likes to say, "Expect the unexpected."

"Hmm," said Natalie. "I will call you back in thirty minutes."

"Okay," Ja-Nay-A said. Watching TV, she soon fell asleep.

Natalie called back at 7:16 PM, the loud ring tone waking up Ja-Nay-A.

She pressed the ignore button on her phone and went over to the computer. She went to Riverbrook High's web site and found the varsity girls' basketball page. As the page opened, Ja-Nay-A closed her eyes, wishing that her name was on the list. When she opened her eyes, she didn't see her name on the list. She stared at the page for several minutes, but her name was not there. In that moment, she hated the girls on the list. She hated Riverbrook. She hated the coach. She hated herself. Ja-Nay-A clicked the power button to turn off the computer screen.

She couldn't hold back the gush of tears. She went into the bathroom and washed her face. She dried her round, medium brown face with a fresh hand towel. A quick glance in the mirror and she saw her naturally red hair. Sometimes she hated her hair, even though her mother and sister also had red hair. Her red hair didn't stop boys from asking her out.

Drake's ringtone blasted from the cell phone. If she didn't answer, it was going to ring again or she would have to turn off the phone.

She pressed the power off button on her phone. No more Drake.

Five minutes later, the house phone rang. Her sister's name flashed in the caller ID box.

Natalie is a pain in the ass, she thought.

She picked up the phone.

"I'm not a starter, Nat." Tears rolled down Ja-Nay-A's face.

"I'm sorry, girl," said Natalie.

"I'm taller than the other girls," said Ja-Nay-A, referring to her six-foot height. She was silent for a minute. "I was starter last year! I don't get it! Coach must hate me."

"I don't know why you didn't make it. Your coach must be blind and dumb."

"I'm a senior. A senior!" shrieked Ja-Nay-A. "My chances of getting a basketball scholarship are gone. How can I tell Mom that I'm not going to get a basketball scholarship?"

THE STARTERS

Chase Anderson

The Anderson's door bell rang. Michael Anderson went into the hall and answered the door. Chase's middle school basketball coach, Eddie Jones, stood in the doorway.

"Hey Eddie," said Michael.

"Hey," said Eddie. "Hi ya doing?"

"Good. Come into the kitchen," said Michael. "We're eating dinner."

"I'm sorry for disturbing your dinner," Eddie said following Chase's father into the kitchen.

"No problem, man."

"Real nice house," said Eddie.

"We been living here since Evan was born," said Michael.

"That's cool."

"Hey everybody," Coach Eddie said when he entered the kitchen.

"Hi Coach Eddie," said Chase with a big smile. She adored and admired her middle school coach.

"Hello," said Chase's brother and sister, Evan and Blake.

"You got a beautiful family, man. Kids look just like the both of you."

"Would you like to join us?" offered Shellie Anderson, Chase's mother. "I'll fix you a plate."

A big, round man who looked like he never missed a meal, Coach Eddie said, "It looks good." He eyed the enticing spread of food on the table. "But, I'll pass. Thanks!" He glanced at Chase. "I just wanted to be here when Chase gets the news."

The whole family looked at Chase.

"What news, Chasey?" Shellie asked.

"You didn't tell 'em?" Coach Eddie said, giving Chase a bewildered look.

Chase finished chewing the food in her mouth, before saying, "No."

"Tell us what?" Michael asked.

"Coach O is going to tell us who the starters are," Chase explained. "We thought she was going to tell us at practice today, but she told us to check the web site at 7."

"I didn't know you were going to find out today," said Shellie. "You're as good as the rest of the girls on the team."

"Mama, I'm just a freshman," Chase said.

"There aren't any freshman boys on the varsity team," Evan said. He was in the eleventh grade at Riverbrook High.

"I heard that she was announcing the starters today, Chase," said Coach Eddie.

"Do you know already? Did she tell you?" Chase asked the man who had been her basketball coach for four years.

"I don't know. I haven't spoken to her," he said with a shrug. "I just know your skills and I think that coach sees your potential. She's a pro basketball player," explained Coach Eddie.

"Chase, I can't believe you didn't tell us," Shellie said.

"Hello," Chase said, her face exaggerated with frustration. "Everybody keeps forgetting that I'm a freshman."

"Coach Remmington is about talent and athletic ability," said Coach Eddie.

"You're a baller!" said younger sister Blake.

"Coach O can be mean sometimes," Chase said.

"You can deal with it," said Michael. "You can't be soft."

"You're not soft when you steal balls from other players," Evan said, laughing. "You're a thief on the court."

"She's a no-nonsense coach. I respect her for that," said Michael. "She has a different approach."

"Yes, she does. She's shaking up the system," said Coach Eddie. "Some of the parents of the girls who were on the team last year and didn't make varsity this year are furious with her. They went to the principal and complained, but Coach Olivia didn't change her mind."

"Oh really," said Shellie. "I didn't hear about that."

"I'm not surprised," said Michael. "I remember when she played for the WNBA. She was controversial then and…"

The grandfather clock chimed at 7 o'clock.

Evan went over to the computer on the desk in the kitchen. He opened the school's web site page and clicked on the varsity girls' basketball page. The rest of the family crowded around the computer.

When they saw Chase's name on the list, everyone shouted.

"Way to go!"

Everyone hugged Chase.

"I told you," said Coach Eddie. "You got skills."

"I can't believe it. I still can't believe I made varsity. I really, really, really can't believe I'm a starter!" Chase said, her voice high-pitched with excitement.

"Snap out of denial," Blake said, snapping her fingers in front of Chase's face. "Wake up and face reality. You are a starter."

"For the varsity team," said Evan.

"I betcha everyone is just as…shocked." Her facial expression changed. "Some of the girls are going to hate me."

"Don't worry about the other girls," her father said. "Coach Olivia is the one who will get the heat."

"You're right about that," said Coach Eddie.

"So don't worry about hurting the other girls' feelings," Shellie said.

"Ja-Nay-A just knew she was going to be starter," said Chase. "She's a senior and she's going to hate me. Heaven is going to hate me too."

"Baby, apparently you impressed the coach. You have to keep working hard," said Michael.

"I worked hard," Chase said, feeling the energy of her excitement pulsing through her blood. "I earned it."

"That's the spirit!" her father said, hugging Chase.

"We're going to celebrate this weekend," said Shellie. "We'll go out to dinner."

"Benihana's?" asked Chase.

"Yes," said Michael.

"We have to tell Grammy," said Chase.

"Shellie, I think I will take you up on dinner," Coach Eddie said. "That food looks mighty good and I'm kind of hungry. I just wanted to hear the news first."

"No problem," Shellie said. "I'll fix you a plate."

"You know what this means, baby girl?" Michael asked Chase.

"Basketball, basketball, basketball," Chase said. "Good thing I love the game."

"If you didn't have the passion, you wouldn't be where you are," said Coach Eddie.

Evan kissed Chase on the forehead. "Way to go little sis. The only freshman on the varsity team," said Evan.

Bailey White

Jennifer Hayes knocked on her daughter's bedroom door. She went inside and saw Bailey lying on her bed, flipping through a *Seventeen* magazine.

"I thought you were studying," said Jennifer.

"I can't concentrate," Bailey said, her eyes scanning an article on make-up tips.

"It's almost time!" Jennifer said with a big smile. "It's almost 7 o'clock."

Bailey didn't understand why her mother was smiling like something wonderful was going to happen. She could tell her mother eleven reasons why she would not be a starter: *there are eleven girls on the team who are better than me.* If she did, her mother would launch into her 'you're an outstanding player' speech. Bailey was not in the mood.

"Let's get it over with," Bailey said, getting up from her bed, giving her mother a fake smile. Bailley had her mother's blonde hair, round face and straight nose, and bright blue eyes inherited from her father. A combination of features that frequently brought comments like pretty, attractive, or beautiful, but Bailey wasn't confident about her looks. She wanted to look like the girls in the fashion magazines.

"I don't why she made the team wait." Jennifer said.

"Who knows? Maybe she wanted to make us go psycho," Bailey said.

"The coach is the boss," said Jennifer.

"I have another word for it and it begins with B too."

"Bailey!" scolded her mother.

Downstairs in the kitchen, Bailey was greeted by her little sister, Darby Hayes, who ran over and grabbed Bailey by the legs, screaming, "Bay-ee, Bay-ee."

Bailey picked up her sister. "It's Bay-lee, Bay-lee."

Darby said, "Bay-ee, Bay-ee."

Bailey smiled and kissed her sister's chubby cheek. She had a head full of curly black hair, dark brown eyes, and barely-brown skin.

"Hi Bobby," Bailey said to her brother who was playing a hand held video game.

"Hey sis," said the five-year-old boy, his eyes never leaving the battle scene on the PSP screen.

"I hope you guys saved me some food," Bailey said. "I'm hungry."

"There's plenty left. Robert's not home yet. He had to work late," Jennifer said. "You have a surprise visitor."

"Who?"

"Me," her father said, coming from the family room into the kitchen. Scott White was blonde with an average-looking face. He was quite tall, well-built, and very athletic. He ran in marathons and triathlons.

"Hi Daddy," Bailey said, when he hugged her and Darby at the same time.

"Hi ladybug," Scott said, giving her a smile that showed slightly crooked front teeth. "Have a good day in school?"

"Oh Daddy, you just want to know if I made starter," Bailey said.

"It's after 7," urged Jennifer.

Bailey looked at the computer on the kitchen desk.

"Are you going to look?" Jennifer asked Bailey.

"Not yet," Bailey said, shrugging.

"I'll do it," Scott said, sitting at the desk. He shuffled some papers to the side of the desk. The computer screen flashed on, displaying different user names.

"What's your password, Bailey?"

Scott looked at Bailey, but she didn't respond.

"Jennifer?" he asked.

"I don't know," Jennifer answered.

"Her password is boyfriend," shouted little Bobby Hayes.

"Boyfriend!" Scott and Jennifer said together.

"Who's your boyfriend?" asked Jennifer.

"I don't have one," answered Bailey.

"You can always talk to me about boys," said Jennifer.

"Mom, please. I don't have a boyfriend. Can we move on?"

"She wants a boyfriend," said Bobby.

"Hush son," said Jennifer.

Scott navigated to the school's web site and found the page listing the starters for the varsity girls' basketball team.

"Come look," Scott said to Bailey.

"Just tell me the bad news," Bailey said in an I-don't-care voice. She put Darby down. "I'm going to fix my plate." She opened a kitchen cabinet and removed a dinner plate.

"Your name is on the list," Scott quietly said.

Bailey dropped her plate. Glass shattered everywhere. Initially calm, her father yelled as if his favorite football team just scored a touchdown.

Jennifer shouted with joy and grabbed Darby who was bending down to pick up the plate fragments.

"I'm sorry, Mom," Bailey said. She went into the pantry to get the broom and dustpan. "I didn't mean to drop the plate."

"I don't care about that damn plate!" Jennifer said. "I'm proud of you."

"You did it, sweetheart!" her father said, kissing her on the forehead. "You are a starter. What an accomplishment!"

"Why doesn't she look happy?" Bobby asked, staring at his sister.

"Yeah, why don't you look happy?" her father asked.

"I don't want to be starter because half the girls on the team don't think I should be on the team and the ones that didn't make it are going to hate me, especially Heaven and Ja-Nay-A."

"You can't worry about what other people think," her mother said.

"If all the seniors were starters, then the other girls wouldn't get so mad," Bailey said worriedly. "But she picked me over Ja-Nay-A and she was a starter last year. Ja-Nay-A is going to kill me!"

"You don't know that she picked you over Ja-Nay-A," Jennifer explained.

"I don't understand the coach's rationale, but I think she has some kind of strategy that we don't see or understand," Scott said. "I'll figure it out when I see you guys play. It won't be a mystery."

"The mystery is: why did she pick me? Does she hate me? Does she want the other girls to hate me?"

"Calm down, Bailey," Jennifer said. "Sit down and I'll fix your plate. Your father is right. We don't understand it now, but we will later."

Bailey sat down and buried her face with her hands.

"I don't know why you're upset," Jennifer said. "You should feel honored."

"Mom, you just don't get it. This is a death threat."

"Don't be so dramatic," Jennifer impatiently said. "This isn't a *Lifetime* movie."

"Some of the girls don't like me. I don't fit in. Some of them are hoping to get a basketball scholarship and they'll think I'm in their way and…"

"Stop it, Bailey," Scott sternly said. "Their problems are not your problems. Be happy and be proud of yourself. I want you to continue to play hard. Be fierce on the court and be strong in that locker room when you're around the other girls. Don't act like you're afraid."

"Yeah Bailey, don't be a wussy," Bobby Jr. said.

"Bobby!" Jennifer gushed. "Where did you learn that word?"

"In school," Bobby Jr. said. "It's a man's word."

"That's not a man's word and you are never to use that word again—not ever. Not in school or at home," Jennifer firmly said.

"Not ever?" Bobby Jr. asked.

"No!" scolded Jennifer. "Give me your PSP and I want you to go upstairs and think about what you just said!" Bobby bounced up the steps.

"Boys," Jennifer said. She picked up Darby. "I'm going to give this little girl a bath."

"You want to get your favorite dessert?" Scott asked Bailey.

Bailey shrugged. "Okay. I didn't eat dinner."

"Do you mind, Jenny?"

"Of course not," Jennifer said. "Desert is always better than dinner."

Scott laughed.

Heaven Jackson

For fifteen minutes, Heaven stared at the names on the starter list. She pressed her face closer to the computer screen and read the names over and over again. Her name was not there. For a brief second, she thought if she closed her eyes and reopened them, her name would magically be there. She opened her eyes and her name still was not there.

Heaven was shocked. She could not believe that her name wasn't on the list of starters.

Her cell phone vibrated so much that it fell on the floor. The throbbing sound annoyed Heaven. Picking up her phone, she read the text messages from other teammates with tears streaming down her face. Heaven turned up the television so her grandmother wouldn't hear her crying.

She didn't understand why certain girls made the team.

She didn't understand why a freshman made the team.

She didn't understand why the coach would ruin her dreams of getting a basketball scholarship. It was critical in her junior year to get a lot of playing time.

Lying down, Heaven rolled across the bed and saw one of her mother's letters. Most of her mother's letters were neatly stacked in the bottom desk drawer. She never ever kept the envelopes. In one of the letters, her mother wrote: *I know you be a starter, baby*. Reading her mother's words felt like needles pricking her heart that made questions pop in her head: *Why did you have to go away? Why did you do it? Why won't you take care of me?* Questions she only thought about when she was upset or depressed. Basketball kept those questions out of her everyday thoughts—some questions had answers and some were answerless. There were the questions that she didn't like the answers.

At this moment: she had one big question: *why didn't I make the team?* She might not like the answer. Coach O was demanding and sometimes blunt and brutal.

Her cell phone kept vibrating. She didn't want to answer sounding like a frog was in her throat. They would hear it in her voice. So, she waited a few minutes. She definitely did not want to tell her boyfriend; but he would find out. Something made her answer when she heard Ja-Nay-A's ringtone. It was a Nicki Minaj song, her favorite artist.

"You cool?" Ja-Nay-A asked.

"Hell no." Heaven could tell that Ja-Nay-A had been crying too. "You been crying?"

"No…"

"Me too."

"Okay…yeah," Ja-Nay-A admitted.

They were silent.

"I'm so freaking pissed," said Ja-Nay-A.

"I don't know why the coach picked the girls she did, but Bailey? She got no real skills," said Heaven.

"And Chase? A freshman? She don't even belong on the team," said Ja-Nay-A.

"It doesn't make any sense," said Ja-Nay-A. "Coach O acts like this year is going to be different. Not with those starters."

"We are going to suck again," said Heaven.

"Well, I was thinking…" said Ja-Nay-A.

"What?"

"Coach said if you make starter don't mean you going to stay starter."

"Those spots aren't guaranteed," said Heaven.

"Remember AAU last year and those girls could not hang," said Ja-Nay-A. "They didn't last the season."

"We can take their spots," said Heaven. "Those girls don't know how to play real basketball."

"We get physical on them and their asses will be sitting on the bench," said Ja-Nay-A. "Just gotta go after two of them."

"Yeah!" said Heaven.

"You down with that?"

"Yeah."

"I don't like Bailey. She think she all that," said Ja-Nay-A. "Got a Black stepdad. That ain't right."

"Girl, that's not our business," Heaven said.

"She won't last the season. I'm not going to make it easy for her," said Ja-Nay-A.

"Gotta go," said Heaven. "I hear my grandma calling me."

Heaven pressed the end button on her cell. She left her bedroom and went down the narrow hall into the kitchen and saw two plates on the counter. Her grandmother was sitting at the table, watching the television show *The Price is Right*. She watched the show every night.

"I've been waiting for you," Grandma said. "We don't get to eat together since you always at basketball practice."

Heaven heated the plates in the microwave. She placed one dinner plate in front of her grandmother and another plate on the opposite end of the small table where she sat.

"Let's say grace," Grandma said, grabbing Heaven's right hand and saying a short blessing.

"Amen," said Heaven and looked at the food on her plate. She wasn't hungry, but knew better than wasting food. Grandma would get very upset. So she picked through the mushy peas, rice and baked chicken.

"So did you get good news?" Grandma suddenly asked.

Heaven looked at her grandmother as if she didn't understand.

A wrinkled smile formed around her grandmother's lips. "About basketball."

"Oh."

"You going to be a ….I forgot what you call it. The first players or is it the top players?" she asked. "You catch my meaning."

Heaven held back the tears that collected in her throat. She didn't want to disappoint her grandmother. Heaven couldn't explain why she wasn't a starter: she didn't know why herself.

Softly Heaven said, "Yes ma'am."

"That's my girl," Grandma said. "I'm proud of you."

Heaven couldn't look into her grandmother's eyes.

Selena Sanchez

"That was delicious, Daddy," Bailey said to her father after eating the last bite of chocolate mousse cake.

"Indeed, it was," Scott agreed. "I better get you back home so you can do homework and stuff."

Bailey was reading through her text messages. She had never received so many messages in one night. There were mostly messages from the some of her teammates congratulating her on making starter. She smiled when she saw the message from Marley: *Congrats. Starter party Friday. Must wear dress. Details later.*

"Bailey," her father said, repeating her name.

"I have so many messages. Marley is going to have a party for the girls who are starters. That's so cool!"

"So cool!" teased Scott.

"We have to get dressed up."

"I like seeing you dressed up like a princess."

"Daddy, I'm not your little princess," Bailey said. "I'm a senior in high school."

"I know, princess."

She glared at him, and then they laughed.

"We need to go Bailey," urged her father.

Bailey scrolled through her messages. "I don't see any messages from Selena."

"So?"

"I wonder if she knows."

"Why wouldn't she know? Your coach posted it online for everyone to see, right?"

"I don't think she has a computer," explained Bailey.

"Text her or call her."

"She dropped her phone in water yesterday."

"She'll find out," her father said, unconcerned.

"I want to make sure she knows," said Bailey.

"It's getting late," Scott said. "I have to get you home. Don't want to upset your mother."

"Her family has a restaurant. It's just at the end of this shopping center. We can go there. I won't take long," suggested Bailey.

Scott impatiently looked at his watch, ready to deny her request. But 'no' turned into 'yes' when he looked into his daughter's concerned face. "Okay. But we're not going to stay for long."

"You're the awesomest dad on the planet," said Bailey.

"Awesomest is not in the dictionary," he said, shaking his head. "Let's go."

Around 8:30 PM, Bailey walked into Los Mexicana restaurant. When Selena saw Bailey, she ran over to greet her.

"You made it," said Bailey. "You're a starter."

"Are you sure?" asked Selena.

"I saw your name on the list," said Bailey.

Embarrassed, Selena said, "Our computer is broke. My brother was going to take me to the library so I could see the list."

"I wasn't sure if you knew, so I'm here to officially tell you that you are a starter!"

Selena shrieked with joy. "Yes! I'm a starter!" She took a deep breath. "Who are the other starters?"

"You and me," Bailey said, and they gave each other high fives.

"Exciting," said Selena. "Who else?"

"Marley, Tequila, and Chase."

"Wow! I can't believe coach didn't pick more seniors."

"I can't believe she picked me," said Bailey.

"I can't believe she picked me," said Selena.

They both laughed.

"We are starters!" said Selena.

"And…. Marley is having a party for us starters," said Bailey.

"Si! Si! Mucho fun!"

Rachel Whitfield

Rachel wasn't looking forward to 7 PM. She cared about making the team. She wanted to be a starter, but she knew that she didn't have a chance.

She was looking forward to dinner at 7; her mother Mary was making scallops and shrimp, broccoli and garlic red potatoes. Rachel didn't tell her parents that the starters were being announced today. If it became a reality, if her name was on the list, she would tell them. She would scream and yell out of her bedroom window. No one would hear the sound of her voice; the houses in her neighborhood were spread far apart from each other.

During dinner, Rachel was unusually quiet.

"What's the matter, Rach?" her mother Mary Whitfield asked. "You seem distracted."

"Nothing."

"How was your calc test?" asked Bernie Whitfield, her father.

"I failed it."

"What?" Her father looked up from the folded up *Wall Street Journal* newspaper.

"Just kidding, Daddy."

"She always gets you Bernie," said her mother.

"She does," her father admitted with a half-smile.

"I talked to Maddie last night. It's still hard to believe that she's in college," Mary said, referring to her older daughter who was a junior in college.

"Honey, why can't you believe it? We have two kids in college." His voice softened. "We just have Rachel for two more years."

"I might stay home," said Rachel. "Go to college online."

The Starters

Mary looked at Rachel, unsure if her daughter was serious or joking. "That's an idea," she said neutrally.

"I don't think it's a good idea at all," her father said. "You're already too shy. That's why I put you in sports. So you can learn how to be aggressive and survive in this doggy-doggy world. People are ruthless…"

"Don't scare her," said Mary.

"The kids in high school are mean," said Rachel.

"See, I know what I'm talking about," said Bernie. "Those high school kids are just going to getting meaner when they become adults."

"Yeah, they're blood sucking vampires," said Rachel.

"Rachel," admonished her mother. "Not everyone is evil."

Bernie snorted. "She's learning about real life."

"I don't like what you're teaching her," said Mary.

After dinner, Rachel went into her bedroom that included her own personal bathroom. She sat in her favorite spot—the picture window. It was her escape from reality, her escape into the world of stories. She picked up a book and began reading a 1,000 page gothic romance. She turned off her phone so she wouldn't be disturbed by text messages or phone calls. She read until 9 PM, studied until 11 PM and hopped in the shower.

Rachel got in the bed and tried to fall asleep. She tried not to think about basketball. Her mind was spinning and twirling. She closed her eyes, but she kept thinking about the starter list. By 1 AM, she gave up. She would have to look at the list of starters. She got out of the bed, turned on her computer and launched the school's web site. She read the starter list.

Her name was not on the list.

Rachel was not surprised.

But now that Rachel officially knew what she knew in her gut, she could go to sleep. She slid between the covers of her queen-sized bed, and closed her eyes. Fifteen minutes later, Rachel was asleep.

CHAPTER 1

MARLEY

"I don't want to hear about the past years when you didn't win," said Coach Olivia. "We're going to have a winning season."

"Are you with me?"

"Yes!" said the five teen-age girls.

"How do I look?" Marley asked her father, while standing next to the reserved table at Dave & Buster's restaurant. She was waiting for the other starters to arrive, checking her watch every other second.

Cooper stared at his iPhone, intentionally ignoring his daughter. He was scanning email, his mind on a real estate business deal.

Wearing a strapless purple dress, Marley removed a tube of lipstick from her Coach purse. She covered her lips with a fresh coat of plum-tinted lip gloss, and checked her perfectly polished fingernails.

"How do I look?" She smiled at him with her most charming smile.

"Why are you begging for a compliment?" Cooper asked, still staring at his cell phone.

"I'm not begging." Marley released a puff of frustration.

"She huffed and puffed and blew the house down," Cooper said, looking at his daughter who was an interesting mix of him and his ex-wife. His chocolate skin; her mother's long black hair. Tall like her mother, but not thin; a round-shaped face like his, with softer features.

Marley realized she was not going to get what she wanted—not this time—so she shrugged her shoulders and looked at her watch. "They should be here any minute."

"Any minute," Cooper agreed.

"I tried calling Franchesca, but she didn't answer…as usual."

"As usual," Cooper repeated, in his most neutral tone. Sometimes the mention of his ex-wife could bring a volcanic eruption of emotion—mostly negative. Even though they divorced when Marley was seven-years-old, Franchesca DuBois had a way of getting in between the corpuscles of his veins.

"Daddy, you didn't invite Sallie, did you?" Marley asked with disapproval.

Annoyed, Cooper looked at Marley. "What did you say?"

"I hope you didn't invite her," Marley said, knowing that she was stepping into forbidden territory. She boldly went anyway.

"No, and if I did," he said slowly and deliberately. "Too bad for you."

"I don't like her," Marley bluntly said. "I don't like any of your "girlfriends," she said, making mock quotation marks with her index fingers.

"That's your problem, not mine."

"I used to want you and Franchesca to get married again, but I realize that love and hate is toxic, especially when hate is ninety percent of the equation."

"I don't hate your mother," said Cooper.

"Then I wanted you both to hurry up and get married to someone else, but that would make everything so insanely complicated," Marley said. "I like things the way they are."

"I'm not a loner type of man. And it's none of your business who I date."

"It is, Daddy," said Marley. "A strange woman in my life is my business."

"Look, I don't have time for this conversation," Cooper said, noticing Olivia Remmington approaching their table. He glanced at his daughter. "Marley, Marley, Marley…you look beautiful, baby."

"I know," Marley said, smiling.

"Hello, Olivia," Cooper said, greeting the coach with a charming smile. He was six foot three, but the coach was taller in her four-inch heels. "Thanks for coming."

"Of course," she said. "I appreciate you having this dinner party for the girls. They're excited." She turned her attention to Marley. "I like that dress!"

"Thanks!"

"Have a seat," Cooper said, pulling a chair out for her.

An attractive caramel-colored skin woman, she had a narrow face and petite features, sometimes hidden by her wild mass of copper-streaked shoulder-length hair. Married and twice-divorced, Olivia blamed her love of basketball for the demise of her marriages.

"This will be an interesting dinner, seeing the girls dressed up," Olivia said, as she sat down. "They wear sweat like it's a scent from Bath and Body Works called funk and sweat."

"The intoxicating odor of funk, sweat and dedication," said Cooper.

"I like that description," said Olivia. "I heard you played football in college."

"Yeah, I was going to play for the NFL until a 300-pound linebacker ran me over."

"Ouch," Olivia said.

"I played semi-pros in Europe for a couple of years, but I had to go to plan B."

"At least you had a plan B," said Olivia.

Cooper laughed. "I didn't have a plan B. I had to make it up. Plan B didn't work. So I went to plan C, D, and E. I've had several business adventures."

"There's Chase and Tequila," Marley said, waving at them. "I wonder if they came together."

Tequila walked towards them in a rush, somewhat awkwardly in her high-heeled shoes. She wore one color from head to toe—orange. Even her wide hoops earrings, the choker around her neck, the bangle of bracelets, and wide-strapped watch were a shade of orange. Tequila swiveled her hips like she was a model for a fashion show with celebrities watching. Her outfit was from a store with cheaply-made, tacky-trendy clothes. Tequila strutted as if her clothes were from a photo spread of Vogue fashion magazine.

Chase followed Tequila to the table, her father Michael Anderson trailing not far behind. Chase had insisted that her mother take her shopping for something new to wear, even though she had a closet full of dresses. Most of her dresses were for church. She was self-conscious about being the youngest on the team, and didn't want to look like she still dressed in the girls' clothing section (she did). She went to two malls with her mother, sister and best friend Kendall before finding a dress that her mother approved. Chase wore a spaghetti-strap, knee-length red and black dress, and black two-inch high heel shoes.

Cooper greeted Chase and Tequila. He didn't have to introduce himself. All the girls knew Marley's father because he watched the practices. He had a tendency to arrive early to pick up Marley from practices, and Coach Olivia didn't complain. Cooper knew how to be discreet and inconspicuous.

Michael Anderson greeted Olivia with a warm smile. He introduced himself to Cooper; the men shook hands. The three adults exchanged conversation about current sports news. They talked about the basketball team and the upcoming season. When Michael turned away to leave, he kissed Chase on the forehead. "I'll see you later."

Chase looked down, embarrassed by her father's public display of affection.

"You lucky, girl. I wish I had a Daddy to kiss my forehead," Tequila said, with unsuppressed longing in her voice. "Thanks for bringing me," Tequila said loudly before Michael walked away.

"You're welcome Tequila," Michael said, turning around to make eye contact with Tequila. "Have fun."

Moments later, Bailey arrived with Selena. Their dresses were almost identical. Everyone laughed when they saw them.

"I hope you didn't plan that. That is so ATL country," said Tequila.

"No," Bailey said. "I didn't know what I was going to wear. I bought four dresses from the mall and this is the one I picked."

"This is my best dress that doesn't look…"

"Straight from Mexico," said Tequila.

"Tequila, that mouth of yours," Coach Olivia said. "It's going to get you in trouble."

"Ain't nothing I ain't heard before," Tequila said.

"You better get it in check," said Coach O.

"I'm not offended, Coach O," said Selena. "I'm proud of who I am. My familia is from Mexico!"

Cooper stood up. "Welcome, ladies, you all look very beautiful."

"In other words, we don't look like basketball players," said Marley.

"But never forget you're ballers," said Cooper.

Everyone laughed.

"There's a time and place for everything," said Coach O. "Never leave that baller spirit on the court. Take it with you everywhere."

"Good evening, everyone," the waiter interrupted. "I'm Dario. I'll be taking care of you," he said with a slight foreign accent.

He was young and handsome, with a mysterious ethnicity; maybe from Egypt, Brazil, Greece, Argentina or some other foreign country. He flashed a heart-melting smile that instantly melted the hearts of the girls.

"Ladies, feel free to order what you like. I'm not saying that to be nice," said Cooper. "You don't have to order the cheapest thing on the menu, so order what you want to eat."

"That's very generous of you, Mr. Woods," said Bailey.

They all nodded.

"Here's the catch. Don't call me Mr. Woods. That makes me feel like an old man."

"Sir, I can't call you by your first name," Chase said, in a serious and respectful tone.

"Definitely don't call me sir," said Cooper sternly. "Some choice expletives might come from my mouth."

Chase's eyes grew wide, shocked by his bluntness.

"Chill, Chase," said Marley. "Daddy isn't going to curse at you. Although I must warn you, I get my foul mouth from him."

"Interesting," Coach O said with a twisted smile.

"So is it okay if I call you Mr. Cooper?" Chase asked, staring at Marley's father with confusion.

"Deal," Cooper said, smiling at a Chase in a way that dissolved her discomfort.

Dario took the girls' orders, with charming individualized attention. He made a point of asking them their names, and each girl smiled wider than the other. As he walked away, the girls giggled like elementary school girls.

"Yum, he's fine," said Marley.

"Behave, Marley," Cooper said.

"She said what I wanted to say," said Tequila. "I would love to…"

"He's super hot," said Bailey.

"Yes!" said Chase.

"Caliente," said Selena.

"Ladies, let me remind you that we are planning to have a winning season. That means no boys," said Coach O.

"What do you mean?" Tequila asked.

"No boys. No serious relationships," said Coach O. "Nothing that can distract you. Boys will distract you in a big way."

"That ain't right. I ain't ever had a coach tell me what to do when I ain't in the gym," said Tequila.

"Tequila, you can speak how you want to with everyone else, but delete 'ain't' from your vocabulary when you're talking to me." Coach

Olivia stared at Tequila before looking at each player. "I'm not a fan of the word 'ain't.'"

"When I was in college we weren't supposed to have girlfriends," said Copper.

"Daddy didn't listen," Marley said with a chuckle. "Voila—me!"

The girls giggled.

"I expect you girls to listen," Coach O said. "Especially if you plan to stay a starter."

Dario brought an array of appetizers to the table. "I know you will enjoy this, Tequila… Bailey… Marley… Selena… and Chase." He made eye contact with each girl as he said their names.

"Dig in," said Cooper.

"What do you mean by that?" asked Bailey. "The part about staying a starter?"

"Just because you are a starter today, doesn't mean you will be a starter tomorrow. You have to perform—always and all the time."

The girls groaned together. They'd heard those words in practice.

"You will hear that for the rest of the season. That's my motto and I urge you to make it yours."

"You always say expect the unexpected," Chase said.

"Yes, I do." Coach O laughed. "I don't do things to be popular," explained Coach O. "I know my style is very different from what everyone is used to. I'm not very popular with certain administrators at the school. I know I've upset some parents."

"Pissed off," said Cooper.

"So you've heard," said Olivia.

"I heard Ja-Nay-A's mom yelling at the principal," said Chase.

"Girls, I don't care about political nonsense. They hired me so the school can have a winning team like the boys."

"The boys games are crowded and fun to watch," said Selena. "Everybody comes to see them play."

"I remember when the girls' games were packed," said Olivia.

"When was that?" asked Bailey.

"I went to Riverbrook way back when the school was predominately white," explained Coach O. "I was the only black girl on the team."

"Really?" said Marley.

"The neighborhoods were mostly all white. Very few blacks or other minorities lived in the area," said Coach O. "That's changed in the past ten years or so. And they rezoned the school district so that brought in kids from areas that aren't near the school."

"I heard you went to Riverbrook, but I didn't know it was true," said Chase.

"It's true. The school has changed a lot since then," Coach Olivia said.

"That's for sure," said Cooper.

"I got a basketball scholarship and played for a D1 school that won games and championships," said Coach Olivia. "I played for the WNBA..."

"I'm going to play for WBNA!" said Tequila.

"I played professional ball in Europe for a team that won games and broke records. I'm used to winning," said Coach O. "I hate to lose!"

"Losing sucks," said Marley.

"Those days are over for Riverbrook girls' basketball team. I know what it takes to win," said Coach O. "I will do what's necessary to win, even if I have to cut all five of you and get new starters."

"Coach, you just playing about getting new starters, right?" asked Tequila.

"No, I'm not." Her tone was stern and blunt.

The girls didn't say a word, but they knew—without an ounce of doubt—that she was serious.

"We kind of stunk last year," Bailey said.

"We were horrible," said Tequila. "We mostly lost."

"I know. I'm here to change that. I'm not here to lose," said Coach O. "That's why I picked you all. So we can win."

"Are you going to tell us why you picked us? I mean, I know why you picked me," said Tequila. "I got skills."

"I picked each of you for different reasons. You will understand why during the season."

"Some of the other girls don't agree with us being the starters," Bailey quietly said.

"I knew my decision was going to be controversial. I knew some of the other girls were going to be mad," admitted Coach O. "But I have a strategy and you just have to trust me."

"How are we going to suddenly become a winning team?" Marley asked.

"I don't want to hear about the past years when you didn't win. This is a new time and era for… us," said Coach Olivia. "We're going to have a winning season. Are you with me?"

"Yes!" the girls said together."

The food arrived. Dario handed each girl their plate, saying their names and evaporating their hearts.

"We're a team. This isn't Marley's team or Tequila's team," said Coach O. "It's going to take a lot of hard work and practice."

"We understand," said Marley, as the other girls nodded their heads.

"We're more powerful as a team. And the girls on the bench are good. They can replace you. Some may need to strengthen certain skills, but I have a team of winners. It's the whole team that's going to make us winners, not just you guys…I mean girls."

"That's absolutely true," said Cooper.

"You're the leaders of this team and I expect certain things from you as starters," said Coach O.

"I'm just a freshman," said Chase. "The juniors and seniors aren't going to listen to me."

"You have to earn their respect. All of you. Practice hard and play harder." Coach O sipped some iced tea. "Play like your life depends on it. Imagine you're on a mountain climbing to the top. If you let go, you fall. It's you or the mountain."

"The mountain is going to lose," said Selena enthusiastically. "Cause I ain't…I'm not falling."

"That's right, Selena," said Coach O. "It's about confidence and attitude."

"That's me," said Tequila, pointing at herself.

Coach O shook her head. "I need to have one hundred percent commitment from you," Coach O said. "Be better than your best." She paused. "Imagine if we have better stats than the boys' team."

"That would be the shit!" Tequila covered her mouth. "Oops!"

"I would love it. They get all the attention…in the newspaper and school announcements," said Marley. "We never get mentioned."

"That's going to change this year. That's a promise," said Coach O. "Like I say in practice…"

"Expect the unexpected," the girls said together.

CHAPTER 2

BAILEY

"Virgin, virgin, virgin!" teased River.
Bailey's faced turned red. "Shh! Don't announce it to the world."
"You can't go to college a virgin."

"Where do you want to go next?" Bailey asked her best friend River Scranton, while shopping at an Atlanta suburban mall with popular teen-age stores—American Eagle, The Gap, Abercrombie and Finch, and Forever 21, along with major department stores, and other stores. It was Saturday, mid-day, and the mall was packed with teen-agers shopping, eating in the food court, going to the movie theatre, or just hanging out.

Carrying several shopping bags, Bailey and River weaved through a crowd of teen-agers, separated briefly by groups of people before catching up to each other. "It's so crowded out here," observed River. "Let's just go into The Gap."

"I thought you didn't like The Gap anymore," Bailey said.

"It's like half-cool," River said, passing two little girls, probably seven- or eight-years old, dressed in softball uniforms: identical shirts with their name and number on the back, knee-length white pants, knee-high socks with stripes on the side, and cleats on their feet. "Look at them." River pointed at the girls after waving at them.

Bailey smiled and waved back at the two girls. "We used to play softball for the same league," she said to them.

"We won our game today," said the girl who had two long blonde pigtails.

"Yeah and I got a homerun!" said the girl with two missing front teeth.

"Cool," River said.

"Your hair is super cool," said the little girl, referring to River's short spiked hair cut: midnight black with wild bursts of pink highlights. River's not-so-original punk hair cut accented her olive complexion and exotic features.

"Thanks!" River said.

Staring at Bailey, one of the girls said, "Your eyes are blue like the sky."

Bailey laughed. "That's a very nice compliment. Thank you very much."

"You're really pretty. You have blonde hair like me," said the little girl. "You could be a model or something. And you're so tall. My mom thinks I'm going to be tall."

"Thank you, but I don't think I'm going to be a model," said Bailey.

"You don't?" the little girl asked, her eyes curious and intense.

"She's a chicken," said River. "Bak, bak, bak!"

"Ignore my crazy friend. I don't like a lot of attention. Photo shoots would make me throw up," said Bailey.

"See, she's a chicken," said River.

The little girls laughed.

"Bye girls," said Bailey as they walked away from the elementary school girls.

River and Bailey browsed toward the junior section in The Gap, as the little girls walked over to the young girls' section. "That used to be us in softball uniforms," said Bailey.

"I was so uncoordinated," said River. "I couldn't hit the ball to save my life."

"You did sometimes. Remember when you got that homerun?"

"They just let the ball roll down the hill and no one tried to stop it. I didn't figure that out for a long time." River picked up a pair of jeans. "I hated softball."

"I loved it," said Bailey. "I actually kind of miss it."

"Remember when I sat on third base playing in the dirt and that girl ran right past me and made it to home base? I was supposed to stop her but I was busy making dirt piles."

Bailey laughed. "That was funny."

"Daddy was so freaking mad, I thought he was going to kill me," said River.

"When he yelled at you in that mean voice in front of everybody, I cried."

"I was scared to go home. I was so glad that Mommy was there… no telling what would have happened," River said, her green eyes darkened, accented by the black eyeliner stretched across her upper and lower eyelids. "I kept telling him that I hated sports, but he wouldn't listen to me. Still doesn't."

"You were so stubborn. I remember when he dragged you out of the car to make you play," Bailey said. "I wondered what other parents thought." She searched through a rack of jeans.

"That he was crazy. He refused to believe that I suck at sports," River said. "He used to make me feel so bad that I was girl. I heard him telling my mother how much he wanted a son."

"Fast forward," said Bailey, "and now you're doing what you like."

"Rock star queen," said River, sorting through a stack of shirts on sale. "And you are a starter on the basketball team."

"Like that's so impressive," Bailey said sarcastically. "I'm not the best player."

"You were a starter when we were playing softball." River picked up a hat, examined it briefly and then put it back on the rack.

"We were like seven or eight. They didn't call us starters, and we didn't even know what it meant," explained Bailey. "This time it's different. These girls are serious basketball players. I seriously don't know why the coach picked me."

"You're just being humble," said River.

"No, I'm dead serious," Bailey said passionately. "There are girls on the team who play ten times better than me. There's this one black girl, Ja-Nay-A. She hates me. She hates me for taking her starter spot. I had nothing to do with it. She scares the shit out of me."

"Tell her, I'll kick her ass," said River.

"You're 100 pounds and she's probably 170 pounds."

"I'll get my dog to bite her in the ass," said River.

"She looks at me like she's going to kill me," said Bailey. "When the coach announced the starters, Ja-Nay-A got in my face screaming at me that it was my fault she won't be going to college."

"I will come to your funeral," River mockingly said.

"That's not funny. I'm really scared of her," she said, her voice rippling with fear.

"Sorry," said River, "I thought I would add some … levity to the situation."

"Levity…funny, ha ha ha! Levity, that's the new name of your band, right?" Bailey asked. "Or have you guys changed the name again?"

"It's still Levity," said River, moving to another row of jeans.

"You're Dad still doesn't know?"

"He'll shit in his pants when he finds out I'm in a rock band."

"He probably will."

"Yeah and he's going to be surprised at the colleges I'm applying to," said River.

"I'm predictable. I'm applying to the schools I've always talked about."

"What Daddy doesn't know doesn't hurt him," said River, shrugging.

"So he still doesn't know about you and Austin."

"He thinks we're just friends."

"Maybe he's just not saying anything."

"I can't believe I like Austin so much. His touch just gives me the shivers and the way he…" River noticed that Bailey looked uncomfortable. "Virgin, virgin, virgin!"

Bailey's face turned red. "Shh! Don't announce it to the world."

"You can't go to college a virgin," River said.

"It's not like there's a checkbox on college applications," said Bailey.

"That's because if there was two boxes: one for virgin and one for non-virgin, no one would check non-virgin," explained River.

"Whatever!"

They tried on different outfits and ended up buying the same pair of jeans and shirt, which wasn't unusual. They dressed alike in elementary school, but never in middle school. They went to the same middle school until seventh grade when there was a racial incident at the school. River's father removed her from the racially diverse public school. He sent River to Independence Academy, a predominately white private school. Bailey and River thought they would be back together in high school, but River's father made her attend a private high school.

Waiting in line to purchase jeans and shirts, Bailey heard her name.

She turned around and saw Diante Johnson who was in her advanced physics class.

"Hey, Diante," she said.

"What's up?" Diante flashed a warm smile. Tall, brown, and good-looking, Diante was a girl magnet at school, and anywhere he went where teen girls hung out.

"Shopping and hanging out with my friend." Introducing them, Bailey said, "This is River and this is Diante."

"Hi," River said.

"Hello," Diante said to River.

"Gap doesn't seem your style," said Bailey.

"I'm actually here with my mother." Diante was dressed in low-hanging jeans and a Polo shirt. "She's in here somewhere."

"That's nice, I guess," Bailey said. "My mother likes to come shopping with me too." She snarled her face. "Hate it."

"I don't mind," Diante said with a slight shrug. "See ya around."

Bailey and River walked out the store, carrying two Gap bags.

"He's cute," River said.

"Yeah, he is," Bailey said.

"You like him?" she asked, strolling past several stores.

Bailey shrugged. "I don't know. He's never acted interested in me."

"This girl started dating one of the black kids in school. There aren't many blacks at Independence, you know," said River. "She's so ostracized now."

Bailey laughed. "Look at my ....family. I'm the fish that jumped out of water and landed on Mars."

River laughed. "Mars is your kind of place."

"Ha Ha!" said Bailey.

"Remember how my Daddy tried to keep us apart when your mom married your step-dad," said River.

Bailey shook her head, an unwelcome memory revisiting her mind.

"He's such a racist. Sometimes it's so embarrassing," said River.

"My grandparents acted the same way. They HATED Robert," said Bailey. "They even tried to get custody of me."

"I remember. Especially the day you wouldn't stop crying because you thought you were never going to see your mom."

Bailey was quiet, remembering her life from six years ago. "Well, they had no choice but to accept our racially mixed-up family," said Bailey. "They adore my little brother and sister."

"So when's your next game?" River asked.

"We're still doing tournament games, but in two weeks we have a home game."

"You know I'm coming," River promised. "I'll bring some of my friends and the band."

"You sure?" asked Bailey.

"Yeah. Why not?"

"You know why! They think Riverbrook is a ghetto school because there are a lot of black kids. Doesn't matter that our SAT scores are high."

"Not everybody in school believes their parents' racial bullshit," River said defensively.

"Some of them do."

"Yeah and I don't associate with them."

CHAPTER 3

TEQUILA

"What time is your mom getting in?" asked Diante.
"Late. She's going out with her creeper new boyfriend."
"You don't like him?"
"Naw," Tequila said.
"You want some company later, devil red?"

The brakes on the school bus squeaked loudly as the driver pulled into Tequila's apartment complex. Tequila sat in the front of the bus because she hated waiting until everyone got off the bus. She sat in the back of the classroom because she wanted to be invisible, but the bus was different. When the bus doors opened, she was the first to get off the bus. Several girls followed behind her.

"Good luck at the game!" one of the girls said, snickering.

"You're going to lose as usual," said another girl.

Tequila ignored them and jetted around the corner, taking the short cut to her building. She wanted to avoid Diante Johnson—who always sat near the back of the bus. Diante was too cute, too cocky, and way too tempting. She did not need any distractions. It was going to be hard enough concentrating on basketball and her classes, especially since the new coach regularly checked their grades. When Coach Olivia told them she checked the status of their grades during the season, Tequila's stomach dropped like she was speeding down a roller coaster ride.

She hated school.

But she loved basketball like Romeo loved Juliet.

Or Edward loved Bella.

Tequila went up to the third floor of her apartment building and unlocked the door. The apartment was silent. The television was off and the video game joysticks weren't sprawled across the floor. Something was wrong. She screamed her little brother's name: "Tevon!"

She looked in the living room and the combination kitchen/dining room area. He usually was watching TV or sitting at the table munching on a hot pocket or macaroni and cheese in a microwavable bowl. She called his name again and looked in the hallway closet. Tevon pretended to act tough, but sometimes he was wimpy, especially if a stranger knocked on the door.

She went down the narrow hallway and looked in Tevon's bedroom, then inside her bedroom and her mother's bedroom. She looked in the closets in all three bedrooms. She went back to see if his book bag was in the living room and didn't see it on the coffee table or on the couch.

Tequila was worried. Tevon got out of school at 2:25 PM and he was usually in the apartment by 3:00 PM. He used to be afraid to come home by himself, but their mother didn't want to pay for after school care. "I was a latchkey kid and so was Tequila," Rashonda bluntly said. "Now it's your turn." Tevon cried for two weeks until he adjusted to being home by himself.

Tequila looked on the calendar in the kitchen to see if Tevon had a doctor or dentist appointment. Nothing was written down on the huge wall calendar that had names, phone numbers, and dates scribbled all around the corners of the pages and in the date blocks. "Tevon! Tevon! Where are you?"

She wondered if he went to his friend's apartment two buildings down, even though he was forbidden from roaming around the apartment complex by himself.

She checked her phone to see if he had called her, but there weren't any texts or missed calls from him. Worry was turning into fear, so she dialed her mother's work number.

Listening to the phone ring, she was tempted to hang up. She did not want to tell her mother that Tevon was not home. Her mother was going to freak out and scream at her, and somehow blame her for Tevon's disappearance.

It wasn't her fault.

A female answered the phone at her mother's job. Tequila nervously asked to speak to "Rashonda Paxton."

"One moment, please."

All hell is about to break loose when Mama finds out that Tevon isn't home, thought Tequila.

"Mama, I can't find Tevon!" she screamed as soon as she heard her mother's voice. "I looked in all the rooms and closets, but he's not here."

Suddenly the living room closet door opened and Tevon jumped out. "Here I am!" Tevon started giggling as if he had just seen an episode of 'America's Funniest Videos.'

A little short to be a fourth-grader, Tevon was a tad chunky. His hair was low-cut and he had big brown eyes and a wide smile that displayed protruding front teeth. "Got you, Tee-Tee! I got you!"

Tequila slapped the back of Tevon's head. "That's not funny."

"Oww," Tevon mumbled, rubbing his head. "That hurt."

She hit him again—just a little bit softer on his shoulder. "Big head, don't be scaring me like that."

"Mama, he was hiding in the closet," she said into the phone.

"I heard," Rashonda said. "I thought you said you looked in the closet."

"I did. I looked in all the closets."

"I'm a good hider," Tevon said, dodging Tequila's hand aimed for his head.

"Tell your big head brother to stop hiding and do his homework," Rashonda said. "You need to do your homework too."

"I know, Mama."

"When is your game?" Rashonda asked. "I need to print your game schedule and put it on my cube at work."

"Game is on Friday."

"I get off work early, so your number one fan will be there."

Tequila smiled. Her mother frequently said she was her number one fan. It was true.

"We got a long practice tomorrow. Coach O has us doing weird stuff like remembering quotes." Tequila added, "Sometimes I think she's crazy, Mama."

"You got to learn how to deal with her." Rashonda lowered her voice. "Just like I got to deal with my crazy-ass boss. She's crazier than a crack addict."

"Crazy like crack head Aunt Dee, huh?"

"Yeah, Quila! Now, fix dinner and do your homework. Make sure Tevon does his homework and takes a bath. You know what you gotta do."

"What time you get off?"

"I get off at 9, but I'm meeting Cedric for dinner."

"Cedric?" Tequila said, twisting her face into an ugly snarl.

"Yes, Cedric!"

"You sure been spending a lot of time with him," Tequila said with distaste spilling from the tone of her voice.

"That's none of your damn business, Quila. I'm a grown-ass woman. Now you do what you supposed to and I'll talk to you later," scolded Rashonda. "Call me if you need me."

"Bye, Mama."

Tequila hung up the phone and looked at her brother. "Why are you scrunching up your face? You look like a monster."

"That's what you looked like when you said Cedric."

Tequila shrugged. "Oh!"

"I like Cedric," Tevon said.

"So what! Go do your homework. I'm going to take a nap."

"You're supposed to do your homework too," Tevon said. "I'm telling Mama."

"Don't be a snitch," Tequila said. "And don't let anyone in."

"I know. I'm not a baby."

"You act like one sometimes."

Tequila instantly fell asleep—but not for long. It was a short nap, but she fell into a deep sleep, dreaming about her father. She was in Brooklyn and she could hear someone calling her father's name, but she couldn't see his face. Just a shadow of a man's face. She hated dreaming about her father. He wasn't in their lives. She hadn't seen him in so long she couldn't remember what he looked like. Dreaming about him only made her think about him—and she didn't like to think about him. Waking up, she forced the dream out of her mind. Frustrated, she hopped out of bed and decided to make dinner.

She went into the bathroom and washed her face. Even without mascara, blush, or lipstick, Tequila saw a beautiful honey-brown skinned girl in the mirror staring back. Her face was long and angular with striking facial features. She had the height to be a model and planned to be on the cover of a magazine one day, while being a famous basketball player. One day in the not-too-distant future.

She went into the living room and heard Tevon snoring on the sofa. His school papers were scattered on the sofa and the floor.

She went into the kitchen and opened the refrigerator door. Tequila grinned when she saw the meatloaf that her mother had made. She just had to make the side dishes. She opened the kitchen cabinet and removed a box of instant mashed potatoes and a can of green beans.

The phone rang and she read the number scrolling across the caller ID box: *Aunt Beatty's number.* Seeing the New York number made her feel like she could see what sadness looked like, even though it was a feeling. So, she didn't answer the phone.

If she were in Brooklyn, she would walk down the street to her two aunts' apartments and scream from the bottom stoop: "I'm a freaking starter on the basketball team." Some neighbors would tell her to "Shut the hell up." Other neighbors would scream, "You go, girl." Her wild and silly aunties would come do something fun or crazy, like throwing a bucket of ice on her from the top floor window.

Tequila had lived in Atlanta for the past three years, but still missed Brooklyn. The feeling never went away. She hated that her relatives could not watch her play basketball. Her mother has nine brothers and sisters, and all her aunts and uncles have lots of kids. She had at least twenty-three cousins. Her family would rule the fans in the stands. She hoped this year that some of her relatives would come to Atlanta and watch her play basketball.

Tequila and Tevon ate dinner while watching the popular carton *Family Guy*. Tevon laughed at every word every character said, funny or not. Tequila only laughed when she thought something was funny.

After dinner, Tevon took a bath and Tequila started doing her homework. She opened *The Sun Also Rises* by Ernest Hemming, a book from her American Literature class, skimming through the book with tiny print and unfamiliar words. A few minutes later, she tossed the book on the floor. She hated reading. She removed the math sheet from the math folder and started working on the equations. She didn't like math either so when her phone vibrated she was happy to be distracted. She saw 'Diante' flashing in the caller ID, and smiled. He was good-looking, smart, and funny—and he was calling her.

"Hey, Diante!"

"Hey, Quila-Quila!"

She laughed. She liked how he repeated her name.

"What are you up to?" he asked.

"Homework and I freaking hate homework!"

"What time is your mom getting in?"

"Late. She's going out with her creeper new boyfriend."

"You don't like him?"

"Naw," she said in a tone that did not invite questions.

"Want some company, devil red?"

"Tevon is still up."

"So, you want some company after Tevon goes to bed?"

The excited smile reappeared on her face, and she missed a couple of heart beats, thinking about the way he made her feel.

"You there?" Diante asked.

"Yeah."

"So, can I come over?"

"I'll hit you back."

Tequila pressed the end button, remembering his last visit. How distracting and fun and hot he was. But then her mother decided to show up early. So, she had to be more careful.

She looked at the time on her phone. She would have more time with Diante, especially since her mother was going out with a new, creeper boyfriend.

A little later, Tevon came into the living room to tell Tequila good night. "I have a present for you in your room." She let him grab her hand and followed him down the hall to her bedroom. Inside, she saw a sheet of construction paper taped on the wall over her bed. The paper read: *You are the best player!*

Tequila looked at her sometimes annoying, but mostly sweet little brother. "Oh, big head. That was sweet."

"Stop calling me big head."

"If you wake up tomorrow and your head has shrunk, I'll stop calling you big head."

Tevon poked out his lips, looking sad and hurt. "Well I'm going to bed," he said, stomping down the hall.

She went into his bedroom. "Thank you, little brother. Go to sleep and I will see you tomorrow."

"Not if I see you first," he said, snickering.

Tequila sat down at the dining room table, and forced herself to concentrate on the confusing algebra equations on the math worksheet.

Diante called again. She stared at his name flashing, her beat beating faster every time the phone vibrated.

She didn't answer.

She didn't know why.

CHAPTER 4

CHASE

"So you're back, bleeder girl," said the point guard from Piedmont High.
Chase fought back tears. "You're it," she said, then snatched the ball away from the girl, ran down court, and scored a lay-up shot.

"Chase, guard number 32," said Coach O. "She's their best player."

"She's super fast," Chase said.

"That's why I'm putting you on her," Coach O said. "You're faster."

Playing Piedmont High, it was the first quarter and they were losing by ten points. Chase dared not say what she was thinking: we're going to lose. She knew the coach would kick her out of the game and they needed her.

It was a home game and the gym was half-empty. In an hour—when the varsity boys played—the gym would be packed. She spotted her grandmother waving a sign with her name. The sign was custom made: Chase in big poster-size letters. Her grandmother brought the sign to every game.

She could always hear her grandmother's voice—loud and squeaky. Grammy screamed during the games—at her, the referees, coaches, and other players. She probably annoyed a lot of people, but her grandmother didn't care. She was 70-years-old and said what she thought—uncensored and unapologetic.

Standing in front of the girl with the number 32 on her uniform, Chase held her arms above her shoulders in a defensive position. She felt sick, but ignored the pain in her lower stomach. Her mission was clear: guard number 32 to stop the other team from scoring.

Chase stared at the girl, thinking: *I'm not afraid of you. You can't pass me. I'm stopping you no matter what you do.* When the referee blew his whistle, Chase ran down court, two steps ahead of the girl she was guarding.

At half-time, Chase felt an unfamiliar pain in her stomach. She thought it would go away, but the pain was sharp and intense. Her stomach would hurt for a minute and then stop.

Mid-way through the third quarter, Chase didn't realize what was happening between her legs as she ran down the court and made a layup. In that moment, she didn't recognize her body's signs that meant monthly visits. She stopped the bleed on the scoreboard; they were no longer losing. Riverbrook now had a six point lead.

When Coach O called a time-out, Chase was ready for a water break. But that wasn't the reason the coach called the timeout.

The coach motioned for Chase to come close to her. Coach O whispered in Chase's ear: "There's a stain on the back of your pants."

Chase looked at her with confusion. She didn't remembering sitting on anything.

"Are you on your period?" Coach O whispered.

Confusion spread across Chase's face. "I haven't had my period yet." Chase spoke so softly that the Coach barely heard her.

Coach O looked at Chase with surprise and compassion, remembering how young she was, even more impressed by Chase's talent and tenacity.

"I don't know if anyone noticed," Coach O said.

"Oh my God," Chase said, as comprehension and embarrassment collided in her head. *People saw blood on my shorts.*

"I'm going to have Marley follow behind you," said Coach O.

"We need Marley in the game," said Chase. "We got to keep the lead."

"Thanks to you, we're ahead. But you need to take care of yourself right away."

Coach O motioned for Marley, whispered in her ear and then the two girls awkwardly walked off the court: Marley followed closely behind Chase.

Layne and Ja-Nay-A checked into the game to replace Chase and Marley.

Inside the locker room, Chase went straight to the bathroom. "I'm so…so…so embarrassed."

"Don't worry about it," Marley said. "I didn't see anything."

"I hope no one else saw…"

"How come you didn't…know?" Marley asked.

"I….I….haven't had my period yet," Chase whispered. "This is my first time."

"Are you serious?" asked Marley, her voice rising in surprise. "I started when I was in seventh grade."

"What do I do?" Chase asked. "I mean I know what my mom told me to do, but it just feels weird, right?"

"Clean yourself up, and I'll find you a pad. You're not ready for a tampon."

Chase felt awkward and didn't know what to say. "Thanks, Marley," stumbled out of her mouth.

Five minutes later, the girls went back to the gym. "Please don't tell anyone," Chase said. "I would die…"

"Don't worry about it. It's a girl thing. It's normal," Marley said, with her arms around Chase's shoulders. "You will be okay. I promise."

Chase and Marley returned to the gym. It was the fourth quarter and the score was tied: 55 to 55. Chase walked over to the coach. "I'm ready to go back in."

Coach O looked at her. "Are you sure?"

"Sure as my name is Chase."

Coach O motioned Chase and Marley to go back in the game and signaled Layne and Jay-Nay-A back to the bench.

"That girl is fast," said Layne, gasping for breath. "I thought I was going to die trying to keep up with 32."

Chase ran back on the court and immediately positioned herself in front of player 32.

"So you're back, bleeder girl," said the point guard from Piedmont High.

Chase paused for a moment, wondering who else noticed her period accident. She could cry in embarrassment or embarrass the girl by stealing the ball from her. "You're it," Chase said, then snatched the ball from the girl, ran down court, and scored a lay-up shot, putting two points on the board for a two-point lead.

Seconds later, the game was tied again.

Marley intercepted the other team's pass, and made a fast break down court, watching the clock with a devilish smile. The score was 57-57. She had to make a basket. Marley swiveled around a player and scored.

Piedmont High now had possession of the ball. Thirty seconds later, they made a basket and the game was again tied.

With less than a one minute on the clock, Riverbrook regained the lead: 61-59.

They had to maintain possession of the ball for the next 33 seconds. They passed the ball to each other until guard 32 from the opposing team came from nowhere and stole the ball. She was headed down court and if she scored, the game would be tied. They would have to play another quarter in overtime.

Chase wasn't going to let that happen.

She ran like a gazelle and blocked the girl from taking the shot, just as the buzzer went off.

Riverbrook High won the game by two points.

The players jumped up and down, hugging and high-fiving each other. Minutes later, the team followed the basketball tradition of both teams lining up in a single row and walking beside the other team, giving each other high fives and repeating, "Good game. Good game. Good game."

The Riverbrook team couldn't stop screaming with joy. They discovered the taste of victory—a new flavor. It was delicious. It tasted as sweet as cotton candy.

Driving home in their mini-van, Chase and her family talked about the game.

"Why did you disappear in the middle of the game?" Evan asked. "They really needed you!" He was tall with an athletic frame from playing baseball and running track. Evan was a younger version of his handsome father: good-looking, medium-brown with distinctive thick eye brows and a warm smile.

"Yeah, what was that about?" asked Blake, who sometimes hated that she and Chase looked so much alike. They were a mixture of both parents: tan skin, dark thick hair, and oblong faces with petite facial features. Blake wore her hair smooth straight down to her shoulders, but Chase usually brushed her hair into a ponytail.

Chase didn't want to tell them that she had her period for the first time—at the wrong time. She dodged their question with a question. "Why didn't Daddy come to the game?"

"He had to work late. Some big project he's working on," her mother said. Seconds later, Shellie's cell phone rang, displaying Coach Olivia's name in the caller ID box. "Your coach is calling."

Shellie talked to the coach for a few minutes. The family heard their mother's side of the conversation:

"She hasn't told me."

"Knew it would happen any day."

"You're right."

"She's a real trooper."

"Thank you. I'm very proud of her too."

"Good night," she said, before ending the call.

"You feeling alright, Chasey?" her mother asked.

"I feel fine! Happy that we won!"

"That's not what I'm talking about," said Shellie.

From her mother's tone of voice, Chase knew that coach had told her mom. "I'm good."

"I'm proud of you," her mom said.

"What are y'all talking about?" asked Evan.

"Nothing," said Chase.

"Chase, I took a nap in your room," said Blake. "Your bed is a mess and there are papers scattered on the floor everywhere."

Evan laughed. "Chase is going to die if you left her room a mess. She's so OCD."

"I am not," Chase said defensively.

"Yes you are," said Evan.

"Definitely," said Blake.

"Why were you in my room?" asked Chase.

"Cause my room was a wreck," said Blake.

"Mommy!" whined Chase.

"Blake, you know better," scolded Shellie. "You know how Chase is."

"Mommy, I was just messing with her. She's always trying to prank me."

DARIAN-BALL-BLOG: NUMBER 1

Our girls' basketball team is starting the season like they know how to play basketball. One of the players had a red moment, but she kept playing. Brave girl.

They won several pre-season tournament games and then won yesterday's regional game against Piedmont High School. How is that possible? I don't think Coach Olivia Remmington picked the best starters for the team, but they may not stay starters for the whole season. That's what I've heard.

But are they are winning because of:
The coach?
The players?
Their defense?
Their offense?

This is just the beginning of the season and the girls are super-hyped. When we get into the real season, will they keep winning? It would be a nice change to have a winning team. Shocking…surprising… super fantabulous.

They're actually winning…for real, for real. The real question: Will it last?

Comments

Madplayer: I got mad skills. But I didn't make the team. They will suck as usual.
Sportsqueen: You must be a boy to even go there!
Seegame: I saw red.
Gamewatcher: I applaud her. She went back IN and they won.
Mindyourbiz: Some things are too private to talk about.
Lovehighsh: Keep winning Riverbrook!
Bxpert: The odds are not in their favor.
Hatebb: I predict a sad, bad season as usual.
Sportsnut: It's possible. We got a real coach.
Iknowsports: The coach is new, but same girls. Just cause they won one game and some pre-season games don't mean nothing!

CHAPTER 5

SELENA

"Umm, spaghetti," said Selena. *"I love spaghetti."*

"I thought you only ate tacos and beans," said a pimpled-face boy behind them.

"Who are you?" asked Eva. *"The food police?"*

"That's stupid," said the boy.

"You eat Chinese food, don't you?" asked Eva.

"Yeah I love Chinese food."

"You don't look Chinese to me, stupid," said Eva.

Selena stood near the entrance to the cafeteria while waiting for her younger sister Maria and cousin Eva. It was the second lunch period—the most crowded lunch of the three school lunch periods. Kids from all races: black, white, Hispanic, Brazilian, Indian, Asian and other cultures walked into the cafeteria.

Selena smiled and waved at the kids she knew. Some of the guys teased her about playing basketball:

"You don't look like a basketball player."

"You're too happy all the time to be stealing balls."

"You popped those threes last week. I can't believe you did that."

"You're not gonna last the season."

"Real basketball girls will eat you for lunch."

"Girl, don't listen to them idiots," said a classmate.

Ja-Nay-A walked passed Selena with two friends. She spoke loud enough for Selena to hear her: "Coach said just because you make starter don't mean you are going to stay starter."

Maria heard Ja-Nay-A's comment. She put her arm around Selena. "Ignore her. She crazy jealous," said Maria who was a year younger. Selena and Maria looked like identical twins. Same round face, olive skin, brown eyes, dark hair and bright smile. Maria didn't have Selena's deep dimples and wore her hair short and curly.

"Yeah," said Eva. "Don't let her inside your brain."

Selena released a frustrated sigh. "You're right."

"Got toughen up, Selena. Kids are going to be saying mean and nasty things about you," said Eva who was her cousin on her father's side. The three of them sometimes claimed to be sisters.

Selena nodded. "That's what Juan said."

"Your brother is smart. He should be in college," said Eva.

"He gotta help Papá run the restaurant," said Selena.

"Let's get some food," said Maria, as they followed other students into the crowded cafeteria.

There were different food options: a cold line for subs, sandwiches and salads; a hot grill line for hamburgers, wraps, hotdogs and fries; and a line for the regular cafeteria-lunch meals.

The girls got in the food line, picked up a tray and utensils as they followed the other students waiting in line. One by one, students placed an empty tray on the steel rack for sliding their tray down the food line. A glass partition hung between the students and the cafeteria workers serving the food. There was just enough room for the cafeteria employee to put food on the students' plates.

The line was moving slowly: a popular dish was being served.

"Umm, spaghetti," said Selena. "I love spaghetti."

Maria smiled. "Me too."

"I thought you only ate tacos and beans," said a pimpled-face boy standing behind them in line.

"Who are you?" asked Eva. "The food police?"

"That's stupid," said the boy.

"You eat Chinese food, don't you?" asked Eva.

"Yeah I love Chinese food!" said the boy.

"You don't look Chinese too me," said Eva. "Estúpida."

Selena and Maria laughed.

The pimple-faced boy's face turned red. The boy's friend punched him in the shoulder and laughed. "That was a stupid thing to say."

"So I'm stupid some times."

"Next, next," said the cafeteria lady.

"I'll have the spaghetti and meatballs, salad and bread," said Selena.

Maria ordered the same meal.

Eva ordered meat loaf, mashed potatoes and peas.

They slid their trays down to the desert area.

Selena ordered chocolate cake. Eva and Maria ordered Jell-O.

They all placed a carton of chocolate milk on their trays. They slid their trays down the row to the cashier and paid. They carefully carried their trays while looking for a place to sit.

Riverbrook had a diverse student population of approximately 2,500 students, but kids had a tendency to sit with other kids like themselves. Not just separated by status and personality: geeks and nerds; pretty; popular; athletes; cool dudes; bad kids; loners; genius kids; rich; middle-class; or poor. There was another layer of separation: race. Sometimes students from different races sat together at the same lunch table.

Selena heard someone call her name. It was a friend from class. "Come sit with us."

The girls sat at table of girls who were friendly with most students. They joined in: eating, laughing, talking—until the end-of-lunch bell rang.

After lunch, Selena was walking down the hall to her class when someone tapped her shoulder. She thought it was her sister—but it was someone unexpected.

Her eyes brightened when she looked into Miguel Alvarez's smiling face. He had thick black hair, dark eyes beneath thick brows and an olive-skin tone. She thought he was the most gorgeous boy in school. He was a star baseball player and girls followed Miguel around like he was a famous movie star. A group of girls regularly went to his baseball games. They called themselves the 'Miguelettes.' They sat together, throwing up signs with his name and screaming his name every time he pitched, batted or ran to a base. He had fans as if he were a professional baseball player.

Selena watched him play several times and he was definitely an outstanding player. His pitches were lightening fast and he ran like the wind.

"Selena bonito," Miguel said with a bright white smile.

His comment that she was pretty left her without words.

"I heard you can hoop."

Still mesmerized to be in his presence, she only smiled.

"I'm coming to see you play," he promised. "You must be pretty good."

She nodded with a big smile.

"Do you talk?" he asked, touching her on the shoulder, bringing her back to the moment.

She laughed. "Sí! Thank you. I'm glad to be on the team."

"You're not just on the team," said Miguel. "You're a starter."

Smiling, she said, "Sí! I still can't believe it."

"I will be checking you out, bonito Selena."

She nodded.

"You lose your tongue?" he teased. "No puede encontrar la lengua."

His words sprinkled with a Spanish accent made her stomach do somersaults. Afraid that she was going to say something embarrassing or stupid, she said, "I have to get to class."

"I will be seeing you," he promised. "Pronto."

Bailey parked in front of Los Mexicano restaurant.

"Thank you, Bailey," said Selena. "Muchas gracias."

"No problem. I don't live far from here."

"My brother Juan picks me up, but he has to leave the restaurant and sometimes we're busy."

"I really don't mind," said Bailey. "Don't sweat it, okay."

"I'm tired," said Selena. "Practice was hard."

"Yeah, sometimes I just want to shower and fall into the bed, but I have to do homework."

"Me too. And I have to work."

"The next few months are going to be crazy," said Bailey.

"Loco, loco," said Selena. "You used to play softball right?"

"Yep, right at Jefferson Park."

"I loved playing softball. We used to watch the boys and older guys play and then someone told my brother that there was a team for girls. Suddenly, I was playing softball. My Uncle Hector signed me up."

"My Dad had me playing softball and soccer when I was five, but I liked softball the best. Hitting the ball with the bat and running around the bases," said Bailey. "That was fun!"

"I used to hit homerooms. Smack the ball out of the field." Selena giggled. "It was a small field."

"It was fun back then, right?"

"Not so much pressure," said Selena. "Mucho fun. Basketball is going to be like that…sometimes."

"You always see the good," said Bailey.

Selena shrugged. "Thanks for the ride. See you mañana."

Selena looked at the clock when she entered her family's restaurant. She was usually there by 5:30 PM. It was 7:30 PM.

"Late," said Felipe Sanchez, Selena's father.

"I was at basketball practice."

"Long time," said Felipe, a short man, with dark hair and a weather-worn face.

"Yes, Papá."

"Too long," said her father, frowning.

A customer interrupted their conversation, so Selena made her way to the kitchen. She put her book bag and gym bag in a storage area reserved for personal belongings.

She went over to her oldest brother Juan. "Should I serve customers?"

"You look a mess," said Juan. He sniffed the air. "Don't smell good either."

He made a funny face that made Selena laugh.

"I was running a lot," said Selena.

"In a field of horse poop?" asked Juan.

Selena went over and hugged her brother. "I don't smell like that."

He laughed. "What's the difference?"

"I'm telling Papá you say bad things about me. You make me cry." She pretended to cry. "He hates it when his girls cry."

Juan picked Selena up and put her in a closet. He pretended to lock the door. "Now you have something to cry about."

"Let me out," she screamed.

"Figure it out, smart girl," said Juan.

A minute later, Selena came out of the closet. "It wasn't locked."

"Muy brilliante," said Juan.

"Yes, I am!"

"Time to be serious."

"Sí!"

"Wash your hands," said Juan.

"I know," said Selena.

"Then you can fold up napkins and stack up dishes for washing."

"Papá not happy I'm late."

Juan shrugged. "He'll get used to it."

"I hope so."

CHAPTER 6

MARLEY

"Focus on academics," Franchesca said.
"I rock all A's, Mother. I take advanced classes and..."
"Getting in an Ivy-league school is the goal."
"For once, be happy for me."
"I'll call you back," said Franchesca.

"Franchesca hasn't called me at all. She didn't congratulate me for making starter," Marley said to Egypt, her cousin. "It's been three weeks." Their fathers, Cooper and Kenneth Woods, were brothers. Marley and Egypt were born three months apart and were both high school sophomores. They acted like sisters, always together, spending the night at each other's houses almost every week. Egypt went to a private school where her father was the head football coach.

"Are you really surprised?" asked Egypt, a tall, light brown, pretty girl with a muscle-packed body. A tennis player, Egypt regularly lifted weights for strengthening as part of her work-out routine.

"Disappointed." Marley sat on the edge of Egypt's bed decorated with a brightly-colored Bohemian-themed comforter and accessories, dominated by red, purple and yellow.

"You know your mother," said Egypt.

"Do I?" she sarcastically asked. "Franchesca left me when I was seven."

"You know enough," said Egypt, standing in her bathroom door, which was accessible only through her bedroom. When her family moved to the house five years ago, Egypt was happy to have her own bathroom.

"I'm going to call her right now," Marley impulsively decided. "She's not going to ignore me like that!"

"That's probably not a good idea," said Egypt. "I don't want you to get your feelings hurt."

"I'm used to it," claimed Marley.

"Not really," said Egypt.

"Sometimes I'm a marshmallow when it comes to my mother."

"You're not a marshmallow when you play ball."

"Your serves can kill someone," said Marley, referring to Egypt's tennis matches.

Egypt shrugged. "Hit the ball or get out the way."

Marley paused, and then said, "Well… I'm calling anyway." She picked up her cell phone, hesitated a few seconds before calling her mother. It rang five times, before going to voice mail. Marley called again; her mother rarely answered the phone the first time it rang. When she finally answered, Marley screamed into the phone, "Mother, I'm a starter! I'm a starter!"

"I know. I got your email and text," Franchesca DuBois said, several hundred miles away in Chicago.

"Daddy had a dinner party for all the starters at Dave & Buster's."

"That's nice."

"The coach is a former WNBA player."

"That's nice."

"We've won two games."

"That's nice."

"Do you think you can come to more of my games this year?"

Silence.

Marley heard her mother whispering, "Stop! Shh!"

"Franchesca!"

No response.

"Mother!"

No response.

"Busy preparing a brief or something?" Marley asked, referring to her mother's occupation as a well-respected attorney for a prestigious law firm.

"No." Franchesca's voice sounded distracted and husky.

"Are you home or out of town?" Marley asked.

"Home."

"I can't believe you're not at work."

"I'm working from home," Franchesca said.

"Are you coming here next weekend? I have a game."

"I don't think so. I'm going to a conference."

Marley activated the speakerphone. "Daddy gave me a necklace for making starter. You know, usually juniors and seniors are starters."

"I want you to focus on academics," Franchesca said. "That's how you are going to be successful in life and make real money."

"I rock all A's, Mother," Marley said defensively. "I take advanced classes and…"

"I just want you to keep your eyes on the prize. Getting into Harvard or Princeton or Yale is the goal, not basketball."

Annoyed, Marley said, "Mother, for once, be happy for me. …I'm happy!"

"I'm glad you're happy. You are very intelligent and athletic. Your intelligence will be your ticket to success," her mother explained.

Marley heard a strange sound—a moan of pleasure. It was a familiar sound which made her uncomfortable. She'd heard those sounds coming from her father's bedroom and sometimes her mother's bedroom.

"Mother, you're busy." She did not want to visualize in her mind what her mother was doing at the moment. "Don't have time for me, right?"

"I always have deadlines…" Marley heard her mother whisper: "Stop that."

"Who are you talking to?" Marley asked.

"Baby, I'll call you later."

Marley disconnected the call before she heard something she did not want to hear. She was angry and disgusted. Her mother could not stop what she was doing for five minutes to talk to her.

"Egypt, she was screwing someone!" she screamed and stomped her feet. "She doesn't care that I'm a starter," Marley said, her small lips quivering.

"She cares," Egypt said in a soft, soothing voice. "She just has a funny way of showing it."

"Yeah, real funny," Marley said, her voice drowning—not dripping—with sarcasm.

"I'm sorry, M."

"Me too, E," Marley said.

They were silent a moment, and in the quiet, they heard a shrill voice screaming.

"Girls! Girls!"

Egypt opened her bedroom door. "Coming, Mommy!"

"I'll beat you downstairs." Marley jetted past her cousin through the bedroom door and ran down the wide hallway with a loft overlooking a large kitchen and family room.

Egypt was right behind her, as they both ran down the stairs into the family room and then into the kitchen.

"Why are you running around in my house? You know better," said Lydia Woods, an attractive, light-skinned woman. In her late thirties, she was a principal for a public high school. "And you're too old for that nonsense."

"I started it," admitted Marley. "Hi, Auntie." She kissed Aunt Lydia on the cheek.

"Marley, Marley, Marley," said Aunt Lydia, shaking her head.

Egypt and Marley laughed.

"Mommy, you always say that," said Egypt.

"Now Daddy says that," said Marley. "I love that shirt, Auntie. You must be the best-dressed principal in the state."

"Thank you. You know I like to shop," said Lydia with a short laugh. "We all do, don't we girls?"

"Guilty," said Marley.

"As charged," said Egypt.

"Tacos," said Marley, her eyes taking in the Mexican-style food on the stove and counters. "Smells good."

"You were expecting my food to smell bad?" asked Lydia.

"That would be E's food," said Marley. "Your food is supreme."

"You're such a kiss-ass," said Egypt, halting mid-sentence. "Sorry."

"Like I don't know you curse occasionally," her mother said.

"Occasionally," snorted Marley.

"I'm not fooled, Marley," said Lydia. "By either one of you."

"What's that supposed to mean?" Egypt shook her head. "Never mind. I'm starving."

"Wash your hands," said Lydia.

"Yes ma'am," said Marley.

"Where's Daddy?" asked Egypt. After washing her hands, she picked up a plate.

"I'm not sure," her mother said. "I don't keep tabs on the man."

Marley and Egypt exchanged looks—they knew she did.

"So, how's school these days, Marley?" asked Aunt Lydia.

"Good."

"You're behaving, right?"

"If I wasn't…you would know," said Marley. "Principal Sanderson would call you." Her aunt had attended the same college as the principal of Riverbrook High.

"Perhaps," said Aunt Lydia. "He might call Cooper."

"You don't want him to call Uncle Cooper," warned Egypt.

"I'd rather they call you, Aunt Lydia, than Daddy," said Marley.

Aunt Lydia laughed. "Cooper has quite a temper."

"Just like Daddy," said Egypt.

"Don't talk about my husband," Lydia playfully said.

Egypt and Marley laughed. They sat down at the table and waited for Aunt Lydia to join them. Before eating, Lydia said grace.

Their dinner was interrupted by the arrival of Derek Woods, who was Egypt's 24-year old half-brother. He wore jeans that hung midway to his butt with a big, shapeless shirt. He was an average-looking, brown-skinned young man with thick eyebrows and moustache. He was funny and charming, and attracted to wild and loud women.

"Hi Mom," he said, greeting his stepmother with a kiss on the cheek. "Hey, guys."

"Guys?" they said together.

"Let me correct myself…Hey E & M." He laughed. "Sounds kind of sexy…"

"Derek, change the subject," interrupted Aunt Lydia with obvious disapproval.

"Yes ma'am."

"How was your day?" asked Lydia.

"I had an excellent day," said Derek.

"Ex-cel-len-tay," teased Egypt with a mock foreign accent.

"How excellent was it?" asked Marley.

"None of your business," answered Derek. "I'm starving. I'm going to shower first."

"You need to," said Egypt. "You smell like dog doo-doo."

"Shut it," said Derek.

"Stop it," scolded Lydia.

After dinner, Marley and Egypt escorted Aunt Lydia to her bedroom—a master on the house's main level.

"Rest and relax, Mommy. I know you've had a long week. We'll clean up the kitchen," said Egypt.

"Thank you, young ladies," said Lydia. "I just might take a long bath."

"I'll do the counters and floors," said Marley, when they returned to the kitchen.

"You have to help me with the dishes."

"Ok," said Marley.

Twenty minutes later, they had finished cleaning up the kitchen, leaving pots and pans on the stove for Egypt's dad to fix a plate.

In the family room, Marley went over to a floor-to-ceiling cabinet that stored at least 500 movies. She found one of their favorite movies.

"E, are you going to make popcorn?" Marley asked, while inserting the movie into the DVR.

"There's nachos."

"Oh yeah," she said.

Egypt tossed Marley a small blanket before snuggling into the corner of the sofa and wrapping a red-plaid throw around herself.

"Let it rip," said Egypt.

Marley started the movie. "One of the girls on the team is a movie freak."

"Like us," said Egypt.

"She's always quoting movie lines," said Marley. "She didn't think she made varsity and when the coach said her name, she had this goofy grin on her face and screamed 'Color me happy!' It was so funny."

"I know that line. That's from…from…*Pretty Woman* with Julia Roberts in it," said Egypt.

"Yep! She was a hooker."

"Who's the movie freak?"

"Chase," said Marley.

"Is she the freshman with the super fine brother?"

"Yes. I don't pay attention to him, but Evan is good looking."

"We should go on a date. Evan and me, and you and J.T."

Marley frowned. "J.T. from your school?"

"Yep."

"I can't stand J.T. The boys at your school are weird or boring or ugly," said Marley.

"Only about 92 or 93 percent of them," said Egypt.

"Evan's going to be hard to get to," said Marley. "His parents are very protective. Chase is naïve because she's so over protected."

"There are ways to get to Evan," Egypt said, smiling coyly.

"Ssh! The movie is starting."

Marley and Egypt shifted their attention to the 56" flat screen TV. Lindsey Lohan appeared on screen.

Twenty minutes later, Derek entered the room, freshly showered and smelling of Axe cologne. "Why are you all watching *Mean Girls* again?"

"Obviously we like it," said Egypt.

"Obviously you're obsessed," said Derek.

"Don't forget you're picking us up tomorrow at the nail salon and taking us to the school for my game," said Marley. "We're playing Forest Hills."

"I know, M," Derek said. "Don't sweat it."

"I just want to make sure you remember and don't get caught up over some ho…ho….ho's house," Marley said, giggling.

"Ho ho's are delicious, but I will ignore that," said Derek. "I'm picking you up at 11."

"That's correct," said Marley.

"I'm surprised Uncle Cooper hasn't bought your spoiled ass a car," said Derek.

"That's none of your business," Marley said Derek. She threw a pillow at him. "I wonder the same thing."

The next morning, Lydia dropped Marley and Egypt at their favorite nail salon. Before leaving, she said, "Derek will pick you up at 11. I'm coming to the first half of the game, but then I have take Egypt to tennis practice."

"Ok, Mommy," Egypt said, before getting out of their green Ford Explorer.

"Thanks, Auntie," said Marley. "See you at the game."

"So E, are you going to be Venus or Serena today?" Marley asked as they walked down the street.

"Depends on who I'm playing against," said Egypt. "And if the coach is acting crazy."

They laughed.

"I feel you," said Marley. "My coach can be loony-toony sometimes."

CHAPTER 7

BAILEY

"*Screw up and coach is going to snatch your ass out of the game.*" Ja-Nay-A pushed Bailey's arm. "*I told you I'm getting my spot back.*"

"*Chill, Ja-Nay-A,*" said Marley. "*We're supposed to be a team.*"

"*Come on, y'all. We gotta get along if we're going to win,*" said Selena.

At practice, Bailey jogged her last lap around the gym. Some of her teammates ran fast to finish quickly; some ran at an even pace; and some ran like they were in a marathon. The goal, this time, wasn't competing with each other, but finishing ten entire laps around the gym. Bailey couldn't wait for the grueling, two-hour practice to end.

Exhausted, Bailey plopped down on the risers, thinking about the two hours of home work she had to do before going to bed. *I'm tired. I want to go home. I want to go to sleep.*

This practice was more intense than other practices. The reason: a game against their local rival school Dalford High.

When everyone finished their laps, Coach Olivia motioned for the girls to sit together.

"You're killing us because we play Dalford, right?" asked Tequila.

"They always beat us," said Zoey.

"They're evil," said Rachel.

"Evil Dalford," Coach O said with a lopsided grin.

"Evil, evil," said Layne.

"Enough, enough," said Coach O.

Some of the girls giggled.

"That was then, but this is now," said Coach O. "Tomorrow's game is a regular season game. We have to come out swinging." Her voice took a commanding tone. "So we have to win!"

"We beat the last game against Forest Hills," said Rachel.

"That was last week. We're playing Dalford and they have an advantage," said Ja-Nay-A. "We'll be playing at their school!"

"Yes, it's an away game. If I had set up the schedule, our first game against them would have been a home game," Coach O explained. "I inherited the schedule, so we have to deal with the cards we've been dealt with. Got it?"

Heads nodded, shoulders shrugged, eyes stared.

"Go to bed, stay off Facebook, eat protein, and get ready to run, steal, score and win." She surveyed her players' faces. "Any questions?"

"You think we can really win?" asked Heaven.

"Never ask me that question," Coach O said sternly, almost indignantly. "I don't walk on a court thinking I'm going to lose. I always play to win—no matter who is on the court."

"What if we are totally, totally losing a game?" asked Kaylee. "What if the score is 75 to 25 and it's the fourth quarter? No way, we can win."

Bailey glanced at Kaylee. *Be quiet. Coach is going to go ballistic.*

"That kind of score is unacceptable. Period." Coach O paused. "What did I say?"

"Un...acceptable," whispered Kaylee.

"I didn't hear you."

"Unacceptable," Kaylee said louder.

"You girls are better players than you think. I expect you to play beyond your potential," Coach O said, emphasizing each syllable of each word. "Last year is last year. It has nothing to do with today. So I don't want to hear about last year's season."

Coach O smiled. "I know you love my quotes. So here's another one: Losers quit when they're tired. Winners quit when they've won."

"And what does that mean?" asked Ja-Nay-A.

"Don't quit for a second, even when we're tired," said Marley.

"Never stop believing you can win, no matter how much time is on the clock," said Chase. "That's what my old coach used to say."

"I like that," said Coach O, before smiling. "I believe in all of you. I wouldn't be here if I didn't. You're winners!"

The girls exchanged awkward glances.

"Say it," said Coach O. "We're winners."

"We're winners," said some of the girls, their voices unconvincing.

Coach tucked the ball on the side of her hip. With a serious gaze, she asked, "Who are you?"

"Winners!" they screamed.

"We *will* win tomorrow. That's what you're going to think from the beginning of the game until the buzzer goes off. Got it?"

The girls stared at their coach; and they shared a similar thought: *she's crazy*. No one would dare say what they were thinking.

"Got it?" Coach O repeated. She heard different responses:

"Yes ma'am."

"Sure."

"Yeah."

"Right."

"Totally."

"Cool."

"I'm melting from your enthusiasm," said Coach O. "I have another quote for you. A famous basketball player, way before your time, said: 'Everybody pulls for David, nobody roots for Goliath.'"

"Huh?"

"What?"

"Who's David?"

"Who's Goliath?"

"It's a story from the Bible," said Chase.

"Even I know that," said Tequila.

"David was a man and Goliath was a giant. They got into a fight," explained Coach O. "The giant was enormous and David was just an ordinary man."

"So Goliath beat the crap out of David?" asked Zoey.

"No, David had a slingshot," said Chase.

"Sounds like he needed a gun," said Ja-Nay-A. "Bang! Bang! Bang!"

"David knocked out Goliath with one shot from his slingshot," explained Marley.

"Yeah for him," Layne said sarcastically, pretending to clap.

"The point is no one roots for Goliath because they expect him to win," said Coach O. "People usually root for the underdog."

"And... we're... the underdog," asked Rachel with a confused expression.

"Yes, Dumbo," said Heaven, sighing.

"No one expects us to win," explained Coach O. "We're going to be playing in front of Goliath's fans, but so did David. He won and so can we," Coach O said.

Realizing that half the players weren't listening or understanding her, Coach O started laughing.

They started at her: curious and confused stares.

"Now that I have your attention. Here is the point: "Dalford is Goliath. Let's kick butt."

"Yeah," said half the girls.

"You better have more roar than that tomorrow. Panthers don't sound like pussycats," scolded Coach O. "You'll be wearing new uniforms and warm-ups."

"Yeah!" the girls screamed with enthusiasm.

"We just have to get your names embroidered on the jackets."

"My mom can do it," volunteered Selena. "She's a seamstress."

"Great," said Coach O. "We'll coordinate everything with the team manager. Rina can help with that."

"We're going to look good when we play tomorrow," bragged Heaven.

"You'll feel even better when you win," said Coach O.

While walking to the locker room, Bailey had one thought: *sleep*. She hoped she didn't have the crazy nightmare about missing a gaming-winning shot. The meaning was obvious; she didn't need a psychologist to know that she was worried about making the team lose.

Bailey rushed to get dressed to avoid Ja-Nay-A. She didn't want a replay of the day the starter list was posted on the locker room door. She didn't have any classes with Ja-Nay-A and they never saw each other during the day. The day the starters list was posted, Ja-Nay-A waited outside of Bailey's chemistry class. Bailey immediately saw Ja-Nay-A as she left the classroom. Fear oozed from Bailey like freshly-sprayed scared-of-you perfume. Ja-Nay-A called her nasty names and threatened to take her starter spot. Bailey didn't utter one word. She couldn't. Her heart was in her mouth.

When the class warning bell rang. Ja-Nay-A ran to her class, leaving Bailey feeling stupid and wimpy. Bailey jetted to the bathroom; she didn't want to pee on herself.

Since that day, Bailey only saw Ja-Nay-A at practices and games. Ja-Nay-A pretended to be a team player in front of Coach O. She knew any player caught fighting would be suspended or kicked off the team. Bailey felt safe as long as Coach O was nearby.

At this moment, Coach O was not in the locker room.

Bailey had changed clothes and was closing her locker door when she heard her name.

Ja-Nay-A's voice sent a chill up her spine.

"Hey B…and I'm not talking about your name," Ja-Nay-A said.

Bailey wanted to ignore her, but knew she couldn't. She was going to have to say something, but whatever came out of her mouth would fuel Ja-Nay-A's anger like turning up the flame on a stove. Bailey did not want a confrontation, but from the look on Ja-Nay-A's face, she had no other choice. She had to stand up to her tormentor or be tormented the rest of the season.

"I'm talking to you Blondie. I know you heard me."

Bailey slowly turned around and looked at Ja-Nay-A. "What do you want?" Her voice was just above a whisper.

"Your spot, Blondie. You're not a real baller. I'm just letting you know that I'm taking your spot!"

Bailey shrugged her shoulders.

"What? You got nothing to say, white girl?" Ja-Nay-A waved her hands in front of Bailey's face. "Oh oh, you so confident. You think you got better skills." Ja-Nay-A stepped closer to Bailey. "I don't know if your rich black step daddy paid for your spot, but you're not going to keep it. I'm just warning you."

"I'm not afraid of you!" The words escaped from Bailey's mouth unexpectedly. The instant she spoke the words. Bailey wished she could stuff the words back inside her mouth.

"How white is that? I'm not afraid of you," mocked Ja-Nay-A. "It's 'I ain't scared of you!'"

"I'm not afraid of you!" Bailey said in a louder voice, hoping the sound of her voice drowned out her pounding heartbeat. "You're not taking my spot."

"Look bitch, I know you want to piss in your pants, but I'm just putting you on notice," Ja-Nay-A said, her voice growing louder by the second. "You screw up and the coach is going to snatch your ass out of the game."

"Chill, Ja-Nay-A," said Marley. "We're supposed to be a team. This isn't necessary."

"Come on, y'all. We gotta get along if we're going to win," said Selena.

Ja-Nay-A glared at Marley and Selena. "Y'all stay out of it!"

"We all in it," said Tequila. "We all up in your Kool-Aid, and we're not going to be fighting or cussing or none of that shit."

"I was trying to get a college scholarship until this bitch took my spot."

"Don't call me a bitch," yelled Bailey.

"What you going to do, hit me?" asked Ja-Nay-A.

Bailey glared at Ja-Nay-A, terrified of what was going to happen next.

"What ya going do? ... I'm waiting."

Ja-Nay-A took a step closer to Bailey—face-to-face, an inch between them.

Bailey balled her hands into a fist; her arms hung low to her waist.

"You start a fight and your ass will be kicked off the team," warned Marley.

"You're not a real basketball player!" Ja-Nay-A said with clenched teeth.

A wave of boldness washed through Bailey's blood. "I earned my spot!"

"I don't know how!" screamed Ja-Nay-A.

"That was the coach's decision. Not hers. You beefing with the wrong person," said Tequila. "I wouldn't mess with Coach O if I were you."

"Well, you're not me," barked Ja-Nay-A.

"I'm not trying to be you," said Tequila. "And I'm not scared of you."

"Look y'all. Enough," said Marley. "We got a game tomorrow."

"We gonna lose anyway. We always lose to Dalford," Ja-Nay-A said.

"Maybe that's why you lost your spot. Cause I'm not planning on losing tomorrow," said Tequila.

"Me either," said Marley.

"Whatever … fake ball players." Ja-Nay-A punched a random locker, causing a vibrating sound that echoed throughout the locker room. "This isn't over," she said, before leaving the locker room.

"OMG," Bailey said, releasing a deep breath of air and sitting down on a locker room bench. She didn't say anything for a few minutes until she realized that some of the other girls were watching her.

"Thanks! I mean thank you, thank you!" Bailey said, looking at Tequila, Selena, and Marley. "I really appreciate you having my back."

"You surprised me, girl," Tequila said. "You stood up to her."

"I surprised myself," Bailey said, shaking her head. "I'm glad it's over." She zipped up her gym bag. "You ready, Selena?"

"Yep," Selena said, with her gym bag, book bag and purse hanging from her shoulders.

Bailey stood up. "We're gone."

CHAPTER 8

TEQUILA

"You were on fire," said Rashonda. "Even rebounded your own shot."
"You play a mean game," said Cedric, her mother's new boyfriend.
Tequila glared at him. "Thank you."

They had won last week's away game against Dalford High School. It was the first time Riverbrook girls' basketball team beat Dalford in seven years.

The stands at the home game for the girls' basketball team were practically empty. Only family, relatives, friends and acquaintances of the team members were there to show support.

Regardless of the empty-looking gym, it was an intense, exciting game against Mitchell High. At the end of the first quarter, the score was 16 to 10, with Riverbrook High losing by six points. Mitchell scored the first basket and maintained the lead. The lead widened as the game progressed, but in the second half, the starters of Riverbrook High School showed why they were starters.

Selena scored a three pointer.

Marley blocked two shots.

Tequila made three lay-ups.

Chase stole the basketball three times.

Bailey scored two baskets.

They could possibly win the game.

THE STARTERS

Coach O deliberately ignored Tequila's ball hog moves. She sensed that Tequila was 'in the zone' and left her in the game. She believed that sometimes a player's selfishness, as long as it got results, can be strategic. Tequila's style of play was aggressive and deliberate. She was scoring.

Four minutes into the last quarter, Coach O decided to put Ja-Nay-A in the game. Ja-Nay-A leaped off the bench, with a toothpaste commercial smile, thrilled by the chance to play, especially since she was taking Bailey's place. Ja-Nay-A jumped into the game with fierceness and determination. She was dribbling the ball down court and didn't notice the opposing player until the ball was swooped out of her hand. Ja-Nay-A yelled at Selena. "You were supposed to be guarding her. We're going to lose."

Coach O blew her whistle and signaled for a 30-second timeout. The girls huddled around the coach, anxiety on their faces, adrenaline pumping through their veins.

"Ja-Nay-A, sit down!"

Ja-Nay-A's jaw dropped open. Her eyeballs were about to drop out of her head.

Before Ja-Nay-A had the chance to ask why, Coach O answered the unspoken question: "I told you the word "lose, loser, losing" should never come out of your mouth when we're playing or practicing. Especially in the middle of a game. I never want to hear that word from any of my players. Period."

Coach turned to Bailey. "Go back in."

Bailey jumped up, excitement pulsing through her veins.

Riverbrook High got the ball back from the opposing team. Marley scored a two-pointer and the game was now 64 to 60, the team losing by 4 points. The point guard from the opposing team got the ball, but seconds later Chase stole the ball and passed it to Bailey who scored a three pointer.

Tequila moved under the net, avoiding the other team's defensive maneuvers and grabbed the ball. Tequila scored two points, and Marley grabbed a rebound. She passed the ball to Tequila, and with five seconds on the clock, she penetrated the other team's defense and scored another two points.

The final score was 64 to 67, in favor of Riverbrook High School.

Riverbrook fans screamed with surprise and excitement.

After the game, Tequila walked over to her mother and they hugged. Not often expressive with emotion, Rashonda embraced Tequila for several minutes. Tequila felt a little awkward because her mother's hugs were usually short pats on the back.

"Baby, you were on fire. On FIRE!" said Rashonda. "I've never seen you play like that!"

"Quila, you still play like a boy," said Tevon.

"Thanks, big head," Tequila said.

"I can't believe this gym is empty," said Rashonda. "The way you girls play, it should be jam packed with people everywhere."

"We sucked last year, so no one pays attention to us," explained Tequila, shrugging.

"Y'all keep playing like today and it will be crowded up in here."

Rashonda was tall and slender like Tequila; they looked almost like twins, except for the age difference. Honey-brown skin, wide eyes, narrow nose and full lips. Tequila's eyes were more slanted, giving her an exotic look. Even though Rashonda had Tequila when she was 18, she looked older than a 35-year-old woman. There was harshness in her eyes and mouth. Rashonda had a hardened, living-on-the-edge-of-survival look that sometimes disappeared when she smiled from her heart. Something she rarely did.

"I'm proud of you, baby," Rashonda said with a radiant smile.

"Thank you, Mama."

"Especially when you pushed those girls and rebounded your own shot," said Rashonda. "That was a New York move."

"You play a mean game," said Cedric Warren, her mother's new boyfriend.

Tequila glared at him. "Thank you," she said, resentful that he was at her game. When she spotted him earlier, she couldn't believe that her mother had brought him to the game. She hated when her mother's boyfriends tried to act interested in her kids. They never stayed around for long.

"You won't have to worry about working when your daughter makes it to the WNBA," said Cedric.

"Ain't that the truth. I know my baby girl is going to take care of her mama." Rashonda laughed. "We could go shopping for mansions this weekend."

"Sure," said Tequila, joking along with her mother.

"Will you buy me the latest Wii game or the newest and coolest video game?" Tevon asked.

"Yeah, and how about a trip to Disney?" Tequila sarcastically said.

"Yeah, man," said brother.

"Quit trying to sound like Usher," said Tequila.

"I'm going to meet your coach. Make sure she knows who I am," said Rashonda. "I'll be right back."

"I'm coming with you, Mama," said Tevon. "I'm getting a new video game! I'm getting a new video game!"

Tequila went to step away, but Cedric positioned himself in front of her. She could smell his strong cologne, as if he just poured it all over his body. It smelled awful. The cologne should have stayed in the bottle. He was taller than Tequila, and very skinny. He had a narrow face, and a curly perm that was popular two decades ago.

"You pretty enough to be on the runway and not on the basketball court." He smiled, revealing a missing front tooth.

Tequila rolled her eyes, wondering why men were so predictable. She felt a creepy vibe from him when they first met. She didn't like the way he looked at her. She sensed that he could be a trouble maker. She knew it was best to stay away from him, like she did with most of her mother's boyfriends.

She felt naked the way he was looking at her, and not the kind of naked she read about it in romance novels. She felt violated by his eyes and the lust that he made no attempt to hide when her mother wasn't around.

"Get a life," she said, walking away from him.

She didn't have time to think about him. She wanted to enjoy her moment of glory. Besides, he probably wasn't going to be around for long. If he managed to get past the two month mark, she would figure out how to deal with him.

He was no different than the other men who dated her mother: acting one way in front of her mother and another way when they were alone. She had learned to avoid being alone with her mother's creepy boyfriends. Not all of them lusted after teen-age girls, but she had a plan for the ones who thought that dating her mother meant they could date her too.

THE STARTERS

DARIAN-BALL-BLOG: NUMBER 2

I thought Coach Olivia was crazy for picking a freshman, a sophomore, two juniors, and one senior to be starters. Insane.

Maybe I was wrong. Since I don't watch their practices (maybe I do, maybe I don't) I just couldn't understand why she picked those girls to be starters. Maybe she wasn't wrong. For the first time in 10 or whatever years, Riverbrook beat Dalford High (our arch enemy) and Piedmont High. And Mitchell High. We are on a winning streak—3 wins, 0 losses.

No one comes to the girls' games. But you should. At least come to one game. You will be surprised in a good way.

I'm impressed with the starters, especially the freshman. Chase runs as fast as lightening. Tequila is from New York and plays like a boy. The team is diverse, just like our school.

Even though Riverbrook is diverse, there are certain sports that are dominated by certain races. There aren't any blacks on the swim team or golf team, and only one black girl plays lacrosse. But the basketball girls are a rainbow of races. That's kind of cool.

Bailey White (her last name is white and she's the white starter) is very good. She plays with intense focus. So does Selena, a Hispanic girl, who can make 3-pointers with her eyes closed. I can't forget about our Marley Woods. Marley, Marley, Marley. Everyone talks about her fashion photo shoot outfits, but she rocks basketball like she rocks designer clothes.

This basketball season might be interesting after all...

Comments

MVP123: I guess you learned not to be so quick to judge. I'm so proud of them. They are so much better than last year.
Mindless: Yeah, white girls can play basketball. Thank you Bailey!
Sportsqueen: The whole team got skills. Don't sleep on Layne, Zoey, Heaven, Ja-Nay-A and the rest of the girls.
Gamewatcher: Riverbrook finally has a REAL girls' basketball team.

Lovehighsh: Coach O is like that little boy in the movie The Sixth Sense. He sees dead people. She sees basketball players. She sees what you don't see. Get it? Don't? You're dumb!
Justagame: Is it the coach or do the girls suddenly realize they can play?
Bestsport: They are really starting something...

CHAPTER 9

CHASE

"I want you to paint me looking young. I don't want to look 70."
"Grammy, you are 70," said Chase.
"Don't make me look like an old witch."
Chase grinned at her grandmother. "You'll look like Queen Grammy."

Chase used her key to open the door to her grandmother's house. She always felt transported to a different place when visiting Grammy's house, transported to a time when she wasn't born yet. A time when there weren't cell phones, iPods, and the Internet. A time before cable TV, computers and microwaves.

Grammy enjoyed talking about the 'the good old days.' She said there were big black telephones that hung on the wall, one television in the house, black and white television programs, no color on TV, and the television screen was fuzzy after 12:30 AM.

Grammy said that everyone knew everyone who lived on the street and neighbors told everyone's business. A neighbor could spank you or tell your parents if they saw you doing something wrong. Chase listened to Grammy's stories, but was glad that she wasn't born back then.

Her grandmother reluctantly moved to Atlanta from Baltimore after her grandfather died and no other family members were around to take care of her. When she became ill with pneumonia, Grammy realized that she needed to be near one of her three children. She moved to Atlanta to be near Shellie, her oldest daughter.

Grammy lived with Chase's family until she found a house. The search for a home for Grammy took the amount of time it takes a woman to have a baby—nine months. Grammy drove the real estate lady crazy. She would complain that the houses were too big, too ugly, too weird, too…something.

When it seemed that Grammy wasn't going to find her own house, Chase's parents decided to look for a house that would include a mother-in-law suite. Chase, Blake and Evan were upset at the possibility of moving out of the house they had lived in since birth. So, when Grammy finally announced she found a house that would "just do" and was twenty minutes away, the family was relieved.

"It will do," Grammy said. "I know it's time for me to get to stepping." She moved out a month later and the Anderson house felt like the Anderson home again.

Grammy moved all her belongings into the new house, and it immediately looked like her Baltimore home. The knick-knacks, pictures, and her special collection of birds were all grouped together exactly as they were before. The curtains were the same, even though they had to be adjusted to fit the different window sizes. Grammy had smiled when her "just do" house almost looked like her old house.

Chase's connection to the past ended when she went into her grandmother's large family room. A huge flat screen TV hung on the wall. There were the latest TV gadgets: remotes for the TV, DVD, and cable. Grammy knew how to work the "fancy contraptions." Michael wrote down the instructions for using the hi-tech TV equipment.

"Hi, Grammy," Chase said to Grammy who was sitting in her favorite lounge-rocking chair.

"Just let me finish watching this judge show about a crazy divorce," Grammy said.

"Okay," said Chase, planting a kiss on her grandmother's baby soft cheek. "I'll get my stuff ready."

Chase walked to the other side of the family room near the large window where her father had placed a folding table and easel. She unpacked her art supplies, neatly aligning brushes and paint bottles on the folding table. She positioned the easel closer to the window.

"Do I need to change clothes?" Grammy asked.

"No ma'am," Chase said. "I'm just painting your face."

Grammy stood up. "I'm going to put on a beautiful blouse, just in case."

Chase shook her head, knowing it was pointless to argue.

When her grandmother returned ten minutes later, Chase was sitting in the lounge-rocking chair: it was the perfect spot for watching the TV.

"Sugah, you know better than sitting in your granddaddy's chair."

Chase jumped up. "You ready?"

"I just need you to brush my hair."

"Yes ma'am." They walked over to the window and Grammy sat in a wide-back chair. "I want you to paint me looking young. I don't want to look like I'm 70."

"Grammy, you are 70."

"Just don't make me look old and wrinkly." She balled up her face. "Don't make look like a witch."

Chase laughed. "You're going to look like Queen Grammy. There's no way I could make you look like a witch."

Chase ran a wide brush through her grandmother's long silver hair. It was as soft as cotton and hung past her shoulders. Grammy rarely wore her hair loose and free; it was always in a ponytail or a bun.

"You know I marched with Martin Luther the King in Alabama," Grammy said. "That was long before you were born."

"You told me."

"That's why I didn't want to come down South."

"I know."

"Things are different. Some things are better and some things are the same. Some things ain't ever going to change," said Grammy.

"It's not like it was back then, Grammy."

"Don't be fooled, Chase. Some white folks aren't ever going to like us and we shouldn't be trying to like some of them. Just because there aren't signs for 'colored folks only' or 'white folks only', don't mean racism is gone. It's just undercover," explained Grammy. "You got to be smarter to see it. You get my meaning?"

"Yes ma'am."

"Don't let anybody look down on you no matter who they are. Shine like a star no matter who's around. God gave you all kinds of talents and you must use them," Grammy said. "Don't want to disappoint God."

"Yes ma'am."

"I don't believe my eyes when I watch you play basketball. I think that some other girl, not my grandbaby out there stealing balls and scaring players with that mean glare you get on your face," said Grammy.

Chase laughed. "When I see pictures of my mean face, I get scared."

"It's a shame your granddaddy never got a chance to see you play. He loved basketball. I can hear him yelling: 'Dunk it! Dunk it!'"

"I think you're ready," Chase said, with a final stroke through her grandmother's hair.

Grammy observed Chase making sure her paint brushes were lined up in perfect order. "Sugah, you just like your Daddy. Got to have everything just right."

Chase smiled. "Drives Blake crazy."

"Your Daddy used to drive your Mama crazy with his perfectionist ways. She learned to live with it," Grammy said. "That's what you got to do to stay married. Your grand daddy used to do stuff that made me mad enough to spit on the floor. Would you believe he never put the toilet seat down? I can't tell you how many times I fell in the toilet."

Chase giggled.

"He did stuff to make my missiles go off, but I didn't fire them." Grammy released a sad sigh. "I miss him."

"Me too, Grammy." Chase picked up a paint brush and dipped it into a color that looked like butterscotch brown. She tested the color on a sheet of paper and kept mixing the colors until she had a darker-hued brown.

"That's what's wrong these young folks. Most of the girls on your team don't live with their parents and that's a real shame. Their parents are just selfish. Downright selfish," Grammy said, shaking her head.

"Mama says everybody has a reason for the things they do and not to judge people," said Chase.

"That's just B.S," Grammy said snorting. "I didn't like your grand daddy on many days, but I didn't leave him. Even when he was as meaner than a snake."

At the moment, Chase wasn't paying attention to her grandmother's words. She was staring at her face, envisioning the painting in her mind's eye. With her narrow face, petite nose and eyes, and narrow lips, she saw how much her mother resembled her grandmother. She understood why people always said that she looked her mother.

Chase wanted to capture her grandmother's hair and the fire in her eyes. She could imagine how she looked when she was young.

"You still there?" Grammy said to Chase.

"Grammy, when I paint I have to concentrate," she said. "I'm painting the picture in my mind before I paint it."

"Are you telling me to shut up?"

"I would never say that."

"No you wouldn't. I'll be quiet after I say this," said Grammy. "I heard you're a woman now."

When Chase discussed her period with her mother, she didn't feel embarrassed. They had talked about menstruation several times over the last three years. Chase felt uncomfortable having *that* conversation with her grandmother.

"I guess."

"You know what that means?"

"I'm not sure what you mean."

"You can have a baby now," said Grammy.

"I know," Chase said, wanting the conversation to end.

"So don't be letting boys go exploring down there."

Embarrassed, Chase blushed. "Grammy!"

"I know you're a good girl, but boys can sweet talk you into things you know that's wrong. The wrong party of your body takes control of your mind and you end up in a whole heap of trouble," Grammy said.

"Yes ma'am."

"Don't let that happen to you. You listen to me!" she said. "I know what I'm talking about cause I been on this earth a long time."

"Yes ma'am," Chase said.

"That's what happened to me…and I wasn't ready," she whispered. "Your grand daddy didn't want to wait."

At first Chase didn't understand what Grammy, but then she understood. That was something she did not want to know about her grandparents.

CHAPTER 10

SELENA

Felipe Sanchez shook his head. "No good. No good."
"She's a great player, Mr. Sanchez," said Coach Remmington.
"Time. Too much time."
"Yes, it's a big commitment."
"Need her at work. School not important. Basketball waste of time."

Selena and Eva sat in the stands in the school's baseball field watching the Riverbrook's baseball team play against Dalford's baseball team. It was the fifth inning and Riverbrook was winning. She sat far away from Miguel's fan club. Eva called them the 'whore club.'

The sun was high above the open air baseball field and it was blazing hot.

"See the phone Juan got me?" Selena asked, showing off her phone.

Eva looked at the touch-screen, smart phone. It was cool looking with fancy features. "Very nice."

"Papá thinks it's a waste of money," said Selena.

"My Papá thinks same way."

"We are in America. Everybody has a phone."

"Mexican-American," said Eva proudly.

"Juan is practical. He wants me to be safe. I have to be at practice late. Maria and Bella have to share a phone. They hate it."

"I would hate it too," said Eva.

"I really need my phone," said Selena. "Coach Olivia is always sending us text messages."

"Are we staying for the whole game?" asked Eva.

"Yeah, why not?"

"Cause it's hot. Caliente!"

"It won't be that much longer."

"Okay," said Eva. "I'm going to get something to drink."

"I know you like number 12," said Selena, with her hands over her eyebrows to block out the sun. "He's cute."

Petite and feisty, Eva dyed her dark black hair different shades of blonde. She would be blonde for a couple of weeks, and then she'd go back to her natural color. She liked the way people reacted to always-changing hair color. "Yeah, I'm going to find a way to meet him."

"I know his name," said Selena.

"You do?" Eva said. "I would find out anyway."

"Ramon."

"Maybe I'll meet Ramon after the game," Eva said, before walking down the risers to the concession stand.

Selena laughed and watched Miguel prepare to pitch. He was focused, and assumed a pitching position, rotating his arm several times before releasing an 80-mile an hour pitch.

"Strike one!" said the umpire.

Miguel pitched to the player again.

The umpire said, "Strike two."

The batter glared at Miguel. He took a couple of practice swings, and then positioned his body for the next pitch.

Miguel made eye contact with the batter as he released a ball that was lightening-speed fast. The player swung at the ball, and missed it.

When Eva returned, Riverbrook was now batting.

"What took you so long?" asked Selena.

"Well, I met this cute boy," she said, handing Selena a bottle of water.

Selena laughed. "You love cute boys."

"He was from Dalford," said Eva.

"Traitor," teased Selena.

Eva shook her head. "I don't care. Mama thinks I should get married when I get out of school."

"My Mama used to say that, but now she says that we have the American infection. She says infección," Selena said in Spanish. "Says she has a little bit too."

Eva looked puzzled. "Your Mama sick? You sick? You don't look sick."

Selena giggled. "Not that kind of sick. She says I dream like I could really touch the sky. You know go to school and have a career. She thinks it can happen for us girls."

"You are loco if you believe in the stars," said Eva.

"So I'm loco," she said, shrugging. "Look, Miguel is batting."

Miguel stood at the base, his feet firmly planted on the ground. When he heard the girls' screams, he looked into the crowd. He practiced his swing several teams before assuming the batting position, with the bat angled on his right side.

"Look at those girls screaming about Miquel," said Eva.

"The Miguettes," said Selena.

"They're crazy," said Eva.

Dalford's pitcher threw a slow, smooth pitch. Miguel didn't swing, and the umpire called a strike.

Miguel swung at the next pitch, sending the ball spiraling in the air high in the sky towards the back of the field. Miguel immediately ran to first base, jetted to second and third base. He heard his teammates yell, "Keep running." Miguel ran even faster as he approached home base. He crossed home base to the cheers of his teammates. He had hit the ball out of the field. Another homerun for Miguel.

The crowd went wild. Girls screamed Miguel over and over, until the next batter approached the mound.

The game ended with Riverbrook winning.

"He's hot and super good," said Eva.

"Yeah, just looking at him melts my heart," said Selena.

"Look at those girls running down there," said Eva.

"I know. Makes me jealous, but I'm not going to act like them."

"Don't."

"Juan would kill me," said Selena.

"Boys don't like girls who chase them."

"Yes they do," said Selena.

"True. Some boys do."

"A lot of boys love it," said Selena. "Look at those girls crowding around the players with their little sexy outfits on."

"Athletes love the attention," said Eva.

"Let's go."

Selena and Eva walked down the riser steps that would take them to the exit. Selena didn't want to watch the girls surrounding Miguel, so she walked away from the baseball field.

Before reaching the exit, she heard Miguel call her name.

"Bonita Selena, wait," he said, running towards her.

She turned around and within seconds he was inches away from her.

"Hola," she said. "Good game."

"Just good?" he asked.

"You hit two home runs and struck out a bunch of players. I think that's just good."

"So you're not easy to impress," he said.

She smiled at him, shrugging. "I enjoyed watching you play," she said.

"Thanks," he said.

"This is my cousin Eva."

"Hi Eva," he said flashing his charming smile.

She smiled back. "Hello," and then headed toward the parking lot. "I'll see you at the car," said Eva.

"I know the season is almost over so I thought I would check you out," said Selena.

"We only have two games left."

"You have the best record on the team," said Selena.

"So know a little something about me?"

Selena shrugged. "Tal vez," she said, meaning 'maybe' in Spanish.

"I want to get to know more about you," said Miguel.

"Maybe you will," said Selena.

"Miguel!" screamed a teammate, running over to them.

"What's up?" asked Miguel.

"Coach wants you to meet someone. A scout or something," said his teammate.

"I got to go, bonita Selena."

"Excellent game, Miguel," said Selena. "Magnífico."

He laughed as he walked away. "You talked more this time."

"Hello, I'm Coach Olivia Remmington," she said while entering her office. Two men sat in chairs that faced her desk.

The younger man stood up. "I'm Juan Sanchez and this is my father, Felipe Sanchez."

"Very good to meet you gentlemen," said Coach Remmington. She was uncertain whether or not to shake their hands, but since they did not offer their hands, she sat in her chair.

"How can I help you?" asked Coach Remmington.

"Selena not play ball anymore," said Felipe Sanchez. "No good. No good."

Coach Remmington was caught off guard. Her gaze shifted from the father to the son. They had two very different expressions.

"Please let me explain," said Juan. "My father's English isn't very good."

Coach Remmington nodded. "Selena is very excited to play basketball with our team."

"Oh, she loves it. She couldn't believe it when you made her a starter," said Juan.

"She's an asset to our team. The girls love her and she's a great athlete."

Felipe shook his head. "No good. No good."

"She's a great player, Mr. Sanchez," said Coach Remmington.

"Time. Too much time, señorita," said Felipe.

"Yes, it's a big commitment," said Coach Remmington. "A lot of time for practices and games."

"Need her at work. School not so important. Basketball waste of time."

"What does her mother think?" Olivia asked.

Felipe shook his head. "She don't think like me. She got stars in her eyes like Selena."

"Mama is quiet, but she understands America ways," said Juan.

Olivia nodded. "Mr. Sanchez, you may not want Selena to play basketball, but she can possibly get a scholarship for college."

"Scholarship?" asked Felipe.

"Scholarships can pay for college," explained Coach Remmington.

Felipe looked at his son. "Is that true?"

"Yes, Papá," said Juan.

"School is very important. Selena's smart and can go to college which will help her get a good job that pays money. She can choose from so many different careers."

"Selena will make a good wife and mother," said Felipe.

Coach Remmington's eyes widened. "Excuse me."

"Let me explain," said Juan. "Papá thinks women should get married and have babies."

"There are lots of professional Hispanic women. More and more Hispanic women and men are going to college," said Coach Remmington. "She can be teacher, a lawyer, a doctor, a judge…"

"I know. I'm still hoping to go to school one day," said Juan. "I want to be a major chef and open a big restaurant like Papadeuax."

"That's great, Juan," said Coach Remmington. "Dreams are important."

Juan paused, pushing down the dreams that simmered inside his heart. "But Papá worries about today. Survival."

"The season will end in February. Maybe March if we go to state."

"That's a long time," said Felipe.

"There are other girls who wanted to be starter. I picked Selena."

"Listen, my father isn't just old school, he's old culture. Our Mexicano culture."

"That's an interesting way of putting it," said Coach Olivia. "I played overseas and respect other cultures." Coach Remmington looked into Felipe's eyes. "The world is changing a lot. Girls have more choices."

"Selena helps at our restaurant. She's a big help," said Felipe.

"I understand," say Coach Remmington. "She has a happy spirit. I think she would be sad if she couldn't play."

Felipe smiled for the first time. "Selena born with a big smile." He shook his head. "No teeth in her mouth."

"Papá, I will help out more and Maria will clean up at night," said Juan.

Felipe said, "Maria got hole in head. Always forget."

Juan laughed. "I will help Maria. I'll make sure she don't forget. And Paco will help."

"He lazy."

Felipe sat thinking.

"Hector is coming back. He needs to work," said Juan. "He will help. He understands what to do."

Felipe remained quiet. "I miss Hector."

"Papá, Selena will cry like a baby if you take basketball away from her," said Juan, looking at his father. "Me and Maria and Paco and Hector will take care of restaurant."

"I do not want this," said Felipe. "I want Selena home to help."

"You don't want her sad, Papá. You don't want her crying."

"No, no, no," Felipe said, shaking his head. "No tears. Her tears make me feel so bad."

"Selena can keep playing basketball, okay Papá?"

Felipe exhaled deeply and slowly shook his head. "Sí."

"Why don't you come see her play?" asked Coach Remmington. "You will see how good she is."

"Too busy," said Felipe. "Work all the time."

Juan stood up. "Thank you, Coach Remmington. Selena talks about you a lot. She admires you."

"Thank you, Juan. Thank you for the team and thank you for Selena. I don't know if I my heart could take seeing her cry either."

Juan laughed. "We always look out for each other. We familia."

"That's a good thing," said Coach Olivia. "Please tell your mother how much we appreciate her sewing the girls' names on their uniforms."

"She was happy to do it," said Juan.

"Muchas gracias for time, sonority" said Felipe.

"You're welcome."

Coach Remmington walked the men to her door. "Good-bye," she said, before closing her door.

Sitting at her desk, Coach Olivia couldn't believe their conversation. She had to respect their culture, but Felipe Sanchez's comments about women infuriated her. Even though she had been around other cultures, she was still shocked by their traditional beliefs and roles for women. Lost in thought, Coach O barely heard the knock on her door.

"Come in," she said.

Ja-Nay-A came in and took a seat.

"Hi, Ja-Nay-A."

"Coach O, I'll get straight to the point. If Selena isn't allowed to be a starter, would you consider me, please?"

"Aren't you the opportunist?"

"What's that?"

"Never mind," said Coach O. "Selena is still a starter."

"Dang!"

"Ja-Nay-A, you have talent. But you need to work on some things. I can put in touch with a personal trainer."

"My parents can't afford a personal trainer."

"He'll work with you. You need to improve some fundamental basketball skills. All is not lost. I can have some smaller schools check you out and set you up for some try-outs."

"Thank you, Coach O. But I think I deserve to be a starter."

"We have a difference of opinion. And I'm the decision maker, here."

"It's not fair. I love basketball."

"I know you love the game, Ja-Nay-A. I'm not intentionally trying to be unfair. I'm trying to do what's best for the team."

Ja-Nay-A stared at Coach O for a second, and then got up before she said something she might regret.

One minute left in the game.

Selena stood at the free throw line, her hands strategically positioned around the ball. She focused on the basketball hoop, not the clock or her family's loud screams:

"Score Selena! Score Selena!"

"Be a shooter! Sea un tirador!"

For one second, she glanced at them. Her brothers, sisters, cousins, and relatives were standing on the top risers, yelling in Spanish and English. It was an away game at Woods Ferry High and her family was the largest group of fans from Riverbrook High who had come to the game, which was forty minutes away. Her mother and father weren't there. Her parents had yet to see her play.

Selena suddenly remembered when she played softball and hit a homeroom. The ball seemed to disappear into the sky and by the time it hit the ground, three players had run to home base, scoring three points. The softball coach had hoisted Selena in the air, shouting: "Blast off, home run!" She remembered that rush of happiness—it felt like her heart had flown from her body and went into the sky and floated among the stars. That feeling was just a moment away. It would take just a moment to propel the ball from her hand and for it to magically drop through the inside of the basketball hoop. She closed her eyes for a second, then regained her focus and shot the ball. It landed inside the net. Her heart floated in the air.

But the pressure was still on. She had to make one more shot to win the game.

The referee threw the ball back to Selena, and she caught the ball. Without hesitation—she positioned her feet and aimed for the basketball net. She made the shot and they were up by one point.

Five seconds were on the clock.

Chase got the rebound and dribbled the ball until the buzzer sounded.

Riverbrook High's girls' varsity team won again. They lined up and slapped hands with the opposing team, repeating, "Good game, good game!"

"Congratulations, girls. I'm proud of you," said Coach O.

"Thanks for being the best coach in the world," said Chase.

"Ditto," said Selena. "Mejor entrenador," she said, meaning 'best coach' in Spanish.

The girls started raving about Coach O, but she quickly stopped them. "Thank you, ladies. You do all the work," said Coach O. "It's time to go. Now, get your stuff. We're leaving in ten minutes."

Selena slipped her warm-up pants over her uniform shorts and put on the matching jacket, with her name embroidered on the right side. She slung her basketball bag over her shoulder and fell in step with Marley and Bailey.

CHAPTER 11

MARLEY

"Sterling and I are getting married," said Franchesca.

"What? Are you serious?" asked Marley.

"You know I'm not the joking type."

Marley glared at Sterling. "My mother isn't the marrying type. She doesn't like being a mother. She dumped me for her career."

"They have more people at their home games than we have at ours," Marley said to Cooper as she stood on the top level riser. They were visitors playing Creekrise High, an away game in their region. The visitors' side of the gym didn't have many fans compared to the army of fans on the home side of the gym. "It's not like they're a good team. They sucked last year liked we did."

"More people are coming to our home games," said Cooper.

"True, true," said Marley.

"You ready to steal and score?" Cooper asked.

"Daddy, you're usually more original."

"This is a nice gym," said Sallie, Cooper's current girlfriend.

Cooper stood up. "You want something from the concession stand?"

"Popcorn, if they have it." Sallie said, smiling at Cooper.

"I'll be right back," Cooper said, taking a step down the risers.

"Franchesca is coming, right?" Marley anxiously asked, standing behind Cooper. "She knows the game is here at Creekrise High and not at Riverbrook?"

"She knows. She said she's coming." Cooper kissed Marley on the forehead. "Be a winner."

Marley watched Cooper maneuver down the risers, stopping to talk to other parents along the way.

Marley had been waiting for this moment—when she was alone with her father's new girlfriend. Marley examined the woman with a critical eye, the way she would look at clothes or jewelry. Sallie was an ordinary brown-skinned woman with a cute hair cut, not the super model or exotic looking woman her father usually dated. She realized that her father didn't have a specific type. He didn't date the same type of woman, but they were always drop-dead pretty. His women sometimes looked like Halle Berry, Kim Kardashian, Beyonce, Kerry Washington, Rosario Dawson, or Paula Patton. He never dated any of them for very long.

Sallie wasn't ugly, but she wasn't pretty either. Marley thought: *If you were a dress, I'd only buy you if you were on clearance.*

Sallie was vice president of a software company and was supposed to be extremely smart.

"Listen, Sallie, I know you like my Daddy, but he never keeps a girlfriend for long."

"So you think you know your Daddy." Sallie flashed a wicked smile. "How do you know I'm not the one he's going to keep?"

"Because you're at least girlfriend number 56."

Sallie looked at Marley for a moment. "I like the number 56. It has a nice sound too it."

"Oh you're a real B," Marley hissed.

Sallie didn't say what she wanted to say. Too many eyes and ears were around. Parents' of Marley's teammates were an earshot away.

"Say something wrong, and if I tell Daddy, your number will be up today," whispered Marley.

"You're a spoiled brat," Sallie whispered with a crooked smile.

"Daddy knows that he spoils me. I'm counting the days until you're gone."

Twenty minutes later, Marley was on the floor for the beginning of the game. All the starters played well, except Tequila was exceptionally aggressive, getting two fouls within the first quarter. The coach took Tequila out of the game and sent in Ja-Nay-A. Tequila mumbled under breath: "It's not fair." Sitting next to Tequila, Marley said, "If you show how upset you are, coach won't put you back in."

Tequila nervously bounced her feet.

"Chill," Marley said. "Don't let them see you sweat. That's what my Daddy says."

"Yeah, yeah, yeah," said Tequila.

They were winning—because the opposing team wasn't very strong. Marley was back on the court, but not playing her best. The coach pulled her to the side during a timeout.

"What's distracting you?" Coach O asked.

Marley looked in the stands, her eyes searching for her mother—a tall, exotic-looking, tan-skinned woman who usually stood out no matter where she was. No sign of Franchesca DuBois.

"When you're on the court nothing matters, nothing but the game. So whatever's on your mind, delete it or you're out."

"Got it," said Marley.

She forced herself to focus on the game. During half-time she was tempted to run up to her father or check her cell phone to find out where her mother was. But there would be consequences: expulsion from the game and possibly future games.

By the time the second half of the game started, Marley decided her mother wasn't coming and concentrated on the game. It immediately showed. She swiveled around players, and scored several shots. She was playing like Marley Woods.

Until Franchesca DuBois arrived with 7:45 minutes on the game clock of the fourth quarter. When Marley saw her mother, she smiled at her and missed a layup. She suddenly turned into fumble fingers. Creekrise High began to score, slowly chipping away at Riverbrook's 15-point lead.

Marley was intensely aware that her mother was watching her every move—right and wrong. Instead of a shot of adrenaline, her mother's presence was a dose of doubtfulness. Marley couldn't even dribble. Her mind was a twisted maze of thoughts and memories that she couldn't shake-off.

She wanted to show off her superior basketball talents to her mother, to prove to her that basketball wasn't a waste of time, to show why she was a starter. But Marley played like a six-grade recreational league player. Every time Marley made a mistake, she saw the disappointment on her mother's face. Hoping for some ray of encouragement, she looked at her father. No encouragement from him. "What's wrong with you?" Cooper screamed. "Play ball!"

Marley missed three shots, let an opposing player outrun her to the basket, and missed a pass. Coach O took her out of the game. Marley was embarrassed to be benched against a team that had a reputation for losing.

When the game was over, Riverbrook lost.

The girls walked down the line of the opposing team, repeating good game to other players.

"What was wrong with you?" asked Heaven.

"We should have won by 20 points," said Layne.

"We shouldn't have lost," said Rachel.

"I'm going to take your spot, Marley!" said Ja-Nay-A.

"Get the hell out of my face," said Marley. "You can't touch me."

"Everybody has off games," said Chase.

"True, but don't let it happen again," said Tequila.

"I know," Marley said and walked over to her mother with hesitance in her steps. "Hey, Franchesca," she said, and gave her a hug. Franchesca wasn't very affectionate and responded with a quick embrace. Her hugs were so brief, that Marley called them air hugs.

"Hi Marley," her mother said, observing her daughter from head to toe. "I got lost trying to find the place. This school is way out in the freaking country."

"I thought you weren't coming," Marley said, unable to hide her disappointment.

"I got detained in a meeting, but I came to see you play," Franchesca said, with a slight smile. "I'm leaving tomorrow night, so I had to see you. What happened on the court? I've seen you play better."

She shrugged her shoulders. "I had an off game."

"That happens. I think this is all a waste of time. You should be thinking about getting into Harvard or Yale."

"I have all A's," Marley said.

"Keep it that way," Franchesca said sternly. "I want to introduce you to somebody."

Marley groaned. She wasn't in the mood to meet another one of her mother's boyfriends. She never liked any of them. She had to give her mother credit: she only dated successful men. She wasn't like Aunt Alana, her father's sister, who dated men Cooper called 'super losers.'

Marley plastered a smile on her face when her mother introduced her to Sterling Price. He was well-dressed, fairly handsome in an older man way, and had an air of success. "It's nice to meet you, Sterling," she said.

"I've heard all about you Marley. Your mom says you take advanced classes and you're a starter and you're in the tenth grade."

"That's me," she said, feeling awkward. She never knew what to say to her parent's 'friends.'"

"I played basketball in college. I went to UCLA," said Sterling. "I love the game, but knew I wasn't pro material, so I went to law school."

"So you're a lawyer like my mother."

"Yes I am," Sterling said. "I'm a criminal defense attorney and your mother does corporate."

"She hates criminal law," Marley emphatically said.

Sterling agreed with a nod. "You know your mother."

"I hate criminals, so why should I defend them?" Franchesca explained.

"Somebody has to represent them. They have rights," Sterling said. "You never know when you're going to be on the wrong side of the law."

"Marley, I want to tell you something," Franchesca said.

Marley looked at her mother who had the biggest grin on her face. She had never seen her mother smile like that, not even when she received a prestigious award for 'attorney of the year.'

"Sterling is my fiancé. Marley, we're getting married," Franchesca said, her voice oozing excitement.

"What?" Marley said, drawing in her breath like she was drowning.

"We're getting married."

"Why are you telling me this now? You didn't prepare me," Marley said. "I didn't know this man existed until now," she said, pointing to Sterling. "Franchesca you can't do this with no warning. That's not fair and very inconsiderate of my feelings."

"I suppose I should have told you, but life is full of surprises," said Franchesca.

"I don't know what to say, except that I never thought you would get married." Marley glared at Sterling. "My mother isn't the marrying type. And she doesn't like being a mother. She dumped me and my father for her career."

"Marley, watch your mouth!"

"The truth comes out of the mouth of babes," Marley said. "Isn't that what they say?"

Franchesca grabbed Marley's arm. "Stop it now. We're going out to celebrate. So you better go change clothes and accept the situation."

"I have to catch the bus with the team. I can't ride home separately. It's a rule."

"I came out of town to see you and drove all the way out here to this back woods country school to see your game. I expect you to ride home with me," insisted Franchesca. "Let me go talk to your coach."

Marley pointed at Coach Remmington. "There she is."

"Come on, introduce me."

Marley rolled her eyes before walking over to the coach, her mother keeping pace in high heels. The sound of her mother's heels clicking against the gym floor caught the coach's attention. "Hey Coach O," said Marley.

Coach O smiled at Marley.

"Coach, this is my mother, Franchesca DuBois," Marley said. Remembering an etiquette class she'd taken long ago, she completed the introduction, "Mother, this is Coach Olivia Remmington."

"Hello. I hear you're doing fabulous things with this team," said Franchesca.

"It's nice to meet you," said Coach Remmington. "Thank you for the compliment," she said, noticing Franchesca's custom-tailored suit and matching Gucci purse and shoes. Coach Olivia immediately understood Marley's anger issues with her mother.

"I need a small favor. As you probably know, Marley lives here with her father and I live in Chicago. I would like her to leave with me so we can spend some quality time together." Franchesca spoke in a polite, matter-of-fact manner. "I'm leaving tomorrow morning."

"I understand your situation, but the girls have to ride back to the school on the bus. That's the rule." Coach Olivia responded in a direct, but polite manner.

"I'm sure you can break the rule this time." Franchesca spoke in a tone that implied compliance with her request.

Coach Olivia did not appreciate Franchesca's arrogant request. "No," Coach Olivia curtly said. "It will open the door for other requests."

Franchesca smiled—a fake smile. "I think you have discretionary power to make exceptions," she said in her lawyer-negotiating voice.

"I'm sorry, Franchesca, but Marley has to ride on the bus with us," Olivia firmly said. "We should be back at the school in forty minutes."

Franchesca stared at Olivia for a few minutes. It was an unfriendly stare. As a lawyer, she knew when and how to negotiate. She realized that she couldn't negotiate this situation to her favor. She also sensed that the coach had formed an opinion about her, and it wasn't favorable.

"I've enjoyed meeting you and I'm sure we'll see each other again Coach Remmington." Franchesca turned to Marley. "I'll meet you at the school."

Marley walked away from her mother. The tears that she held at bay made their way through her self-protective I-don't-give-a-damn fortress. She quickly wiped them away. When she got on the bus, she found a seat near the back of the bus. Marley usually sat up front and talked about the game and whatever else the girls talked about. This time she was as silent as a rock.

Her mind didn't know how to process her mother's engagement.

Marley even ignored her phone for a while. She finally picked it up and saw that her father had texted her ten times: *What's wrong? I'm not talking about the game.*

She shot back a simple message: *She introduced me to her fiancé.*

Before Marley pressed the send button, she knew that she was sending a bullet to her father's heart. That text was going to hurt him too.

A half hour later, Marley said good-bye to her teammates before trudging off the school bus. She slowly walked towards her father's car parked in the school's parking lot. It was chilly and windy, but her father was standing outside the car. She was not surprised by her father's face: she saw the pain of her mother's rejection. Her father was a womanizer, but she knew that he was still hurt that Franchesca had chosen her career over her family. Marley and her father had a strange, unspoken bond because they both felt the same sense of rejection. It hurt them in different places, but it also connected them.

A sudden memory of her parent's fighting jumped inside Marley's brain. Copper asking her mother: "How could you love your career more than your child? I'm more a mother to her than you are. Explain that!"

Marley stood still in the next room, listening, but wishing she didn't have to hear them argue. She could have run into her bedroom and blasted her music, but she always listened—even when she knew she shouldn't...even when she knew she didn't want to hear what was being said.

"I'm not the wicked witch of the west. I love Marley, but I have an excellent position with a respected law firm," Franchesca had said. "I graduated from Harvard Law School. I'm not going to throw that away."

That memory disappeared when Cooper hugged Marley for several minutes. Her father's hugs were warm and comforting, not forced and fake like her mother's. He kissed her on the forehead. "It will be alright."

"Daddy, I'm tired. I just want to go home."

Cooper took Marley's overstuffed sports bag and dropped it inside the back of the SUV. Just as he slammed the trunk shut, Franchesca drove up, and parked behind them. She hopped out of the car.

"Hi, Cooper," she said walking over to him. "How are you?"

Cooper stared at the woman who once was his wife, the woman who still had a way of getting inside his armed-guard protected heart. He said nothing, because he had nothing good to say.

"Obviously Marley told you the news. I'm marrying a real man," she said. "He understands my ambition and independence."

"I don't care who you marry," Cooper said with controlled calmness. "I don't like the way you told Marley."

"She's okay," Franchesca said, dismissively. "Surprised, but she'll be fine."

Calmness lost, Cooper screamed, "You're so damn oblivious. You're so freaking self-absorbed that you don't even see what you're doing to your daughter. You don't even care."

"I saw that she wasn't happy when I told her. Frankly, she was rude and obnoxious to my fiancé," Franchesca said. "But she'll adjust. She has to. She has no other choice."

"Why are y'all talking about me like I'm not here?" Marley interrupted. "I'm not invisible. Just like I wasn't invisible when you used to argue in front of me when I was little."

"I know you hear us, Marley," Cooper said to his daughter. "But I'm defending you." His gaze landed on his ex-wife. "You could have told her at dinner. She was already upset that you were late for her game. You distracted her game cause she was so busy wondering if you were going to show up that she couldn't concentrate."

"She's wasting her time playing basketball."

"Well, don't come to any more of my games," screamed Marley, hurt by her mother's negative attitude about basketball and the unspoken words between them.

"And then you introduce her to your fiancé without warning!" Cooper's voice grew louder with each word.

"She knew I was dating someone," Franchesca said.

"Franchesca, you're always dating someone," Marley said. "You never told me you were serious."

"Look, I don't need to explain my decisions to you," Franchesca said to Marley. "Stop calling me Franchesca."

"You were wrong. You are insensitive and uncaring," Cooper accused. "You will never change."

"My insensitivity as you call it isn't *your* problem."

"It is—when comes to Marley. *YOUR* daughter!"

"I know she's my daughter. Stop telling me that."

"You don't act like it," Cooper said. "You *NEVER* have!"

"Stop, okay," Marley pleaded. "Just stop. Everybody is looking at us." Marley had seen the stares and whispers of her teammates as they departed from the bus and went to their parents' cars, while watching an unplanned episode of a reality show courtesy of Marley's soap-opera-like life.

Franchesca and Cooper glared at each other.

"You're right. Let's move past this episode. Come on, Marley let's go to dinner," Franchesca said. "I thought you would have changed clothes, but you can come like you are. We're not going anywhere fancy this late."

Marley looked at her mother with absolute disbelief. *How could you think that I want to go to dinner after this nightmare scene?* In a calm, but steely voice, Marley said, "I'm going home!"

"No, you're going to dinner with me," Franchesca insisted. "That was the plan."

Marley released a gush of anger. "I have homework and I'm exhausted."

"You've stayed up late to do homework before," Franchesca said.

"I don't want to go to dinner with you and that Sterling man. I don't want to fake it," Marley said. "I can't play nice tonight," she said, her voice cracking with emotion. "I really…really can't."

"You're going to dinner with us. I changed my plans so that we could spend some time together," Franchesca said with nothing's-stopping-me determination. "I was supposed to catch a flight tonight."

Marley was quiet for a minute. "I just want to go home," she said in a soft, sad, lost voice.

Franchesca grabbed Marley's hand. "You're coming with me."

Marley yanked her hand away and stepped back. "No, I'm not!"

Franchesca looked at Cooper and then Marley. "You're not going to disrespect me." She moved towards Marley when Cooper stepped between them. "Leave her alone," he calmly said. "Let her be. She's going home with me."

Sterling got out of the car and walked towards them. "Is there a problem?"

Cooper flashed Sterling a don't-mess-with-me look. "This isn't your problem, man."

"There is no problem," Marley cried, with tears coming down her face. "I just want to go home!" Marley opened the car door and got inside her father's car. It was warm inside.

Marley watched her mother and father exchange angry, vile words. Franchesca had the determined look on her face that she wasn't backing down. But Sterling said something that made her throw her hands up in resignation. She knew that her teammates were watching them—the ongoing Cooper-Marley-Franchesca saga. At the moment, Marley really didn't care.

Franchesca got in her car, with Sterling on the passenger's side. Her mother drove slowly and waved at Marley before driving off. Marley didn't wave back.

Cooper got into the car and put the car in drive. He looked at Marley before taking off. Neither said a word. He didn't put on the radio or play a CD or plug-in his iPod. No words. No music. No discussion about the game. No conversation about Franchesca, just the silence of their thoughts.

It was a loud, long drive home.

DARIAN-BALL-BLOG: NUMBER 3

Marley, Marley, Marley. Your family is a reality-show drama. A rich daddy and a bitch for a mommy. I heard she's a kick-ass, money-making attorney. We know why you dress like your clothes come from Beyonce's closet. Maybe it's the money, but I only feel a teeny-weeny bit sorry for you. Your mommy shows up and you crumble while playing.

Buckle up solider, especially if you're going to keep your starter spot. Ja-Nay-A and Heaven are breathing down your neck and they got skills. Coach O hasn't promised anyone that they will be starters for the whole season. So, Marley, Marley, Marley, keep your mind off your personal life when you play. Just some friendly advice.

Oh yeah, we lost our first game of the season. We lost to a team that has a losing record like us. But we are winning team! We still have more wins than losses: 4 wins, 1 loss.

Comments

MVP123: Leave Marley, Marley, Marley alone.
Mindyourbiz: She played okay. Not her best, but okay...
Sportsqueen: So they lost. And they will lose again.
445River: You are a hater. Get a life!
Lovelaugh: Don't get her Daddy mad.
LuvBB: I hear her Mommy is the B word.
Madplayer: It sucks they lost. But the season is just beginning.
Gamewatcher: Darian, how do you know so much?
Iknowsports: Are you a spy?
Rocksports: Too bad we lost to a team that sucks, but whatever...
Justagame: I think our players all of sudden have alien powers.
Lovesports: You have a point. Most of girls are the same from last year. But they play differently. What's changed about them? Maybe the girls had alien blood transfusions or are drinking alien juice in their Gatorade bottles.
Ibelieve: They could have turned into aliens. It's possible. There really are aliens. We are not the only ones on this planet.

Madplayer: It was going to happen eventually. They are going to lose. Face it. They are the same girls from last year unless aliens take over their bodies when they get on the court.

CHAPTER 12

BAILEY

"You're extremely cute," said the cutest boy in the party.
Bailey smiled back at the dark-haired boy. "Yes, I am."
"You don't go to Independence. I would have noticed you."
"I go to Riverbrook," Bailey said.
"My Dad calls it the N-school."

"This is my best friend, Bailey," River said, introducing her to Megan, a girl who went to her private high school, Independence Academy.

"Hi Megan," Bailey said. "Nice to meet you."

"Hello," Megan said. "You and River have super unique names. I have the most common name on the planet. There must be at least ten Megan's in our school. You probably know some Megan's."

Bailey laughed. "I know a few Megan's. Sometimes I wish I had a normal name."

"I love my different name. I got teased when I was little, but I stopped caring a long time ago," said River.

"She doesn't care about much of anything," said Bailey. "Except music and boys."

"Some boys," River said. "I'm selective about who I obsess over."

"How long have you been friends?" Megan asked.

"Since kindergarten. We both went to public school until I was forced to come to Independence Academy in the seventh grade."

"I've never been to public school," said Megan.

"I've been in public school my whole life," said Bailey.

"Bailey is the star player on her school's varsity basketball team."

"That's cool," said Megan.

"I'm not the star," said Bailey. "I'm a starter, but I'm not the star of the team."

"I play lacrosse and volleyball," said Megan, a tall, thin-as-a-rose-stem white girl with dark brunette hair. "I'm the only girl on the rifle team," said Megan with a gleam of pride in her dark brown eyes.

"A rifle probably weighs more than you," observed Bailey.

"I hear that all the time," said Megan with a chuckle.

"She can shoot anything. I told her she should be a spy or something," said River. "Remember that show *Alias*? She could be Sydney. Or that bad-ass chick in Covert Affairs."

"That would be exciting, and I'll give myself a cool name like Skye or Rembrandt," Megan said.

"Or Luminous or Storm," said River.

"But I will probably be a boring accountant like my dad," said Megan.

"Bor-ing!" River said.

"I don't know what I want to be. I never admit that to my parents," Megan said with a spurt of nervous laughter. "I do love sports."

"I hate sports," said River.

"We know," Bailey and Megan said together and laughed.

River grabbed Bailey's hand. "Let me show you around and introduce you to some of my friends."

They walked through the multi-level million dollar house with seven bedrooms, five baths, a showcase kitchen, and 50-seat theatre room with a mini-stage. The house had been professionally decorated. It was Jared Woodruff's house, a member of River's band. His parents didn't mind Jared having parties. Sometimes the parties were supervised; sometimes they weren't. It was the band's regular practice spot, and they were going to perform for their friends in the theatre room in the next hour.

Bailey met lots of River's friends: a flurry of names, faces, and comments about parents and professions. Bailey had met some of them before and she never pretended to go to a private school or be different than who she was. She didn't always reveal that her stepfather was black, but if it came up she would proudly talk about her family. Most kids rarely asked that kind of information. It was the parents who wanted to know. It was the parents who made comments like: "Oh dear, you have a black stepfather," "You're the one whose mom married a black man" or "That must be difficult for you." They would act embarrassed or concerned, but not very convincing. Over time, Bailey learned not to care what people thought of her or her family, whether they were black or white.

After a while, most of the kids were in the theatre room. River's band "Levity" was getting ready to perform. River was the lead singer. Excitement sparkled in River's eyes, no doubt helped by the alcohol mixed in her drink.

As River joined her band members on the mini-stage, Bailey went over to the bar area with food and drinks. She scooped up some peanuts and the "bartender" offered her a drink. "Virgin or non-virgin?" he asked. Bailey laughed, and before she could answer the bartender had poured some type of drink in a fancy glass. She took a sip and immediately knew it was an alcohol-mixed drink. She shrugged, and kept the drink. She found a seat near the front of the stage, and got ready to watch River perform. She was proud of River—she was doing exactly what she wanted to do.

Bailey was still searching for her niche…her passion. She stumbled into sports—but didn't think she was an incredible athlete. Looking at River singing on stage, happiness glazing from her eyes—she knew River had found nirvana.

Bailey had another drink, and began to feel a little buzz. She rationalized that it was just a little alcohol. She wondered where the boy was that River had wanted her to meet. River said he was "deliciously handsome" but wouldn't give her any physical details.

Levity performed non-stop for almost an hour, the crowd getting more excited and drunk with each song. When it was over, Bailey was ready to go. It was Friday night and she could stay out late, but she had a game on Saturday at 3 PM.

A boy suddenly crashed into her. Bailey noticed that he was cute and could tell from his glazed eyes that he had consumed plenty of alcoholic drinks. "Sorry," he said with a grin that showed perfectly-straight, glistening white teeth. His black hair was parted down the middle, chin-length, with one side tucked behind his right ear while the left half of his hair swung around his face.

"You're extremely beautiful," he said.

"Yeah, I am," Bailey said, smiling, her confidence boosted by a couple of alcohol-filled drinks.

"You don't go to Independence because I would have noticed you."

"I go to Riverbrook High," Bailey said.

He raised an eyebrow. "That…multi-cultural school," he said. Pausing, as if searching for the right words, he added, "Isn't that the politically correct way to put it?"

Bailey looked at him with new eyes—the cute boy had completely disappeared. "You have a problem with people who aren't like you?"

He stuffed his hands in his jean pockets. "My dad calls it the N-school. You know what word I'm talking about. It rhymes with trigger."

Bailey's face darkened with anger. "If I had a gun, I'd pull the trigger on you."

He laughed. "So you're feisty. I like feisty girls."

"No. I'm just not a racist." Bailey's eyes were cool, distant.

"I'm not either," he said with a shrug. "But I hear it so much from my parents I guess it's kind of rubbed off."

"That's no excuse. Don't you have your own brain?"

"Yeah." He peered into her eyes, confused by her hostility. "My brain is checked out now." He moved closer to her and whispered. "That girl over there. That's Nicki. Her Dad used to play in the NBA."

"So?" Bailey said, looking at the tall, slender black girl who was laughing with a group of kids.

His dark eyes were thoughtful as he considered his response. "My best friend dates her."

"So."

"Nicki is real cool. She's smarter than a lot of other kids. But that's not me."

"What does that mean?" asked Bailey.

"Dating other types of girls."

"I guess you wouldn't go out with me."

"You're freaking hot! Your eyes are skylight blue." He stopped when he realized what Bailey wasn't listening.

"I don't meet your criteria."

The boy leaned closer in. "You're hot and look like a fashion model," he said. "That's on my criteria."

"My step-dad is black," she said bluntly. "And my little brother and sister are bi-racial."

"You just need to adopt an Asian kid and an African kid and you'd have a little United Nations." He laughed. "Your family is almost the regular people version of Brad Pitt and Angelina Jolie."

Bailey stared daggers at him. "You're an asshole."

"I'm proud of it," he said, with an obnoxious grin.

River walked over to them.

"You were awesome, dude," Bailey said. "The band sounds good and your voice is just incredible."

"They are a combo of Fall Out Boys and Paramore," said the obnoxious boy.

"And River sounds like the girl from Evanescence," said Bailey.

"We're going to see their asses on MTV one day," said the obnoxious boy.

THE STARTERS

Her hair and body drenched in sweat, River said to Bailey, "So, you met Matthew Charles." She patted Matthew's head. "This is who I was going to introduce you to."

"Him?" Bailey said with obvious dislike. "He's disgusting and he's twisted in the head."

River glared at him. "Matthew, what did you say to her?"

"I didn't know she was your friend. You're right, she is freaking hot," Matthew said. "Her eyes are blue like the Caribbean ocean."

"Ugh," Bailey said. "Spare me Matthew Charles." She grabbed River's hand and headed away from the boy who could have made her heart spin like a top—until he opened his mouth.

"Dude, what did he say?" River asked.

"He's a racist," Bailey said, her voice full of indignation. "He started talking about this black girl who goes to your school. When I told him that my step dad was black and my little brother and sister are bi-racial, he made a crude joke out of it."

"Matthew's cool, he just doesn't know how to be politically correct. He doesn't think for himself. He's a daddy's boy."

"Too bad for him," said Bailey. "He's handsome, but I don't like assholes."

"Sorry, dude. He's really not as bad as you think."

Bailey's head was starting to swirl. "I think I had too much to drink."

"What?" River said, shocked. "You had a drink...alcohol?"

"Yes."

"You're finally starting to have fun. It's about time."

"You don't have to drink to have fun," said Bailey.

"Okay, grandma. I bet you feel different," said River.

"Yeah, I should have been a drunk a long time ago," said Bailey cynically.

"A lot of kids drink, get high," River said, shrugging.

"I noticed." Bailey paused. "What about you? You don't do it every day, do you?"

River snorted. "You know I indulge."

"I mean…"

"I play around with… stuff," she said. "You know me, Bailey. I like to be adventurous and experiment sometimes…"

"I like to play it safe," admitted Bailey. "You should be careful experimenting."

"One day you're going to have to indulge in some of life's … delights," said River.

"Sounds like danger to me," said Bailey.

"Living on the edge sometimes won't kill you."

Bailey snickered. "I don't know about that."

"Dude, I see those drinks got you relaxed," said River. "You feel different, right?"

Reluctant to admit it, Bailey paused. "A little."

"It makes me feel like I can be me," said River. "Freer."

"I like me, normal me," said Bailey. "Just like I like normal you."

CHAPTER 13

TEQUILA

"I'm not going to read this," Tequila rudely said to her teacher.
"That's your choice. Feel free to exercise that choice," said Mrs. Bernard. "But the consequence is in-school suspension."

Tequila hated school.
Despised going to class.
Disliked teachers bossing her around.
Hated doing homework.
If it weren't for basketball, she would have quit school when she turned sixteen. But then she wouldn't be able to play basketball.
And her mother always threatened to kill her if she quit high school.
Sometimes Tequila wondered if her mother would really do it, but then her mother had a don't-F-with-with me side.
Tequila hated school from the moment she stepped into a classroom with gum-plastered desks, wobbly chairs and torn-up textbooks. She was only 6-years-old. Her mother actually thought moving to Atlanta would change her attitude, but Tequila felt the same: school was boring, hard, confusing, and a waste of time.
Her mother—even though she did not graduate from a high school, but had a GED—was adamant about her kids graduating from high school.

When Tequila was suspended in the fifth grade—for spitting on a boy—she learned just how serious her mother was about school.

"You quit when you were 16," Tequila had smart-mouthed her mother as they walked that day from her elementary school to their apartment in Brooklyn.

Rashonda was silent while they walked back to their apartment in the projects. They walked five blocks in silence, her mother stopping occasionally to speak to people and complain about "my bad-ass child."

Tequila kept looking at her mother because it was unusual for her to be quiet. Tequila was only ten-years-old and she knew her mother's silence was deadly.

They made it to their apartment. Tequila's heart quivered as they walked inside. She knew she was going to get punished. Her mother removed a wide leather belt from the dresser drawer. But then she handed Tequila a toothbrush and bar of soap. "Clean the bath tub and shower."

It took three hours to clean the shower and tub. Tequila never spit on another boy again.

Her attitude about school never changed. Each grade got harder and harder. It showed in her report cards. Some years she had B's and C's, D's and F's would find their way on her report card which caused an instant fight with her mother.

"You're not going to be a drop out like me," Rashonda screamed when Tequila barely passed the seventh grade. Tequila heard that threat every year, sometimes every week since she started high school.

That memory flashed in Tequila's head in her American Literature class. The teacher asked the students to take turns reading the classic novel, *The Great Gatsby*. Thinking about reading out loud in front of her classmates made her head spin. Tequila kept looking at her watch, hoping the bell would ring before it was her turn.

At the beginning of school year, she had been mistakenly placed in an honors literature class. She immediately knew she was in the wrong class when she didn't recognize a single face. Tequila was moved out of that class the very next day. Even though she was with kids who read on her reading level, she didn't want to read in front of them. Some of them stumbled over words like she would. Still, she didn't want everyone to know that she read like a sixth grader. If she took her time, skimmed past unfamiliar words, she could understand the story.

Reading out loud was worse than sitting in a blazing hot room with no windows or air conditioning.

Jessica, a white girl with bright red hair and black clothes that matched her black eyeliner, volunteered to read the next section. She was a weird girl—one of the gothic girls, which Tequila had never seen until she moved to Atlanta. All the kids at her school in Brooklyn were black, so she wasn't used to having classes with white kids, Asian kids, Hispanic kids, and foreign kids from places like Brazil, England and Russia.

She wondered why they wanted to leave their country and come to the United States. She hated leaving New York and coming to Atlanta, but at least she was in the same country. She didn't understand why they believed America was such a great country. They had been brainwashed. She laughed when one kid said, "it's a land of opportunity." Eventually she got used to walking around in a school where black faces weren't the only faces in the school.

Jessica, with a flair for the dramatic, read the book like she was in a Broadway play. She giggled when finished. "It's so romantic."

"Excellent job," Mrs. Bernard said. "Tequila, it's your turn."

Tequila looked at her watch. She was going to sound like a stuttering idiot after Jessica's Oscar-winning performance.

Mrs. Bernard, a middle-aged woman, short and stout, patiently waited for Tequila. The teacher loved arts and theatre, and told the class about her career as a young actress. Tequila did not care, nor did most of the other kids.

"Tequila, you can begin on page 55."

Tequila looked at the words on the page. Foreign words were scattered on the page.

Tequila had a choice: be embarrassed or refuse to read.

"You know, this will help you with your SAT," said Mrs. Bernard.

"Basketball is my ticket to college," Tequila said, trying to distract the teacher. "It's my thing."

"Tequila, colleges also look at your grades. Academics are very important even in the world of sports," said Mrs. Bernard.

"I guess," Tequila shrugged.

"I hear you're an excellent basketball player."

"Thank you," Tequila said. "I've been playing since I was a little girl. My big brother taught me, but he's dead now." Tequila hoped that mentioning her brother's death would get the teacher's sympathy. "He got killed by a gang."

"I'm sorry to hear that. There's death in literature and lessons to be learned about how decisions can affect your life."

Tequila looked at Mrs. Bernard with confusion. *What did that story have to do with her?*

"What do you mean?" Tequila asked, stalling for time.

"We'll get to that," Mrs. Bernard impatiently said. "Go head, Tequila. Start reading page 55."

Tequila looked at the words on the page—words that looked like scrambled letters. The thought of reading in front of her class made her head spin.

"Mrs. Bernard I don't like this story. Can I read something different?"

"No you may not. You have to read what everyone else is reading. No exceptions!"

"I think the story is depressing."

"Are you refusing to participate in class?" Mrs. Bernard sternly asked.

Tequila looked around the classroom. All eyes were on her.

Sympathetic eyes.

Disapproving eyes.

Curious eyes.

You-so-stupid eyes.

"Mrs. Bernard, Tequila can hoop. I think she gonna be famous one day," said Phil who hated school like Tequila. "She got skills, give her a break."

"That's nice, but Tequila must read like everyone else," said Mrs. Bernard.

Tequila swallowed. "Can I read another time?"

"No, Tequila. Start reading now," Mrs. Bernard said, very impatiently and sternly.

Tequila read the first sentence. The fifth word in the second sentence was unfamiliar. So, she stopped. "I'm sorry, Mrs. Bernard. I don't want to. I'm not into reading."

"I see. Remember the rules. My rules are very clear." She pointed to the rules posted on the wall in the front of her classroom. "Must participate in class room activities is rule number one. No sleeping is number five." Rule number five was often ignored; Mrs. Bernard pretended not to notice the kids who slept almost every day.

"Are you choosing not to participate?"

Tequila looked at the book and didn't answer.

"Tequila, are you going to read as I directed?"

"No," Tequila said, annoyed and embarrassed. "I don't want to!"

"Well, then," said Mrs. Bernard, her lips pursed together. "That's your choice. But the consequence is in-school suspension."

Tequila was quiet for a moment, rethinking her decision. She didn't want to go to in-school suspension. The kids in suspension were really bad or crazy or out-of-control. "I don't want to read in front of the class," said Tequila, while gathering her book bag and purse.

"Immediately report to in-school suspension," said Mrs. Bernard, turning to her computer. "I will email them now so they will be expecting you."

Tequila glared at Mrs. Bernard and left the room. As she took two steps away from the class, the bell rang.

If only the bell had rung one minute earlier, she wouldn't be going to in-school suspension.

She saw Marley while walking to the administration building and immediately thought about Coach O. In that instant, she deeply regretted her decision.

Her mother was going to be furious.

Coach O was going to go ballistic.

Reading like a sixth grader in front of her class made her stomach queasy. Not playing basketball was going to make her vomit.

The moment Coach O found out that she had in-school suspension would be the same moment that her playing time would disappear.

Tequila realized she had made a huge mistake.

CHAPTER 14

CHASE

"Mommy, there's a 'For Sale' sign in our yard," Kendall screamed.
"I know," Regina said.
Kendall looked at Chase. "I don't want to move!"
"I don't want you to move either," said Chase.

Chase watched the junior varsity girls' basketball team playing a rival team. She still couldn't believe that she wasn't on the court playing with them. Several of the girls on the JV team were her teammates on the eighth grade middle school basketball team. Coach Eddie had predicted that Maya and Chase would make the varsity team.

Chase did.

Maya did not.

The fact that Chase made the varsity team changed her relationship with some of her eighth grade teammates. During middle school, they went together to movies, birthday, skating and bowling parties, and sleepovers. Now in ninth grade, Chase still hung out with some of them. Some friends became associates—speaking when they saw each other, but no texts or phone calls.

Some were obviously envious—especially Maya. No matter how they really felt, most of the girls congratulated Chase for making the varsity team. Not Maya. She stopped speaking to Chase when the varsity team was announced. Chase was hurt that Maya stopped being her friend. She had what her mother called: *a life lesson.* "Not everyone will be happy for your success, including friends," her mother had said.

Her best friend Kendall Whitlow was thrilled that she made the varsity team. She even decorated Chase's locker at school with streamers, balloons and a 'congratulations banner.' They lived next door to each other and had been friends since they were five-years-old.

While watching the junior varsity team play, Chase remembered the many games they played together. Chase shook the memories away and focused on the game. "Defense! Defense!" Chase screamed at Riverbrook JV player Faith. The tall, healthy girl held both arms high above her head to stop an opposing player from moving past her. The girl dribbled the ball, waiting for a chance to move past Faith. Kendall snatched the ball from the girl, made a fast break towards the front court, and made a lay-up shot.

Screaming happily, Chase jumped up and down: the JV team was winning by ten points. "Go Kendall," she shouted, rooting for her best friend. "Go Kendall!"

One minute later, the buzzer sounded, signaling the end of the game. Chase stepped down the risers and stopped to speak to Kendall's mom.

"Hi, Miss Regina," she said, hugging the tall woman, her long braids brushing against Chase's cheek. Regina Whitlow smiled back and commented about the game. "They're better than they were during the pre-season tournament," said Regina.

"Yes," agreed Chase.

"I talked to your mom. You're coming home with me," said Regina.

"Okay," Chase said, before walking through the small crowd of parents to the players' bench. Girls were milling around, discussing the game and gathering their belongings.

"I'll be right back girls," said Regina.

"Good game," Chase said to Kendall.

"Thanks!" said Kendall who had a round brown face with large expressive eyes, a broad nose, and full lips. She resembled her mother, except for the splattering of moles across her mother's face.

"She didn't make as many points as I did," said Maya.

"I wasn't counting, and it doesn't matter," said Chase.

"I bet it matters to your big-time coach," said Maya.

"So you decide to talk to me today," Chase said, returning Maya's unfriendly glare.

"You supposed to be Kendall's best friend and you don't come to all her games."

"That's none of your business," said Kendall.

"Maybe you need to be hanging with the varsity girls," said Maya. "That's where you belong and…"

"Shut up, Maya," Kendall said. "Because you don't make any sense and that's why no one listens to you."

"You don't tell me to shut up," said Maya. "This is between me and Chase."

"Get over it. Coach O made the decision two months ago," said Chase. "There's nothing you can do but try-out next year."

"You giving me advice?" Maya stepped closer to Chase. "You're not my mother or boss."

"You need to get out of my face," said Chase. "Step away from me."

"Let it go," said Kendall.

"What y'all going to do?" Maya said, swaying her head back and forth.

"You're going to get yourself kicked off the team," said Kendall.

Maya noticed that junior varsity Coach Harris was watching them. She didn't want to get on the coach's bad side. "Whatever, robotics, girl," Maya said to Kendall.

"Yeah, I can build a robot," said Kendall, who was in the advanced science and technology program. Kendall caught grief for being the only black girl on the robotics team. "What can you build?"

"Whatever, whatever!" Maya said, walking towards the locker room with her sports bag dangling from her left shoulder.

Thirty minutes later, Chase and Kendall were riding in Regina's SUV. The girls were singing a current Beyonce song. When the song was over, Kendall asked, "Mommy, how was your day?"

Regina released a deep sigh. "Interesting."

"That tells me a lot," Kendall said. "I had an interesting day. I learned about a sensory device that can make robots aware of their surroundings."

"That's intriguing," Regina said, turning into their neighborhood.

"What? Can it breathe?" teased Chase. "So weird."

"So are you, Ms. Perfectionist."

"That's not weird, just a little strange," said Chase, laughing. "But making robots, that's out there."

"My robot's name is Cleopatra."

"Just getting weirder…"

"Well, I'm proud of my weirdness," said Kendall.

"You're just both unique," said Regina, looking through the rearview mirror at Chase and Kendall in the backseat.

Regina drove pass several homes and then turned left into the driveway of a two-story brick front home with a black door and black shutters framing the windows. She reached up to the visor and pressed the garage door opener. The sound of the garage door opening didn't block out the scream from the back of the car.

"Mommy, there's a *For Sale* sign in our yard," Kendall said, her voice skating the thin edge of panic.

"I've been trying to prepare you for this," said Regina. "I told you that when I got laid off, I would have to find a job soon." Her voice was soft and soothing.

"I don't want to move, Mommy." Big tear drops fell from Kendall's eyes. "I don't want to move! I hate that Daddy moved out!" Kendall hysterically screamed.

"Baby, I don't want to move either," Regina said with restrained emotion. "I'm really trying to get a job so we don't have to."

"Maybe you and Daddy…"

"Kendall, we've already discussed this," Regina firmly said.

"It's shocking to see the sign," Kendall said. "This is a nightmare. I didn't think it would ever really happen." She looked over at Chase. "I don't want to move away from Chase."

"I don't want you to move either," Chase said, sounding as sad and distraught as Kendall.

"I understand, girls," Regina said. "I don't want to move either. I'm going to do whatever I can so that we don't have to move."

"You promise, Mommy?" asked Kendall, her voice sounding like a five-year-old.

"I promise, sweetie pie," said Regina.

They were quiet, until Chase brought up the holiday. "You guys are coming over for Thanksgiving like usual?" asked Chase.

"Of course, we're coming. We love holidays with your family," said Regina.

"Would you believe we have a game next Tuesday, two days before Thanksgiving?" said Chase.

"That's the life of a baller," said Kendall.

"I love Thanksgiving." Chase removed the vase and candle sticks from the middle of the dining room table and placed them inside the credenza. Shellie came into the room with a bag from a local dry-cleaner. Inside the plastic wrapping, a tablecloth hung between two hangers.

"That's my favorite table cloth," said Chase.

"It's *my* favorite," said Blake.

"Well, my dear daughters," said Shellie, 'it is my absolute *favorite*."

Blake wiped off the dining room table that had been lengthened with table extenders. "The table is ready for *our* favorite tablecloth."

Chase and Blake covered the dining room table with a plastic, foam-backed white table protector.

Shellie carefully removed the tablecloth. "Your hands are clean, right?"

"Yes ma'am," said Chase.

Blake nodded her head.

Shellie unwrapped the heavy-linen tablecloth. She neatly spread it across the table. It was medium white, with scalloped edges around the border. Little brown turkeys were finely-sewn all around the tablecloth.

"It is so beautiful," gushed Shellie. "My grandmother, your great grandmother made it."

"We know," said Chase.

"I always feel guilty eating on it," said Shellie. "Grandmother always used it on Thanksgiving day. She used to make us iron it. Ugh, that was so much work. That's why I put it in the cleaners."

Blake laughed, imagining her mother ironing the tablecloth.

"Thanksgiving wouldn't be the same without it," said Blake.

"That's why I have this thin plastic cover to protect it," said Shellie.

"Good idea, Mommy," said Blake.

"We're going to have three tables this year," said Shellie. "Two for adults and one for kids."

"That's not fair," said Blake.

"We've always done that," said Shellie.

"Not three tables."

"We invited the Smith's, Cornwell's and Washington's from church," said Shellie.

"And Tequila from my team. Her mom and brother are coming too," said Chase. "Kendall and her family always come."

"Of course," said Shellie. "You know they are always welcome."

"Next year I'm inviting my whole class," said Blake. "Or the cast from my play."

"Then we'll just set up more tables," said Shellie.

Later, the kitchen counters were crowded with meats (turkey, ham, chicken, and roast beef) and main dishes (macaroni and cheese, yams, greens, green beans, mashed potatoes and more); some were prepared by Shellie and some by her guests. There was a separate desert table, which included Grammy's specialties: sweet potato pie, pound cake, coconut cream pie and other deserts: lemon pie, chocolate cake, carrot cake, cookies and cheesecake.

Dinner was set to begin at 6 PM. Every one who'd ever been invited to the Anderson's for dinner knew that dinner started at 6 PM sharp. If late, you would have to eat the second round of dinner.

People began arriving at 4:30 PM. Some knew each other or introductions were made.

Tequila and her family arrived at 5:30 PM. Chase answered the door. "Ah, you're not late," teased Chase.

Rashonda laughed. "Quila sometimes is in her own time zone."

"I can't wait to eat," said Tevon.

Shellie entered the front hall. "Welcome to our home," Shellie said. "Come in, come in."

"Thank you, Shellie. I really appreciate the invitation," said Rashonda.

"We believe holidays are a time to be with family and friends. So make yourself at home."

"I made some banana pudding," said Rashonda, holding a casserole dish.

"My mom makes the best banana pudding in the world," bragged Tevon.

"Is that so?" asked Shellie.

"That's a fact, girl," said Rashonda, handing the banana pudding to Shellie.

Rashonda and Shellie laughed.

"I'm sure we will enjoy it," said Shellie.

"Tevon, the boys are downstairs in the game room. There's some kind of video game war going on," said Chase.

"Yeah man! They are toast!" said Tevon.

"We're watching movies," said Chase.

"Yeah, movie chick," teased Tequila.

"Be in the kitchen by 6 so we can say grace and eat," said Shellie.

At 6 PM, family and guests crowded in the Anderson's kitchen.

"Everything looks delicious."

"Can wait to eat."

"Homemade cranberry sauce!"

"Stuffing with pecans!"

"Thank you all for sharing this Thanksgiving Day with us," said Michael. "We always say grace and then we…"

"Eat like pigs," said Evan.

Everyone laughed.

"Daddy, please don't say a two hour grace," said Blake. "We're hungry."

"We have a lot be thankful for, don't we?" asked Michael. "Our health, home, family, friends, and jobs."

"Yes, Daddy," said Blake. "And I'm grateful for everything and I'm sure everyone is too."

"You just want to eat," teased Evan.

"So do you," said Blake.

Michael looked around the room at the different people in his house. He was proud to share the moment with them. "Please bow your heads."

Michael was silent for a minute, and then said a relatively short Thanksgiving blessing: three minutes instead of his five to seven minute grace that sounded like a mini-sermon.

"Wow, Daddy, that was the shortest grace you ever said," said Blake.

"You want me to keep going?" asked Michael.

"We want to eat!" said Blake.

After the Thanksgiving feast, guests scattered into different rooms. Some of the girls watched movies and most of the boys played video games. Some guests played pool or ping-pong. A roomful of mostly men invaded the family room, watching the football games.

Chase suggested playing Taboo, but no one was interested.

Around 8:30 PM, people started leaving.

Rashonda said to Shellie: "I enjoyed meeting everyone. Thank you for inviting us to your house for Thanksgiving."

"You're welcome," said Shellie. "I'm glad you came. Tevon seemed like he had fun."

Rashonda laughed. "When that boy is playing video games, he's in heaven. Shellie, I've never been to your church. I'm not a big churchgoer, but I like the people I've met here. I think I will visit your church one day."

"We've been going to our church since Evan was born," said Shellie. "I hope you come visit. Let us know when you plan to come."

"We will," said Rashonda.

"Tequila, are you ready for those tournament games tomorrow?" asked Shellie.

"Yes ma'am," said Tequila. "I had to get a tutor or the coach wasn't going to let me play …cause I kind of dissed a teacher."

"You didn't have to tell her that," said Rashonda.

"No problem. There are very few secrets on the team," said Shellie. "I'm glad Coach Olivia is working with you and if we can help in anyway, let us know."

"Thank you, Miss Shellie," said Tequila.

"We'll see you guys at the tournament," said Shellie, before closing the door.

CHAPTER 15

SELENA

"Selena, there were probably 40 of your relatives at the game." Heaven giggled. "Did they come in one van?"

The laughter stopped and no one spoke.

"That wasn't very nice," said Marley.

"Y'all looking at me like I'm crazy," said Heaven. "You've seen a million Mexicans get out of one car."

The girls were exhausted. The Riverbrook High girls' varsity team had played three games in the Thanksgiving tournament: won two games and lost one game.

The tournament was not over.

Riverbrook was in the winners' bracket, waiting to play Jackson High, a team outside their regular region who had also won two games and lost one game.

The winner of the Riverbrook High and Jackson High game would win the Thanksgiving tournament in first place.

Tired, yet excited, the girls sat on the bleachers waiting for the next game. They listened to their iPods, talked to each other, admired boys, or hung out with their family members who had traveled to a school seventy miles away to see them play. Chase sketched people and things of interest in her sketch pad.

Selena and Bailey were listening to Bailey's iPod, one ear pod in each of their ears, both bobbing their heads to a John Mayer song.

"This is chill music," said Selena.

"We'll play something else before the game," said Bailey. "Something to get us fired up."

"Tequila always listens to Drake or Biggie or Eminem," said Selena.

"You know Biggie is from New York and he reminds me of my brother who died. He was a Biggie fan." Tequila shrugged. "And I just like Eminem. All that anger gets me ready to beast out."

"I like Eminem too," said Bailey.

"I'm going to the concession stand," said Tequila. "Be right back."

"Hey Selena," said Miguel.

Selena looked up, surprised, but happy to see Miguel. "What are you doing here?"

"I came to see you play."

"I didn't know you were here."

"I saw you bust that three pointer," he said. "Magnificent."

She smiled, highlighting her deep dimples. "Gracias."

"I saw some of your family," said Miguel. "Your brother is so funny. He was standing up the whole time you're out there."

"That's my older brother Paco. He el loco," said Selena. "We're in the same grade."

"Same grade?" asked Miguel.

"No good in school." She shrugged. "He comes every day, but not serious about learning. He failed a grade. My big brother Juan is real smart."

"Good luck on the next game. I can't stay. I have to pick up my little sister."

"How old is she?" asked Selena.

"She's only seven. She's at a friend's house," said Miguel. "You'll meet her. She thinks she's my shadow."

Selena laughed.

"I was watching the other team play," said Miguel. "Their guard really can't handle the ball, so your little freshman can shut her down and y'all can win."

"I'll remember that," said Selena.

"I'll be seeing you soon," said Miguel.

"Sí," said Selena.

After Miguel walked up the risers, Bailey said, "OMG, you're friends with Miguel, he's one of the cutest boys in school!"

"I guess so. He always speaks to me with that melt-your-heart smile," Selena said, grinning.

"He's gorgeous," said Bailey.

"I know," said Selena. "So many girls like him, so like I can't be sure if he really likes me."

"He must like you," said Bailey. "He came all the way out here to see you play. This is the middle of nowhere."

"I hope he likes me for me," said Selena. "He's got a fan club of stalkers."

"They're more than stalkers. They're slores," said Bailey.

"My cousin Eva says they're whores," said Selena.

"Whores, slores," said Bailey. "The boys' basketball players have them too. Slores galore."

"Slores?" asked Marley.

"You know how some girls are about the boys' teams. Especially the boys who are stars of their team and get a lot of attention. Slores follow the boys around like they're rich already," said Bailey.

"They are so obvious," said Marley. "Walking around in booty skirts and no underwear. And they try to get pregnant by them. They're after that money."

Selena laughed a little. "I can't compete with them. And I'm not having a baby just to get money."

"You're not like them," said Bailey.

"I know," said Selena. "That's what worries me. Miguel might not really like me if I'm not like them."

"You don't want to be like them," said Marley.

Not far away on the bench, Tequila motioned to them. "Coach wants to meet with us and then we have to go warm up."

On the bus ride back to the school, the girls were loud, giddy and silly. "We're going to keep on winning," said Coach O. "We caught them off guard because they expected…"

"Us to suck like we did last year," interrupted Heaven.

"Expect the unexpected," said Chase. "Right Coach O?"

"Yeah!"

"I just can't believe we won the tournament," gushed Selena.

"Neither can I," said Layne.

"It's a miracle, especially against that last team," said Bailey. "They hardly ever lose."

"I think other schools will finally start to respect us," said Marley.

"That's right. So we're going to switch up our plays," said Coach O. "Thank Selena for those last shots. You stayed cool under pressure and that's important. Very important."

All the girls clapped. "Go Selena, Go Selena, you're a shooter," they said, singing to the beat of a rapper's song.

Coach didn't interfere with their celebration: singing, dancing, bragging and teasing. She did interfere when Heaven made a racially insensitive remark.

"Selena, your family really comes out to support you," said Heaven.

"That's cool," said Zoey.

"I wish my relatives were here to see me play," said Tequila.

"My dad travels, so he can't make many games," said Rachel. "I'm used to it."

"My mom and dad work at the salon," said Kaylee. "They come to home games."

"Selena, there were probably a hundred of your relatives at the game." Heaven giggled. "Did they come in one van?"

The laugher stopped and no one spoke.

"That wasn't very nice," said Marley.

"Y'all looking at me like I'm crazy," said Heaven. "But you know there's some truth to what I'm saying. You've seen a million Mexicans get out of one car."

"Heaven Jackson, you will be quiet," said Coach O, standing in front of the girls. "I will not tolerate any type of racist remark whether you think it's true or not."

Fury was etched on Coach O's face. "I will not tolerate racism or stereotypes or sexist comments or anything that is negative, mean or nasty because it is absolutely unnecessary."

The girls were uncomfortable and quiet.

"Just because you make something funny doesn't make it okay," Coach O said, her voice ripe with indignation. "Do you understand me?"

She glared at Heaven.

"Yes ma'am," said Heaven, her eyes downcast.

"Does everyone understand?" asked Coach O. "Because that applies to every last one of you."

The girls responded with various forms of agreement:

"Yes."

"Yes ma'am."

"You're right."

"We have a racially diverse team. How are we going to be racist amongst ourselves?" Coach O asked and waited for a response.

No one spoke.

"When I played at Riverbrook a million years ago, I was the only black girl on the team. I heard my share of racial insults," she said, her eyes searching the faces of her players. "I think the fact that our team is diverse means we should celebrate our differences. We're going to play some teams who don't like us for various reasons, but we must be united."

Coach O paused, thoughtfully. "That means acceptance and mutual respect among each other. I'm not saying that you have to be best friends, but on that court you better be best friends, and off the court you show each other respect."

A long awkward silence followed. The girls looked at each other, not sure what to say or do.

"I'm sorry, Selena," Heaven said. "I really wasn't trying to offend you. I was trying to joke, but it was a bad joke."

Coach O looked at Heaven. "Thanks for apologizing without me having to tell you to."

"I accept your apology. And we don't have to talk about it anymore." Selena shook her head. She didn't like confrontation or conflict. "I don't want to think about it anymore. I just like being happy."

They were quiet for several long minutes, and then Selena started singing a song by Kool and the Gang, *Celebrate Tonight.*

"*Celebration! We're going to celebrate and have a good time!*" sang Selena.

"You're such a cheerleader," teased Tequila.

"*Celebrate good times: come on!*" Chase joined in, clapping her hands.

"*Celebrate good times: come on!*" sang Tequila, Marley, and Zoey.

Soon everyone joined in, singing the infectious lyrics. "*Celebrate good times, it's time to celebrate,*" including Coach O, the assistant coach, and team managers.

Everyone laughed when they finished singing the song.

"Y'all so silly," said Tequila. "My Mama used to sing that song all the time."

The bus pulled in front of the school and everyone went their separate ways. Selena got into an old van that was probably fifteen-years-old. It had been painted several times and was an odd shade of purple. Her family and friends called it the Barney van. She hopped in the van, which she was surprised to find empty.

"Where is everybody?" she asked Juan.

"I took them home," Juan said." I helped Papá close the restaurant so we can straight home."

"Thank you, Juan," she said, leaning back in the front passenger van seat. "I'm so tired."

"A long day, little sis."

"Let me tell you what happened on the bus," Selena said.

Juan gazed at her, recognizing from the serious tone of her voice that something was wrong.

"Heaven made a joke about the whole family coming to see me play."

"The bunch of Mexicans in a van joke," said Juan.

"Sí! But Coach O got furious." Speaking fast, she said, "She told off Heaven and told us that she wasn't going to tolerate any type of racial comments about anybody. She was mad and serious."

"You got a good coach. She's probably been called some names."

"Coach O told us she was the only black girl on the team at Riverbrook years ago. I think that's why she was so offended by what Heaven said. Everybody got real quiet," Selena said. "I don't think anybody will say anything like that again."

"Your couch is tough," said Juan. "She stands up for what she believes and she knows how to handle situations. That's cool."

"I wish Papá would come see me play."

"Maybe," said Juan.

With a sudden burst of enthusiasm, she said, "He'll change his mind one day soon."

"My little sister with eternal sunshine in her eyes."

CHAPTER 16

MARLEY

"Who reads that Darian blog?" asked Rachel.

"I do," said Zoey.

Everyone nodded their heads except for Tequila.

"Sometimes she's funny, but people make whack comments," said Bailey.

"Yeah, like calling us aliens," said Elise.

"See, that's why I don't read crazy shit like that," said Tequila.

"Let's make a pledge," said Marley, talking to the team of basketball girls gathered around her brightly-colored, full basement which consisted of an office, a game room with a pool table and ping-pong table, a theatre room, and a big open area with a huge sectional sofa.

A brightly-lit large Christmas tree stood in the corner of the main room, decorated with gold lights, red and gold bulbs, bows, ribbons and Christmas accessories.

"No talking about basketball," said Bailey, sitting on the sectional sofa.

"We played two games last week," said Elise.

"And we won," said Rachel.

"Ganadores!" said Selena. "It means winners in Spanish."

"Maybe we should celebrate being ganadores," said Zoey, mispronouncing the Spanish word for winners.

"Ganadores" said Selena.

"Well I'm celebrating that we don't have to see or talk about basketball for seven days," said Layne. "We don't even have to play until after Christmas."

"I'm ready to give my best friend a break." Tequila laughed. "You know, my basketball is my best friend."

"Pathetic," said Layne, shaking her head.

"I'm going to kick the ball out of my room," said Heaven. "He gets on my nerves anyway. He won't stay still."

Some of the girls laughed.

"So no talking about basketball," said Selena. "Makes us loco."

"It's secret Santa time," Marley announced.

"Good. I didn't want to have to beat Heaven again," said Ja-Nay-A, coming into the main room. "She sucks at pool."

"You cheated," said Heaven. "That's why I left."

"Don't feel bad," said Layne. "I kicked her ass."

Tequila laughed. "Layne beat you in pool, Ja-Nay-A?"

"She cheated," said Ja-Nay-A.

"Girl, I didn't cheat. You didn't think I knew how to play," said Layne.

"You little hustler!" said Ja-Nay-A.

"Never under estimate me," said Layne. "Expect the unexpected."

All the girls laughed.

Minutes later, the girls sat win various places—on the floor, the sofa, or chairs.

"So, who's going to go first?" asked Rachel.

"What if we just went around the room, starting with me," suggested Heaven. Before anyone answered, Heaven removed the present from her gift bag. "I like! I like!" she said, holding up a black sweater for everyone to see.

"I'm next," said Layne. She took out two tee-shirts. "Tee-shirts," she said. "One says, 'Stare at my boobs and you will go blind' and the other says 'I'm the shit." She added, "That's a true statement."

Everyone laughed.

"Someone knows me well. Zoey, did you get these?" asked Layne.

"I'm not your secret Santa," said Zoey. "Seriously, dude."

"You can't wear those to school," said Rachel.

"Watch me," said Layne.

The girls laughed.

"I don't want you to get in trouble," said Rachel, concern in her voice.

"Thanks, Rach. I did get sent home for having a tee-shirt that said F-CK Teachers. The 'U' was missing but they still sent me home." Layne laughed. "Freedom of speech, right?"

"I got perfume," said Ja-Nay-A. "Thank you Secret Santa, whoever you are."

"Did Santa get you some deodorant too?" asked Layne.

"Layne, me and you about to go down," said Ja-Nay-A, with eyes narrowed. "I know I smell bad after practice. I wear men's deodorant because I sweat so much."

"None of us smell good after we play," said Marley.

"I got perfume too," said Rachel. "Britney Spears perfume! I don't know if my secret Santa was trying to be funny, but I like Britney Spears." In a high-pitched voice, she added, "I don't care if you all laugh at me."

"Gag me," said Zoey. "I can't wait for Lady Gaga's perfume. It's supposed to have blood in it."

"You want to smell like blood?" asked Rachel. "That's gross."

"I just love Gaga, so whatever her perfume smells like I will be smelling like it" said Zoey. "Even meat."

Some of the girls laughed.

"I can't believe someone bought me black Converse sneakers," said Zoey, after opening her present. "What's wrong with the pair I wear?"

"They're holey," said Chase.

"And smelly," said Ja-Nay-A. "I got nerve, right? I got smelly arm pits and Zoey got funky feet."

"You know what's really crazy," said Layne. "Zoey has at least ten different sneakers. Different colors. But she wears the same black pair all the time. Drives her mother insane."

"Thank you. I will drive my mother insane with my new pair of black sneakers," said Zoey.

"You're twisted," said Kaylee.

"I'm next," said Chase. She closed her eyes before pulling out a sketchpad, and a set of paints and brushes. "I love it," she gushed. Chase put the gift bag on the floor.

"Are you sure you checked everything in the bag?" whispered Layne.

Chase smiled as she dug through the tissue paper and removed a movie gift card.

"Thank you, Layne," said Chase. "My secret Santa!"

"No I'm not, Movie Chick," said Layne.

"Yes, you're my secret Santa, dude," said Chase.

"My turn," said Selena. A set of matching earrings, necklace and bracket and shirt were inside her gift bag. "Beautiful. Mucho gracias," said Selena. "I will wear them the first day we go back to school."

"Let's not talk about school," said Tequila. "It's my turn." She jumped up from the sofa and removed a small Coach clutch from her gift bag. "I can't believe it." She stared at the wallet. "How? Who? We were supposed to spend $25. I can't believe anyone on my team would buy me a fake."

"I'm sure it's not a fake," said Layne. "Just be happy."

"I am very happy. Thank you very, very, very much!"

"Your turn, Bailey," said Tequila.

Bailey rummaged through her gift bag, before showing off a manicure and pedicure set from Bath and Body Works.

Kaylee flashed a gift card from Hollister from her mysterious Secret Santa.

"I'm glad I didn't get Marley, no offense," said Kaylee. "You're the girl with everything."

"I know my Daddy spoils me, but he taught me to be grateful whenever I get a gift from someone. No matter whom the gift is from or what it is," explained Marley while opening her gift. "I truly appreciate my…Starbucks card. Is someone trying to say I'm a Starbucks addict?"

"You have Starbucks every day." Zoey laughed. "But so do I."

"Your turn, Elise," said Rachel.

Elise unwrapped the latest James Patterson book, along with a gift card from Borders. "So someone noticed that I read a lot."

"All the time. You and Rachel are always reading," said Tequila. "I don't understand why."

"It's how I escape," said Elise.

"Me too," said Rachel.

"There are better ways to escape," said Tequila.

"Who reads that Darian blog?" asked Rachel.

"I do," said Zoey.

Everyone nodded their heads except for Tequila.

"I don't have time," said Tequila.

"Sometimes she's funny, but people make whack comments," said Bailey.

"Yeah, like calling us aliens," said Elise.

"See, that's why I don't read crazy shit like that," said Tequila.

"Since we are playing better, winning more games and it's basically the same group of girls …maybe we have been invaded by aliens," said Rachel.

"Yeah, I think my blood is green now," said Zoey.

"My blood is vampire dark red," said Rachel.

"I want to know who's writing the crap," said Layne.

"Me too," said Elise.

"I don't give a crap," said Heaven.

"Do you think it's one of the team managers? Rina or Poppy. They're always around," said Chase.

"I like them, but they are kind of strange," said Zoey.

"Rina is intense. She does her job and keeps to herself," said Layne. "I wouldn't want to be team manager. Washing uniforms and bringing water bottles. Gross!"

"Where are they?" asked Rachel.

"Some party for team managers," said Marley. "Sounds lame."

"They're lurkers. They don't talk much," said Elise.

"Poppy's only shy when she doesn't know people. She talks to the Magnet kids," said Kaylee. "She's a math geek like me. She's not a good writer."

"Poppy talks sometimes, but she says the wrongs things at the wrong time," said Marley. "Kind of awkward and weird."

"You think everybody is weird," said Layne.

"I am curious," said Zoey. "I might have to do some checking to find out who the slore is."

"She doesn't have to be a slore," said Bailey.

"She's telling our business, so she's a slore," said Zoey.

The girls played games, danced, sang Christmas songs and had fun together. Basketball was not mentioned during the Christmas party. Two hours later, parents started arriving to get their daughters.

"Coach O bought us all presents. Make sure you get one before you leave," said Marley. "They're right by the door."

"Where is our mysterious Coach Olivia?" asked Layne.

"She's in Europe. Says she has family over there," said Marley.

"You know she played over there," said Zoey.

"I heard that," said Tequila.

"She'll be back the day after Christmas for our tournament," said Marley.

"Thank you for hosting the secret Santa party," said Chase.

"Hey, I'm an only child," said Marley. "I love doing stuff like this."

The girls left with a trail of 'thank you,' "have a good Christmas," "see you at the tournament," comments. They smiled when picking up the Victoria Secret's gift bags Coach O left for each team member. Some peeked inside: perfume, lotion, shower gel, and pajama bottoms.

Marley and Cooper cleaned up after the team left. Cooper maintained a clean, neat and everything-in-its place home. Marley knew it would be futile to argue about cleaning the house.

"I'm glad Franchesca decided to go away for the holidays because I wasn't ready to see her yet," said Marley. "Or that Sterling person."

"You have to accept it," said Cooper.

"You haven't accepted it," observed Marley.

Cooper looked at Marley, surprised by her astute observation, but did not respond. "We've been divorced for a while, little girl. Your mother has a right to move on. I don't agree with a lot of things she does when it comes to you, but she is your mother."

"I didn't want to see Sterling Price. What kind of name is that?"

Cooper laughed.

"Ah-ha, I made you laugh."

"A little."

"I'm glad we're having Christmas dinner over E's house" Marley said. "I don't have to go to iceberg Chicago to visit Franchesa."

Suddenly, they heard the doorbell.

"Oh no," said Marley.

"What?"

"It must be Sallie."

"She's out of the picture."

"Oh that's so sad. Why? What happened, Daddy?" she asked with outrageous insincerity.

"None of your business, M," said Cooper. "Now open the door for your cousin."

"Yay! E is here!"

She went to the door and opened the door for Egypt. They went into the kitchen. "Hi, Uncle Cooper," said Egypt, kissing him on the cheek.

"Hey, E." He noticed her coat. "Cute jacket."

"Thanks!"

"Daddy, can we go upstairs to my room?"

"Clean up downstairs first."

"Awww," whined Marley. She picked up two plastic trash bags.

"I'll help," said Egypt, following Marley into the basement.

Downstairs, they dropped plates and trash into the garbage bags.

"M, I have to tell you something."

"What?!"

"My mom is trying to have a baby!" said Egypt.

Marley stopped and stared at her cousin. "Stop playing!"

"Yes, I heard her and Daddy talking about it."

"Are they serious, serious?"

"Yes. Mom says she's been waiting for the right time, but she's running out of time."

They were quiet for a while.

"Are you cool with it?" asked Marley.

"What can I say? What can I do? I'll be going to college soon, so I won't grow up with her or him." Egypt frowned. "That sucks."

"You're right," said Marley.

"It will be…different," said Egypt.

"OMG!"

"What?"

"What if Franchesca decides to have a baby?"

"And? What can you do about it?"

"Nothing. I'll be mad. She didn't exactly want me, E," said Marley. "Why would she want another baby?"

"I don't know, M," Egypt said in a compassionate voice.

"The more I think about it, there's no way she'd get pregnant," said Marley. "She's so into her career. Aunt Martina is a super career woman like my mom, but Aunt Laurel is really into being a mother. I wish my mom was more like her."

"I think my mom would be happy," said Egypt.

"I think it would be tragic if Franchesca had a baby," said Marley.

"Let's think about something us," said Egypt. "Put on some Christmas music."

"I'm so glad Christmas dinner is at your house," said Marley.

A few minutes later, the popular 90's girl group TLC's Christmas song was playing. *"Have a Merry, Merry Christmas and a Happy New Year…"*

DARIAN-BALL-BLOG: NUMBER 4

Winter break is over. How do you feel: Glad? Mad? Sad?

Anything interesting happen over winter break? Usual stuff: Christmas, presents, Hanukkah, Kwanzaa, Feliz Navidad, New Year's. Here's a space to add any other holidays I may have forgotten: (_____).

Break-ups and make-ups. Happy or crazy family visits. Nothing-to-do days. Sleep-til-noon days.

Vacation is so over.

The girls' basketball team didn't get much rest over the break. They drove all the way to South Carolina and placed third in the Christmas tournament. I heard some of the players on the other teams were college players in disguise (just kidding). Maybe. Well our girls came in first place in the Thanksgiving tournament.

Tournaments don't count in our local region ranking. So it kind of doesn't matter. Sort of. We're mid-season and we have 9 wins, 2 losses.

Check out the game highlights on the school website. About time they started showing the girls' games on the web site.

Yeah people, there really is a girls' basketball team at Riverbrook High.

Finally.

Comments

MVP123: Tournament games don't really count.
LoveBB: The team is so much better than last year.
Mindyourbiz: They won their games before the holidays.
Moreball: They came in third in a tournament that doesn't count. So what?
Ballzone: What do you expect? They are still trying to be a real team.
Marsball: Remember they are aliens.
Iamfrom: You are the alien.
Sportsqueen: If they have special powers. I hope they zap you to Mars.
Shooter: Their powers are only good on the court. Sort of like superman is only superman when he has on his cape.
Lovesports: You are crazy if you believe in aliens.

Ibelieve: Don't knock what you don't know. I believe in aliens. You really think there are only humans in the universe. Do you even know how big the universe is?

Realworld: I believe what I see. They are not playing like they did last year. Aliens!

CHAPTER 17

BAILEY

"What are you doing?" Bailey's teacher asked.
"Looking at my text messages," she whispered.
"You know what you have to do," Mr. Morgan said.
"Please!" pleaded Bailey.
"Get caught texting and you have to read one of your text messages."

Bailey discretely looked at her text messages, hoping her physics teacher, Mr. Morgan, didn't notice her cell phone sandwiched between the pages of her textbook. She half-listened to Mr. Morgan's monotone voice, while eyeing the number of text messages from Matthew Charles—19 messages. When she had received his first text message last night, she immediately called River.

"What's up, ladybug?" River had answered, using Bailey's elementary school nickname.

Annoyed, Bailey asked, "Why did you give Matthew my phone number?"

"You didn't tell me not to."

"Dude, you should have asked me first!"

"Dude, you would have said no," explained River. "He made a sick-o first impression and he wanted to make it up to you. He's been bugging me since he met you."

"I don't care. He's an ass," Bailey said.

"He's not as bad as you think he is," River said. "He had a little too much to drink and said things he shouldn't have said. And he didn't know you were the friend I wanted him to meet."

"He's still an asshole."

"Give him a second chance," said River.

"Why should I?"

"Because he's cute," River said

"So!"

"Because he thinks you're totally hot."

"So!"

"You have to lose it eventually."

"What?" Bailey asked.

"Your virginity."

"Not to him!" said Bailey.

"I heard he's pretty good," said River. "My sources are reliable."

"You better *not* be the source."

"No way," River said. "Friends don't sleep with each other's boyfriends, old or new."

"Not always true."

"I know, I know. A lot of girls at my school do, but I don't," River said. "Me and Matt are just friends. Remember I date his best friend, Austin. He rocks my world."

"Words I don't expect to hear from you"

"Really, give Matt a second chance," insisted River.

"No way."

"You got to give it up to someone." In a taunting voice, she added, "You don't know what you're missing."

"And what's going to happen if I don't?"

"You'll turn into Cruella De Vil from 101 Dalmatians. She was mean and evil," said River.

"That movie scared me to death when I was little," admitted Bailey. "She was so evil."

River mocked Cruella De Vil's mean voice: "Get me those puppies!"

Bailey laughed. "You're crazy you know that, right?"

"I've always been crazy. That's what you love about me."

"Bye, you traitor," Bailey said.

In class, Bailey was surprised to see that Matthew was blowing up her phone. She did not respond to any of Matthew Charles' 19 text messages, yet he continued to text her. On impulse she decided to open one of the messages. Forgetting she was in class, Bailey laughed when she read, 'This is Matt the ass.'

"Care to share what you find so amusing in your textbook?" her teacher asked.

Mr. Morgan stared at her with that I-know-you're-using-your-phone look. Guilt was written all over her face. "I was reading my text messages," she whispered.

"Oh what a surprise," quipped Mr. Morgan. "It's the surprise of the 21st century, like Steve Jobs inventing the iPhone."

"Everybody knows Steve Jobs invented the iPhone, so it's not a surprise," said a girl in the class.

Mr. Morgan looked at the girl. "Precisely my point."

"Back to Ms. White and her inappropriate texting in class," said Mr. Morgan.

"I'm sincerely sorry," Bailey said.

"You know what you have to do," Mr. Morgan said.

"No, Mr. Morgan," Bailey pleaded. "Please."

"It's one of my rules. Get caught texting and you have to read one of your text messages."

"Can you make an exception?" asked Bailey.

"Have I ever made an exception?"

Bailey didn't answer. She saw on his stern face that he wasn't going to change his mind.

She sighed and scrolled through her messages.

She heard her classmates chuckling with anticipation of her humiliation.

Mr. Morgan leaned over and pointed to a message. "Read that one."

Bailey read the text message in a low whisper: 'Sorry I was an idiot. Give me a chance to be a jerk. Matt the ass.'"

Everyone one laughed, including Mr. Morgan.

Bailey wished she could turn invisible and walk out of the class unseen.

"Class, I guess we've had our amusement for the day. Now, let's get back to work."

Bailey didn't hear anything else that came out of Mr. Morgan's mouth. She just stared at the clock. When the bell rang, she jumped out of her seat and ran out the door.

She heard several students say: "Matt the ass, Matt the ass" or "Who's Matt the ass?"

Not wanting to hear their guesses and mean comments, Bailey rushed down the hall to get away from her classmates.

"Don't be embarrassed," said Diante Johnson.

Without looking, she knew who it was. She glanced back at him, but kept walking.

"Half the class has been caught texting and had to do the same thing," said Diante.

"That was humiliating and horrible," complained Bailey.

"Not as horrible as Casey's text," Diante said. "Something about what color lipstick did you have on last night?"

"I knew she was a rainbow girl," said Bailey, remembering the girl's red-blotched face.

"Me too, but her text had so much sex in it that Mr. Morgan made her stop reading it," said Diante.

"Her text was way worse than mine," agreed Bailey.

"Yep."

"Reading my text was embarrassing. I wanted to melt into my seat."

"I'm melting! I'm melting," Diante said, imitating the wicked witch of the west's infamous finale scene in *The Wizard of Oz* movie.

"That was a horrible imitation," said Bailey, laughing.

"At least I made you laugh."

"You did."

"So, do you like Matt the ass?"

Bailey stared at Diante, unsure if he was serious or joking. He looked at her with curious eyes. "No, he's an ass," Bailey said. "He's texted me a million times but I haven't answered."

"Everyone deserves a second chance," said Diante.

Bailey shrugged. "I don't think so."

"What if I text you?" Diante asked. "Would you hit delete or reply?"

"Depends on what you say," Bailey answered. "Anyway, you don't have my number."

"Yes I do."

"How?" Bailey asked. "I don't remember giving you my number."

"You didn't, but I have it," Diante said with a cocky grin. "Guess I'll have to text you to find out if you reply."

Bailey looked at him, not knowing what to say.

"Got to get class," Diante said, darting around the corner.

Bailey quickly shot River a text: *Got in trouble cause of Matt the ass.*

River zipped back a reply: *What did Matt do?*

Bailey's reply: *Got caught using cell phone in class. Had to read a text from Matt to class.*

River: *Embarrassing! None of his business. Teacher should be fired.*

Bailey: *Yeah. Diante tried to make me feel better.*

River: *Who's that?*

Bailey: *You met him at the mall.*

River: *The hot black dude?*

Bailey: *Yea. Wants to text me.*

River: *Lose it to him. I heard they're good in bed.*

Bailey: *Asshole comment. You know I hate stuff like that. Don't offend me!!!!*

River: *Sorry!!!*

Bailey ran to class and grabbed a seat just as the bell rang.

CHAPTER 18

TEQUILA

"I got your spot, dummy," said Heaven. "My grades are good. We don't need you."

"F you," said Tequila.

"Leave her alone," said Layne. "You know she's mad."

"She's trying to get you to act crazy so you'll get kicked off the team," said Marley.

"I can't believe this crowd," said Tequila.

"Me either," said Marley, watching the large groups of people coming into the gym.

"Wow," said Chase.

"People are finally coming to our games," Tequila said, her eyes roaming the crowd.

The girls were sitting on the floor, their legs extended as they stretched while doing pre-game warm-up exercises.

The gym was crowded because both the girls' and boys' varsity teams were playing against Maysville High, a rival school in the southern part of the region. Maysville High usually went to the regional playoffs.

It was an extremely important game.

Practices had been grueling. Coach O prepared them mentally with a quote: *Good, better, best. Never rest until your good is better and your better is best.* She made them repeat the motto until they could say it without thinking.

"Look," Bailey said, pointing at the risers. "Some of the boys from the basketball team are here."

"I like to watch them play," said Kaylee.

"The crowd goes bananas," said Layne.

"There's Tariq, Steve, Mike-Mike, and Quinton." said Tequila.

Selena waved at her family and relatives, sitting on the top rows. "Selena! Selena!" they screamed.

"I love my familia. I love how loud they are."

"I love how they root for us," said Rachel.

"I wish Papá would come see me play," said Selena.

"He will one day," said Chase.

They stood up and started practicing their shooting drills.

"We finally have a crowd and I'm not going to get any tic." Tequila stomped her foot. "No tic."

"Sorry Tequila," said Selena.

"Yeah, I got your spot, dummy," said Heaven. "My grades are good. We don't need you."

"F you," said Tequila.

"Leave her alone," said Layne. "You know she's mad."

"She's playing you," said Marley. "Trying to get you to act crazy, so you'll get kicked off the team."

Tequila looked up and saw her mother heading towards the bench. "Oh no!"

"What's she going to do?" Chase asked.

"Try to get Coach O to let me play."

"Oh gosh," said Selena.

"She shouldn't do that," said Marley. "That's going to make Coach O even madder."

"I know," said Tequila.

Tequila watched her mother talking with Coach Olivia. From a distance, everything about the conversation seemed wrong. She could tell that her mother immediately aggravated Coach O. She even saw Coach O tried to stay calm and cool. But then her mother said something that made Coach O angry. Coach signaled to a security guard. In that instant, her mother realized that she had gone too far. Rashonda closed her mouth and walked away.

A few minutes later, Coach O walked over to Tequila.

"I had to remind your mother about the rules. I make the decisions about who plays and when they play," said Coach O. "She seems to think I'm easily persuaded or intimidated. When it comes to basketball, I'm the boss. I take this game very seriously."

"I know, I know," said Tequila. "She was just trying to help me."

"I'm not surprised that she wants to see you play. Most parents have something to say about their kids playing time. But, I was offended by her comments about me forcing you to go to a tutor. I'm trying to help you," explained Coach O. "You're benched because you walked out of class and disrespected a teacher. You got a tutor and then quit going to him."

"I didn't like him. He was psycho-killer strange and he…"

"Get another tutor and you can play again," said Coach O. "I need to know that you are trying to improve your grades."

"I'm serious, Coach O. That tutor was weird," explained Tequila. "He picked his nose and smelled like vomit."

Coach O looked at Tequila with I-don't-give-a-damn expression. "Vomit might smell good if you get your feet back on the court."

Tequila looked down at her feet before looking at Coach O. "I'll get another tutor," Tequila humbly said.

"When you get another tutor, you can play again. Do we understand each other?" asked Coach O.

"Yes ma'am."

Tequila sat down, wondering how she was going to sit through another game without playing. It was pure torture.

No tic.

No playing time.

No dribbling.

No shooting.

No scoring.

Just sitting.

Tequila was in can't-play basketball hell.

The packed gym with the screaming crowd and screeching buzzer aggravated Tequila like flies buzzing around her ear. She squirmed on the bench like a fish flipping around on land, gasping for air. Tequila wanted to play…she wanted to do something…she wanted to help her team win…but was stuck on the bench. It was an extremely close game. They won by three points.

The torture didn't end when the game ended.

She had to endure further torment—her teammates complaining that she let the team down. Tequila rarely felt guilty, but she did during the game. She ignored the girls' comments in the locker room:

"You suck."

"You let us down."

"You're a loser."

"You're stupid."

Tequila wanted to hit somebody. But she didn't give in to the temptation to take her frustration out on one or all of her smart-mouth teammates.

A few hours later, the game was over and Tequila was home. She was glad to be home. She took a shower, and plopped on the sofa. She channel-surfed, but nothing caught her attention on television. Her mother apologized for making a scene with the coach.

"I thought I could convince her to let you play," said Rashonda. "But she's stubborn."

"I know."

"I didn't appreciate what she said about your education. She practically accused me of neglecting your education," Rashonda said, still annoyed. "She doesn't know how hard I've been trying to get you to like school your entire life."

"I know, Mama. I have to get another tutor and get better grades or I won't get to play."

"She's harsh. But you gotta do what you gotta do to play," said Rashonda. "Get another tutor."

"Okay, I will," Tequila said.

"Well, I'm going out for a little while," said Rashonda. "I'm going to meet Cedric."

"Mama, I don't like him."

Rashonda stared at her daughter; this wasn't the first time she said something about the men she's dated. "He's my friend …for now."

"Why don't you date someone with money?"

Rashonda placed a hand on her hip and angled her head forward. "Why don't you introduce me to a man who has money?"

Frowning, Tequila shrugged.

"I won't be long." Rashonda kissed Tequila on the forehead. "Go to bed and don't wait up."

"You know I do. I worry until you get home."

"Stop worrying about everything."

After her mother left, Tequila's cell phone rang. She looked at the flashing light: it was Diante.

"Sorry you didn't get any playing time," said Diante.

"Sucks."

"I can help you with your homework so you can play again."

"Coach O is a bitch," said Tequila.

"I can take your mind off basketball and school. I'll make you feel better," Diante promised.

"I…have homework to do," Tequila said thinking about the coach's warning to stay away from boys.

"I'll help with your homework," said Diante.

"Well…" said Tequila.

"I know your mom is gone. I saw her drive away with some man."

Tequila was quiet for a second. "I don't like him."

"I can be there in five minutes. I'll take your mind off things."

Twenty minutes later, Diante rang the doorbell. She touched-up her makeup and put on fresh coat of red lipstick before opening the door. "Don't want to wake my brother," she whispered.

"Hi," he said. "Those devil red lips."

"Hey," she said with a soft, seductive smile.

"Your coach should have let you play. You would have made a huge difference."

"That's what's up. You know it."

"Just like I know what to do to make you feel better."

Diante wrapped his arms around her neck and pulled her close. He kissed her lips.

She felt his breath inside her mouth as his lips covered her lips, pulling her into a tornado of feelings that left her breathless and thoughtless. Another kiss, another caress. A kiss that turned into caresses and kisses in many places. It was a kiss that erased basketball from her brain. It was a kiss that left her body dizzy and her mind frozen.

DARIAN-BALL-BLOG: NUMBER 5

Tequila Paxton's feet never hit the court. The team almost lost. You could see Tequila going crazy-insane on the bench. But the coach was just cool and controlled, even when the team was down by 15 points and it was obvious that Tequila could have made a difference. Ja-Nay-A and Heaven got some much deserved playing time.

The coach left Tequila on the bench because she's an average student. (I heard she walked out of class.) Who gives a crap? She balls like a boy. She scores 15 points on average and some games she scored over twenty points. Basketball is her passion. Let her do her thing. She's not the best student. She quit going to her tutor. So Coach O risked losing a game because she needs a tutor? What was she thinking? Tequila I'm on your side. I think Coach O is being unfair.

Comments

MVP123: Tequila should work on her grades if she wants to play.
Mindyourbiz: Coach O cares about winning but she cares about her players' education. I respect her for that. Tequila, get a tutor!
Schoolsucks: Coach O is a crazy to bench a player than can score.
Sportsqueen: Who cares about her grades if she helps us win?
Lovegames: I'll tutor the girl if that means we can win. But I have a D average.
Iknowsports: You would hate being benched.
Evespy: How do you know so much about the team?
Justagame: You spy on them in the locker room? Creepy.
Gamewatcher: The coach is stupid to not play Tequila because she walked out of class. I walk out of class all the time. Not that anyone cares.
Lovehighsh: They might play better if they had more fans.
Player: There were more people at the girls' game than ever.
Hategirlsbb: I just go to the game to watch them lose. But they haven't lost many games. Maybe I'll stop going.
Iknowsports: Maybe coach should switch up her starters. Not naming any names.

Madplayer: Get it together Tequila. The coach is queen of the team.
Justagame: It ain't that serious.
Ibelieve: Maybe Tequila needs to drink the alien juice. It might make her smart.

CHAPTER 19

CHASE

"Chase, this is Ms. Karen's son, Jamal Thompkins."
Jamal got up and gave Chase a hug. "What up? What up, Chase?"
"Nothing much," Chase said, noticing her mother's unhappy expression.

Cooper offered to take Chase home after basketball practice. While in the car, Cooper, Marley and Chase sang along with the latest rap song. Chase thought she knew all the words until she heard several curse words in the chorus. When Cooper saw Chase's mouth drop open with shock, he pressed the channel button for another song. "My bad," said Cooper.

"That's okay, Mr. Cooper. I just didn't know what they were... really saying," explained Chase.

"You'd be surprised at what they say," Marley said. "Sometimes the lyrics are really nasty."

"And very disrespectful to girls," said Cooper.

"I guess that's why my parents don't let us listen to the unedited versions."

"Your parents are good people," said Cooper. "They are the rare couple who stays together through thick and thin."

"You're real lucky to have a normal family," said Marley.

"Thanks!" Chase said.

"There are all kinds of definitions for normal family," said Cooper. "We're the normal dysfunctional family."

"Yeah, Daddy. The new definition of dysfunctional family," Marley said with mock pride.

A classic song from Earth, Wind and Fire poured from the car's speakers. "I know there aren't any inappropriate words in this song," Cooper said, turning up the song 'Reasons.'

"I love this song," said Chase.

"Me, too," said Marley.

They all sang, laughing and straining through the super high-pitched falsetto parts.

"That's my favorite part," said Chase. "I can't sing at all. My little sister has a voice. Blake can really, really sing. She almost sounds like Whitney Houston and Christina Aguilera."

"She has a real voice," said Marley. "She seems really sweet."

"Blake drives me crazy sometimes," said Chase. "She knows I like things neat, but she'll unmake up my bed just to bother me."

Marley laughed. "That would make me mad too."

Cooper pulled into Chase's driveway, turning down the music as his foot pressed the brake.

"Thank you, Mr. Cooper," Chase said, before opening the car door.

"You're welcome. Anytime, baby baller."

Chase grinned. "See ya at school tomorrow, Marley."

"Good night." Marley made the peace sign. "Peace out, C."

Chase pulled out her key from her book bag, noticing the unfamiliar car in the driveway. She opened the door and waved at Cooper and Marley as they drove away. The house was unusually quiet when she went inside. No sounds of music, television, laughter or loud voices. It was too early for everyone to be upstairs in bed.

She planned to eat dinner, take a shower and do her homework. It was going to be a late night: she had a major chapter test in science tomorrow.

"Mommy... Daddy," she said. "Where is everyone?"

"We're in the living room, Chase," her mother said.

Chase went into the kitchen and saw her plate in the microwave. The sight of roast beef, mashed potatoes, broccoli and dinner rolls made her stomach growl with her hunger. She wanted to heat up the food and eat, but instead followed the sound of strange voices into the living room.

Chase was surprised to see her family gathered in the rarely used formal living room, but even more surprised by the two strangers sitting on the loveseat. From the uncomfortable looks on everyone's faces, she knew something serious or bad—maybe both—were happening.

Her father introduced her to an anorexically-thin black woman whose head was bald like an eagle. "Chase, this is Karen Thompkins."

"Hello," Chase said in a suspicious voice.

The woman extended her hand. For a reason she couldn't phantom, Chase was reluctant to shake the woman's hand. But she did: it was the polite and proper thing to do. The woman's hand was bony and her handshake was limp.

"Chase is our basketball player," her father said. "She's on the varsity team and she's only in the ninth grade."

"That's very impressive," said Karen.

"Your game must tight, little girl," said the boy sitting next to Karen.

Chase drew her eyebrows together and gave him the once over. There was something familiar about his face, but she couldn't figure it out. She looked at Karen and decided that the woman must be his mother. Still, there was something familiar about his face.

"Chase, this is Karen's son, Jamal Thompkins," said her father.

Jamal got up and gave Chase a hug. "What up? What up, Chase?" She didn't hug him back; she just stood there stiff and unfriendly.

"Nothing much," Chase said. She looked at her brother and sister who seemed to be distracted and confused. Blake whispered something, but Chase didn't understand her. She looked at her mother. Chase couldn't decode her mother's bewildered expression.

"We're going to go," Karen said to Michael. Chase noticed the woman seemed to focus her attention more on her father. "Sorry for the surprise visit."

Her father seemed uncomfortable and awkward. Everyone seemed out of character.

"Life is full of surprises," Michael said.

"It was nice meeting you all," Karen said, rising from the sofa.

"Yeah," said Jamal, nodding his head.

Michael stood up and moved towards the front hallway.

No one said anything during the awkward silence.

"I mean y'all cool," Jamal said. "Real people."

"Come on, Jamal," Karen said, moving toward the door.

Jamal got up, a half-smile on his face.

"We're going to go, Michael," Karen said. "Sorry again for the surprise visit."

After they left, Chase went into the kitchen to warm up her plate. Evan and Blake came into the kitchen, looking as strange as they did in the living room.

"Who are they?" Chase asked Evan and Blake.

"Something fishy is going on," Blake said.

"What do you mean?" asked Chase.

"They got here about an hour ago. Mama made us go to our rooms while they talked."

"You didn't sneak downstairs and listen?" Chase asked.

"No. Daddy used his mean voice so we stayed in our rooms," said Blake.

"What do you think, Evan?" Chase asked.

"You're not going to like it," said Evan.

"What does that mean?" Blake said.

"Bad news," Evan said, pouring soda into a glass. "Mama was forcing herself to be polite, but she was steaming inside."

"Kids, I want you to come into the family room," said Michael. "Chase, you can bring your plate."

A few minutes later, Chase, Blake and Evan sat on the sofa in the family room and stared at their parents, not knowing what to expect.

Chase knew trouble was brewing. She didn't know what kind of trouble. Her friends teased her that she had the perfect family: both her parents were together, she and her siblings had the same parents. Some said they lived like the television show 'The Cosby Show.' It was on television before she was born; but she'd seen the show on Nick-at-Nite plenty of times. Chase loved watching the show, especially when Bill Cosby danced goofy and made silly faces. That's how her Daddy acted, dancing without much rhythm. But unlike Mr. Huxtable on the show, Michael was very good at fixing things around the house.

Chase didn't realize how hungry she was until she'd eaten everything on her plate, including the two rolls, not thinking about the carbohydrates she was consuming. She wasn't exactly following the coach's protein and vegetable diet—at least not tonight.

Chase decided Evan was right. Whatever their parents were going to say they were not going to like. She had a feeling their lives were on the verge of weirdness—like a snowstorm in July in Miami. She didn't know why; maybe it was the strange and odd expressions on her parents' faces. Not sadness like when Grandpops died or when Daddy's brother was killed in an accident. Not worry like the time Daddy thought he was going to lose his job.

Something was wrong…very wrong.

"Kids, we're not going to beat around the bush, trying to prepare you for what we are about to say. We're just going to be straight forward and honest," Michael said. A deep frown carved creases into his forehead. "The boy you just met is my son. … Your half-brother."

Chase's eyes widened. All her breath left her body.

"I don't freaking believe it!" Blake said, covering her mouth. She looked at her mother, waiting to be chastised for using a quasi-curse word, but her mother was silent.

"I knew it!" Evan said. "He looks like Daddy, and Mom was acting fake nice like she really wanted to scream."

"I didn't know about him," Michael said.

"Obviously I didn't know either," Shellie said with hostility in her tone. She was quiet for a minute, struggling with her thoughts and feelings. "I don't know how I feel."

"What happened? I mean we know how it happened. I don't like thinking about how we got born. You and Mommy…yuck," Blake said, with much exaggeration. "But I'm taking health so I know a little something about sperm and eggs…and how they meet up."

"Karen was my high school sweetheart. We were boyfriend and girlfriend in high school," explained Michael.

"Oh," Chase said, feeling hollow inside.

"How come she didn't tell you?" Evan asked.

"I went to college and we dated for a while until I met your mother. Karen met someone else and they got married and he raised Jamal as his son."

"Sounds like a soap opera to me," said Blake.

"So, why does she look so frail?" asked Chase.

"Because she's sick," said Michael.

"Oh," Chase said.

"Chase, is that all you can say: Oh! Oh?" asked Blake. "Don't you get it? She's seriously sick. She wants Daddy to take care of Jamal!"

"Oh…Oh!" Chase said, her eyes wide with absolute understanding.

"Duh, big sis," said Blake.

"I had a long day and I'm tired," Chase explained. "I'm shocked. I just can't believe this!"

"Whatever! I'm not ready to have another brother," Blake yelled.

"Don't be selfish," said Evan.

"He's not our problem," hissed Blake.

"How old is he?" Evan asked.

"I guess about four or five years older than you," Michael said.

"What about his Dad?" Chase asked. "The man that's been taking care of him all his life?"

"They're divorced and that's when Jamal found out the man he thought was his father wasn't his real father," explained Michael.

"She lied to him about his father. That wasn't nice," concluded Blake. "So she's not a nice person." She folded her arms across her chest. "I don't like her."

"It's more complicated than that. We don't need to get into all the details right now," Michael said wearily. "You just need to know that you have a brother."

"But why do we really need to know this?" asked Chase.

Michael looked at his wife and then his three children. He was struggling with the shocking and unwanted news that he had another son. He didn't know he really felt. But he was most worried about his family. They were going to be hurt about something that happened almost twenty years ago.

"His mother has cancer and he might have to live with us," he said.

"No thank you," Blake said dramatically. "I like things just the way they are."

"Me too," Chase said.

"We've done community programs at church. We've fed the homeless. We even let a family we didn't know stay with us," said Michael. "How can we turn away family?"

"He's not family," said Chase in a cold voice.

"Mommy, how do you feel?" Blake asked.

"It's uncomfortable for me. I'm not thrilled, but I know it's the right thing to do," Shellie said, in a quiet voice that hid deeper emotions. "I know you all know it's the right thing to do."

"But you don't always have to do the right thing," challenged Evan.

"It's not like you're going to get struck by lightning if you don't do the right thing," said Blake.

"I knew you would be shocked, but I thought you would have some compassion," Michael said, stunned by his children's cold, almost uncaring reactions.

"Everything will change!" Chase exploded with dramatic emotion. "I know everything will change!"

"That's life, baby. Things change. Nothing stays the same. You have to adjust and be adaptable," said Shellie. "Believe me, I'm not saying this easily."

"It's just like when you're playing basketball," Michael explained. "The coach gives you a play, but you adjust the play when you're on court, don't you?"

"Yes. All the time," Chase said. "That's just a game. This is real life."

"You're right. This is real life," Michael said, his voice brimming with sadness.

The room went silent.

"I'm sorry for this...situation," Michael said. "I know this is going to be difficult, but we will deal with this together." He paused. "All of us."

"So what's next?" Evan asked.

"We're going to get to know him. He's not moving in anytime soon. We'll have them over for dinner or maybe go out to dinner somewhere," said Michael.

"Is he a good kid or a bad kid?" asked Chase.

"Does he get into trouble?" asked Blake. "I don't want a thug living with us."

"He's had a rough time," said Michael. "Losing the man he thought was his father and now the possibility of losing his mother hasn't been easy for him."

"I hope he doesn't come here starting drama," said Chase.

"You should make sure he's your son. You should go on the Maury Povich show," said Blake.

Everyone laughed—a nervous laugh.

"This is more detail than I planned to share, but I already had his paternity checked," Michael said, in a voice hemorrhaging guilt. "I wasn't going to introduce you to someone and not have the facts," explained Michael.

Chase hopped up from her seat, anxious to get away from the confusing, painful situation. "I have homework to do," said Chase. "Can I be excused?"

Sensing Chase's distress, Michael wrapped an encouraging arm around her. "Family meeting is over," said Michael.

The kids bolted from the room.

CHAPTER 20

SELENA

"Papá got Mama a rose," said Selena.
　"That's for you," said Maria.
　"Me. Who left it?"
　"That baseball player. He's super caliente."

By the time she arrived at the restaurant, Selena was glad to see that there were no customers. Very few customers came in after 8:30 PM. Remembering that she had two tests to study for, Selena immediately began her nightly clean-up routine. She was starting to hate the restaurant, even though she had spent almost every day of her life there since she could crawl. She usually did her chores without complaint, but she was mentally and physically tired.

　"You're doing some of my chores," said Selena, realizing that her sister had been doing both of their chores. She had noticed before, but never said anything until now.

　"You're busy. I know practice is mucho hard," said Maria.

　"Mucho, mucho gracias," said Selena. "I have to study. I can't get bad grades or I can't play."

　"Like Tequila?"

　Selena nodded.

　"See, that's why I'm helping you," said Maria.

"Te amour," said Selena. "I don't want you to have to do everything."

"You can clean the back tables. Won't take long," said Maria.

Her father came around the corner, and greeted Selena with a smile and a kiss on the cheek. "Hola, amor."

"Papá, we won! I made the last two shots that made us win the game!" Selena jumped up and down, even though her feet never left the ground. "It was unbelievable, Papá. I wish you could have seen me."

"Somebody got to take care of our place. Es así como vivimos," he explained in Spanish, waving his hands in the air, and then repeated in English, "This is how we live."

"I know, Papá," Selena said. "I really want you to see me play. Just one time. I'm really good."

"Bonita niña," Papá said. "El baloncesto no es para chicas," he said, repeating his belief that basketball wasn't for girls.

Selena stared at her father but kept the words in her mouth that she wanted to say. She was tired and he wouldn't listen anyway.

So, she started cleaning the back seating area of the restaurant. Selena sprayed the tables with cleaner, wiped the tables off, and cleaned the salt and paper shakers. She wiped off the menus and stacked them into two piles: one for the kitchen and another pile underneath the hostess station. As she placed a stack of menus under the hostess station, she noticed a flower on the counter top of the hostess station.

"Whose flower is this?" she asked, but no one was nearby to answer.

She picked up the red rose and felt its beautiful, delicate petals. She smiled, thinking the flower was for her mother, Rosa. Her parents had been married for twenty years, but her father would sometimes be unexpectedly romantic. Her mother was only 16 when she married her father. She couldn't imagine marrying anyone at 16 or even 20. She planned to go college, but still didn't know what she career she wanted to pursue.

Her sister Bella, who was in middle school, came out from the kitchen.

"Papá got Mama a rose," said Selena.

"That's for you," Bella said.

"Me?"

"Who left it?"

Maria joined the conversation. "The baseball player. The one that sometimes makes you forget you have a tongue."

"Handsome Miguel," said Selena.

"He asked for your cell number, said he was going to call or text you, but I didn't give it to him," said Maria.

Frustration flashed in Selena's eyes. "Why didn't you give him the number?"

"Papá was standing close. He doesn't know that Juan got us phones."

"El secret," said Selena.

Maria placed her fingers on her lips and moved her fingers as if she were closing a lock.

"It's a beautiful rose," said Selena, tenderly touching the rose.

"He wrote you something on a napkin," said Bella.

"Where is it?" Selena asked excitedly. "Where is the napkin?"

"I think I might have thrown it away," Maria teased.

"I will throw you away," said Selena. "Hand it over."

Maria dug it out from the underneath the stack of menus. "I didn't want Papá to see it."

"Oh, gracias," said Selena. "Did Juan see him?"

"Juan was in the kitchen," said Maria.

"Good," said Selena.

"Miguel came right up to me and asked for you. He thought you were going to be here. I think he wanted to surprise you."

"Oh," Selena said, flattered.

"I warned him about Papá. He can't do stuff like this in front of him," said Maria.

"Nada en absoluto!" Selena opened the flap of the napkin that had the restaurant's name in the corner.

"You are more beautiful than a rose." She showed it to Maria and Bella. "He wrote it in Spanish."

"Romantic," said Bella.

"He has a lot of pretty girls chasing after him," said Selena.

"Look like he's chasing after you," said Maria.

"Or he's just playing with me," said Selena.

"Why would he do that?" asked Maria.

"I don't know. I don't understand boys," she Selena.

Maria laughed. "They are mystery."

"He congratulated me when I made the team," she said. "He came all the way to my Thanksgiving tournament to watch me play."

"So….he must like you," said Bella.

"Why you act scary like he's Diablo?"

"Not diablo, maybe playboy," explained Selena.

"Oh," said Bella.

"You know all the girls follow him around like he's already famous. Eva calls them the Miguettes," said Selena.

"Maybe that's why he likes you," said Maria. "Because you don't act like the other girls."

Selena fingered the rose, smiling with a glow in her eyes. "I can't believe he gave me this rose."

"So you like him?" asked Bella.

"Sí! Sí!"

"So you will talk to him tomorrow at school," said Maria.

"I will thank him for the rose and hope I don't say something stupid," Selena said.

They heard their father's voice.

"You better hide the flower from Papá or he's going to ask you a hundred questions," said Maria.

Selena went into the kitchen and returned with her book bag. She carefully slid the flower in the bag, protecting the petals as much as possible.

Their father came out of the kitchen, giving orders. "Rápido! Rápido! Let's go home." Bella was behind him.

"I'm ready," said Maria.

Selena was removing a textbook from her locker for her next class. When she closed the locker door, Miguel was standing there with a silly grin on his face.

Selena returned his grin. "You come from nowhere. I didn't see or hear you."

"I surprise you," he said.

"Thank you for the rose," said Selena. "That was a surprise."

"Surprise because it came from me?" Miguel asked, leaning closer to Selena. "You smell so good."

"Thank you," she said.

"I was surprised to get a flower from you," said Selena. "Muy bonita flower."

"You get flowers from other boys?" asked Miguel.

"You give flowers to other girls?" she asked.

They stared at each other; neither one answered the other's question.

"You are beautiful and interesting," said Miguel.

"Is that all you can say about me?" she asked with a flirtatious smile.

"I have mucho to say. Later," said Miguel. "Can I take you out on a date?"

"I have practice every day."

"So do I," said Miguel. "What about Saturday? Do you like carnivals?"

"Love them," said Selena.

"Go to the carnival with me next Saturday?" asked Miguel. "I'm going to a tournament this week."

Selena looked at clock on the wall, realizing that the bell would soon ring.

"Si."

"Can I pick you up from your house at 6?"

"I'll check with my parents, but it should be okay."

"I'll call to get directions" said Miguel.

Practice was over, and Selena was getting ready to leave. She zipped up her gym back, and closed her locker. She heard a loud echoing sound. Someone was banging on the locker door next to hers.

Ja-Nay-A was knocking on the locker as if it were a regular door. Selena looked at her. "What's up?"

"Stuff you don't know."

"Maybe I don't need to know," Selena said. "Don't want to know."

"I'm just waiting for your father to come back and see Coach O," Ja-Nay-A said.

"What are you talking about?" asked Selena.

"Your father wants you off the team!" Ja-Nay said, with an evil smile.

Selena's eyes were wide with confusion and bewilderment. "What?"

"I'm going to take your spot when he does. That's what Coach O said," said Ja-Nay-A.

"You're lying! You're just being mean," said Selena.

"Ask your brother Juan. He was there. He's cute."

"Don't talk about my brother or my father," said Selena, her voice loud and edgy.

As Layne and Zoey came around the corner, they heard the conversation.

"Selena, don't believe her," said Layne.

"Go ask your father," said Ja-Nay-A.

"I know he doesn't like me playing basketball," said Selena.

"He's never been to one of your games," reminded Ja-Nay-A.

"What's wrong with you?" asked Zoey, stepping closer to Ja-Nay-A. "Why are you bothering her?"

"I was a starter last year and I'm supposed to be starter. This is my senior year."

"You need help," said Layne.

"I know a therapist you can see," said Zoey.

"The only therapy I need is to be a starter. So as soon as Selena is gone, I'll get it back."

Selena tried to hold them in—but tears fell down her face.

"You're not tough enough to be starter," said Ja-Nay-A.

"I guess you weren't good enough to be starter," Layne shot back.

"This is between me and Selena, but we can go there if you want to Layne."

"Dude, this is ridiculous," said Zoey. "You're not starter and you need to get over it."

"Coach O says expect the unexpected. So that means me and Heaven still got a chance," said Ja-Nay-A.

CHAPTER 21

MARLEY

"Come with me. Some of my boys are partying down the street."
"You have to bring me back here before 11:30," said Marley.
"So...you coming?" asked Quinton.
"Yeah, why not," said Marley.

Cooper followed the female voice of the GPS navigation system, directing him through a large subdivision of look-alike houses. "I'll pick you girls up at 11," Cooper said to Marley and Egypt as he parked in front of a brick, two-story house.

"Uncle Coop, thanks for driving us," Egypt said.

"I've heard Nadia's parties are real cool," said Marley. "A lot of basketball players are going to be here and everyone is hyped because we've been winning games."

"All because of you," said Egypt.

"I get my points in, but I won't take all the credit," said Marley. "It's a team thing."

"Your coach is a pro. She knows what she is doing," said Cooper. "Otherwise the team would suck like last year."

"I love Coach O," said Marley.

"Have a good time," said Cooper. "Watch what you drink. If you put your drink down, get another one. Someone might put something in your drink."

"Mommy said the same thing," said Egypt. "She called it the date rape pill."

"Boys will slip it in your drink to get you to do what they want you to do," said Cooper. "Don't be crazy and don't do anything stupid." Cooper sternly glared at his daughter and niece. "Either one of you."

"Yes, Daddy," Marley said with a mischievous grin.

"We're going to be wild and crazy girls," joked Egypt.

"Like the girls gone wild videos," said Marley.

"That will be the last video you ever do," warned Cooper. "Now, get out of my car." Both girls hopped out of the car.

"Can we stay till 12?" Marley asked, leaning into the car window. "We're going to seem so lame leaving at 11."

Cooper considered their request. "Okay."

Marley and Egypt went inside the crowded house. Marley knew most of the kids and introduced Egypt to some of her friends. They entered a room with no furniture. A DJ was spinning music in the corner, surrounded by two large speakers, blasting the latest songs. They got pulled into a dance-off by friends: free-styling dance moves against other kids, mostly girls. The throbbing music was like a tornado funnel cloud—sucking everyone into the middle of the dance area.

They danced to song after song—hip-hop, rap, rock, dub step and pop—until they were hot, breathless and thirsty. Marley squeezed through the crowd and went into a large eat-in kitchen. The countertops were filled with different foods and drinks. Marley spotted a large punchbowl, picked up a plastic cup, and poured some punch into her cup. She sipped the punch, tasting some type of alcohol mixed in with the punch's fruity flavor. She considered throwing the cup away and getting a can of soda, but decided to drink the alcohol-flavored punch. She looked around: most of the other kids were drinking the punch.

As she sipped the punch, a cute boy she saw in the school cafeteria on Tuesdays and Thursdays approached her. "I'm Phil," he said, an awkward smile on his acne-filled face.

"I'm..."

"Marley Woods," he said, finishing her sentence.

"So you know who I am," she said, blushing.

"Yeah, and I kind of want to get to know you," he said. "Is that possible?"

"Maybe," she said. "Music is too loud to talk in here."

Phil nodded. I'll be right back," he said. "Then we can find some place quiet."

Marley watched him walk towards a girl she knew, and decided not to wait for Phil. Instead, she looked for Egypt. She found her dancing in the middle of the floor surrounded by a bunch of boys screaming, "Go Egypt! Go Egypt!" She was about to dance along with Egypt, when a deep voice from the ceiling called her name. "Hey, Marley Woods."

Marley looked up at the six feet, seven inches tall basketball player whose head almost scraped the ceiling. "What's up?" she said to Quinton, one of the top scorers for the boys' varsity basketball team.

"You. I've been watching you."

"Creepy," she said. "That's my cue to leave."

"I'm talking about on the court. You got skills, baby."

"Thanks!"

"And you're beautiful," he said.

"I know," she said.

"And you're a diva," he said.

"I am what I am," Marley said, smiling. "Thank you for noticing."

"You're a trip." He laughed. "Pretty chocolate skin and that beautiful hair," said Quinton.

Marley smiled, before changing subjects. "I heard about the Christmas banquet for the boys. Y'all went to the Sun Dial restaurant. My Daddy takes me there a lot."

"Yeah, we had an after party. I invited you on Facebook but you didn't show," he said.

She shrugged. "Couldn't make it. Glad I didn't. I heard what happened."

"Someone has a big mouth," said Quinton.

"I heard your coach found about someone having weed and benched some of the players."

"Not me. I left before Coach got there." Quinton flashed a devilish grin. "We know how to party."

"Our Christmas party was nothing like that. We had a Secret Santa party at my house. Just the team," said Marley. "It was cool."

"I heard Coach O ain't no joke. She can be nice and she can be…"

"Mean," finished Marley.

"Not as mean as our coach," said Quinton. "He's for real crazy. He should be in a psych hospital."

"But y'all have a winning record."

"You record is good. Real good," he said.

Quinton tilted his head sideways, eyeing Marley from head to toe. "I've been trying to get with you, but your Daddy got a tight grip on you. I'm surprised you're here."

"Daddy is protective. But I get out. I do my thing. I have fun."

"Wanna have some fun with me?"

Marley twisted her lips and stared at the good-looking boy with a charming personality. He was scouted by top college recruiters and already had a bunch of girls dying to date him. "Depends on what you're talking about," Marley said.

"Let me add a little something-something to your cup."

Quinton motioned to one of his friends, who brought over a book bag, and removed a bottle of rum. Marley watched him pour some alcohol into her cup. The thought to say "no thanks" evaporated from her mind the second it entered her conscience. *Why not experiment*, she thought.

She sipped the drink, shook her plastic cup and drank some more. "My father would kill me if he saw me. Coach O would be disappointed. And, I think Coach Tillman would be mad if he saw you drinking."

"Coach can't control what I do all the time," said Quinton. "I'm not on the court right now."

"My father tries to control me 24/7. Sometimes I just want to scream at him to leave me the hell alone."

"Your Daddy isn't here, so you can do what you want."

"I like that," Marley said, the affects of the alcohol gliding through her veins and clogging her brain cells. "I can do what I want to do!"

"How about going with me? Some of my boys are partying down the street."

Marley took another sip of the drink. Her head spinning from the alcohol, she felt like a different person. She ignored her father's voice in her head: *Don't do anything stupid.* She thought: *I'm just going to have fun. What would Franchesca think?* "You have to bring me back here by 11:30. Seriously."

"Scout's honor," Quinton said.

"You're no boy scout, but you better have me back here," said Marley. "You don't want my Daddy to kill you."

"I got you," said Quinton. "You don't have to worry." He took a few steps closer, a charming smile on his handsome face. "So…you coming?"

Marley looked at him, his smile melting her resistance. "Yeah! Why the hell not?"

"You know I like the way you dribble a basketball," he said. "You got handles."

She shrugged her shoulders. "Give me a sec. I have to tell my cousin I'm leaving," she said, scanning the room for Egypt. When Marley didn't see her, she sent Egypt a text, and then followed Quinton to his car.

Quinton drove two blocks away and she could hear music blasting as they pulled into the driveway.

"Whose house is this?"

"My mama and I stay here," said Quinton. "I have a little brother and sister too. But they aren't here. They're visiting my auntie."

"I'm an only child."

"You're spoiled, I can tell," Quinton said. "When I get to the NBA I can spoil you big time."

"I'm not one of the girls trying to having a baby by you because I think you're going to the NBA," Marley said, with a defensive tone. "I got my own dreams. I'm going to make my own money."

Quinton leaned over and kissed her on the lips. It was an unexpected kiss that made the walls of her stomach collapse. She turned her head away. "Stop."

"Chill, Marley, we just going to have a good time." He got out of the car and walked around to the passenger side.

"Who else is here?" she asked, when Quinton opened the door.

"Everyone who ain't at Nadia's house. What do they say? The usual suspects."

"Oh," Marley said, almost regretting her boldness.

"Don't worry. It's cool." He laughed. "Sometimes we get crazy."

"Good crazy or bad crazy?"

"You'll find out," said Quinton, escorting Marley down the walkway to his front door.

An hour later, Egypt was looking for Marley at Nadia's house. She read Marley's text and then sent her a text message: *Where r u? Your dad will be here any min.* Questions ran through Egypt's mind: Where is she? What is she doing? Why isn't she back by now? What if Uncle Coop gets here before Marley? What if something happened to her?

Egypt went outside and watched the cars go in and out of the cul-de-sac. She didn't know what car Marley left in. She didn't know what to do or who to call.

Suddenly, Marley got out of an old black Cadillac. Egypt ran over to her. "Where the hell you been?"

"I went to Quinton's house. There was a party over there too."

"Uncle Coop is going be here any minute and you look…a mess."

"I don't care," said Marley, her eyes wide and glazed.

"Her Daddy will kick your ass if he sees you," Egypt said to the boy she didn't know.

"I'm not scared of some old dude," said Quinton.

"Don't call my Daddy old. He's a playa," Marley slurred. "Women stalk him."

"I ain't finished with you, Marley," said Quinton. "I'm feeling you, girl."

"You can feel whatever you like," said Marley. "It's a free country."

Quinton laughed. "I'm going to roll up out of here."

Marley waved at Quinton as he drove away.

"You're drunk," said Egypt. "Uncle Coop can't see you like this."

Egypt and Marley went inside Nadia's house and found a bathroom. They looked through the cabinets under the sink and found mouthwash. Neither wanted to use a stranger's bottle of mouthwash, but they did anyway. They wiped off their faces and squirted on some perfume.

They went outside and saw Cooper standing in front of the car, his arms folded across his chest, his eyes staring at them as if had been watching them the whole time they were at the party. Their legs almost quivered as they approached the car. Marley stumbled off the curb and Egypt helped her up.

"I told you not to be stupid," Cooper said with false calmness.

Marley looked at her father. "I'm not stupid. You always say I'm supremely smart."

"Be quiet, M," whispered Egypt. "Don't make it worse."

The girls got in the car. Before shutting the door, Cooper cupped his hand around Marley's face.

"You've been drinking," said Cooper. "I can smell it!"

"I…I…I," Marley stuttered.

"Shut up," warned Egypt. "Keep your mouth shut."

Cooper got in the car. "You're too young to drink. When you drink you lose control. You do things you wouldn't ordinarily do."

"I found out this boy Quinton from the varsity team is in love with me." Marley giggled. "I think he is so fine."

Egypt covered Marley's mouth.

"Did he do anything?" Cooper stared at Marley as if he had x-ray vision. "Did you let him touch you?"

"Maybe he did. Maybe he didn't," said Marley. "Maybe I wanted him too."

"Marley, I should beat your ass," Cooper yelled. "I stopped spanking you a long time ago, but that doesn't mean I can't punish you. You're on restrictions."

"I hear you and your girlfriends doing it. What do you think I'm thinking when I hear you doing I-T?"

"Don't be smart with me, little girl. Don't try and make me feel guilty," said Cooper. "It's not going to work. I'm trying to let you grow up. You need to learn how to handle yourself in certain situations, when there's alcohol around and boys trying to get in your pants."

"Daddy, I was just having fun," Marley said in a sweet voice.

"Having fun can be dangerous. And if you're trying to be grown, I'm going to teach you about being grown. You aren't going to like it."

Egypt knew that tone of his voice wasn't a good sign. "Uncle Coop, you can take me home, please."

"Egypt, you are in trouble too. Your Daddy and Mama can curse me out, but I have a lesson for both of y'all."

Cooper didn't say anything else during the thirty minute ride to his house. When they arrived there, he directed the girls into the family room.

"Stay here," he said. "I'll be back."

Egypt whispered, "Uncle Coop is freaking mad."

"He'll get over it," said Marley, giggling. "He never stays mad at me for long."

Cooper returned, holding a tray with three bottles of liquor and two shot glasses.

"Daddy, what are you doing?"

"You want to know what it feels like to drink... to get drunk?"

Marley and Egypt looked at each other. Neither answered his question.

"You're going to find out. You're going to drink until you get drunk. That will end your curiosity."

"My head is already spinning and I want to go to bed," complained Marley.

"So you were drinking?"

Neither said a word.

"Don't lie to me!"

Drinking was the last thing Marley wanted to do. Lying to her father was the wrong thing to do. "Yes, Daddy. I'm very sorry," she said in a soft, heart-melting voice. "Everyone else was drinking and I was having fun like everyone else."

"What about you Egypt?"

"I had the punch, Uncle Coop," said Egypt. "I knew it was spiked."

"You want to know about drinking, so I'm going to teach you about it."

"Uncle Cooper, I really don't like the taste of alcohol."

"I already feel ...sick," said Marley.

"What were you drinking?" Cooper asked.

Marley shrugged her shoulders, not wanting to admit that she drank more than the spiked punch.

"You shouldn't drink till you're grown. And you should know what you're drinking. But I know you will be tempted to experiment. And I know that peer pressure is intense..."

"So you understand the pressures of being a teen-ager and you're not going to be mad anymore," interrupted Marley.

"I'm disappointed, Marley. Extremely disappointed and angry. But I'm going to teach you a lesson that hopefully you and Egypt will never forget." He gave them two shot glasses filled with some dark-colored alcohol. "This is rum. Drink up."

Marley whined. "This isn't funny, Daddy!"

His face balled into an angry knot, he asked, "Do I look amused?"

"I want to go home," said Egypt.

"You're here for the good, bad and ugly."

"Drink it...one gulp," Cooper commanded.

Slowly they brought the small, half-empty shot glasses to their lips. They looked at each other with the same pitiful expression, before sipping the dark rum.

"This is nasty," complained Marley.

"Yuck," said Egypt.

Cooper partially refilled their glasses.

"Please Daddy, no."

"Lesson is not over," he said, gesturing for them to drink more.

Reluctantly they drank from the shot glasses. When finished, they quickly put the glasses on the coffee table.

"We understand," said Marley. "We're too young. We don't know what we're doing."

"It's not healthy," Egypt added.

"Is that so?" asked Cooper, pouring more rum into the tiny shot glasses. He gave them the glasses. "Drink up."

"This tastes like a chemical," Egypt said in between sips. She gulped the last sip. "No more. Please!"

Marley dropped her shot glass before finishing, and jumped up from the sofa. "I think I'm going to be sick," she said running into the bathroom.

"I don't clean up vomit," Cooper yelled.

CHAPTER 22

BAILEY

"Flowers for the pretty girl,"
Bailey knew who it was before she turned around: Matt the ass.
"You give flowers for a theatre or dance performance," she said.
"You performed on the court and you were outstanding."
"Thank you," Bailey said, taking the flowers.

For the first quarter of the Riverbrook girls' basketball game, the team played like sixth graders. They had home court advantage against Williamson High. They had beaten the team before, but the girls were playing like the basketball was a hot potato. Riverbrook couldn't keep their hands on the ball.

The tip-off ball went to Williamson High and the first half of the game was played on their side of the court. Williamson High maintained constant control of the ball, making a series of layups that put them in the lead by 10 points going into the second quarter.

Coach O called a time-out and blasted the girls about their mistakes and sloppy plays. She noted that the point guard from Williamson High frequently stole the ball and threw it down court for an almost guaranteed basket by the post player. She chided the girls for not seeing the obvious and adjusting their strategy.

Bailey, Marley, Chase, Heaven and Layne started the second half of the game. They initiated a more defensive game and scored 12 points. With regained focus and strategy, Riverbrook began to catch up. By the end of the third quarter, Riverbrook had an eight-point lead.

Believing that they were going to win, the girls reverted back to their sloppy habits: ball turnovers, missed shots, and bad passes. The opposing team ran a full press and within three minutes they had a six-point lead. Riverbrook panicked and scrambled to regain their lead but their movements were erratic and thoughtless. Coach O sketched out plays on the play board, but the girls didn't execute them on the court. She rarely screamed from the sidelines, but she was clearly frustrated with her team.

When the end-of-game buzzer sounded, Riverbrook lost by four points.

Disappointment was painted on all the players' faces. After lining up with the Williamson team for the 'good game' ritual, Coach O walked off the court.

Sweaty and exhausted, Bailey went over to her family.

"You played well," Jennifer said, patting her daughter on the back.

"Y'all came back strong in the second half, but fell apart in the fourth quarter," said her stepfather Robert.

"I know," said Bailey. "We were on a winning streak…"

"You've only lost a few games," said Jennifer. "You have a great record."

"Your coach has to identify why you're losing," said Robert. "Is it the teams you're playing, the girls who are playing, or your rotations? She tries to mix the starters with the rest of the team but sometimes that doesn't work."

"Tequila is still benched." Bailey shrugged.

"I'm surprised she didn't put her in," said Jennifer. "But she must serious about the grades."

"Coach is going to be disappointed if we start losing a lot."

"Your coach isn't going to let that happen," said Robert. "She's smart and strategic. The team has done very well with her coaching."

"Bay-ee, Bay-ee," said Darby. "Pick me up."

"I'm stinky and sweaty," said Bailey, while picking her sister. "Stinky." Bailey wrinkled her nose.

"Stink Bay-ee," Darby said, giggling.

"Silly girl," Bailey said, and kissed her on the cheek.

"Bay-ee play with ball," said Darby.

Bailey lightly tickled Darby's belly. "Yep."

Little brother Bobby stood next to Bailey's knees. "I can beat you," said Bobby Jr.

"Oh yeah?" said Bailey.

"I can dunk on you," said Bobby, Jr. "I got moves. I play basketball on the Wii."

"We'll play at home," said Bailey. "I'll beat you."

"I'll beat you real bad," said Bobby, Jr.

Chase and Layne approached Bailey. "Coach is having a team meeting," said Layne.

"We're about to be yelled at," Bailey said, handing Darby to her mother.

"Hi, Darby," said Chase, smiling at the pretty little girl.

"Hi," said Darby, dressed in a pink polka dot dress with a matching hat.

"Can you say Chase?"

"Ch…Ch… Cha… shh," said Darby.

"That's my name," said Chase.

"Good game, Chase and Layne," said Robert.

"Thanks," said Chase.

"Thank you, Mr. Robert," said Layne.

"I'll see you at home," Bailey said, amidst hugs and kisses from her family.

Chase, Bailey and Layne headed towards the locker room.

'Bailey, can I ask you something?" asked Chase.

"Sure," said Bailey.

"This may be a weird question, and my mom would say I'm being rude and nosy, but…"

"What?" Bailey asked as they walked into the locker room.

"Was it strange or awkward or weird when your Mom married your stepfather?" asked Chase. "I'm not being a hater. He's black; you and your mom are white. I just wonder how it felt for your family to change like that."

"It was super weird at first," Bailey admitted, a gust of breath blowing from her mouth. "My mom's parents were mad and embarrassed. They didn't like Robert. People used to stare at us like we were aliens from planet Mars," explained Bailey. "They still stare and talk about us, but we ignore them."

"I'm sorry," said Chase.

"My mom lost some of her friends and my dad was a little crazy at first. He wanted total custody of me, but then he came to his senses," said Bailey. "I didn't want to leave my mom. Eventually my grandparents accepted Robert and they love my brother and sister."

"I came from a school that was all black," said Tequila, joining the conversation. "So it was a big shock to come to the South and see people from other countries and races. Honestly, I've never seen so many bi-racial kids."

"My stepdad is cool. I really like him," Bailey explained. "It took a while, but Robert gets along with my dad and now my life is normal…for us."

"My mother wouldn't think it was normal," said Rachel.

"What's normal anymore?" asked Marley.

"What's the color of love?" asked Selena.

"That sounds like a question my crazy lit teacher would ask," said Tequila. "And I don't really give a crap."

"People should do whatever makes them happy," said Layne.

"Yeah, we shouldn't be getting all serious anyway. We just got a beat down," said Heaven.

"Yeah, Coach O's beat down is going to be worse," said Ja-Nay-A.

Tequila banged her fist on the locker door, causing a loud echoing sound. "I'm so freaking mad that she won't play me. She's going to ask me if I have a tutor."

"Do you? Cause if you don't, my feet will be hitting the court," said Ja-Nay-A, edging closer to Tequila. "Taking your spot!"

Tequila put her hand in Ja-Nay-A's face. "Step back. I meet my new tutor on Monday, not that it's any of your damn business," said Tequila.

"If you don't keep your new tutor…" taunted Ja-Nay-A.

"Coach is going to make us do suicides at practice on Monday," complained Zoey. "I just know it."

"I just want to play," said Tequila.

"Whose fault is that?" asked Ja-Nay-A.

"Shut up!" barked Tequila.

"Chill," said Layne. "We're in enough trouble with Coach O."

They were quiet for a few minutes.

"Have you guys read what was in the Darian blog the other day?" asked Marley.

"Yeah, I wonder who she is to be writing all that stuff about us," said Chase.

"She knows a lot. Too much," said Zoey.

"We don't think it's the team managers, Poppy and Rina," said Chase.

"Maybe someone has cameras in our locker room and the gym," said Zoey.

"You're paranoid," said Layne.

"Paranoid. She said we're aliens cause we're playing better," Zoey. "Aliens? Really?"

"She didn't call us aliens. One of the blog readers said we're aliens," said Rachel.

Chase shook her head. "When did we become aliens?"

"You know the day we drank that green drink," said Layne. "It was in a Styrofoam cup."

"Maybe it was purple or pink, depending on how we mixed it," said Ja-Nay-A, laughing.

"What are you talking about?" asked Chase.

"Something from a rap song about getting high," said Marley.

"I didn't drink anything green," said Chase. "I don't do stuff like that."

Several of the girls cracked up.

"We didn't drink anything green or pink or purple. We were just joking around," said Layne. "You are so naive, Chase."

Chase shrugged her shoulders.

"I'm not an alien," Rachel. "I don't care what that blog says."

Everyone laughed.

"Time to get our heads caught off," said Layne.

Five minutes later, the girls were dressed in their warm-up suits in the meeting room next to the locker room. Some sat on benches and some sat on the floor while waiting for Coach O—impatiently and nervously waiting. They usually were talking, laughing, arguing, or teasing each other.

But no one said a word. They were silent—the whole team.

Coach O came into the room with a lopsided smile. "This is strange. Twelve girls, I mean young ladies, and no one is talking."

"We know you're extremely mad at us," said Rachel.

"I can beat that," said Layne. "She's infuriated with us."

"Pissed," said Zoey.

"She's F-ing mad at us and she should be," said Ja-Nay-A.

"You know how I feel about profanity," said Coach O. "Let's not get off track here," she said. "I have a homework assignment for you."

"Homework?" said Ja-Nay-A, scowling.

"We didn't expect this," said Marley.

"Expect the unexpected," said Heaven, sarcastically.

"You're jumping to conclusions," said Layne. "She's not done."

"I want you to do research on teams who were losing during the season, but then won their championship."

The girls looked at Coach O with confusion and bewilderment.

"Let's make this interesting. It can be any sport and give one reason why they became champions."

"This sounds intriguing," said Rachel, smiling.

"Of course you would say that," said Zoey. "You're strange."

"I like being strange!" shot back Rachel. "I like being me."

"You have until Wednesday," said Coach O.

The girls looked at each other, not sure what to say.

"I'm giving you this assignment to remind you who you are," said Coach O. "Winners!"

"I thought you were going to eat us alive," said Chase.

Coach O laughed. "I like my food cooked. Not enough room for you girls in my stove."

"I know you're kidding," said Rachel.

"Yes, she is," said Layne, patting Rachel on the back.

"See you on Monday." Coach O turned and left the room.

Bailey left the locker room, and went out the gym's back entrance to the parking lot. As Bailey walked to her car, she heard a voice.

"Flowers for the pretty girl."

Bailey knew who it was before she turned around: Matt the ass. She hadn't seen him at the game. He surprised her when he came to her last game which was almost thirty miles away from Riverbrook. He had screamed her name until he was hoarse.

Bailey smiled at Matt. "You give flowers after a theatre or dance performance," she said, taking the mixed bouquet of flowers.

"You did perform. You performed on the court and you were outstanding," he said.

"But we lost," she said.

"That was one game," he said, shrugging.

She smelled the flowers. "They're beautiful."

"So are you," said Matthew.

She stared at him. There was something different about him. Something about the way he looked into her eyes. Something about the way he was making her feel. "Thank you," she said, blushing.

"Want to get something to eat?" he asked.

"Yeah, I'm starving."

A week later, Matt sent flowers to Bailey at school. Bailey expected something sarcastic or sweet would be written on the card. Nothing sentimental; the card simply read: *To Bailey, From Matt*. The next week, he brought flowers to her basketball game. It was an away game—the school was fifteen minutes away. One day at school, Bailey received a text from her mother: *Flowers from Matt at house*.

The flowers kept coming.

Matt hand delivered flowers to Bailey at another home game. It was the seventh bouquet of flowers. "I can't call you Matt the ass if you keep bringing me flowers," Bailey said.

"That's what I thought," said Matt, grinning.

"So am I supposed to call you Matt the flower guy?"

Matt stared at the girl who had unexpectedly whittled her way into his heart, even though she represented everything his father complained about the demise of racial definition in America. His father believed that races should stay separated. Matt didn't care what his father thought. He was thinking with his own mind, drawing his own opinions about people, race and politics. He smoothed a strand of hair away from Bailey's face. "Matthew is a strong name. Matthew Charles is a fine name. It's my real name."

"Matt the ass is … just so distinctive and memorable," said Bailey with a smirk, before bursting into laugher.

DARIAN-BALL-BLOG: NUMBER 6

This is a short blog. Riverbrook lost. They just fell apart and lost to Williamson High. It's simple: we need Tequila. She got mad basketball skills.

But I ain't blow-up-the-school mad. We haven't lost many games. We are mentioned in local newspapers and the local online dispatch news. I heard that some schools even scout us to see us play. That's major. M-A-J-O-R! That means other teams are taking us seriously. FI-NALLY! Much respect to Coach Olivia Remmington. You put Riverbrook on the basketball map. We in there now!

Comments

MVP123: I'm still proud of them. They are so much better than last year.
Mindyourbiz: They had a bad game. Every team has a bad game.
Hailey9: Tequila should be playing. I heard all she has to do is get a tutor. She should listen to the coach if she wants court time.
Sportsqueen: They lost focus. It was inevitable.
Halftime: She'll be back. She learned her lesson.
Gamewatcher: Maybe Tequila wasn't thinking. But sitting on the bench, I betcha she was regretting her decision.
BBdreamer: For you Lauryn Hill fans, she says Consequence is no coincidence. No playing time is consequence. Sorry boo.
Eyesonyou: Don't dis your teacher. Karma is a B.
Lovehighsh: More people come to their games.
Hategirlsbb: They lost this game. So what? They've been winning.
Iknowsports: The coach should switch up her starters. Not naming any names.
Madplayer: I'm telling you the coach was wrong to cut me. I can help them win.
Justagame: You win and you lose.
Fanfever: I watched them last year when they sucked. I go whether they win or lose.
Thinkyoucanplay: I won't name any names but not all the players can play.
Sportsqueen: Some people like to swim in the pool of haterade.

CHAPTER 23

TEQUILA

"He stared at my boobs and smelled liked pee, so I stopped going to him,"
said Tequila.
　"Your coach found out and benched you," said Lindsey.
　"I gotta play basketball. That's what I do."
　"Let's get you back on the court."

Tequila stepped inside the school's library. She looked up at the sky high ceiling with paintings high above her head. She felt like a midget inside the enormous room. The library was a maze of long aisles with rows and rows of books stacked several feet high to the ceiling. Somewhere in the mysterious and unfamiliar place, there were private meeting rooms for tutoring and group study. She had a tutoring appointment with Nathaniel Mitchell in room 131.

There were no signs or arrows pointing to the rooms, so Tequila asked the librarian for directions to room 131. "Go past the next three rows and then make a right," the librarian said with a deep Southern accent. "There are arrows on the floor leading you to the study rooms in the back."

"Thanks," Tequila said.

"Let me warn you: cameras are in those rooms," the librarian said.

Tequila nodded and followed the woman's directions. Within five minutes, she found the room. She knocked on the door before opening, and saw someone who didn't match the name of Nathaniel Marshall. A blonde girl, who strongly resembled Blake Lively from the *Gossip Girls* TV series, stood up and greeted her with a big smile.

"Hi, Tequila. I like your name. It's so cool."

Tequila glared at her. "You mean ghetto, don't you?"

"No, no," the girl said, "not at all."

"You're not Nathaniel Marshall. He's a boy."

"He's hot," the girl said.

"My other tutor was nerdy and I couldn't stand him. He stared at my boobs," explained Tequila. "He smelled like pee and picked his nose, so I stopped going to him."

"Your coach found out and benched you." The girl glanced down at her notebook. "It's in the notes."

"Yeah." Tequila shrugged.

"I'm Lindsey Athens," she said, sitting down at the round table. "I don't want to look at your boobs because mine are better than yours anyway."

Tequila's mouth dropped open. "What?"

"I only pick my nose in my bathroom at home."

Tequila's lips twirled into a lopsided smile when she saw the half-smile on Lindsey's face. She sat in a chair across from Lindsey.

"I don't smell like urine. I'm a Victoria's Secret freak. I love their perfume," Lindsey said, removing a bottle of Heavenly perfume from her purse. She sprayed some on her wrist. "Like?"

Tequila whiffed the jasmine-scented smell. "Yeah." She laughed. "You're kind of funny, Lindsey."

She shrugged. "Sometimes."

"So let me tell you what's up. I don't want to be here. I hate school. I hated school since I was a little. But my coach won't let my play cause my grades suck. I like Coach O, but sometimes I think she's …crazy."

"I heard she's tough," said Lindsey.

"I love basketball and I have to stay on the team," Tequila said. "All I care about is basketball."

Lindsey looked at Tequila for a moment before responding. "Well…I already know everything you just told me. Almost everything."

"Oh?"

"I've seen you play," said Lindsey. "You're amazing."

"Thanks."

"I'm a cheerleader. I know the girls' don't pay attention to us."

"Not really. Sorry."

"The boys love when we cheer," said Lindsey. "But, let's talk about how I can help you stay on the team."

"You're kidding."

"No, I'm serious."

"Okay, Miss Georgia Peach," said Tequila, her eyebrows raised, suspicion on her face. "You're telling me that you're cool tutoring a hood rat from New York."

"If you want to call yourself a hood rat, that's on you. If I say I don't see color, I'll sound fake. I'm not your typical Southern girl. Hating people just because of their skin color is stupid." She met Tequila's skeptical gaze. "We are all people. We're all God's creatures," Lindsey said with the passion of an old-fashioned preacher.

Tequila stared at the skinny girl with long blonde hair, a broad-shaped face, sparkling brown eyes and pink-coated lips. "Are you for real?"

"I do make some exceptions. My stepdad is from New York and he's a mean son of a bitch. I won't say I hate him, but he's my least favorite person on the planet."

"A wicked stepfather."

"Wicked, wicked. But, he's got money. We got upgraded when my mother married him."

"My mom needs someone like that. All she dates are losers."

"My mom was the same way until she met Curt the turd," Lindsey said with a vicious laugh. "That's what we call him behind his back."

Tequila burst out laughing.

"He is a turd," said Lindsey, shrugging. "And he knows it."

"You're ...really funny," Tequila said.

"Let's get started on your homework."

Scowling, Tequila uttered, "Ugh."

"You're going to stay on the team," declared Lindsey. "It would be cool if we make it to regionals."

"Okay," Tequila said with a frustrated sigh. "I need help with reading and math."

"Got you covered like a blanket," Lindsey said.

"If you say shortie, I will scream."

"I listen to rap. Drives my mom and Curt the turd insane, but oh well," said Lindsey. "Your coach got your teacher to agree to let you read certain pages from *The Great Gatsby*. We'll practice reading together and then you can volunteer to read in class."

"Is you crazy? I never volunteer in class." Tequila frowned. "I hate reading."

"You have to, but you'll be prepared and you won't be embarrassed," Lindsey said in a reassuring voice.

"I guess I don't have a choice," said Tequila.

"You love basketball and you're not getting kicked off the team."

"You are...I don't know what to call you Blondie, girl, but you are different."

Lindsey slid a book across the table. "I'll take that as a compliment."

Tequila shook her head and looked up, noticing the camera in the corner. "The librarian wasn't lying."

"There are cameras all over this school. Let's stop wasting time, girlfriend," Lindsey said with intentional exaggeration.

"Okay, Blondie," said Tequila.

"Let's dive into the stereotypes," said Lindsey.

"I'm swimming in them," said Tequila. "And you know black people don't swim."

They looked at each other for a second, and then burst into laughter.

"No more stereotypes," Lindsey said.

"Deal," said Tequila.

The tutoring session lasted an hour. Tequila became less resistant and defiant by the time it was over. They scheduled the next tutoring session in two days.

"I got to go," said Tequila, glancing at the clock on the wall. "I have to catch The Dummy bus." When Lindsey looked confused, Tequila explained, "The bus that takes home students who need extra help."

"I'll take you home," offered Lindsey.

"You don't even know where I live," said Tequila.

Lindsey shrugged. "Doesn't matter."

"I live in Darlington Place. It's not exactly the best apartment complex. Coming from New York, we thought it was paradise. There's a swimming pool and tennis courts," said Tequila, "but then we got schooled when we saw other apartments."

Twenty minutes later, Lindsey dropped Tequila in front of building 17 in the apartment complex.

"Thanks, Lindsey," said Tequila. "For tutoring me …and driving me home."

"You're welcome," she said.

Before Tequila closed the car door, Lindsey said, "We used to live in building 20."

Shocked, Tequila's eyes widened. She watched Lindsey angle a wide curve in an older-model black Jeep Cherokee.

Tequila walked up to the third floor. She opened the door to her apartment, and flicked on the light switch, but the apartment remained dark. She flicked on other light switches and turned on lamps, but not an ounce of electricity surged through the bulbs.

She had a sinking feeling in the pit of her stomach. It was a familiar feeling. Ever since they moved to Atlanta, the lights, water or gas would sometimes be shut off. They had even been evicted last year and Tequila worried that it would happen again. Her mother was saving money so they could buy a house. Tequila wanted to believe that they would really move into their own house. But without relatives in Atlanta, Tequila often worried how they were going to survive.

Tequila called her mother while opening the blinds for some light. Tears welled in her eyes.

"Mama," she said, relieved her mother had answered on the first ring. "The lights are out." As the words came out of her mouth, tears crawled down Tequila's face.

"Baby, calm down. I was hoping the lights would be on by the time you got home," Rashonda said, the words rushing out of her mouth in a quiet tone. "I went to the electric company on my lunch hour and they said the lights would be on before five."

"It's dark in here!"

"I'm sorry, honey."

"Are we going to be alright?"

"Yes. In New York, they don't cut your lights off if you are a few days late. You gotta be months behind, but Atlanta don't give a shit," Rashonda angrily said. "When I remembered that today was the due date, I went straight over there to pay those crazy people."

"We're not going to get kicked out?"

"No. Stop worrying. It's not going to happen again."

"Everything okay with work?"

"I promise you everything is fine," said Rashonda. "I'm saving for us to get a house."

"I know," Tequila said, unable to hide the doubt in her voice.

"Did you meet with the tutor?" her mother asked. "I'm not comfortable with you being alone in a room with a boy."

"The tutor is a girl and she's cool. I couldn't deal with another weird boy," said Tequila. "Her name is Lindsey. She's a white girl and I like her. She brought me home."

"Was she helpful?"

"Yeah! She's real smart, and she doesn't make me feel stupid," explained Tequila. "Where's big head?"

"Tevon went home with a friend. Some boy named Lucas," Rashonda said. "I'm glad that boy finally has friends."

The apartment suddenly was ablaze with lights.

"Mama, the lights are on!"

"I told you not to worry," Rashonda said.

Tequila wiped away her tears. "Yeah, you did."

CHAPTER 24

CHASE

"Chase, this is Maggie McDonald. She's a reporter," said Coach O.
"Hello. Nice to meet you," said Chase.
"Can I interview you?"" asked the reporter.
"Yes ma'am."

"Practice shooting drills for the next thirty minutes," said Coach Remmington. "Work in groups of three."

Chase teamed up with Marley and Ja-Nay-A, and started shooting from the left side of the basketball hoop. She positioned her hands on both sides of the ball, arched her hands, and aimed for the basketball net. She missed the shot. Ja-Nay-A threw the ball back to her and Chase continued to shoot. She missed more baskets than she made.

"What's wrong with you?" Ja-Nay-A asked.

"Nothing," said Chase.

"You shouldn't even be on the team," Ja-Nay-A said, hostility swishing in her words. "You're just a ninth grader."

"Leave her alone," Marley said. "Everybody has their bad days."

"Like when your Mama showed up and you turned into a mummy on the court," said Ja-Nay-A. "Couldn't dribble or shoot."

Marley calmly dribbled the ball as she moved towards Ja-Nay-A. Face-to-face, she whispered between clenched teeth, "Stay the fuck out of my business."

"Mother, I don't want you to get married," Ja-Nay-A said in a mocking, little girl voice.

"Don't talk about my family!" Angry, Marley said, "We can settle this. Let's go outside now!"

"Come on, girls," said Chase, looking to see if Coach O was watching them. "You guys are going to get kicked off the team."

"Ja-Nay-A stay out of my business," said Marley.

"Glad it ain't my life," said Ja-Nay-A.

"I don't want your life," said Marley, and then smiled. "Hmm…. you're not a starter!"

"I get a lot of tic," Ja-Nay-A said with arrogance.

Marley stared at Ja-Nay-A with the steely gaze of an assassin. "I'm not worried about you."

Ja-Nay-A looked at Chase. "I might take your tic."

"I'm not worried," said Chase, dribbling the ball.

"You better be, Miss Little Girl with the perfect home life," said Ja-Nay-A. "I forgot. You're a big girl now," Ja-Nay-A giggled. "Since you got your period."

Chase glared at Ja-Nay-A before throwing the ball at Ja-Nay-A's stomach with such strong force that Ja-Nay-A fell backwards on the floor. "Your turn," Chase said before walking towards the gym's exit door.

"That hurt," wailed Ja-Nay-A, holding her stomach. "I'm still taking your spot."

Chase ignored Ja-Nay-A and walked away. Chase knew why she was missing baskets: she couldn't stop thinking about Jamal—her new brother. Her father's son—the stranger. She didn't want him to come live with them. Chase knew it would change everything. *If only he never ever came to our house.*

Chase's hand was on the door to leave the gym, when she heard Coach Remmington call her name.

Chase turned around and walked towards the coach who was sitting on a bench next to a woman she had never seen before.

"Chase, this is Maggie McDonald," said Coach O. "She's a reporter with the local paper."

She greeted the woman with a warm smile. "Hello, Miss McDonald. Nice to meet you," said Chase.

"Hello there," the reporter said, extending her hand to Chase. "Come sit with me," she said, leading Chase to the first row of the risers. The reporter sat down and Chase sat beside her. Coach Olivia sat a few spaces down the row.

"I'm hearing good things about the team. Quite a change from last year," said Maggie, a short, dark-skinned woman with a small face and a short hair cut that resembled Halle Berry's trademark hair style.

"I wasn't here last year. I know we had a bad rep," said Chase.

"Oh, you're the freshman," said the reporter. "The youngest player on the team."

"She's our baby baller," said Coach O.

"Do you mind if I interview her for the article?" Maggie asked Coach O.

"Not at all." Coach O said, before turning to Chase. "As long as it's okay with you, Chase?"

"Sure."

"I will be back after you interview Chase," said Coach O.

"Are you comfortable Chase. Need water or anything?"

"I'm fine," said Chase.

Maggie flipped open a notebook and uncapped an ink pen. "Let's get started."

"Were you surprised when you made varsity?" asked Maggie.

"I was shocked. My eighth grade coach said I could make varsity but I didn't believe him," said Chase with a rush of excitement in her voice. "Then when I heard there was a new coach and she was pro basketball player, I thought: no way am I going to make the team."

"So it was a good surprise?"

"Yes ma'am," Chase said, smiling. "I'm happy and so excited to be on the team."

"Your family must be very proud of you."

"Yes. They come to all my games. My grandma is so loud I can always hear her voice." Chase said, noticing the reporter writing what she was saying in her notebook.

"You must have some incredible skills," the reporter said.

"I don't like to brag, ma'am," said Chase. "I just love playing basketball."

The reporter observed Chase's polite demeanor. "You seem like such a sweet girl, but your coach described you as a force of intimidation."

"Wow, she said that about me?" said Chase, her eyes sparkling.

"She sure did."

"I kind of turn into a different person on the court," explained Chase. "I get focused and aggressive. I don't know what happens to me."

"Oh really?"

"My little sister says I'm like Beyonce," said Chase. "I don't know if you know this, but Beyonce says she turns into another person on stage. She becomes Sasha Fierce when she performs. She even has an album with that name."

The reporter laughed. "I know about it."

Chase cracked a proud smile. "I guess I'm kinda of like that. I get this crazed-out, dazed-out look on my face. When I see pictures of me playing basketball I don't recognize myself."

"You need some fierceness to survive in this world. Be proud of your accomplishments," said the reporter.

Chase nodded.

"I hear the team is better this year. You're winning more games," said the Maggie. "Why do you think the team has improved?"

"That's easy. Coach O," said Chase. "She knows what she's doing and she brings out the best in each player. Plus, she's really serious about us playing together as a team."

"I'm coming to your next game, so I can see Little Miss Fierceness."

"Thank you, Miss Maggie," said Chase.

"Thank you for talking with me," Maggie said.

"You're welcome," said Chase.

As Chase walked away she realized that thinking about her unwanted brother had interrupted her concentration. She forced herself not to think about the boy she didn't want to know about. She went back on the basket and started shooting—with a lot more accuracy. Tequila practiced with her, taking turns at different positions on the court. Chase noticed some of the girls on the team talking to the reporter.

She threw the ball back to Tequila. "The reporter is a good thing, right?" asked Chase.

From the foul line, Tequila shot the ball straight into the hoop. "It's all good. Unless she says something bad about us." Tequila noticed the newspaper photographer pointing the camera towards her. She dribbled the basketball three times and then dropped it inside the hoop. A perfect shot. A perfect picture.

"I hope the photographer is taking good pics of us," said Tequila as Coach O walked over them.

"So, do you like Lindsey Athens?" asked Coach O.

"Who is she?" asked Chase.

"Tequila knows," said Coach O.

"She's my tutor," said Tequila.

Sensing the conversation wasn't about her, Chase stepped a few feet away, and continued to practice shooting baskets.

"I like her Coach O. She's a different kind of person for me. She's white, blonde and a perky cheerleader," said Tequila. "She has real country accent. She acts dingy sometimes, but she's really smart."

"That's good," said Coach O. "I need to know that you are going to work with her." She made eye-to-eye contact with Tequila. "Stick with her for the rest of the season."

"I will," Tequila said. "She tutored me the same day we met and we're getting together on Monday."

"Whether you like her or not, you're going to have to deal with her," Coach O firmly said. "That's the only way you're going to play."

A soft grin spread across Tequila's face. "Lindsey's cool, she's my tutor. I'll keep seeing her."

"You do that and you can play again. You have problems with her or have to find another tutor, you will be benched for the rest of the season," Coach O said in a matter-of-fact tone.

Tequila's grin disappeared. "Are you for real?"

"I don't play about education," said Coach O. "We do understand each other, right?"

"Right." Tequila watched Coach O walk away, feeling angry that she had so much control over her life. She threw the basketball from half court; it bounced off the backboard and dropped through the net.

CHAPTER 25

SELENA

Miguel threw two more balls. He hit one jug so hard, the milk jug shattered.

"Man, what you do that for?" asked the man from behind the counter.

Miguel whispered in Selena's ear: "Pick out the biggest stuffed animal."

She pointed to a huge brown teddy bear with a red bow around the neck.

"Don't come back here. You can't play no more. Got it?"

Miguel just laughed. "My twin brother can."

During Riverbrook's morning announcements, Tianna the PantherTV reporter mentioned that the girls' varsity basketball team was featured in the local newspaper. She read a section from the paper: *"I'm just a freshman. I'm so excited to be on the team,"* said Chase Anderson, the youngest player on the team.

As soon as Chase heard her name, she jumped up from her seat. She asked her teacher to be excused from class so that she could go to the front office to read the article. Her English teacher didn't object.

Chase zoomed down the hall, pushed opened the door to the front office and was surprised to see half the girls' basketball team in Henry Nickels' office, the school's athletic director. He was usually stern and strict, but for this unusual occasion, he relaxed his rules.

Selena was holding the newspaper, a proud, goofy grin on her face. Her two ponytails flipped in front, hanging down her chest. "There's a picture of Ja-Nay-A and Marley shooting."

"That was the day I was going to fight you for talking about my mother," Marley remembered.

"Sorry," Ja-Nay-A said.

"I spoke to the reporter for a few minutes," said Selena. "I didn't think she was going to put my words in the paper."

"Well, she did," said Mr. Nickels, a short, thin man with thinning gray hair and a wild gray beard. He played tennis in his youth; but no longer had an athletic body.

"I just love playing basketball. It makes me so happy when I score," Selena said, reading her quote. She looked at everyone. "That sounds so lame," said Selena.

"Cheerleaderish," said Zoey.

"Sounds just like you," said Layne.

"Whatever," said Selena, giggling.

"I'm the one that should be upset," said Bailey. "There's a quote from all the starters, but me."

"Yeah, but there's a picture of you," said Tequila. "It's a game shot."

"Yep," Bailey said with a proud smile.

"This is so cool," said Marley. "An article about us."

"That means a lot," said Heaven. "Scouts will come check us out."

"Hell yeah," said Ja-Nay-A, her mind considering the possibility of being scouted by a college recruiter.

"Okay, ladies," said Mr. Nickels. "Time to get back to class. I think Coach Remmington posted the article in your locker room."

"Can we make a copy, Mr. Nickels?" asked Marley. "I have lots of people I want to mail it to."

"Good idea," said Tequila. "My family in New York would be so proud of me."

"Okay, okay," said Mr. Nickels. He took the article from Selena and handed it to his administrative assistant, Mrs. Madison. "Make fifty copies."

"Thank you," said Selena. "I'll put it on the wall in our restaurant."

"Just hurry, girls. Get your copies and get back to class," said Mr. Nickels.

"It's probably online," said Marley. "I'm going to look it up."

Selena and Miguel held hands while walking around the carnival at a state park. It was a large carnival with variety of amusement rides and games. They had been at the carnival for over an hour and saw girls and boys they knew from school. Some of the girls were flirty-friendly to Miguel, but rudely-unfriendly to Selena. Miguel always introduced Selena, forcing some girls to speak to Selena whether they wanted to or not. Boys were respectful and casually friendly.

Strolling through the fair, Miguel stopped at a toss-a-ball game to win a prize. He glanced at Selena and asked, "Want a stuffed animal?"

"Sure."

He placed money from his pocket on the counter. "I'm playing," said Miguel.

Wearing a beat-up Atlanta Braves cap, the short, older man from behind the counter put three balls on the counter. "This isn't as easy as it looks, bud. You got to knock down all three milk jugs."

"You don't who he is," warned Selena.

"Yeah, yeah," said the man. "He plays for the Braves."

Miguel swung his arm around several times as if warming up before throwing a pitch. But he didn't throw the ball.

Selena giggled.

He then narrowed his gaze, and threw one ball, knocking a milk jug down to the ground.

"One down, two to go," said Selena.

"You don't doubt me, do you?"

She grinned. "No."

Miguel threw two more balls, knocking down two more milk jugs. He hit one jug so hard, the milk jug shattered.

"Bud, what you do that for?" asked the man from behind the counter. His face was red and flustered.

"Sorry," said Miguel, with a casual shrug. He turned to Selena and whispered in her ear: "Pick out the biggest stuffed animal."

Selena flashed a soft smile that did not betray that chill that traveled down her body when he whispered in her ear. She pointed to a huge brown teddy bear with a red bow around the neck.

The man from behind the counter handed the furry bear to Selena.

"Thank you," she said.

Frowning, the man from behind the counter rudely said, "You can't play this game no more."

"It's not that serious, man," said Miguel.

"Yes it is. No one wins from me, you hear," said the man, his voice rising with indignation. "Don't come back here. You can't play no more. Got it?"

Miguel just laughed. "My twin brother can."

"I won't let your twin brother play neither, you hear me?"

Miguel narrowed his gaze at the man and turned around. He took Selena's hand and they walked away, laughter ringing in the air.

"You are silly," she said. "Thanks for winning the bear for me."

"You're welcome. Hey, come on," said Miguel. "Let's get on the Ferris wheel. The line is short."

They rushed over to the line for the Ferris wheel. A few minutes later, they were strapped inside a Ferris wheel passenger car.

"You're not scared are you?" Miguel asked, noticing fear swirling around her brown eyes.

"Sometimes it makes my stomach queasy."

"Do you want to get off?"

"No," she hesitantly said.

"We can get off, but we have to do it now before the ride starts."

Selena looked around, heard the sound of locks snapping and suddenly the ride lurched forward. "It's too late!"

"You will be alright," he said, "unless a tornado comes and spins the Ferris wheel away."

She laughed. "That's not funny."

"But you laughed," he said, snuggling close to her.

"I'll try not to think about," she said, as the Ferris wheel slowly rotated upward to the sky.

They were quiet for a few minutes.

"So what are thinking about?" Miguel asked.

"Family stuff."

"La familia. Never forget family."

"I know."

"I can tell something is bothering you," he said.

It took Selena a minute to respond. "My father hates that I play sports. He thinks only boys should play sports."

Miguel shrugged. "He's from Mexico."

"I love my Papá, but he is out of touch with reality."

"My Papá was the same way."

"Was?"

"He died when I was 10. He played baseball and was very good."

"Sorry, Miguel," she softly said. "I don't mean to make you sad."

"I try to remember the good times. He was a mean man sometimes, because he didn't make it to the pros, but he was good man and took care of us."

"I understand."

They were quiet for a few minutes, watching the people miles away on the ground look smaller and smaller as they rose higher and higher in the sky.

"I can't look down anymore," said Selena.

"Just look into my eyes," said Miguel.

"Okay," she said, not wanting to admit that staring at him had the same effect—it made her stomach queasy.

"My Papá went to the coach and told him that he didn't want me to play basketball."

"So you're not going to play? It's the middle of the season?" Miguel asked, concern simmering in his voice.

"My brother Juan. Ah, Saint Juan," she said, with warm affection. "He went to the coach with Papá and somehow convinced my father to let me stay on the team."

"Saint Juan," said Miguel.

"Saint Juan didn't tell me. He didn't want me to know."

"He was just protecting you."

"You know who Ja-Nay-A is, right?"

"Yeah."

"I guess she overheard Coach O talking to Juan and Papá and then she waited and told me. She caught me off guard because I didn't know that Papá had talked to my father."

"And she wasn't nice about it."

Selena inhaled a breath of air. "She said she was going to take my starter spot."

"You're still a starter right?" he asked.

"Sí."

"When did your father see your coach?"

Selena frowned. "I don't know for sure. I think it was a while ago."

"Has Coach O said anything to you?"

"No."

"It gets ugly in sports. Some of the other kids' parents on the baseball team tried to buy their kids' playing team," said Miguel.

"My old Coach Winston took money from the parents. But then there was that scandal and they got rid of him."

Selena shook her head. "I remember."

"Our new coach has honor," said Miguel. "He's fair and believes in his players. And he doesn't take money."

"Coach O is like that."

"So don't worry about Ja-Nay-A or losing your spot," said Miguel. "Just keep playing like you do."

She shook her head as he stroked his hand across her right cheek.

"You're so sweet and adorable, but not on the court," said Miguel. "You're a little monster."

Selena's eyes grew wide. "You are loco. First you say I'm sweet and then you say I'm a monster."

"You're a mean monster on the court. Stealing balls, blocking shots, and popping threes."

"Well you almost hit people with balls going 80 miles an hour. That's not very nice," said Selena.

"We're two monsters," said Miguel. "We belong together."

She laughed. "I'm not a monster."

"No, bonita. You are the sweetest girl I know."

He kissed her lips, a long kiss that sent chills through her body. She closed her eyes and enjoyed the feel of his lips on hers.

When she opened her eyes, he said, "Your kiss is sweet too."

She blushed, and looked away.

"It's okay," he said. "I'm not trying to rush you."

The Ferris wheel jerked in the air, swaying as it began to glide down the opposite side.

He held her hand.

"It was nice talking to you about stuff," she said.

"I'm a good listener and friend," he said.

She nodded, a trace of a smile gracing her face.

The Ferris wheel moved again, getting closer to the ground. They heard a creaking sound.

"It sounds like it's about to fall apart," said Miguel with mock exaggeration.

Her eyes widened and then she realized from his expression that he was joking. "Trying to scare me. It's not working."

"I know you don't scare easily."

"We're not that far from the ground," she said, looking out of the Ferris wheel car. "Maybe I should push you out here."

"I said you were a monster," Miguel said, with a soft kiss. "A beautiful monster."

DARIAN-BALL-BLOG: NUMBER 7

Hey! Is it too early to talk about our ranking in the region? I'm going there. Regional games are the regular games we play against other teams during the main basketball season. (School board and athletics directors decide stuff like that.) Region games count because those games determine our season record and whether we play in the regional championship games. Now that's clear: there's good news: We have a winning record: 10 wins, 3 losses. Really, Truly, Absolutely. We are more than half way through the season. Only 7 more region games to go. We have to win. We have to get more points on the board than the other teams.

Maybe it's too early to talk about winning the region championship. Maybe it's way too early to talk about sweet 16 and elite 8. Definitely too early to think about going to the state championship. Maybe it's not. But it is possible. So let's start thinking about the possible now.

We're coming to the end of the regular season so the championship season is almost here.

We have way more wins than losses. Going to the state championship is not a fantasy, is it? We got to keep winning…winning…winning.

Shooting.

Scoring.

Winning.

Team, click your sneakers together three times and you just might land in Oz… that is Championship Oz. Oh for you retards who don't get it: I'm making a comparison to the Wizard of Oz. Got it now?

Comments

Girl8ball: We didn't make it to region championships last year. How are we going to state?

Alleyoop: Dream on. Dream on. The impossible dream.

Basketqueen: Boo to haters. Yay to dreamers.

Irockball: I think it's possible. I also think it's possible that we share the universe with other beings from other planet.

Knowtoomuch: How do you know so much about the team?

MVP123: Riverbrook can make it to regionals. Got to have a game plan.
Ibelieve: I believe there is a bigger plan in the universe. Maybe it includes Riverbrook.

CHAPTER 26

MARLEY

"*Why get excited about love? It has an expiration date,*" said Marley.
"*You'll understand when you fall in love,*" said Aunt Martina.
"*I'm never falling in love,*" said Marley. "*It makes people stupid.*"
"*Love is complicated.*"
"*I'm going to date boys who like me more than I like them,*" said Marley.

A scream of frustration was trapped inside Marley's lungs, but she had to contain it. She was on a plane that had been circling over Chicago's airport for over an hour. "*Get me off this freaking plane!*" was ready to explode from her mouth like a lit firecracker. But she kept the words inside her mouth. She didn't want the other passengers to think she was a crazy teen-ager.

There were over 1,000 songs on her iPod, but Marley was tired of listening to her favorite songs, favorite playlists, and favorite artists. She had seen the movie they were showing on the airplane's movie screen. She flipped through the pages of a book she'd hastily bought before boarding the plane. It was a boring book. She almost bought *Green, Eggs and Ham* by Dr. Seuss—at least it would have been made her laugh for a few seconds. She tried to fall asleep, but catching some Z's was as impossible as catching clouds in the sky.

So, Marley sat bored and restless on the crowded plane. The worst thing in the world was waiting for something she didn't want to do or someone she didn't want to see—her mother. She didn't like Chicago, hated the cold weather, and rarely enjoyed their mother-daughter visits.

Marley suddenly remembered something a woman told her on a plane trip to Chicago a while ago: a human heart breaks into a million pieces when the hurt comes from a tender spot in the heart. It was as if the woman knew how much her mother had broken her heart. She had pierced her heart's tender spot. Marley preferred when her mother came to Atlanta.

She didn't feel so displaced.

She didn't feel so confused.

She didn't feel so controlled.

Marley wondered how she ended up with two control freaks for parents. Her mother was more controlling than her father. Her mother was a control freak twenty-four hours a day; she always had to be productive which meant Marley had to be productive too. Her father was a control freak about certain things: the house and car had to be clean; his business was very organized. Yet, he was fun and spontaneous. Last year, they went to the Bahamas two weekends in a row, "just for the hell of it." Egypt and her father Kenneth went with them and they all had fun. It was two brothers and their daughters on vacation.

Marley wasn't sure what to expect during this visit with her mother. It would be their first time together after her mother's ridiculously-insane, inappropriately-timed engagement announcement. She was shocked when her mother called and apologized for what she called a 'momentary lapse of judgment.' Her mother rarely apologized. Marley had wanted to say that "you're just not that into me," a title from a book and movie. Even though the book and movie were about romantic relationships, Marley thought it described how her mother felt about her. Franchesca was into her career, not her daughter.

Marley tried not to let thoughts about Franchesca roam through her mind. She did not understand her and decided that she might not ever understand her mother. Maybe she would later—when she's an adult.

Almost ninety minutes after the scheduled landing time, the plane finally touched the ground. Marley screamed, "Yeah!" before she realized the word had left her mouth.

She sent a text message to her father: *We landed. FINALLY!*

Marley trailed behind other anxious-to-get-off-the-plane passengers and followed the airport's signs to baggage claim. She knew where to go from her numerous trips to Chicago. She also knew from past visits that she might be forced to go to a business meeting with her mother. That is, she'd be waiting in a room while her mother was in a meeting.

Walking through the airport, a memory blasted through her mind. Her mother had sent her to elementary school with a 102 degree temperature because she had to be in court. As usual, her father picked her up from school and took her to the doctor and scolded Franchesca for "irresponsible parenting." Marley didn't know why that particular memory invaded her mind while riding the escalator that led to the baggage terminal. Memories had an unpredictable way of showing up announced to remind her of things she did NOT want to remember.

When she arrived in the baggage area, she kept an eye out for her mother. She watched the luggage circling around the carousel, looking for her two Louis Vuitton suitcases. An older white man tried to talk to her, but Marley ignored him. Her father warned her long ago not to talk to people in the airport. She had learned the hard way that her father was right. One time—a stranger introduced himself and said he knew her father. She was walking towards the airport exit door with him when her father spotted them. She had never seen her father so afraid and angry; he screamed Marley's name and the strange man ran into the crowd of people. Her father called the police, but the strange man had disappeared. She was only ten, but she would never let that happen again.

She spotted her luggage at the same time she saw a text from her mother: *Running late. Sent limo. Meet you at house.*

Marley stared at the text with the same disappointed feeling she felt when she received the exact same text many times before. Almost every time she came to Chicago. Yet, the disappointment always hit her like a punch in her stomach. Marley felt like crying—and didn't know why. She deleted the text and refused to let one tear drop fall from her eyes.

Marley knew what she had to do: get her luggage and find the limo man. She pulled her luggage from the carousel and headed towards the transportation area. She immediately saw the limo driver, holding a card with her name. She approached the older black man with a raisin-wrinkled face. "I'm Marley," she said.

"Good to meet you," he said, with a smile that showcased bright white teeth that contrasted against his dark skin. "Let me get those bags for you, young lady."

"Thank you," Marley said.

"Don't look like a wilted flower, little lady," he said with an island-tinged accent.

"I was on the plane forever, circling around," Marley complained. "I was going crazy."

"That was out of your control," the old man said.

"Huh?"

"The airplane circling the sky was out of your control. Nothing you can do about it, eh?"

Marley shrugged. "No."

"So, why make you crazy?"

Marley laughed.

"So the pretty little lady can laugh," said the old limo driver. "Follow me, please."

An hour later, Marley arrived at her mother's penthouse condominium. Franchesca opened the door before she could knock. Marley was shocked when her mother wrapped her arms around her waist. It was an awkward hug. "Marley, sweetheart."

"Hi, Mother."

"I'm glad you're here. You look so pretty," she said.

"Thank you," Marley said, observing that very little had changed in the interior designer-decorated condo. The furniture was very modern with black and white as the dominant theme.

"Your plane was late, so we're late for our appointment," Franchesca said.

"What appointment?"

"We're going to the spa," said Franchesca. "Your favorite place."

A slow smile spread across Marley's lips. Total pampering. Facial, manicure, pedicure, and massage while listening to music with some kind of Indian or Iranian sound. It was one of her favorite things to do with her mother, but something they didn't do very often. Maybe this was going to be a good visit.

Marley put her luggage in her bedroom—which was very different than her bedroom at her father's house. Both rooms were filled with expensive, modern furniture and decorations, and 500-count thread bed sheets. Her bedroom at her mom's was photo-shoot ready, but her room at her dad's was picture perfect clean. In a word she could describe the difference; her bedroom at her mother's felt like a hotel, and her bedroom at her father's felt like home. A home and a hotel—what a world of difference. She used to complain, but now she adapted to wherever she was staying at the moment.

Marley freshened up and met her mother in the living room. Franchesca was gazing out the window at the skyline—building after building of skyscrapers competing to reach the sky.

Franchesca turned when she heard Marley. "Ready?"

Marley smiled. "Yes, I am."

"I like to see you smile," Franchesca said with rarely-expressed tenderness, before leading Marley to the door.

Marley enjoyed every moment at the spa. It was paradise—a total escape from reality. She didn't want it to end. But her mother was a time-conscious person with a tight schedule, planning every moment of her days and nights.

So from the paradise of a warm spa retreat, Marley went outside to the frosty cold night air of Chicago. She had on two sweaters, a thick winter knee-length parka and boots, but she felt naked in the below-zero, freezing temperature.

They went to visit Aunt Martina, her mother's sister, who also had attended an Ivy-league college and had a successful career as a financial investor. Martina and Franchesca were very alike in their intense pursuit of careers and financial success. Marley liked being around Aunt Martina because even though she was a workaholic, she had a fun, playful side, which her mother seemed to be missing.

Alone with Aunt Martina, she was enjoying herself until her aunt mentioned her mother's fiancée.

"She told me you weren't happy about it," said Aunt Martina.

"I was so shocked I didn't know what to think or how to feel."

"He's a nice man and I've never seen her crazy about any man, except your father."

"Well that was a long time ago," said Marley, unable to recall a memory of her parents being happy together. "What happened to their…love? Why do people stop being crazy about each other?"

"I don't know," said Aunt Martina. "If I knew the answer to that million dollar question I'd be a millionaire."

"I heard you already are," said Marley.

"Don't believe everything you hear," she said with a mischievous grin.

"Love seems crazy, unreal and undependable. Why get excited about something that has an expiration date?" Marley asked. "At least you know when milk is going to be bad. The date is stamped on the carton."

"You're rather cynical to be so young," said Aunt Martina. "Love is complicated."

"Look who I have for examples. Parents who dislike each other."

"When you fall in love, you'll understand."

"I'm never falling in love," said Marley. "It makes people stupid."

"You don't like a boy in high school? I know boys hit on you."

"All day long," Marley said with a cocky tone. "I like this one boy, Quinton. He's a star athlete and the girls lose their mind about him, but I'm not trying to be one of those I'm-going-to-have-his-baby girls because he's going to be star. I'm not a groupie."

"That's smart."

"I like boys who are smart, but they have to look good. I mean they got to be hot like a movie star."

"Those are the ones to watch out for," warned Martina.

"I'm not going to get seriously involved with any boy. Not one that's going to make me act crazy. I'm going to like boys who like me more than I like them," said Marley.

"Think you got it all figured out?"

"I think that's what you do," said Marley. "I've never seen you lose your mind over a man."

"My dear niece, don't think you have me all figured out."

"Okay." Marley laughed. "Egypt's always in love. But it's usually with someone different and it doesn't last long."

"That sounds like Egypt," said Aunt Martina. "I better warn you. Your mother is going to take you to dinner with Sterling tomorrow."

A strange expression came over Marley's face.

"Aunt Martina, my stomach really hurts," Marley said, doubling over and holding her hand against her stomach. She made an ugly face. "I think I'm going to throw up."

"You're smart as hell, and you're a great basketball player, but your acting skills are horrible," said Aunt Martina.

Marley fell onto the floor and crunched into a ball. "I'm sick. So sick," she wailed. "I think I should go to the hospital."

"You need something a lot more serious than a stomach ache before Franchesca takes you to the hospital."

Marley sat up. "How can I make my head feel hot like I have a 102 degree temperature?"

"Not going to work," Aunt Martina warned. "Were you hoping that your mom and dad would get back together?"

"Please, I'm too smart and logical to think something so typical of divorced kids," said Marley.

Martina shook her head. "I know that's what you were hoping for."

Marley stared at her aunt for a moment, noticing—not for the first time—how much the two sisters looked alike. Somehow she could be honest with Aunt Martina who didn't have children and lived a very organized and structured life like her mother. "Maybe," Marley half-confessed.

"On a happier note, tomorrow you will visit Laurel—our crazy sister with too many children," said Aunt Martina.

"I love visiting Aunt Laurel," Marley said, her voice full of excitement. "She has four beautiful kids. I adore my little cousins. They are so much fun."

"She's just a mommy now," Martina said with undisguised disappointment.

"She's a wonderful mommy." Marley wished her mother was more like Aunt Laurel—a doting, caring, super-involved mom.

"She's a great mom, but she threw her career away. She has an MBA from a great school and she's doing nothing with it," said Aunt Martina. "Nothing."

"Maybe she's doing precisely what she wants to do."

"Hmmm...the wisdom of Marley Woods," Aunt Martina said, kissing her niece on the forehead.

Marley loved every moment she spent with Aunt Laurel and her four noisy kids who were under ten-years-old—two girls and two boys—and their cluttered and chaotic house. She hated every second of the dinner with her mother and Sterling at one of Chicago's finest restaurants. She was charming and polite during dinner, behaving the way her mother expected. After all, she was going to be leaving the next day.

That's what she thought until they returned to her mother's condo. Sitting in front of the warm, blazing fireplace, they were watching a movie that Marley had seen several times, but she didn't tell her mother.

Breaking the silence, Franchesca said, "Your father told me about the drinking incident."

Marley stared at her mother, uncertain what to say.

"That was a very unorthodox way of teaching you a lesson," Franchesca said, her tone dripping with disapproval. "Were you drinking at that party?"

Marley sighed. "Yes."

"You know better, Marley!"

"And I don't want to ever drink again," said Marley.

"I know you will be experimenting with things, Marley. You're exposed to all kinds of things in high school."

"You have no idea. I've seen kids making out in the hallway, girls kissing each other. Kids come to school high…"

"You don't have to do what everyone else does."

"Mother, I know I shouldn't have done it," she said, remembering why she did it: to make her mother angry. She knew that was not a good excuse.

"I don't agree with your father's tactics. You and Egypt could have gotten sick."

Marley rolled her eyes. "I don't want to think about it."

"Okay. Listen to me: I want you to stay for an extra day," said Franchesca. "We can spend more time together and you can meet Sterling's family."

Marley's eyes widened almost the size of golf balls. "Mother, I have to get back," she said, with controlled emotion.

"You'll just miss one day."

"I have a game tomorrow," she stated, agitation leaking through her tone.

"You can miss one game," Franchesca casually said. "You're out of school tomorrow."

"I know, but we have a game anyway. I can't miss it! My team needs me."

"Marley, your future is in academics, not sports," her mother explained, with thinly-veiled patience. "You can be a lawyer, an architect, an engineer. Respected professions that make real money."

"I love playing basketball. I can't let my team down. It's a very important game," she said passionately. Marley tried to hold back the tears, but her cheeks were wet with tear drops.

"We've had this conversation about basketball a million times. I've already changed your ticket," said Franchesca. "I have a surprise planned for you." Her voice filled with excitement, she said, "It's something you will absolutely love."

"I don't care. I just want to go back home!" demanded Marley.

"This is your home too!"

"No, it isn't!" Marley went into her bedroom and shut the door. This was so typical—every visit seemed to end with them fighting.

Marley sent her father a text: *She changed my ticket. Doesn't want me to leave until Tues. I need to be back for tomorrow's game.*

When her father didn't respond in thirty minutes, she called him.

He answered after one ring and said, "I got you a ticket for 10 AM. You'll leave after Franchesca goes to work."

"She'll be furious."

"I'll pick you up. Meet you at baggage claim."

"Daddy, she's going to be so…so freaking mad."

"I know. But it won't be the first time your mother is …so freaking mad."

The next morning before leaving, she wrote her mother a note: *"I'm sorry I have to leave. I don't want to let my teammates down. Please don't be foaming-at-the-mouth-mad. Please try to understand. I really love basketball. Love, YOUR DAUGHTER Marley!*

At the airport, Marley thought about texting her mother, but decided to wait until she was safely on the plane. Right before take-off—the moment passengers are directed to turn off cell phones—Marley sent her mother a message: *On the way to ATL. Can't miss game. Sorry. Don't be mad.*

Watching the 'sending message' display on her phone, she knew that her last three words were meaningless. Her mother was going to be extremely, furiously, revengefully mad—madder than a disturbed wasp nest.

Marley slept on the plane. When it landed as scheduled, she made her way through the Atlanta airport to the baggage claim area. She got her luggage and then saw her father parked in front of the airport. Cooper got out of his car. After she came through the sliding glass doors, he greeted her with a hug and a kiss. He put her luggage in the back of the SUV and got inside the car.

"You okay, baby?" he asked.

"I hate Chicago. It is so freaking cold. I could never live anywhere that's as cold as Antarctica," said Marley.

"That's one of the reasons why I left St Louis."

"I don't want to let my team down. I can't let them down, Daddy, but Franchesca's going to be furious."

"Don't worry about the … wrath of Franchesca," said Cooper, repeating a comment about Franchesca they often joked about.

Marley laughed. "Well…I'm here now. She can't snap her fingers and bring me back there."

"If she could, she most definitely would."

Marley pretended to shiver. "That would be scary if she had that much power."

"She thinks she does," he said, chuckling. "Don't worry about it now. I have your uniform and sports bag," said Cooper. "Just get your mind focused on the game."

"This is a serious game," said Marley. "Coach O warned us that Swanson plays dirty."

"Go in there to win," said Cooper.

"Yeah, we are champions," said Marley, repeating the words she had heard from Coach O at least a hundred times.

"Let's go champ," Cooper said, driving away from the airport to the frantic beat of a rap song.

CHAPTER 27

BAILEY

"She called Bailey the N word!" shrieked Chase.

"I couldn't let her get away with that!" Tequila yelled.

"Put me in coach," demanded Heaven. "I'll take her out. She already has four fouls. I'll make sure she fouls me and then she'll be out of the game."

Swanson High was one of the five schools that were not in Riverbrook's regular playing region. Winning or losing to Swanson wouldn't affect their region win and loss record, but it would affect their spirit and reputation. Coach O didn't believe in losing any game, against any team, even scrimmage games. Coach O wanted everyone to know that they were a winning team, no matter who they were playing.

Swanson always beat Riverbrook, so the pressure to beat Swanson High School was intense. Swanson expected an easy victory. But Coach O planned to change that expectation. Riverbrook had to beat Swanson, especially if they wanted to change their reputation as a team that always loses. They had to beat tough teams inside and outside their region if they were going to be taken seriously as a team to watch and beat.

The girls were quiet on the bus ride to Swanson. Tension was in the air when they entered Swanson High School, located in a small town in rural Georgia. The game was going to start in an hour. It was an odd day and time for a game. It was Monday and school was out for a teacher workday.

The gym was packed with Swanson fans. They were dressed in all-American colors: red, white and blue.

Swanson fans booed the Riverbrook team as soon as they entered the gym.

The girls felt like they had entered a foreign country and were unwanted guests. In enemy territory, they were the targets of eyes that expressed more than just an obsession to win. Swanson High was known for winning their regional playoffs and had won two state championships. From the hateful posters, the mean-spirited cheers, the unfriendly stares—Swanson had no intention of losing.

As Riverbrook's varsity girls walked to the designated visitor's side, they felt a thick cloud of negative energy—dark and hate-filled.

For the first time, the girls felt afraid.

Coach Remmington saw the girls' fear and immediately took them into a private room.

"What was that? You went in there looking like chickens," said Coach O. "Now they think we are afraid. They think they're going to win. They think you were intimidated."

"We were…I mean I thought we were supposed to…" said Ja-Nay-A.

"Act afraid," Kaylee softly said.

Coach O looked at each player. "But you weren't acting, were you? I could see the fear on your faces."

"They look scary," said Rachel in a nervous voice.

"You were supposed to *pretend* that you were afraid. So we could catch them off guard. That was the objective," said Coach O in a reprimanding tone. "You do know what pretend means don't you?"

"We know what it means," Heaven said, shaking her head. "I got a bad vibe when I walked in. They looked at us like they hate us. I've never seen that look before."

"I could almost feel their hatred," said Marley.

"They screamed racist words at us. Mean things. Even the grown-ups said mean things," added Selena. "Ellos son malos como el diablo."

"I don't know what you said, but I know diablo means devil," said Tequila.

"Sí, diablo people," said Selena.

"They look very scary," said Layne.

"Someone said they were going to pull out my red hair," said Zoey.

"Didn't I tell you this was going to happen?" Coach O asked.

The girls looked at each other.

"I didn't think it was going to be this bad," said Marley. "We are in hick country."

"Hicksville," said Elise.

"The players look mean," said Chase.

"Did you forget to put on your big girl panties, baby baller?" asked Ja-Nay-A.

"Shut up!" said Chase.

"Stop it now," scolded Coach O. "Listen to me. Remember our strategy. Pretend to be afraid." In a louder, stronger voice, she said, "PRETEND!"

"I'm not afraid," said Marley, in an unconvincing voice.

"If you are afraid, hide it. Conceal it. Fake it. Hide it in the pit of your stomach. Whatever you do, don't show it," said Coach O.

"Poker face," said Zoey. "Like the Lady Gaga song. I got my Poker face."

"Show no emotion. No excitement. No fear," said Coach O.

"Then we stop pretending after the tip-off," said Chase.

"Yes, baby baller," said Coach O.

"I'm not baby baller today!" Chase said with a sudden burst of fierceness.

"So now you got on super girl panties!" said Marley.

"Can I borrow a pair?" whispered Rachel.

"We just all got to go hard!" said Ja-Nay-A.

"From start to finish," said Coach Remmington.

For the first time since they entered Swanson High School, they laughed.

"You all have on super girl panties underneath your super bad uniforms, right team?" said Coach O.

They shook their heads, a sprinkling of smiles on some of their faces.

"Sí," said Selena. "Super uniformes malos."

"Now, let's play ball!" said Coach O. "Let's kick ass!"

Riverbrook's girls' varsity basketball team returned to the gym, but they couldn't quite shake their fear and apprehension. They walked to their designated side of the court, and quietly prepared for the game. Coach O usually gave a brief prep talk while the team circled around her, but she did not. She communicated with arm movements and the players understood.

The five Riverbrook starters hit the floor along with the Swanson team. Tequila moved into tip-off position: standing opposite a girl who was thicker and taller, facing front court—the direction of the basketball hoop for Riverbrook to score for the first half of game. Tequila didn't make eye contact with the Swanson players. She pretended to be nervous and afraid… until the buzzer sounded.

Game on.

Tequila screamed in the girl's face, distracting the player and hitting the ball in the direction of their front court, with Marley grabbing the ball mid-air. She passed the ball to Chase who caught it, ran down front court and made a lay-up.

Within three minutes of the game—passing the ball, running like lightening, shooting with accuracy—Riverbrook had a six-point lead. They fought hard to keep the lead, with a tit for tat battle—they would score and then Swanson High would score. The starters concentrated on the game, ignoring the nasty, roaring cheers for Swanson. They followed Coach O's advice: *don't look at the crowd.*

With each microsecond, the game was even more exciting and intense.

Twenty seconds before the end of the first half, a Swanson player flagrantly fouled Bailey. The opposing team played with rule-breaking aggressiveness—which was precisely what Coach Remmington wanted. Bailey was nervous as she eyed the basketball hoop and positioned her body to make two free throw shots. Her gaze wavered towards Riverbrook fans—shouting and rooting for her. But Riverbrook's cheers were drowned out by Swanson fans' loud chant: *Miss it! Miss it! Miss it!*

Bailey's palms were sweaty and the ball slipped out of her hand. She picked it up, dribbled several times and scored two points.

The other team got the rebound and tried to score, but the buzzer sounded. At half-time the score was 32 to 26 with Riverbrook in the lead.

The tension in the air was as thick as a brewing summer thunderstorm.

Both teams began the second half with fierce determination and aggression. Swanson was ahead by four points when the third quarter ended. The game was fast paced, both teams taking turns scoring points. The referees called fouls on several players.

During the fourth quarter, Bailey caught a rebound and dribbled up court. She was stopped by the opposing team's strong defensive maneuvers. They stood in front of the basket perimeter, their arms stretched outward to the side. Bailey dribbled while her teammates got into position to run a penetrating defensive play. A girl from the other team stepped into Bailey's face: "You Ni**er! You Ni**er-lover!"

Tequila and Marley heard what the girl said; both felt a gush of anger wash through their bodies like that they never felt before. Anger now ruled their concentration. Bailey was so distracted that the girl stole the ball from her. As the name-calling girl dribbled down court to score, Chase ran past the girl to stop her from making a layup. Hands in the air, Tequila stood to the right of the basket; she spun in front of the ball-stealing player, elbowed her in the shoulder, and intentionally tripped the girl. The referee called a flagrant foul on

Tequila and the other team scored two free throw shots from the foul line.

Coach O called a time out.

The girls ran over and before Coach O could ask them what happened, Chase blurted out what the girl said. "She called Bailey the N word!"

"I couldn't let her get away with that!" Tequila yelled.

"Put me in coach," demanded Heaven. "I'll take her down, she already has four fouls. I'll make sure she fouls me and then she'll be out of the game."

"I like the strategy, but not the reason behind it. But do it," Coach O thoughtfully said. "I'm angry too girls, but we can't let anger control our plays."

"I know her," Bailey said, upset and angry. "We went to middle school together and then she moved away. We were friends, but I don't remember her being…racist."

"They're furious. We're beating them and they're not used to losing," said Coach O. "Stay cool, score and beat them like they never been beat before. Keep scoring. We gotta win now girls."

Heaven tightly guarded the name-calling player. Heaven was body-to-body with the girl. The girl backed up and ran straight into Heaven, knocking her on the floor. The referee called an intentional charge. The name-calling player had five fouls and was benched for the rest of the game.

Heaven stood at the free throw line. Before she took a shot, she would smile at the name-calling player and then shoot. She smiled at her both times, and scored two baskets.

"You…" Heaven screamed, but intentionally did not finish her sentence. She just wanted to agitate the benched player who was having a difficult time containing her rage. It was an aggressive fourth quarter. Coach O ran full press plays and strong defensive strategies. Riverbrook's lead grew with each shot. With every basket scored, Swanson's chants grew nastier. Racist words were hurled at them. Blatant threats shouted.

The buzzer sounded. Riverbrook won: 62 to 55.

The Swanson crowd ran onto the floor, screaming at the referees and the players. Sensing the escalation of unsportsmanlike and violent behavior, laced with racial tension, Coach O had asked the school bus driver to park in the front of the school. As the crowd rushed down to the court, Coach O told her players: "Run to the bus!"

Coach O didn't follow the normal end of game protocol, concerned that slapping of hands and the fake "good game" might lead to a riot. As they got on the bus, various objects were thrown at them. Some of the girls were hit by soda cans and rocks.

Coach O got on the bus last, and made sure all the girls were there. The bus sped away and the girls hurled questions all at once.

"I didn't get my stuff."

"I'm scared."

"We should have called the police."

"The police were there. Swanson police."

"I'm worried about my family."

"I'm calling my dad and he's not answering," said Marley.

Coach O signaled for them to be quiet.

"I told everyone to leave one by one," said Coach O.

"You did?" asked Kaylee.

Rachel burst into tears. "I think I peed in my seat."

"That's okay," said Zoey, putting her arms around Rachel. "That's why I sat next to you."

Marley handed Rachel a towel from her bag.

"I had a bad feeling when I walked in there. And when crowds get out of control, crowd madness and hysteria takes over," said Coach O. "It can lead to a dangerous situation." She took a deep breath. "I didn't want anyone on the team hurt or your family or fans who came all the way out here getting hurt."

"This is so crazy," said Tequila.

"I didn't call the police, because frankly they would have been local police and I think they would have made things worse," said Coach Olivia.

THE STARTERS

"I can't believe they acted like that!" said Rina, the team manager.

"You would think it's the 1960's," said Marley.

"Marley, I asked your Dad to tell everyone to leave—discretely. I didn't want to be obvious, but I knew Riverbrook folks needed to leave before the game was over."

"I can't believe this," Chase said, her eyes misted with tears.

"The fact that we started off winning, shocked them. They almost caught up twice, but they had never been beaten like that," explained Coach O. "They couldn't handle it. I felt it."

"I can't believe she said that word to me." Bailey looked at her teammates. "Or any of us. ...I didn't know what to say. I should have said something back. I feel so stupid," said Bailey, her voice filled with hurt and rage. She wiped tears from her eyes.

"I had your back. I tripped the bitch," said Tequila.

"I fouled her out," Heaven said proudly.

"And that really made them mad," said Layne. "Coach, you told us to pretend we were afraid. I didn't think we would get attacked."

"I'm surprised and not surprised," said Coach O.

"What do you mean?" asked Marley.

"I played against them when I was a student at Riverbrook a long time ago. I was the only black girl on the team."

"The only black girl!" said Heaven, shock riveting in her voice.

"There weren't many blacks in the school district back then," explained Coach O. "I was called the N-word to my face at games and sometimes at schools. It happened more than once and my coach at the time ignored it." Her voice grew heavy with resentment. "My coach was very racist."

"Really?" said Tequila.

"My parents were angry and indignant. They made complaints against the school and even to the board," explained Coach O. "Nothing was done. I had to suck it up." Coach O was quiet for a moment. "But, I will file a formal complaint against Swanson. I will make sure they are reprimanded some kind of way."

"I'm glad we beat them racist…MotherFather people," said Marley.
"We kicked their asses," Tequila proudly said.

Back at Riverbrook High, parents' cars were lined up waiting for the bus's arrival. When the bus pulled into the school's parking lot, the girls immediately jumped off the bus. They were swarmed by family, friends and fans, congratulating them on beating a team that Riverbrook had never beaten before. The parents who knew about the incident at Swanson were obviously relieved.

It was wonderful victory, but Bailey felt excited and nauseated at the same time. She didn't expect to see her father, but it was obvious on his face that he knew what happened.

Bailey was reluctant to talk about it with her father; he would be furious and it would reignite his resentment with her mother for marrying a black man. It brought back memories that Bailey did not want to relive; how he exploded when he found out who her mother was going to marry. It took a long time for her father to accept her black stepfather and Bailey did not want to go back to that time of tension and confusion.

"Are you going to talk about it?" her father had asked when they were in the car.

"Maybe later," she said. "I'm fine, Daddy."

"I'm very angry that someone would call you that word." He banged his hand against the steering wheel. "And you're not even black… If I could find that girl I would…"

"Daddy, you would only get in trouble," she said calmly, hoping to calm the rage she saw on his face.

"I thought about going out there and finding out where that girl lives. I want to do something. Even if it's just pressing charges," Scott said with clenched teeth.

"I hardly ever see you get mad like this."

"You're my little girl. And it angers me that anyone would say something like that to you."

"I'm pissed because I know…." she paused.

"I guess I didn't expect something like that from a kid," said Scott. "I know parents are going to speak their mind."

"Kids say a lot of racist and mean things Daddy. More than you think. A lot of the kids who go to school with River are very racist."

"I know," he said. "Some private schools kids self-absorbed brats."

"We have girls from different races on our team, and we won fair and square," Bailey said. "Well…we did play more aggressive than normal."

Scott was quiet before answering. "I know."

Ten minutes later, he pulled in front of her house. Scott kissed her on the forehead. "I heard you played extraordinarily well under extreme circumstances. I just wanted to congratulate you. Good game and I'll see you later." She got out of the car and waved at her father.

Her mother opened the door as soon as heard a car pull into the driveway. "Are you okay, baby?" Jennifer asked.

"I'm fine," she said. Inside the house, she told her mother and stepfather what happened in detail. As Bailey described the game, she saw her mother's face get redder and redder the angrier she became. Her stepfather was angry and appalled, but not shocked. She told her mother who the girl was, and her mother remembered the girl's family moving away to escape the diversity of the middle school. "Suzanne Boyd, right?"

"Yes, I went to her birthday party twice. I didn't think they were *that racist*," said Jennifer.

"I didn't tell Daddy I knew her. He's so mad I think he would go find her."

"That doesn't surprise me," said Jennifer. "You know how protective he is of you."

Bailey told them what happened to Coach O years ago when she played at Riverbrook.

As they comforted Bailey with words of encouragement, the doorbell rang. Robert answered the door and ushered Coach Remmington into their kitchen.

"I'm sorry for arriving without advance notice, but I wanted to apologize in person for the events that occurred at the game," said Coach O.

"There's nothing for you to apologize for," said Jennifer.

"Their actions are not on me, but I hate that Bailey had to experience such a racist insult. I hate…don't want to use that word, but it's affected the whole team. That concerns me." She paused. "I'm going have to do some team building exercise or some counseling to help them process what happened."

"That would be helpful," said Robert.

"I don't know if Bailey told you about my experiences when I was a student at Riverbrook."

"Yes, she did," said Robert. "Unfortunately, some things change and some things stay the same. I deal with racism in corporate America every day."

"You have to rise above the negativity, even when it's racism," said Coach O. "I don't want it to escalate. I don't want the kids to retaliate. I'm going to talk to the parents."

"Smart move," said Robert.

"I intend to file a complaint with the high school sports commissioner," said Coach O. "I don't know if they will do anything to reprimand Swanson, but I'm not letting them off the hook easily."

"Bottom line is Riverbrook won," said Robert.

"Yes we did," Coach O said with a proud smile. "I must admit it was personal and it felt good to beat them. They beat us when I played them years and years ago." Coach O looked at Bailey. "If you don't want to play the next game, I understand."

Everyone's eyes were on Bailey. "Marley had to sneak away from her mother and fly back from Chicago to play with us." Bailey looked at her mother, stepfather and coach. "I'm not going to let some girl's racist remark stop me," she strongly said.

Jennifer hugged her daughter. "I'm proud of you, baby."

DARIAN-BALL-BLOG: NUMBER 8

Bailey was called the N word when they played Swanson High School. The freaking N word! Can you believe that? Just thinking about it makes me want to search the internet and find out how to make a bomb and blow up that racist, redneck school. I'm for peace and love and fake racial harmony. But when people cross the freaking line, I think about peace and love and revenge.

Swanson was mad because we were beating them. I admit that I didn't think Bailey belonged with the starters, but she's proved herself and got real skills. They crossed the line. How dare that Swanson B dis her? Racist name calling is so wrong!

Breathe.

Breathe.

Breathe deep.

Our team handled it. The girl had four fouls and Heaven got in the game and purposely fouled the girl, so the racist witch flew out on a flaming broom to the bench (not really). She was out for the rest of the game. Benched. That's where she belonged for showing no disrespect. That's what you get, you child of evilness.

The whole school was out of control: the team, the fans, the parents, the administrators. What's wrong them? As soon as our team walked into the building, the Swanson fans were nasty, racist and uncivilized.

Check out how Coach O played them. She told the girls to go in there and pretend that they were scared and intimidated by them. Our girls faked them out. Because when the game began, their fake fear morphed into super basketball powers and we beat them. They were so mad at us that our girls had to run to the bus. The crazy Swanson fans threw rocks and cans at our girls. Riverbrook fans drove over 50 miles to show support had to sneak out and leave before the beginning of the fourth quarter. Coach O was concerned that there was going to be a riot or something. Ain't that crazy?

Maybe we should do something to retaliate. Anybody bold enough to drive over there and teach them a lesson? Well, maybe not. I heard Coach O wants to take the high road. How about the high road of slashing tires of cars in the school's parking lot. Spray painting the building with not nice words.

I'm not really serious or trying to get kids to retaliate. Just mad. Just venting. So don't do anything. Period. Not a thing! I'm crystal clear, because I'm not taking the blame for more madness. Riverbrook: Hear me loud and clear - no retaliation.

Comments

Girlball: How dare they? Don't they know this is 2012?
Mindyourbiz: I'm with you! We should go to Swanson High and teach them a lesson in respect.
Alley hoop: Stop racism now!
Basketqueen: Sounds like they grew up on the backwoods of some redneck hole. Yeah, let's take the high road and let them be backwards ass stupid.
Radicaldude: I know how to make a bomb! It's not hard!
Sportsqueen: We just think it's different.
Trackball: Don't they know we have a black president? This is a different world.
MVP123: Some people don't ever change. Will never change. Don't want to change.
Knowtoomuch: Who are you really? You know way too much.
Realme: I can't believe what happened! I'm glad they got out of there before someone on our team got hurt.
Sportshigh: We punked them. Ha Ha Ha!
SwishScore: Coach O told the girls to pretend they were afraid. They pretended to pretend (they were really afraid). The Swanson girls didn't know they were being faked. That's how we squashed them.
Nochange: Life was simple when people stayed on their side of the fence.
Nochange: Bailey's family is all mixed up racially. Her Mama should know better.
Nochange: Maybe that's everyone should stay with their own race. Swanson was just standing up for what they believe!

THE STARTERS

Darin: I don't comment on what people say, but Nochange you're banned from this blog.

BBhigh: I know Bailey felt bad. I bet her Dad wants to kick someone's ass.

Fromwayback: I've been to her house for sleepovers….the girl who said that word. She lived in our school district. Her parents were strange back then. Had a confederate flag and I didn't even know what a confederate flag was. She's a goner from my Facebook.

Mindyourbiz: Let's kick Klan ass.

Sportsqueen: I love how Coach O keeps her cool.

Gamewatcher: Glad Tequila tripped her and Heaven fouled the girl out the game.

Yeahitsme: They shouldn't be allowed to play ever again.

CHAPTER 28

TEQUILA

"You did that on purpose," Bailey said to Tequila.

"I think what you did was on purpose," said Tequila.

"I can't be guilty about something I don't know about it," said Bailey.

"Yeah, right."

Saturday afternoon. Tequila and Tevon walked around the food court at the local mall, trying to decide what to eat. Tevon couldn't make up his mind, so Tequila decided they would both get pizza since there wasn't a line at the pizza place.

They ordered pizza and drinks and carried their food to a vacant table. They sat down and starting eating. Tequila half-listened to Tevon talking about a brand new video game. He begged her to take him to the video store in the mall. Tevon sounded like a robot on repeat: *video store, video store, video store.*

"Okay, okay," Tequila said. "Don't ask again."

Sipping soda, she looked around the crowded food court and almost choked on her drink when she saw two faces that she didn't expect to see together: Diante and Bailey walking to a table.

"WTF?"

"You're not supposed to curse," said Tevon.

"Leave me alone!"

Tevon looked at his sister's face. "What's wrong?"

"Shut up!"

"I didn't do nothing."

"Sit here. Don't move. I'll be right back."

"Okay," he slowly said.

"I mean it, Tevon! Don't freaking move!"

Tevon looked at Tequila, worried and nervous.

"I won't move," he gently said. "I promise."

Tequila got up and walked over to Diante and Bailey. They were now sitting at a table with food from a popular fast food restaurant.

"Hey!" she said, with obvious irritation.

Diante looked at Tequila. "Hi."

Bailey greeted Tequila with a friendly smile. "Hi, Tequila!"

"Hi, Tequila?" she said, her tone hostile.

Bailey's expression changed. "What's wrong? You okay?"

"Ask Diante."

Bailey suspiciously looked at Diante. "What's going on?"

"Nothing," he said, without making eye contact with Bailey.

"Nothing?" repeated Tequila.

"Me and Bailey are just eating," Diante said. "Chill, Quila."

"Don't tell me to freaking chill," Tequila loudly said.

"Whoa! What's going on here?" asked Bailey.

"Are you dating him?" Tequila asked Bailey.

Bailey looked at Diante and then Tequila. "That's none of your business."

"So, do you know about Diante and me?" asked Tequila.

Diante stood up and grabbed his food. "Let's go, Bailey."

"I want to know what's going on." Suspicious, Bailey stared at Diante. "You told me you're not seeing anyone."

"Not really," said Diante. "Not seriously."

"Let me tell you this, Bailey," said Tequila. "Let's just say we have exchanged body fluids."

"What?" Bailey said confused. Understanding dawned. "Oh, yuck! Yuck. TMI."

"Quila, you know what's up," said Diante.

"I don't know what's up," said Bailey. "So I'm leaving."

Bailey grabbed her purse and left the table.

Diante watched Bailey leave the food court and turned towards Tequila with a charming smile. "I didn't know it was like that," he said. "Devil red."

"Screw you," said Tequila.

Tequila went back over to the table where Tevon was sitting.

She slumped into the seat and didn't say a word.

Tevon stared at her.

"Stop staring at me."

"You alright?" he tenderly asked.

"Yes."

"Why are you crying?"

"It's suicide time. Five times," said Coach O, referring to the practice drill that required the girls to run from the back wall of the gym to the quarter mark of the gym, then sprint back to the back wall, and then run to the half-way point of the gym and sprint to the back wall again. They would turn around and run to the third-quarter mark of the gym, then turn around and run back to the original starting point. From there, they would run the entire length of the gym, from the back wall of the gym all the way to the opposite side of the gym, and then run back to their starting point. They would go back and forth, stopping and starting at the different points, returning to the back wall and running again to a designated quarter mark in the game.

The girls lined up near the back wall in the gym for the suicide drills. They were in a runner's position, waiting for the coach to blow the whistle.

Coach O blew the whistle. The girls took off running, but not all of them ran at the same pace.

The faster girls ran to the first set of orange cones, about a fourth of the way to the other side of the gym. They stopped, turned around and ran back to their starting point.

Chase, Layne, Marley, Tequila and Ja-Nay-A ran to the next set of cones—half-way point of the gym—and returned to the starting point, the other girls trailing behind them.

When the other girls returned to the starting point, they ran towards the half-way point of the gym, but they were now running at their own individual pace.

Chase, Selena, Layne and Marley and Ja-Nay-A ran to the next set of orange codes. They turned and ran back to the starting point. From the starting point, they ran all the way to the other side of the gym. Almost done, they accelerated to see who ran the fastest. Chase came in first, Marley second, Tequila third and Selena fourth.

After all the girls finished the first round of suicides, Coach O directed them to line-up from the starting pointing and repeat the suicide drill.

The girls didn't complain. They were used to the drills, except today they had to do five additional suicides.

Chase came in first place most of the time, with Marley close on her heels and Tequila not far behind. Layne, Selena and Elise would sometimes come in fourth or fifth or sixth place.

"We're going to beat you one day, freshie," Layne said to Chase.

"Yes, we are," said Marley. "Maybe we should put marbles in her sneakers. That will slow you down."

Chase's mouth dropped open.

"We're just kidding," said Layne. "You're the prankster. You put whipped cream on the toilet seats."

They all laughed.

"We're going to get you one day," said Layne.

"Yeah, marbles in your sneakers. That will slow you down." Marley grinned. "Just joking, Chase."

"Oh," Chase said, laughing. "My brother says I'm gullible."

Marley and Layne exchanged a look of agreement. "You'll get there."

"Just so you know, I'm the master of faster," bragged Chase.

"I'll be right back girls," said Coach O. "When you're done with suicides, start the dribbling exercises."

The girls formed two lines about a few feet from the basket, while facing the basket, but on separate sides of the basket. Elise dribbled the ball to the basket, made a lay-up shot and then threw the ball to Ja-Nay-A in the other line. Ja-Nay-A dribbled to the basket and made a lay-up. Ja-Nay threw the ball to Tequila who dribbled to the basket, and dropped a lay-up shot. She threw the ball to Bailey with such force that the ball hit Bailey in the stomach making her fall backwards to the floor.

"Hey, Bailey's on the floor," said Layne.

Bailey stumbled to stand up, and then walked over to Tequila. "You did that on purpose," she said angrily "You threw the ball when I wasn't looking."

Tequila shrugged. "I think what you did was on purpose."

"What's your problem?" asked Bailey.

"You know."

"I can't be guilty about something I don't know about it," said Bailey.

"Yeah, right."

"He lied to me."

"You don't know who you're dealing with." Tequila laughed dramatically. "Little Miss Sunshine. You can't handle him."

With a cool, steely gaze, Bailey said. "I don't care. I don't care about him. I don't even talk to him anymore. He's a liar."

"I'm just supposed to believe you, huh?" asked Tequila.

"Believe what you want. I told you what happened."

"So it's 'my bad'," said Tequila, before getting nose-to-nose in Bailey's face. Bailey stared back without fear.

"I don't have anything to say to you," Bailey eventually said.

Tequila glared at Bailey and then walked away.

Layne went over to Bailey. "What was that about?"

"Unnecessary drama," said Bailey.

"Sounds interesting." Layne could not contain her curiosity. "Are you going to tell me or is it a secret?"

Bailey was quiet for a moment, deciding whether or not to tell Layne. She didn't confide in many girls at school. "I went out with this guy that Tequila was kind of seeing. But I didn't know. He didn't tell me or I wouldn't have gone out with him."

"Depends on the guy," said Layne. "I might."

"Doesn't matter," said Bailey shrugging. "If a guy is dating a friend or someone on the team, I don't want to date or talk to the guy."

"Like I said, it depends on who he is." Layne laughed.

Bailey and Layne were laughing together, when they heard Coach O blow her whistle and motioned for the team to gather around her. They all sat on different rows on the risers.

"What's a good quote?" asked Coach O.

Some of the players groaned.

"I know," said Rachel. "Good, better, best. Never rest. Until your good is better and your better is best."

"Very good, Rachel," said Coach O. "That's one of my favorite quotes."

"You brainwash us," said Ja-Nay-A.

"I expect that kind of comment from you," said Coach O. "I want to talk to you girls about an incident that happened at school." She paused. "It's about something a student did."

"Oh," said some of the girls.

"I already heard about it," said Ja-Nay-A.

"Me, too," said Marley.

"What are y'all talking about?" asked Chase.

"You're such a baby," said Layne.

"No, I'm not!" said Chase.

"Look, I need you all to pay attention," said Coach O, and then waited for them to look at her.

"One of the basketball players on the boys' team is in serious trouble."

"Mike-Mike," said Heaven.

"Yes," said Coach O.

"What did he do?" asked Elise.

"He texted a picture of his body part to a girl," explained Coach O.

"Yeah, he sent a picture of his penis," said Zoey.

"Yuck," said Rachel with a look of disgust.

"That is gross," said Selena.

"Nasty," said Chase.

"The girl's parents saw the picture on her phone and called the police."

"The police?" asked Heaven.

"Really?" said Zoey.

"This is a very serious," explained Coach O. "He can go to jail. He's been suspended from the team."

"But he has a scholarship," said Tequila.

"It doesn't matter. What he did was illegal," said Coach O.

"That's really messed up," said Marley.

"Real messed up," said Heaven.

"There are consequences for your actions," said Coach O. "Some consequences are very painful."

"He's dating Natalie. I don't think he meant any harm," said Heaven.

"Yeah, but why is he sending pictures of his body parts to another girl?" asked Marley. "That's what I heard."

"Doesn't matter if he sent it to his girlfriend," said Coach O. "The charges are criminal. I'm telling you this to warn you girls." Her voice turned stern. "I don't want to hear about anything like this about my team. You will be kicked off. Period."

"We would never do anything like that," said Chase.

"I hope not," said Coach O. "Receiving or sending any kind of naked pictures can get you a serious criminal charge. And, I recommend you not to text about sex either."

The girls were quiet.

"You have to be careful. We've already talked about Facebook and Twitter and Instagram. Don't post crazy pictures because it will come back to haunt you. You may think you're just having fun, but a picture with a bottle of beer in your hand looks bad."

"Yes ma'am," said Chase.

"Yes, ma'am," said Rachel.

"That's so crazy," said Ja-Nay-A. "They want to control how much fun you have."

"You're in control of what you show to the world," said Coach O.

Marley sighed. "I guess so."

"You all understand me. If you're caught with inappropriate or crazy pictures on your phone or Facebook, the same thing can happen to you."

"I can't believe it," said Elise.

"Listen to me and I'm very serious: I won't tolerate it. I can't save you from criminal consequences. I hope you carry yourselves with dignity in all situations."

The girls were quiet, looking at each other with curious and confused stares and a scramble of unshared thoughts.

No one spoke until Coach O said, "So, now that we got that out of the way, we need to talk about the next game."

"We got this coach," said Tequila. "We've been winning."

Ja-Nay-A gave Heaven a high five. "Like the song says, 'We run the court."

"Yeah, we're going to win, right girls?" said Marley.

"Cockiness is the biggest downfall of success," said Coach O.

"What's wrong with being confident?" asked Layne.

"There's a thin line between cockiness and confidence," said Coach O. "Let's not end up on the wrong side."

DARIAN-BALL-BLOG: NUMBER 9

Three more games in the regional season. Three more games left to play. Three more teams to defeat. Our record: 13 wins, 4 loses.

They are going to win.

Not hopefully.

Not maybe.

Definitely.

We gotta win the next games.

Gotta! Gotta! Gotta!

Go Riverbrook Girls!

Go Panthers!

Comments

Mindyourbiz: Win, win win!

Girl8ball: I hope they can do it! I know they can do it!

Basketqueen: Drink the alien juice. You get superpowers.

Radicaldude: I can mix them some red bull and some cough medicine they will be unstoppable. They might be high, but they will be unstoppable.

Irockball: What does Nike say: just do it!

MVP123: Even if they lose the next games, this has been their best season.

Yeahitsme: Bring it!

Fromwayback: Coach got to play the best girls. This isn't the time to be fair.

Sportsqueen: If they focus and don't make mistakes...just maybe they can do it.

Gamewatcher: I love watching Tequila. She's a beast.

Ibelieve: I'll take to the aliens. Put in a good word.

Lovehighsh: They got their paws up. Claw, scratch and win.

Superfan: These last games are going to be packed. Get there early.

Hategirlsbb: I can't believe they've won more games than they've lost.

Iknowsports: The starters got to go hard. Chase runs faster than a panther.

Justagame: I really hope they go to regionals and win. I would be happy if they just won regionals.
Irockyoudon't: Dream big, dude!
Fanfever: They run the court. Yeah!
Thinkyoucanplay: I'll admit it. I have been wrong about them. Go girls!

CHAPTER 29

CHASE

"I hate strangers coming into my house," said Kendall.
"Maybe your mom will get a job soon," said Chase.
"We don't have much time," said Kendall.
"What?"
"Mommy says we have to sell soon or we will have to move."

"Everybody keeps talking about Darian's blog," said Kendall. "She doesn't talk about the JV team, but we wonder who she is."

"We were talking about it at practice yesterday," said Chase. "Coach O asked us if someone on the team is writing the blog or telling someone what happens in practice."

"And?"

"Everyone denied it."

"No one's going to admit it to Coach O," said Kendall. "She's too intimidating."

"Coach O didn't care until the blogger started talking about going to Swanson for revenge. Everyone was so mad," said Chase. "But my mom says revenge was going to make things worse."

"Yeah, my mom says retaliating wouldn't get us anywhere," said Kendall. "Anyway, do y'all suspect someone?"

"I don't know. Rina the team manager hardly says anything. She's a math whiz but they say she can't write," said Chase.

"So what about the other team manager?"

"Poppy does her job, but she doesn't really care about the team. She doesn't care when we win or lose," said Chase. "All she cares about are boys."

"So who is it?"

"We don't know," said Chase. "Heaven and Ja-Nay-A used to get real mad about the blog, but not anymore."

"That's because she's not dissing the team anymore," said Kendall.

"Exactly," said Chase.

"It will be interesting to we find out she is," said Kendall

"Darian could be a boy," said Chase.

"That would be creepy. I think it's a girl," said Kendall. "You have a boy's name."

"True. I really want to know who she is," said Chase. "She knows a lot."

"Whoever she is. She writes some interesting things and the blog comments are funny," said Kendall.

"Yeah, we're aliens because we've been winning," said Chase.

Kendall laughed. "I always thought you were from another planet."

"Ha, ha ha!" said Chase. "So are we going to take the fliers out?"

"Yeah," said Kendall. "I'm surprised my mother hasn't figured it out. She knows how much I don't want to leave."

"She probably doesn't think you would go that far," said Chase.

"I wish I could do more," said Kendall. "Like make somebody give her a job." A sad, heavy sigh blew out of her mouth.

"I'll stand guard," Chase said to Kendall, walking down the three steps from Kendall's porch.

"Okay," Kendall said.

Chase went to the corner and watched the cars speed down the busy street, on the look-out for the black SUV that Kendall's mother drove. She also had to make sure her parents weren't driving by. Chase turned and gave Kendall the thumbs up—no familiar cars were coming. Kendall ran over to the real estate flyer box in her front yard, filled with fliers describing the house she lived in since she was five-years-old.

Kendall pulled out the sales fliers, leaving two in the box. She ran back into her house, Chase trailing behind her. Kendall put the fliers in her book bag and planned to throw them away the next day in school.

They went into the kitchen, and prepared their plates from the food in the refrigerator. They heated up the spaghetti in the microwave. They fixed a bowl of salad and baked some garlic bread.

"Has anyone looked at your house lately?" Chase asked, even though she didn't want to hear that her best friend might be moving out of the neighborhood.

"Unfortunately," Kendall said, twirling spaghetti around her fork. "Two people came this week."

"Oh," said Chase, sounding as sad as she felt. "Maybe we should write something on the fliers that would scare people off. Murder happened here in big red letters."

"I kind of like that idea," said Kendall. "If Mommy found out she would be so mad."

They ate in silence for a few minutes.

"I hate it. I hate it, hate it!" Kendall suddenly screamed. "I hate strangers coming into my house and looking around my room." The outburst brought a stream of tears down her face.

"I'm sorry," Chase said. "I would hate it too. We have to pray that your mom finds a job soon so you won't have to move."

"We don't have much time," said Kendall. "If she doesn't have the money to stop whatever it is they do to make you move out, then we will have to move."

"What!" said Chase.

"Yeah," whispered Kendall.

"We have to pray that God acts quickly," said Chase. "My mom says miracles happen every day."

Kendall closed her eyes. "Please, God help us. Help us right away. Please help my mom get a job so we don't have to move." She peeked at Chase whose eyes were closed. "Amen."

The girls were quiet and then Kendall said, "I'm getting used to my Dad not being here. I'm getting used to going back and forth between my house and his apartment." She paused. "I can't help thinking that if they hadn't divorced, then we wouldn't have to sell the house. Our lives would be the same. Normal like yours."

"My life isn't normal anymore. It has changed a lot. I have a brother that has a different mother," said Chase.

"Lots of people we know have half brothers and sisters," said Kendall.

"I know, I know," Chase agreed. "Other kids' families are all mixed up, but it's…strange for me."

"It might happen to me if my dad marries Miss Ivory and they have a baby," said Kendall. "That would be so strange."

"At least you like Miss Ivory," said Chase.

"You don't know anything about your brother. He's probably nice."

"Yeah, we're having dinner with him next week," Chase said with mixed emotions. "That's going to be awkward."

Their conversation was interrupted by the arrival of Kendall's mother, announced by the sound of the garage door opening.

"Hi Mommy," Kendall said to her mother, when she entered the kitchen from the garage door. "You look nice in your business suit."

"I just came from a job interview," explained Regina.

"You did? How did it go? Did they like you? Did you like the job? Are they going to hire you?" Kendall asked, her voice rising in excitement with each question.

"Whoa, too many questions! And I don't have answers," Regina said with a hopeful smile. "It looks good, but I won't know anything for sure until next week."

"That's enough time, right Mommy?"

"Hi, Chase," said Regina.

"Hi, Miss Regina."

Looking back at her daughter, Regina asked, "Time enough for what?"

"So we don't have to sell."

Regina's facial expression went from a ray of sunlight to a cluster of clouds. "I don't know, honey." She released a deep breath. "I know you hate when people come to look at the house, but someone's coming in a half hour."

Tears formed in Kendall's eyes. "Can I go over Chase's? I hate being here when strangers are poking around MY house."

"Yes, baby," Regina said, her hidden emotions poking through the cracks in her voice.

"Grammy is picking me up to take me to the movies. Can Kendall come with us?"

"Of course."

"Grammy is funny," said Chase. "She whispers through the whole movie, but she's not really whispering."

"Sometimes she takes us to classic movies," said Kendall. "I don't like the black and white movies."

"They're not my favorites either, but that's what Grammy likes," said Chase. "I'm used to them now."

"Chase, I heard your team is on a winning streak," said Regina.

"Oh yeah, we're taking it all the way this year, Mommy," said Kendall.

"We lost a game two weeks ago," said Chase.

"You still have way more wins than losses," said Kendall.

"Yup. We have one more regional game and we'll know how we rank," said Chase.

"I hear you're one of the star players," said Regina.

"Thank you," said Chase, blushing.

"That coach has definitely made a difference," said Regina.

"I love her. She can be a little mean and intense, but we're better players and she knows what to do…she's just awesome," gushed Chase. "I really, really admire her."

"I'm excited for you guys. We will definitely be at your next game," said Regina.

"Mommy, is Daddy still coming to get me this weekend?" asked Kendall.

"Yes," said Regina.

"Ok, but he doesn't want us to sell the house, right?"

"Kendall, stop asking so many questions. Go over Chase's house and think about something else for a while," said Regina.

"There is that cute guy in my class," said Kendall. "I stare at him the whole class. I'll think about him Mommy."

"He is fine," said Chase.

"Girls, go…leave…before I wave my magic wand and turn you back into five-year-olds who don't think boys are cute," said Regina.

DARIAN-BALL-BLOG: NUMBER 10

One more region game left to play. Our last game is against our big, bad rival—Dalford.

We beat them before.

We'll huff and puff and blow them away.

Yeah, let's beat them again.

Comments

Girl8ball: Huff and puff and blow them away. Ha! Ha! Ha! Lame! Lame! Lame!

Mindyourbiz: Dalford, don't you know by now that we are some winning witches. Coach O ain't going to let them get this far. We about to beast out.

Ibelieve: Drink the alien juice. That's where they get their superpowers

Aleyoop: If I was Dalford, I would bow out before they blown out.

Basketqueen: Let's not to be too cocky. This is the first year that we've been good.

Coolnerd: We did it before, we can do it again. There is an equation for that but I don't think anyone cares to know about the probability of repeatability.

Irockball: Look, let's just do it again. Win again.

MVP123: We are the champions. Rock on!

Yeahitsme: Oh say can you see…a Dalford victory. I can.

Fromwayback – Dalford just got a big reputation from years ago. Guess what? That was then, this is now!

Mindyourbiz: Girls be ready. All of y'all.

Sportsqueen: No bad passes.

Gamewatcher: Coach O should be given an award for taking the team this far.

Lovehighsh: Panthers are fierce and mean. That's how we got to play.

Hategirlsbb: Huff and puff and blow their school down.

Iknowsports: Riverbrook runs the court.

Justagame: It's more than a game now, it's about conquering. I see you Marley outsmarting the other team.

Irockyoudon't: I believe they can fly.

Fanfever: It's gonna be a heart stopping game. When it's over, we got to have more points on the board.

Thinkyoucanplay: We will rock them.

CHAPTER 30

SELENA

"We're going to regional playoffs so we don't need team drama," said Layne.

Ja-Nay-A said, "If we win regionals…"

"…We'll play in the sweet sixteen," said Rachel.

Everyone turned. "How long have y'all been standing there?" asked Tequila.

"Thirty seconds. I heard everything that was said," said Rachel.

"So everyone knows," said Bailey.

"No secrets around here," said Selena.

Selena heard a deep throaty voice. One second it was loud and jovial and the next second it was quiet and serious. The voice alternated between Spanish and English.

It was a voice she knew, but had not heard in several years.

Selena followed the sound of the voice, towards the back of the restaurant. She clearly heard her brother's Juan voice. She knew Juan's voice. But the other voice made her heart pound.

She screamed and ran past the bar area. She screamed: "Hector! Hector!"

A wide crooked smile spread across Hector Sanchez's face when he saw his cousin. "Selena, Selena."

Selena jumped into Hector's arms. He picked her up and she wrapped her legs around him. "I can't believe my eyes. Are you real?"

"Pinch me," he said.

She ran her fingers threw his wild black hair. She kissed him on the cheek.

"Selena you are too big for Hector to hold you like that," Juan said.

Selena balanced her legs to the floor, embarrassment on her face.

"You are not my little primo anymore," said Hector. "You used to always run and jump into my arms."

"Sí, I was a crazy little girl."

"You were crazy about me. Nothing wrong with that." Hector stared at Selena, admiration in his eyes. "You are not a little girl anymore. You are muy bonita."

"Thank you, cousin Hector." Selena shook her head. "I didn't know you were coming. We haven't seen you in a long time."

"Not since my Papá died," said Hector.

"Sí, le echo de menos," said Selena, saying that she missed her cousin in Spanish.

"Where have you been? What have you been doing?" she asked.

"You're not a little girl, but you're not a grown up either," he said, avoiding her curious gaze.

Selena looked confused.

"He doesn't want you to know," said Juan.

"I had to get away. I grew up in this restaurant," Hector said, rubbing his goatee. "Every time I saw your Papá I thought of my Papá."

"My Papá still here," said Selena. "He loves you."

"I know. I love Uncle Felipe. He was like my second papa. When my Papá died every time I saw your papa my heart would shake like there were jumping beans in my chest. Sounds crazy. I couldn't stop thinking about Papá." Hector was silent for a second. "Papá would think I was weak. He didn't like weak. But it still made me crazy."

"You always been loco, Hector," said Juan.

Hector laughed with a hacking cough, a congested sound from his chest.

"I'm happy to see you," said Selena.

"I saw your sisters and everybody big now."

"You going to stay with us?" asked Juan.

"My Mama. She cried and cried when she saw me. Made me feel so bad."

Juan lightly jabbed Hector. "She lost her husband and then she thought she lost her son."

"Don't make me feel so guilty, man. I stay here to help with restaurant."

"That will make Papá happy," said Selena.

"Selena I hear you play basketball," said Hector. "How did that happen?"

"I don't know," she shrugged. "I tried out for the team and made it."

"She's very good," said Juan. "She's the star."

Selena kissed her brother on the cheek. "Mucho gracious."

"I remember when you played softball. You were good."

Selena smiled, remembering how Hector used to teach her how to bat.

"Papá hates it," she said in a low whisper, shaking her head.

"Cause you are a girl," said Hector.

"Sí."

"We in America and girls can do different things," said Hector. "Maybe one day your Papá will understand."

Juan shook his head.

"Maybe I can help him understand," said Hector.

"Papá will change his mind," said Selena.

Hector laughed. "It will be like the old days," said Hector, "when we made tortillas together."

"Papá will be smiling from ear to ear," said Selena.

Hector walked around the restaurant. "I miss this place."

"Welcome back," said Juan. "You read to work? We have more customers now. Very busy."

"That's good." Hector tapped Selena on the shoulder.

She turned around and smiled at her cousin.

"I'm coming to your game."

"We beat them at their school, so we can beat them at our school," said Selena, before the team came out of the locker room. The girls ran into the gym—finally packed with fans to see the girls' game. It was Riverbrook's last regional game against their main rival: Dalford High.

The buzzer sounded.

Riverbrook scored the first basket. Seconds later, Dalford High scored. By the end of the first quarter, Riverbrook was in the lead. It was a close lead, and it was going to be a second-to-second game.

Every move, every play, every second counted.

Chase dribbled the ball down court and passed it to Selena and then Marley bounce passed the ball to Tequila. Bailey was positioned to make a shot.

"I'm open," said Bailey.

Tequila didn't pass the ball to Bailey; she passed the ball to Marley who repeated the play. This time when the ball was passed to Tequila, the other team stole the ball. Dalford ran down court and scored.

Coach O patted her shoulders with her hands, signaling a time-out.

The girls ran over to the bench. The players on the court sat down while the other girls stood up.

"Tequila, why aren't you passing the ball to Bailey?" asked Coach O.

"Put somebody else on the block," said Tequila.

"You don't run my plays," yelled Coach O. "Pass to Bailey."

Tequila rolled her eyes at Bailey. "She's going to miss."

"No I'm not! I make my shots!" yelled Bailey.

Tequila shot back. "Not all the time."

"No one does," said Marley.

"What's wrong with you?" asked Selena.

Timeout was over and the starters returned to the floor. Marley felt the tension between Tequila and Bailey, so she set up plays that didn't require them to pass the ball to each other. At times, they had to. When Tequila showed reluctance before passing the ball to Bailey, Coach O pulled her out and sent in Ja-Nay-A.

Riverbrook started scoring basket after basket. Dalford couldn't penetrate their defense and began to make sloppy moves. Riverbrook was relentless with an intense, unstoppable press. By half-time, Riverbrook was in the lead by twenty points.

Tequila asked Coach O if she could return to the game, promising that she would follow the rules.

So, the starters played the third quarter with the same momentum. Dalford occasionally scored, and attempted to close the gap in the score. But they were behind, so when Chase stole the ball, Riverbrook was in position to maintain a 20-point lead. Coach O sent in Ja-Nay-A, Heaven, Kaylee, Lane and Zoey until there were three minutes on the clock. The starters returned to the court and finished the game with a 35-point lead.

Fans from the stands ran down the floor to hug and congratulate the girls.

Selena's family surrounded her and screamed: You are the best in Spanish: *Tú eres el mejor*. Soon half of Riverbrook joined in screaming: *Tú eres el mejor*.

Thirty minutes later, after the excitement of winning died down, the girls went to the locker room.

As Selena opened the locker door, she heard Tequila's loud voice. "Bailey, where are you?" Tequila came around the corner near

Bailey's locker. "I was looking for you. Were you hiding from me like you were hiding Diante?"

Bailey ignored Tequila, as she flipped open her locker door.

"Diante Johnson?" asked Selena. "What does he have to do with it?"

"It's none of your business, Selena," said Tequila.

"You know there aren't many secrets on this team," said Selena.

"She's been dating him behind my back," said Tequila.

"I didn't know you were doing stuff with him," said Bailey. "He never told me he was seeing you."

"Did you ask?"

"No! I thought if he was involved with someone he wouldn't ask me to go out with him," said Bailey.

"You're stupid," said Tequila.

"Don't call me stupid," huffed Bailey. "I have a 4.0 GPA."

"Who gives a shit? You're stupid about boys. He's not going to tell you."

Hearing the conversation, Ja-Nay-A came around a row of lockers and turned down the row of lockers where the other girls were standing. "She's right," said Ja-Nay-A. "They don't always tell you about other girlfriends."

"I know," said Bailey. "I just didn't know that Diante was like that."

"You don't know him the way I do," Tequila said with a sly smile.

"If I knew, I wouldn't have gone anywhere with him," explained Bailey." I just don't do that."

"Some girls do. They will screw your ex or current boyfriend in a minute," said Ja-Nay-A.

"It depends on what he looks like," said Zoey, giggling as she joined the conversation, her bag slung over her shoulder. "I wouldn't mess with a friend's *current* boyfriend."

"So are you his girlfriend?" asked Selena, standing on top of the locker room bench. "Diane's girlfriend?"

"Hell, no," said Tequila. "I don't want to be his girlfriend, anyway."

"So why are you mad at Bailey?"

Tequila sighed. When she saw Diante at the mall, she was shocked to see him with someone else. Even though they had never discussed dating others, she was devastated to see him with another girl. "I don't know."

"You and Bailey better work it out or you won't be playing in the next game," warned Selena. "Coach will know if you're not playing like normal. She probably already knows something is wrong."

"We're going to regional playoffs and we want to win, so we don't need team drama," said Layne.

Ja-Nay-A said, "If we win regionals…"

"…We'll play in the sweet sixteen," said Rachel.

Some of the girls turned around. "How long have y'all been standing there?" asked Tequila.

"Thirty seconds. But I heard everything that was said all the way on the other side of the locker room," said Rachel.

"So everyone knows," said Bailey.

"No secrets around here," said Selena.

Wearing Hello Kitty pajama tops and bottoms, Selena quietly eased out of her bunk bed careful not to wake up her two sisters and cousins sleeping in the two bunk beds which dominated their bedroom. She walked down the hallway of the 20-year old ranch style home, passing her brothers' bedroom and the bathroom. Her parent's bedroom was the last room at the end of the hall. She headed in the other direction, but could hear her father snoring.

Selena walked down the steps to the next level, which included a small kitchen, living room and small bedroom. She went to the lower level, a basement area that had been remodeled by the previous owner to include a family room, small bedroom and bathroom.

Selena went into the small bedroom which was her mother's sewing room. There were two sewing machines, two mannequins, and a work table, along with piles of material and bolts of fabric and sewing accessories. Her mother was intently stitching a hem on a dress, when Selena kissed her on the forehead. Rosa looked up and smiled, her black hair was pulled into a tight bun.

"Hola querida mamá" Selena said.

"Usted debería ser," her mother said. "You should be sleep," she repeated in English.

"Homework."

"You work too hard like your Papá."

"Papá only wants me to work in store."

"I know bebé."

"You work hard too, Mamá."

"I have five dresses to make for quinceaneras," said Rosa, referring to dresses for Sweet 15 parties.

"Oh Mamá, I want to help."

"No, no," she said, shaking her head. "You are too busy."

"Bella's sweet 15 is not until summer."

Selena sat on the corner of the sofa and opened her text book. This was her favorite time to study. The house was quiet and she enjoyed being in the presence of her mother.

"Are you glad Hector is here to help Papá?" asked Selena.

Rosa didn't answer, but continued hemming the wide bottom of the dress.

"I was happy to see Hector," said Selena.

Rosa shook her head. "Hector bad news."

"Papa needs his help."

"He gone long time," said Rosa.

"He missed his Papá. I miss Uncle Roberto."

"Gone long time."

"Mamá, why you upset?"

"Hector used to be a good boy. But he got dark side. Roberto knew. He tried to hide it."

"I don't understand," Selena said, flipping through an American History book.

"Diablo in him," her mother said.

"Mamá! That's bad to say. Papá trusts him."

"Papá don't see bad when it's familia."

"Mamá, Hector is good."

"I not trust him," She muttered, "Juan knows."

"Knows what, Mamá?"

"Nada, Selena," said Rosa in firm voice. "Do homework, so you can go to bed."

"Si, Mama!"

"You like that baseball boy?"

Selena answered with an ear-to-ear smile. Her mother looked up and saw her daughter smiling. It made Rosa feel happy and sad. Happy that her daughter found a boy that made her smile and sad because she did not know if the boy would one day make her cry.

"No entregas tu corazón," her mother said. "Don't give your heart away. He got to work for your heart."

DARIAN-BALL-BLOG: NUMBER 11

We beat Dalford! It was out last regular season game. That means the regular season is over. Our record 15 wins, 5 losses. We rank third in our region. An epic season. Last year it was 2 wins, 18 losses. Not bad for our team of winners-in-disguise. Coach O had a strategy for winning and it worked! She is a super coach.

Now the regional play-offs begin.

Ranking third means we don't play the best teams in the first round. So, we can start strong and go all the way!

Here's the weird thing: there is a possibility that we might play Swanson in the regional games. I despise them. The thought makes we want to vomit. It depends on how all the teams play and rank in the other regions' brackets. Swanson is second in their region. Let's just hope they get knocked out by another team because if we play them again it will be UGLY. If we HAVE to play them, we HAVE to beat them again. I don't think they should be allowed to play at all because of their nasty racist behavior at our game. But that's just my opinion.

Here's my prediction: We are going to win regionals!

Comments

Girl8ball: We won! We won! Dalford lost and they were so mad!

Aleyoop: I applaud you girls. You never give up even when the other team is winning.

Basket queen: They play like a real team.

Cool nerd: I like one of the starters a lot. The one with the really pretty blue eyes. Can we go out?

Trackball: We are winners!

MVP123: Gonna be regional champs!

Yeahitsme: Dalford is probably still in shock! The whole region is in shock!

Fromwayback: Our glory days are back. My mom said we were good when she went to Riverbrook 15 years ago. We're good again! Selena keep shooting those threes.

Mindyourbiz: Yay Riverbrook.

Sportsqueen: Coach O is the best coach in the world.
Fanstalker: The BEST of the BEST!
Lovehighsh: Why not? We've gotten this far.
Gamewatcher: Here's the question: can we win regionals?
Hategirlsbb: We got to keep huffing and puffing.
Iknowsports: Regionals ain't going to be easy. We'll be playing teams we've never played before.
Madplayer: True. But we're on a winning streak.
Justagame: Coach O probably got a plan for regionals.
Irockyoudon't: They gotta keep flying.
Fanfever: They gotta fly higher to win regionals.
Thinkyoucanplay: The sky's the limit, right? We're going to regionals stronger and better than ever!
Mindyourbiz: Beating Dalford, you know what that means, right? We are a force to be reckoned with.

CHAPTER 31

MARLEY

"I wish you understood that I love basketball."

"I do understand," said Franchesca. "I just want you to have a specific goal."

"Mother, I'm thinking about being a nurse."

"What? A nurse! You can be a doctor, a brain surgeon, a neurologist!"

Marley heard her name over the classroom's intercom. Her brows drawn together, she checked her watch. It was 11:15 AM and class had just started. She had no idea why she was being called to the front office. It didn't matter. She was happy to get out of advanced geometry.

While walking towards to the front office, she decided that Coach Olivia must have called a special meeting for the team.

Marley walked in the front office and heard her name as soon as she stepped inside. "Hello there, Marley," said Mrs. Connor, an older, gray-haired woman who had worked at the school for over thirty years.

Marley smiled at Mrs. Connor who frequently wore different colored wigs. She had on a multi-colored wig. Mrs. Connor was known for wearing different colors and styles of wigs, with dramatic-looking make-up. Students often peeked in the office just to see what kind of wig Mrs. Connor had on. Marley wanted to laugh when she saw the pink and blonde curly wig on Mrs. Connor's head, but glanced away before giggles erupted from her mouth.

"Hi, Mrs. Connor," Marley said.

"I've got my fingers crossed that you girls keep winning," said Mrs. Connor. "I'm so proud of y'all!"

"Thanks! Coach O is working us hard," said Marley.

"I hear she's a pistol," said Mrs. Connor. "But we like her," she said with a loud snorting laugh.

"I like her too," said Marley.

"Your mother is here," said Mrs. Connor.

Marley's smile instantly disappeared. As soon as she saw her mother, she wanted to leave. Her mother was on the phone and didn't immediately see Marley. If Mrs. O'Connor were not there, Marley would have slipped out the room.

Franchesca turned around and saw Marley. She ended her call, and hugged Marley. "Hi, sweetie."

"Hi, Mother," she blandly said.

"I came to take you to lunch," said Franchesca. "You've been avoiding me, young lady."

You don't answer the phone. You don't care about anything I have to say. You disagree with everything I do.

Marley kept those thoughts to herself. She would prefer to go back to geometry class, but she didn't want to make a scene. So she played the good daughter in front of the office staff.

"Where do you want to go?" Marley asked.

"I don't care for Olive Garden, but it's nearby. We can beat the lunch crowd."

"Okay," said Marley, following a few steps behind her mother.

Franchesca's phone rang; and she answered: "Franchesca Dubois."

Marley could tell from her mother's tone that it was a business call.

She saw Quinton in the front entrance hall. She waved at him, hoping he stayed where he was.

But he walked over to her.

"Marley, are you ditching school?" Quinton asked, noticing her standing by the front exit door. He was dressed in jeans and a polo shirt.

Marley rolled her eyes. "My mom is taking me to lunch."

Quinton glanced at Franchesca who was dressed in an expensive, tailored brown suit and high-heeled brown shoes. He could tell the shoes were some type of designer shoes.

"That's your mom?" he asked, giving Franchesca an admiring look from head-to-toe, the way he would look at a girl his own age. "Now I know why you are so fine."

Marley gave him a bored look. "I'm prettier."

Quinton laughed. "Okay, okay. Funny and smart."

"You forgot pretty," she said.

"Beautiful, gorgeous, hot," he said.

Marley smiled.

"You heard about Mike-Mike?" Quinton asked.

"He messed up big time," said Marley.

"I'm not going out like that," said Quinton. "I'm about to sign with a D1 school."

"Cool."

"I heard y'all kicking ass in regionals. Killing teams you've never played before. You coming up big time."

Marley laughed. "Y'all ain't the only one with skills."

"Marley," interrupted Franchesca. "Let's go."

"See ya Quinton," said Marley.

She followed her mother out of the school's main entrance door.

Parked right in front of the school, Marley just had to walk a few steps to the car. She got inside the rented Lincoln Cadillac.

"Nice car," she said to her mother.

"It will do," said Franchesca, pressing the radio buttons until she found a station that played music from the 80's and 90's. "I'll change it if you want to hear that demeaning rap music," said Franchesca.

Marley shrugged. "I don't care."

"I thought we should spend some time together. We haven't seen each other since you came to Chicago and ran away with your father's help."

"Mother, I didn't run away. I left you a note and I told you how I felt about missing that game."

"You'll learn that other things in life are more important, but I'm not going to argue about that today. It's over. All is forgiven."

"So you forgive me for being a team player," Marley said sarcastically.

"Let's move on, Marley."

"How's Aunt Martina?"

"She's great. She's finally dating someone."

"Really? Does she like him?" Marley asked with genuine interest.

"I think so."

"How's Aunt Laurel and the kids?"

"Oh, those kids are out of control. I don't know how she does it. I keep thinking that one day she's going to wake up from this mommy madness and get a real life."

"Mother, she likes her life. She's happy. Why don't you see that?"

Pulling into a parking spot at Olive Garden, Franchesca stopped to look at Marley. "That's an interesting observation."

"Whatever that means," said Marley.

"I mean you might be right and I never considered that possibility."

"Why? Because you don't like being a mother," she said with unconcealed bitterness.

"I love you Marley. I know you don't think I do, but I do from the bottom of my heart."

Franchesca's phone rang, but she pushed the ignore button. "I wasn't ready to be a mom. I was so…determined and driven to have a career that it just seemed more natural than being a mother." Franchesca stopped, her face full of self-reflection. "Your father, as weird as it may sound, was always better at it than me."

"That's very weird, Mother. It's against human nature. Sort of why women have ovaries and a womb and men donate the sperm."

Franchesca looked at her daughter as if she had just met her for the first time. She was smart, but also had an unexpected insight about people. "True."

"You agree with me?"

"I don't know how to change certain things about myself. Somehow I'm missing the mom gene," Franchesca admitted. "I will never tell Cooper, but he's a good father. A better father than I'm a mother."

Marley didn't know what to say. Her mother's moments of honesty were rare.

"I don't agree with sports, but…"

"Mother, I love basketball. Daddy isn't making me do it," explained Marley.

"Maybe not, but…"

"There's no but," said Marley. "It's something I want to do. I love the game."

"I understand that, but I just want you to have a specific goal."

Marley didn't say anything for a few minutes. She scrolled through her text messages. An impish grin on her face, she said, "Mother, I'm thinking about being a nurse."

"A nurse! Are you crazy? You can be a doctor, president of a company, a brain surgeon, a neurologist!"

"Grandma is a nurse."

"Women of her generation didn't have opportunities to be a doctor or lawyer."

"There's nothing wrong with being a nurse," said Marley.

Franchesca's cell phone rang. She looked at the name.

"I have to figure out how to make things better between us," admitted Franchesca. "I don't want to talk about this nursing thing. Not now. But I need to take this call. Go in and get us a table, okay sweetie."

"Sure, Mother," said Marley, and then opened the car door.

Marley went inside the restaurant. She was greeted by a hostess who escorted her to a booth. While waiting for her mother to come inside the restaurant, she sent Egypt a text: *I told F I want to be a nurse.*

Seconds later, Egypt shot back a text: *You would hate it. Why would you tell her a lie?*

Marley felt a twinge of guilt. She sent Egypt another text: *Why would she believe me?*

DARIAN-BALL-BLOG: NUMBER 12

We won! We won! We won the regional championships! I can't freaking believe Riverbrook won the FREAKING CHAMPIONSHIP FOR OUR REGION! I take that back. We had a winning record for our regional season: 15 wins, 5 losses. And now we won the regional playoffs. We came in third place during the season, but going to regionals was like a new beginning. We played teams we never played before, some teams I never heard of. Some of the games were edge-of-your-seat close. Winning by 1 or 2 points. But we won.

Press Start and we did!

Press Win and we won!

Because we have a team of kick-ass players.

Go Riverbrook girls' varsity team. Coach O you are freaking awesome! You rock basketball!

We are getting closer to the super serious competition level.

Fiercer competition.

Unbelievable tension.

Heart-pounding exciting.

Let's do this, girls! We are on the prowl. Panthers get your paws up!

Winning Sweet 16 is next. Press Play!

We are taking over.

Comments

Mindyourbiz: I can freaking believe it!

Aleyoop: You go girls. You were serious and intense in every game. That's how you won.

Basketqueen: You are real basketball players. What a difference a year and a coach can make.

Coolnerd: I don't think Ms. Blue eyes will go out with me. I'm scared to ask her out or any girl. I just dream about her.

Irockball: The team is unbelievable!

Ibelieve: I believe the girls have super alien powers.

MVP123: I predicted it: We are regional champs!

Fromwayback: The games were so exciting. I couldn't wait to watch them play.

Mindyourbiz: It's the alien Gatorade.

Fanfever: So we ain't gonna lose. We gonna take on sweet 16 like gangsters.

Thinkyoucanplay: That's the only way we gonna win.

Sportsqueen: I'll say it again: Coach O is the best coach in the world.

Hategirlsbb: We got to keep huffing and puffing.

Madplayer: Our girls are rough and tough. Marley Marley, Marley, we need your super basketball IQ.

Iknowsports: The competition is gonna be rougher and tougher.

Gamewatcher: Winning regionals means we are going to sweet 16. Cool. So so cool.

Lovehighsh: It was scary going to regionals and we won. So let's not be afraid to go sweet 16 and expect to win!

Justagame: I wonder if Coach O really thought the team was gonna go this far.

Irockyoudon't: Coach hates to lose. You can tell.

CHAPTER 32

BAILEY

"I was sitting here," Bailey said.

"You must be that girl who goes to that racially diverse school," said a girl that Bailey didn't know.

Bailey ignored the girl's rude comment. "Well, this is my seat."

"Not anymore," the girl said. "I'm here now."

"She's sitting with me," said Matt, nodding at Bailey.

"She's not one of us, Matt," said Kristin. "You can do better."

At the popular coffee shop, where River's band Levity was going to perform, Bailey stood by a table near the front of the stage. She had arrived early, watching the band set-up and checking out the people coming in.

When Matt came through the doors, she said, "Hello, Matt." An ear-to-ear grin was plastered on Bailey's face.

"Oh my God, you finally smiled at me. A smile from your eyes," he said, wearing blue jeans and a tee-shirt with Levity scrawled across the front. Bailey wore the same tee-shirt. "Does that mean I'm forgiven?" asked Matt.

"It just means I won't call you Matt the ass … unless you revert back to your evil ways," said Bailey.

"Matt the ass is gone," Matthew declared.

"Thanks for coming to my games," said Bailey. "Some of the regional games were far away."

"You played like I've never seen you play before."

"Thanks!"

"I won't miss your sweet 16 games," said Matt. "Watching you play turns me on."

Bailey's cheeks turned red. She smiled and looked away.

"You're sweet." He kissed her on the forehead.

Other people started coming into the coffee shop which also was a small venue for local and up-and-coming artists. Most of the kids in the coffee shop were from River's private school. Bailey knew some of the kids; they frequently came to Levity's shows. Bailey spoke to several kids and was surprised when some of them congratulated her team for winning the regional basketball championship. Matt introduced her to other kids, and they exchanged conversation about the growing popularity of Levity.

"More and more people are coming to see them," said Matthew. "Radical, man."

"Radical," said Bailey.

"What are you doing for spring break?" Matthew asked.

Bailey gave him a blank look. "Spring break?"

"Yeah, the week when you don't have school."

"I know what it is. Why are you asking me about it?"

"Because a group of my friends are going on a cruise," said Matthew. "I was wondering if you want to go."

Bailey looked surprised.

Matthew didn't understand her response. "Somehow I've insulted you?"

"No. I just wasn't expecting an invitation like that from you."

"Oh. ... as you will discover, that is, if you let me, I'm not such a bad guy," Matt said.

She shrugged. "River told me about the cruise. She's been bugging me from the beginning."

"You should come with us. You'll have fun."

"I usually go on spring break with my family, my little brother and sister." She considered her options. "My mom did say I could go someplace different since this is my senior year."

"So…come with us," Matt urged.

"I don't know yet. Why do you want me to go?"

"I like you Bailey. I wouldn't have texted you like a maniac if I didn't like you."

"Why me?"

"I've been in private school my whole life with all these self-absorbed, spoiled brats. You're different," Matthew said, staring intently at Bailey. "You're normal and you're so damn beautiful."

Bailey blushed. "Thank you."

"So will you go?"

"I'll think about it," she said, blazing Matthew with a bright smile.

Bailey turned toward the stage, and waved at River who was adjusting her microphone. Out of the corner of her eye, Bailey spotted River's father coming into the coffee house. "Oh no, I don't believe it," she said.

"What?" asked Matt.

"River's dad is here," said Bailey. "He hates, hates, hates her singing."

"I know. She told me he's like Mr. Anti-Everything."

Bailey went over to the small stage, and got River's attention. "Your dad is here."

"No freaking way," River said, looking around until she saw him. Seeing him intensified her normal pre-performance butterflies: ten thousand butterflies fluttered around her stomach instead of one thousand butterflies.

"I wanted you to know before you started singing and saw him."

"I might have peed in my pants," said River.

"You better perform your butt off, dude," said Bailey, giving her best friend a tight hug. "Good luck!"

Bailey headed over to River's father, a tall, gray-haired man who looked older than his age. "Hello, Mr. Banks."

"Well, hello Bailey," Mr. Banks said. "I'm not surprised to see you here."

Bailey nervously laughed. "I think she's got an awesome voice."

"I thought she was a shower singer," he said, noticing the crowded room. "I didn't expect to see a crowd."

"The crowd keeps growing every time."

"Spoken like a true friend and fan," he said.

"I'll see you later, Mr. Banks. Enjoy the show." On impulse, Bailey added, "Rock on, dude!"

Mr. Banks laughed. "You've grown up or you've been around my wonderfully precocious daughter too much."

Bailey went back to her table, and saw an unfamiliar blonde girl sitting in her chair. Without exchanging a word, she decided the girl was arrogant and snobby.

"I was sitting here," Bailey said to the blonde girl sitting rather closely to Matt.

"You must be Bailey," she said. "You go to that racially diverse school."

Bailey ignored the girl's rude comment. "Well, this is my seat," she said bluntly. "You need to get up."

Offended, the girl looked at Matt for support.

"She's sitting with me," said Matt, nodding at Bailey.

"Well, now she's not," the girl insisted.

"What's your problem, Kristin?" asked Matt. "You're being ridiculously rude."

"She's not one of us, Matt," said Kristin. "You can do better."

"Get out of my seat," said Bailey, with a sudden burst of I'm-not-letting-people-push-me-around. "Go back to your microcosm of a world."

"So you can use big words. Who cares? My father is a millionaire and I will be going to Yale just like he did."

"Did I ask about your unimpressive, out-of-touch-with-reality world?"

"Kristin, leave now. I'm serious," said Matt. Kristen glared at Bailey, and then reluctantly stood up. "Her stepfather is black. Her little brother and sister are black."

"Yes they are and that's none of your freaking business," said Bailey.

"Go away, Kristin," said Matt. She opened her mouth, but Matt escorted her away from the table before she could say something else offensive.

From a distance, Bailey watched them talking. Angry words were spilling out of their mouths. Matt walked away while Kristin was talking, her face full of fury. Matt came back over to Bailey's table.

"She's psycho. What's wrong with her?" asked Bailey.

Matt ran his fingers through his black hair. "She's my old girlfriend," he admitted. "I'm sorry for what she said to you. I'm sorry for how she treated you."

"You have interesting taste," Bailey said, her brows furrowed together. Somehow she couldn't help wondering if acted like an asshole with all girls.

The lights grew dark and the sound of River's clear pitch voice spun her mind to the present: her best friend was singing and she sounded like a real star.

Levity's performance at the coffee house was a shorter set than they played at their friend's huge basement. The reaction was still the same—a volcanic eruption of applause and praise.

For just a second, Bailey made eye contact with her best friend. She saw a different girl: River was in her 'performing' zone. River had transformed into her alter-ego: rock star diva.

DARIAN-BALL-BLOG: NUMBER 13

Yes, I started out as a hater. I said bad things about the team. Now, I'll EAT my words and VOMIT them. Our team isn't a group of losers... they are winners. Riverbrook has a winning record for the regular season. We won regionals and now we are two games deep in the sweet 16. How sweet is that? Sweet as a box of frosted flakes. That is my favorite cereal—a mouthful of sugar. Crunch, crunch! Yum, yum! Delicious!

Coach O may be demanding, but she is calculating and she knows what the hell she is doing. Go Riverbrook girls' varsity team! We are feeling you starters: Chase, Marley, Selena, Bailey, and Tequila. You rock basketball! I can't leave out the rest of our beasting team: Layne, Zoey, Elise, Heaven, Ja-Nay-A, Rachel, and Kaylee because when you go in—you go all the way in.

Go Riverbrook. Panthers on the prowl.

Comments

Girl8ball: To win they have to make the impossible possible. It's possible. Other teams have won the sweet 16 when no one believed they can do it. We can do it girls!

Gamewatcher: It's possible because we won regionals and now we are playing the best 16 teams in the state. We ARE one of the best. We BELONG!

Ibelieve: They have to get to that alien state of mind.

Mindyourbiz: 14 games to win.

Aleyhoop: You go girls. 14 games to go.

Basketqueen: You are real basketball players. What a difference a year and a coach can make. I refused to believe that Bailey can play. I was wrong. She is like a pittbull.

Coolnerd: In my dreams, Ms. Blue eyes loves me.

Irockball: The team is unbelievable!

Hategirlsbb: We got to keep huffing and puffing.

Iknowsports: The competition is so intense.

MVP123: One minute we're winning, one minute we're losing.

Yeahitsme: It's like being on a roller coaster ride.

Fromwayback: I thought regional games were exciting. Sweet 16 is a different level of excitement.

Mindyourbiz: Fear and tears.

Sportsqueen: What's sweet about sweet 16? It's 16 games of blood and sweat. If you make it through.

CHAPTER 33

TEQUILA

"So she wouldn't have sex with you?" asked Tequila.
"We never got that far. She's different."
What does that mean?"
"There was no ...connection between me and Bailey."
"Too bad for you."

Tevon sprinkled water over Tequila's face. In a deep sleep, Tequila opened her eyes while wiping water droplets from her face. Seeing Tevon's face just inches away, she bolted straight up. "Stop!" she screamed. "What are you doing?"

"Waking you up!" yelled Tevon.

"Why are you bothering me?"

Tevon laughed. "You look so funny. I wish I had a camera. You looked crazy."

"You know better than waking me up like that," said Tequila. "What's wrong with you? I was taking a nap." She closed her eyes and whispered as calmly as she could. "I'm tired Tevon. Coach O has been working us like dogs."

"Bark, bark," growled Tevon. "Bark, bark."

Tequila flopped back down on the bed and pulled the blankets over her head. "Go away."

"You have company."

From under the blankets, Tequila said, "Stop lying."

"I'm not a liar," said Tevon, offended. "Diante is REALLY here."

She wiggled her head from under the blanket. Tequila stared at her little brother. His big brown eyes were sincere and serious. "He's really here?"

"Yes," he whispered.

"OMG!" she screamed.

"He's waiting for you."

She washed her hands over her face. "Tell him to wait until I'm ready."

"Okay."

Tevon stared at his sister, trying to find the nerve to tell her something else.

"Go now," Tequila gruffly said.

"You kinda need to fix your face. Make-up is smeared all over your face. You always look really pretty when he sees you."

Tequila's eyes turned into narrow slits. "Get out of here!"

Tevon ran out of Tequila's room as she jumped out of the bed in her panties and bra. She went into the bathroom and washed her face, brushed her teeth and did a quick wash-up. She slathered on the Victoria Secret lotion she got from Coach O for Christmas. Her eyes scanned the closet, where most of her clothes were piled on the floor. She picked up a Riverbrook tee-shirt, sniffed it and slipped it over head. She put on a pair of short-shorts. She applied shiny red gloss across her lips, and brushed her in hair in short, quick strokes.

Tequila took a deep breath and went down the hallway. She had been so focused on the upcoming games that she had very little time to think about Diante.

When she thought about him, she had one thought: He had never taken her on a date. Not a real date.

She walked into the small living room. "What are you doing here?" she asked, without a trace of warmth.

"I came to play video games with Tevon," he said, hoping that she would laugh. Her response was a cold stare, so he said, "I came to see you, Quila. You won't answer my calls or texts."

Tequila sat on the opposite end of the worn, plaid sofa, obviously trying not to sit near Diante. "That should tell you something," she said dryly. "That I don't want to talk to you. That I have nothing to say."

Sitting on the other end of sofa, he said, "It told me that I need to talk to you in person. Face-to-face."

"Why?" asked Tequila.

"So we know what's up."

"You're dating Bailey."

"I went out with Bailey… but we didn't hit it off."

"That's not my problem," said Tequila.

"No, but I still want to talk to you. I want you to know that nothing's happening between us."

"Okay."

"It never felt right."

"Why? …Because she's white."

Diante stared at Tequila, wondering how to explain something that he really didn't understand. Diante shrugged. "I don't know why. We just didn't hit it off."

"So…she wouldn't have sex with you?"

"That's not what I meant. We never got that far anyway. She's the type of girl that you got to work for it."

"What am I?" Tequila asked, hurt and offended. "What does that mean?"

"There was no… connection with Bailey. She's different. She was cool to talk to in school. But that was it. It was awkward when we were out together. We didn't have anything to talk about it. I think she felt the same way."

"Boo-hoo." She sat back on the sofa, and pretended not to care. "Too bad for you."

Diante stared at her, struggling for the right words to say.

"Now that I'm up, I gotta study," said Tequila.

"There was a connection between us, right?"

"Believe what you want to believe."

"There was a vibe with us from the start. You know what I'm talking about. That's why you wouldn't sit next to me on the bus. You avoided me at first." Diante crept closer to Tequila on the sofa.

"I should have kept ignoring you."

"But you didn't."

"So! I didn't! But that was then." She paused before saying, "Now I know who you really are."

"There was something that drew us together, devil red. You know it."

"Don't call me that!"

"Okay." Changing the subject, he said, "Your team is beasting. Y'all won the regional play offs."

"I was there," she said sarcastically.

"It's because of you, Miss WNBA."

"A year ago, I would have said that. But we are a team. I know what it means to be on a real team," said Tequila. With a don't-doubt-me look, she said, "I do my thing on the court. I'm going to get my points."

"That's the cocky Tequila I know."

She laughed.

"At last," said Diante.

"What?"

"You laughed."

"You said something funny."

"Can we start over again? Can I take you out?"

Tequila laughed again. It was more a snicker than a laugh.

"What's so funny?" Diante stared into Tequila's brown eyes. "I'm serious."

"You've never taken me out."

"I'm not all bad. I have helped you with your homework. I have a good GPA."

She ignored what he said. "It doesn't matter. We're not dating. We're just friends." She then repeated what he said when she saw him at the mall with Bailey. "That's what's up, right?"

"I didn't mean to hurt your feelings," Diante said with sincerity in his voice.

"You should have thought about that before you started getting with other girls."

"I didn't think about what I was doing. I didn't think about how I feel about you."

"Why would you go out with someone on my team? That was foul."

"That's why I'm here…to apologize."

"Yeah, right," she said.

"It's not like I tried to date your sister or best friend."

"Diante!"

"Okay. I shouldn't have dated your teammate. I apologize."

"I don't want your apology, Diante. You only want one thing."

"I like being with you. I'm serious. I really mean it."

Suddenly, Tevon came in the room and kicked Diante in the shin.

"Ouch! Hey man, that hurt." Frowning, Diante rubbed his shin.

"Don't be mean to my sister," said Tevon, hands clenched together, holding his fists in front of his chest in a fighting position.

"Little man. I'm not going to fight you," said Diante.

"You scared?" asked Tevon.

"Yeah, I'm real scared," said Diante.

"Tevon, go back to your room," said Tequila. "I got this."

"I'll hurt him if he tries to hurt you, Quila." Tevon gave Diante an evil stare. "You've been warned."

When Tevon left, Tequila giggled. Diante started laughing.

"You'd be in big trouble if my family from New York were here."

"I better watch my back."

An awkward silence weighed heavily between them.

"Seriously, I want to see you again, Devil Red."

"I said don't call me that," Tequila said without any hint of joking.

"What if we went to the movies?"

"Oh really," she said skeptically.

"Oh really," he said seriously. "How about Friday?"

"Practice."

"Saturday?"

"Game."

"I'll be there," said Diante. "What about after the game?"

"I'm busy."

"If you win, will you go out with me?"

"We are going to win!"

"So, will you go out with me after you… win?"

Tequila stared at the boy who made her heart beat faster than tires spinning one hundred miles an hour on the highway.

"Maybe yes. Maybe no."

DARIAN-BALL-BLOG: NUMBER 14

Sweet 16 is still going on. The competition is fierce. Some of the games are won at the buzzer. Overtime. And double overtime. Sometimes I feel like I'm going to have a heart attack—a real heart attack and I'm only a teen-ager. Some of the teams are scary, when all the players are 6 feet and taller. We are playing against the best-of-the-best—teams that win year after year. We are truly the underdog—but underdogs do win.

We are almost there. Closer and closer to victory. Girls, we are rooting for you!!!

So, I'm going to say it again: Keep on winning!

Comments

Girl8ball: Unfortunately, they can't lose one game.
Mindyourbiz: Hey, they haven't lost yet. Don't jinx them idiot.
Aleyhoop: Don't stop winning girls. Get it! Get it!
Basketqueen: They got basketball swag.
Coolnerd: Those eyes watch everything that's happening on the floor.
MVP123: We are on a roll!
Yeahitsme: No one would have predicted that our loser team is now a winning team at Sweet 16.
Fromwayback: Sports is so unpredictable. Never know what's gonna happen until the buzzer ends the game.
Mindyourbiz: That's why it's exciting. Don't sleep on Heaven and Ja-Nay-A.
Sportsqueen: Yeah, we in to win it. We are!
Gamewatcher: We watch. We scream and shout. The team is scoring and scoring. Keep it up!
Lovehighsh: They are actually going to the next round in Sweet 16. This is a story of the underdog becoming the top dog.
Iknowsports: I'm so nervous watching their games I could pee on myself.
Madplayer: I can't stay mad at Coach O forever. She didn't pick me for the team. But, we are rocking the basketball world.
Justagame: Winning is about playing with spirit and guts. Our girls are bleeding sweat, tears and determination.

Irockyoudon't: They got it. They are so close to winning the 16.
Fanfever: They are unbelievable. Coach O is a miracle worker.
Thinkyoucanplay: They are playing against teams that are beasts. And they have become beasts.
Hategirlsbb: Every time they get on that floor, they prove themselves. Don't doubt them.

CHAPTER 34

CHASE

"We thought this would be a good time to get to know your brother," said Michael.

"We get it, Dad," said Evan.

"This is weird," said Blake.

"From Mars weird," Chase said.

It was their favorite Japanese restaurant: Benihana's. The Anderson family went there for special events—birthdays, anniversaries, and celebrations. Every since they were little kids, Evan, Chase and Blake enjoyed watching the Japanese chefs throwing knifes, the fire flames shooting in the air, and the slicing, dicing and flipping of food while preparing hibachi-style meals. The show was fun. The food was excellent.

But someone was new to this family outing—their brother from another mother.

His presence was uncomfortable.

Their conversation was awkward.

Chase kept glancing at her watch, anxiously waiting for when they would leave. While eating dinner and talking during the meal, she learned more about her brother than she wanted to know. She concluded that he was thuggish and wild. She could tell from her father's conversation that he wanted to save him. Her father was involved in different church ministries, but it's different if the person you are helping is family—a stranger from your family.

"We thought this would be a good time to get to know your brother," said Michael, with eyes on Chase, Evan and Blake.

"We get it Dad," said Evan.

"This is weird," said Blake.

"From Mars weird," Chase said. "I feel like I should be in a movie or something."

"Yeah, a reality show. Where are the cameras?" said Blake, looking around the restaurant. "What would we call it: The Anderson Family's New Addition?"

"Enough," scolded Shellie.

"We'd be a boring reality show," said Blake. "Unless Chase starts having sex and I get a boob job and turn gay and Evan becomes a male escort and Jamal gets arrested for…"

"Blake, have you lost your mind? Don't you say anything like that again!" reprimanded Michael.

"Yes, sir," said Blake.

"This is our new real life," said Evan. "We have to adjust."

"Yeah, sure," said Chase.

"I know you guys didn't expect me. I just blow into your world from nowhere." Jamal was uncomfortable and it showed on his face. "I ain't expect my mom to get so sick." He looked away, not making eye contact with anyone. "She's real sick."

"We know," Shellie said in a comforting voice. "But you will get through this. We've been praying for her. We're here to help."

"Thank you," Jamal said. "That means a lot."

"We are a church going family," said Michael.

The Japanese waitress brought everyone the same desert: orange sherbet.

Jamal tasted the desert. "This is good," he said.

"We always order the same thing at this restaurant," Blake said.

"Sometimes Mommy will get apple pie," said Chase. "What's your favorite dessert?"

"Peach cobbler," said Jamal. "My Mama loves to bake cakes. She makes birthday cakes for parties."

"She must be pretty good," commented Shellie.

"She is. Don't tell anybody, but I got baking skills too," admitted Jamal. "I help her bake. Sometimes she has to make a lot of cakes at one time."

"That's nice of you," Shellie said.

"I might be a chef," Jamal said.

"That's a good profession," said Michael.

"I'm just thinking about it," said Jamal.

"I'm going to be an actress or lawyer," said Blake. "I'm kind of …dramatic."

"I can tell, Blake. You are a drama queen," said Jamal. "No offense."

"Whatever," Blake said.

"What about you Evan? You probably going to be a doctor or something big time."

"Nope. I want to be an engineer or go into computers," said Evan. "My dad is a computer geek, but so am I… as much as I don't like to say it."

"And you little baller," Jamal turned to Chase. "You want to play for the WNBA, right?" Jamal asked.

Chase shrugged "I don't know about that. They don't make a lot of money, but it would be fun."

"In one of the regional games, Chase scored the winning basket," said Michael.

"Seriously?" Jamal said.

"Yeah," Chase said. "The team picked me up and carried me around. It was mad crazy."

"I bet you loved it," Jamal said.

"She did," said Shellie. "Every minute of it."

"We're playing in the sweet 16 now," said Chase. "I have a game in two days."

"Intense," said Jamal. "Y'all can't lose."

"Believe me, I know. The whole team knows," said Chase. "We're trying not to go bananas thinking about it."

"That's hard," said Jamal. "Good luck!"

"Thanks!" said Chase.

"They could possibly go to state," said Michael.

"I get chills just thinking about," Chase said grinning.

"You got it going on little sis," Jamal said.

Chase flashed Jamal a look that said I'm-not-your-sister.

Noticing the hostile look on Chase's face, Michael said, "We encourage our kids to pursue their dreams. They should have a plan to get there and a back-up plan."

"I plan to be a star one day. I'm going to win American Idol," said Blake. "Or The Voice."

"She's only told us a thousand times," said Shellie, shaking her head.

"I'm not the only artist in the family," said Blake. "Chase can paint like crazy and Evan loves to draw."

"Y'all some talented people," said Jamal. "I don't know if I'm going to fit in."

An awkward silence followed.

"Sometimes it takes a while to find out what you like and what you're good at," Michael said. "You have plenty of time."

"I like to draw too," Jamal said. "I started doodling and then I started drawing a super hero. I don't what I'm going to name him, but he's got weird super powers. Kind of like Hancock. The movie with…"

"Will Smith," said Chase.

"Weird powers," said Evan, laughing. "That sounds cool."

"I do sketches of my mom. When she's sick and when she's feeling good," Jamal said, unable to hid the sadness in his face. "I want to remember everything about her."

Chase looked at Jamal with empathy—for the first time. "I painted my Grammy."

"For real?" asked Jamal.

"Yes. She wanted me to make her look like she's forty, but she's eighty."

Jamal chuckled. "That's funny. Maybe me and you got something in common. Evan and Blake, we might find out that we like some of the same things."

"Probably," said Shellie.

"A big maybe," said Blake, skepticism in her voice.

"So *you're* the one I have to work hard to win over," said Jamal.

"My Daddy says no man should get me or Chase easy," said Blake. "I think that includes you, bro, bro."

Everyone laughed.

Chase watched Blake performing on the stage of her middle school auditorium. She was playing the lead actress in a former-Broadway musical play: *Once On this Island*. TiMoune was the main character's name, a peasant, so Blake was dressed in peasant garb. In the story, TiMoune saved the life of the rich boy who lived on the other side of the island. He was in a car accident, and she nursed him back to health and fell in love with him. When he recovered from the car accident, he returned to his wealthy plantation. TiMoune was heart-broken and left her village to look for him.

From watching Blake rehearse and practice singing around the house, Chase knew every song in the play. So did everyone in the family. At home, Chase would sing along with Blake. Other times, she would scream: *Blake stop singing*. Eventually, Chase grew to like the songs.

When Chase was in the sixth grade, she had a very small part in the classic play *Annie*. Chase recited her lines with no emotion. Singing and acting didn't interest her. One year Blake convinced Chase to perform a Destiny's Child song with her at the school's talent show.

A proud smile was on Chase's face as she watched Blake dancing and singing like a professional. She had to admit that her little sister was super talented. Blake sang her last song and then the rest of the cast came on stage for the finale song. Chase noticed tears drop from her mother's and grandmother's eyes. They cried every time they saw the play—even at rehearsals.

Evan stood in the back of the theatre with a camera, filming the play. He loved recording events and often filmed her basketball games.

The cast bowed as the crowd stood, clapping and cheering.

"She was so good," said Grammy.

"Yes ma'am," said Chase.

"I don't know where she got it from," said Grammy. "Nobody in my family can sing or dance."

"A mystery gene," said Chase.

"Look at those people crowding around her," said Grammy. "She's going get a big head."

Chase chuckled. "She already got a big head."

Grammy leaned over and whispered in Chase's ear. "Yeah, well, don't tell her that I think she already has a super gigantic head."

"Ooooh, Grammy."

"I'm speaking the truth."

Their conversation was interrupted by people they knew from their church who came to watch Blake's performance.

"Tell Blake she's going to be a star one day."

"You must be proud of your grandchildren."

"That girl can really sing."

"What a talented family."

"We're going to see her on TV one day."

"And you, Chase, your team is in the sweet 16. That's a big accomplishment for a team that was at the bottom last year," said Mr. Winters, her eighth-grade math chapter.

"I'm excited and nervous," said Chase.

"I've been watching you play. Some of the teachers came across the street to watch the high school games."

Chase grinned. "Sometimes I can hear Ms. Lloyd screaming my name."

They both laughed.

Her grandmother chimed in. "I wondered who was louder than me at the games."

"We're very proud of Chase and we're so happy that the school is doing better in sports. That's good for our reputation," said Mr. Winters.

Blake ran over to them and hugged Chase from behind. "I was so good. I killed every scene," she bragged. "I'm going to take over. Look out Beyonce and Britney and Rhianna because I'm coming and taking your spotlight."

"Chase is definitely not modest," remarked Mr. Winters.

"If I'm good, I'm good. What's wrong with me saying it?" bragged Blake.

"You are very good, sis. Amazing!" said Chase.

"You rule the basketball court, but I rule the stage," Blake giggled.

CHAPTER 35

SELENA

"*My friends will think I'm loco now,*" Miguel said.
"*They're teasing you?*"
"*They can't believe I'm getting so serious about one girl.*"
"*Who?*" she asked.
"*You silly.*"

Felipe Sanchez stared at his daughter Selena like he was watching a stranger. It was his first time seeing Selena play basketball and he couldn't believe his eyes.

His daughter…his little girl had an unfamiliar expression on her face. She was dribbling the ball up and down the court like she knew what she was doing.

Selena had control.

She passed the ball to her teammates.

Selena had power.

She ran down court to block a shot.

Selena had speed.

She dropped the ball in the net.

Selena scored at least 12 points.

His daughter was unbelievable. She was an amazing athlete. His daughter. He was in awe and had to admit that she was an excellent player. His little chicka.

His daughter was playing almost like a boy.

Felipe was a quiet man. He didn't scream and shout like the rest of his family. He intently watched her every move, his heart beating wildly, his eyes glowing with pride.

When Riverbrook won the game, Riverbrook fans went wild. "Sweet 16! Sweet 16! Sweet 16!"

Felipe didn't understand what they were saying or why. He was just proud that his daughter's team won. "Go Riverbrook! Mi chica bonita!"

Selena was so thrilled to see her father, that she quickly patted the other team's hands, and said "Good game." She practically ran across the gym and greeted her father who had made his way to the gym floor from the top of the risers.

"I'm so happy you came to my game," gushed Selena. "Mucho gracious."

"Proud of you mi niña," her father said, calling her his little girl.

"Sí, it makes me happy to see you here Papá," she said. "Muy feliz."

"You are good…que son Buenos," he said. "I had to see with my own eyes."

"It's real Papá," she said. "I'm real."

"I don't know what this all means. Women should get married and have babies," her father said. "But America is different. Some things good and some not so good."

"Sí, Papá."

"I try to understand…comprender algunas," he said. He slapped his head with a weather-wrinkled hand. "I still think Mexico."

"I know," she said. "I'm very happy now."

Selena wrapped her arms around her father and expressed her deep feelings of love for him. "Te quiero a padre."

Smiling, he said, "Mi chica bonita."

"Gracias padre," Selena said.

"We're close to winning sweet 16. Papá, this is big…muy importante grande."

Felipe smiled at his daughter. "That make you happy?"

"Si!"

"So it make me happy," her father said.

Selena nodded her head.

"Got to go back to work, now." Felipe pinched the bridge of his nose between his thumb and forefinger. "Can't leave Paco there long. He loco."

"Tres loco," said Selena, giggling.

Sitting in Miguel's car in the student parking lot, Selena watched him open the glove compartment and remove a small gift bag. The parking lot was mostly empty.

"Something special for you," said Miguel.

Selena flashed a curious look at Miguel and then took the gift bag. Her heart was pounding.

"Open it," he said.

She removed the tissue paper and howled with pleasure when she saw a necklace with two connecting hearts dangling from the chain.

"For me?"

"Of course," he said.

"Wow," she gushed. "Gracias!"

"My friends will think I'm loco now," he said.

"Loco cause of me?"

"They can't believe I'm getting so serious about one girl."

"Who?" she asked.

"You silly."

She laughed. "Just making sure."

"I think about you day and night," he said.

"I think about you night and day," she said.

"You're my girl now, right?" Miguel traced his finger from the top of Selena's forehead to her lips.

It was a slow evening at Los Mexicana. Not many customers came into the restaurant, but Juan knew that the next few days were going to be busy with the shopping center's food tasting event. He was in the back of the kitchen surveying the food supplies to determine if more food would be needed.

"Always slow at beginning of week," said Hector, standing near the sink.

"Sometimes we run specials on Monday and then we get a crowd," said Juan.

In the front entrance of the restaurant, two Hispanic men came into the restaurant.

"Would you like a table?" asked Bella, working as the hostess for the evening.

"We are looking for Hector," said the taller man, with several tattoos.

Bella didn't answer. She turned around and immediately went into the back kitchen, pushing through two sets of doors, separating the kitchen from the customer area.

"Hector there are two men looking for you," said Bella. "They look very mean."

"There are mean people in this world," said Hector, as he moved to the customer area of the restaurant.

Observing the nervous look on Bella's face, Juan followed Hector.

"I can handle this," said Hector.

"I'm coming," Juan firmly said.

Hector greeted one of the men with a warm smile and a handshake. "Hola Raul." He was tall and thin, with a thin, narrow face.

Hector nodded his head at the other man who was shorter and wider. They were both in their mid 20's, and neither looked like they worked normal jobs.

"You've been a hard man to find," said Raul, with a suspicious glare.

Hector shrugged. "I wasn't hiding. I'm with my family."

"Families don't need to know certain things," Raul said, in a flat, serious tone.

"What does that mean?" Juan asked.

Raul ignored him.

"Hector different man now. I lost my mind when I lost my Papa," explained Hector.

"That doesn't change things for us," said Raul.

"Those days are over," said Hector. He looked at Juan and then met Raul's intent gaze. "This is not the place," Hecor said, his voice cold and harsh. The tone was unfamiliar to Juan.

Raul nodded his head. "Familia."

Selena sauntered into the restaurant. Tired from practice, she managed to smile at her cousin. "Hola Hector."

"Hola." In a curt tone, he said, "Go in the back with your sister."

Selena looked at Juan and saw the suspicious expression on her brother's face as he looked at the two men. She stared at the two men who were talking to Hector. She didn't trust them for some reason.

"Pretty girl," said Raul.

Selena refused to make eye contact with either men. She heard her brother tell the men not to look at his sisters. "Never look at my sisters," said Juan, in an edgy-dangerous sounding voice. Selena couldn't remember ever hearing Juan sound like that.

"This is America." Raul laughed. "Supposed to be a free country."

The shorter, wider man spoke volumes with a venomous stare directed at Hector and Juan.

Juan looked at Selena. "Go in the back." Without another word, she hurried into the back room.

"It's best that you leave," Juan strongly said. "No food or drinks."

"Hector knows that's not why we are here."

"I will call you Raul and we meet in two days, but don't come back here," said Hector. "Not around my familia."

The men moved toward the exit door. Raul turned and smiled. "They are pretty."

Juan followed the men out the restaurant. "Don't come back here!"

Juan watched the two men get into a fairly new truck with large silver-rimmed wheels.

Before going back into the restaurant, Juan cornered Hector. "I don't know where you've been or what you've been doing. But I won't have that around here. You are not going to put us in danger." Juan grabbed his cousin's shoulder. "So if you need to leave again, then leave."

"Uncle Felipe is happy that I'm here," said Hector. "It makes him think of happy times."

"Those men are not about happy times," said Juan. "I'm not stupid, Hector. Don't put us in danger."

"I would never do that," said Hector. "I love my familia."

"You need to stay away," said Juan.

CHAPTER 36

MARLEY

Marley speared a scallop with a fork and put it inside her mouth. She coughed, and the scallop plopped out of her mouth. "OMG."

"What's wrong?" asked Quinton.

"OMG!"

"Marley, what's wrong?"

"OMG!" *she whimpered.*

"Your food is ready," the waitress said to Marley and Quinton. She placed a plate filled with sizzling scallops and shrimp, a loaded baked potato and broccoli in front of Marley. The waitress presented Quinton with a steak, baked potato, and salad.

"Thank you," Marley said.

"Are you finished with the oysters?" the waitress asked.

"Yes, they were delicious."

"Did you enjoy them?" the waitress said to Quinton.

"No."

When the waitress left with the plate of oysters, Marley said. "I can't believe you wouldn't even taste one."

"They look like they were looking at me," said Quinton. He made circles with his fingers around his eyes.

"You're so silly," said Marley, laughing. "You don't know what you're missing. I wouldn't eat them until one day my Daddy made me. I took one bite and spit it out my mouth."

"In a restaurant?" asked Quinton.

"Yes, and Daddy looked like he was going to strangle me, but he just laughed."

"That's it?"

"No, he made me eat another one."

Quinton laughed.

"He said I spit it out before I really let my taste buds enjoy the taste. Something crazy like that."

"What did you do?"

"He showed me how to eat them properly. I did exactly what he did and they were good. I was shocked. So I ate another one."

"Are you really that easy?" Quinton grinned. "I just show you what I want... like where I want you to kiss me and you'll..."

Marley glared at him. "No, I'm not easy like that!"

Quinton cut a piece of steak. "What a surprise," he said sarcastically.

She gave him an impish grin and took a bite of her food. "This is a nice change. It's been crazy. School. Practice. Homework. Games. Sweet 16 madness."

"Yeah, it's been crazy for me. Plus, I have to take care of my little sister," said Quinton. "Sometimes I pick her up from daycare and cook dinner for my little sister and brother."

Marley twisted her eyebrows into a knot. "Really? Somehow I can't imagine you doing that."

"I gotta help my moms," said Quinton, taking a bite of his steak.

"I hear you."

"I could live with my dad, but I didn't want to leave my mother by herself with my little sister and brother," said Quinton. "The man she married was crazy and I'm glad she didn't stay married to him long."

"That's very chivalrous of you," said Marley.

Quinton laughed. "You're so damn smart sometimes."

"It just comes out. I'm not trying to show off or anything."

"I know," he said. "If you don't mind me asking, how come you live with your dad? You're a girl and your mom doesn't seem like she struggles with money like my mom."

"My mom is a career fanatic. She's a lawyer. That's what she loves to do more than anything on this planet." She gazed at him with a distant stare. "It makes me so mad and hurts my feelings that her career is more important than me."

"Sorry Marley," said Quinton in a tender voice.

They ate in silence for a few minutes.

"Our coach can't believe the girls' team is in the sweet 16. He's excited for y'all but at the same time, he gets on us harder. He says we'll look bad if y'all have a better record."

"We don't. You lost only one game the whole season."

"We do what we do," bragged Quinton.

Marley speared a scallop with a fork and put it inside her mouth. She coughed, and the scallop plopped out of her mouth. "OMG!"

"What's wrong?" asked Quinton.

"OMG!"

"Marley, what's wrong?"

"OMG!" she whimpered.

"Marley, what's wrong?!

"My daddy is over there," she whispered.

"Oh shit!" Quinton said, trying to soften his deep voice. "I thought you said he was going to a meeting."

"That's what I thought."

"And you said he doesn't like this restaurant," said Quinton. "What's he doing here?"

"I don't know. Maybe he didn't see us. Let's get the check and get out of here."

Within a few minutes, the waitress came to their table. "Can I get you something else?"

"We need the check. We gotta go. Sorry for being so rude," Marley said, digging through her purse for her wallet.

"Marley, I got this. I brought you here. I'm a gentleman." He handed the waitress a credit card.

"Please hurry," she said to the waitress.

One minute passed.

Two minutes passed.

"Relax, Marley," said Quinton.

Three minutes passed.

Four minutes passed.

Marley had her eyes closed.

"Are you praying?" asked Quinton.

"No…I probably should. If I don't see him, then maybe he won't see me."

Neither spoke for a few minutes.

"See who?"

Marley didn't open her eyes. That voice. She knew it was her father.

"Hello Quinton," Cooper said. "How are you?"

"I'm fine, Mr. Woods. How are you?"

"It's a beautiful night," said Cooper, sliding in the booth beside Marley.

"Yes it is," said Quinton.

"Did you enjoy your meal?"

"Yes, sir," said Quinton.

"Did you Marley?" asked Cooper.

"Yes," she whispered, her eyes still closed.

"Marley, open your eyes," he said. "You're not five."

"I'm sorry, Daddy. I should have asked you. I was just tired of…"

"Stop," he commanded.

Marley opened her eyes. She expected to see her father's dark anger look. He was slightly smiling.

"You're not mad?"

"Of course I am. You disobeyed me," said Cooper.

"I apologize on Marley's behalf," said Quinton. "I convinced her to go to dinner with me."

"How chivalrous of you," said Cooper.

Marley and Quinton smirked at each other and laughed.

"What's funny?" Cooper asked.

"Marley said I was…chivalrous…when I told her I take care of my little sister and brother. She just said it ten or fifteen minutes ago."

"Daddy, how did you find me?"

"I have my ways."

"E told you," said Marley.

"No. I don't have to ask her. I just check…GPS."

Marley's eyes widened. "On my phone?"

"Yes, baby."

"Oh…I forgot about that," Marley admitted.

"I didn't," said Cooper.

"I'm so sorry, Daddy," she said in a soft, baby-sounding voice.

"Are you sorry that you had dinner with Quinton?"

"No. I mean yes. I mean no." Marley dropped her head low, and placed both hands on her forehead. "I'm sorry that I didn't stay home like you told me to. So it's like a double sorry."

Cooper stared at Marley and Quinton for several minutes, knowing that they were nervous and uncertain of his actions. "You get a buy," said Cooper.

"Like in basketball?" asked Marley.

"Yes. You have a game in a few days and then there's the championship game. I don't want to add more pressure and stress on you."

Marley wanted to smile in relief, but was hesitant. She didn't want to do anything to change his mind. "Daddy, are you going to punish me later?"

"No."

"Really?"

"Marley, do I lie to you?"

"No you don't." Confused, but relieved, she sweetly said, "Thank you, Daddy."

"You're welcome." Cooper stared at Quinton, and then at Marley. "I'm taking you home. You know that, right?"

"But," Marley said.

"I understand, Mr. Cooper," said Quinton. "I appreciate your… chivalry."

"That's a stretch," said Cooper, before laughing.

"Daddy…"

"We had our little funny moment," said Cooper. "Marley has to concentrate on basketball. Just like you. She doesn't have time to see you or talk to you. Do you understand me, Quinton?"

"Yes, sir. I do. Sweet 16 is her number one priority."

"You're a quick learner," said Cooper.

The ride home from the restaurant was uncomfortable. Cooper did not say a word. Marley was too afraid to speak. She felt uncertain and suspicious. He was being nice right now, but she expected him to punish her when they got home.

She sent Egypt a text: *Daddy found out that I went to dinner with Q. He didn't ground me or act crazy. What's wrong with him?*

Egypt sent back a text: *Be afraid. Very afraid.*

Marley sent another text: *Thanks, E for making me feel worse.*

"So, what did Egypt say?" asked Cooper, breaking the silence.

"Are you psychic Daddy?"

"I know you, baby girl."

"I love you Daddy."

"Me too," said Cooper.

"With all my heart," said Marley. "You're the best Daddy in the world."

"No more sucking up," said Cooper. "When you get home, shoot 200 baskets."

"For real, Daddy?" complained Marley. "It's late and I went to practice earlier."

"I can always come up with something more interesting," said Cooper.

"Okay," Marley reluctantly said. "Two hundred baskets."

CHAPTER 37

BAILEY

"What if a date someone who is black, white, Indian or whatever?" Bailey asked.

"Are you trying to tell me something?" her father asked.

"I don't know if I will marry a white guy. I might marry someone from a different race."

"I already know that," said Scott.

"Oh." She paused. "Why did you cheat on Mommy?"

"Daddy, museums are creepy," Bailey said, after her father paid admission into the Atlanta's High Museum of Art. "There are dead things in here."

"I think you will like this exhibit," Scott said.

"Paintings and artistic stuff aren't my thing. You've been trying to get me to like art since I was a little girl," said Bailey. "I still don't like it."

"You think I don't know you don't like this place. I want you to know about different things," explained Scott. "You might date someone who's an artist. Or discover some type of art that you like."

"Right Daddy," she said cynically. "I would much rather go to the Lady Gaga concert."

Scott put his hands around his throat as if choking himself. "Gag me!"

THE STARTERS

"I've hinted every way I can. After a while, I figured you were just ignoring me."

"No, just prolonging the agony." They rounded the corner to enter a room with paintings featuring 19th and 20th century American artists. Scott pulled out two tickets and playfully flashed them in Bailey's face.

Bailey screamed. "Lady Gaga tickets! Thank you, Daddy. I love you Daddy."

They caught the curious stares of snobby art browsers, but Bailey didn't care that she was not adhering to proper museum behavior, her loud voice echoing in the massive, high-ceilinged room. With a heartfelt hug, she said, "Thank you, Daddy!"

"You're welcome."

She stared at a grotesque picture of a naked woman whose stomach was layered with rolls of fat when she suddenly remembered basketball. "Oh my God!" she gasped. "I hope the concert isn't on the day of a game."

"I already checked. That's why I ended up paying so much money," said Scott. "I purchased the tickets last minute, but the seats are close to the stage."

"Yes! Yes!" Bailey screamed for a second before an unwelcome thought entered her mind. "Are …we going together?" she asked, hoping the answer was no. Her father went to all types of concerts, even the ones most parents wouldn't be caught dead watching.

"We're going to see Jimmy Buffet together," said Scott. He kept up with latest songs, but was a dedicated Jimmy Buffet groupie (known as parrot heads). Scott had attended over thirty Jimmy Buffet concerts all over the world. Bailey realized that a lot of people didn't know who Jimmy Buffet was and her father didn't care.

"Jimmy Buffet," she said in a quiet voice that loudly communicated disappointment.

"Got you," he said, joking. "River's going with you and I checked her schedule."

"You are the awesomest Dad on earth," she said with the excitement of a seven-year-old girl buying a new doll at an American Girl store. "You think of everything."

"I didn't bring you here just to torture you. I thought you might like the exhibit of Annie Leibovitz' photographs."

The name sounded familiar, but Bailey wasn't sure who he was talking about. "Is she the old lady who takes the weird photos? Even some nude pics."

He shook his head. "She took the photos of Miley Cirus that caused a bunch of controversy."

"Yeah, Miley was naked. Everyone was talking about it for a while, but no one cares anymore," said Bailey.

"Fame. You're hot one day and then you're not," said Scott.

"Whatever her name is, she's kind of old to be a photographer, but she still rocks."

Scott laughed. "I think you'll like her photos. Very artsy and creative."

"We'll see if I agree," she said.

As they made their way through the different exhibits, they also discussed colleges. During her junior year, Scott had taken Bailey on several college visits.

"Any new college offers?" he asked.

"Yes," she said.

He looked at her. "Well…"

"UGA, Vanderbilt, Georgetown and … Spelman."

"Spelman? Really?" he asked. "The black college?"

"Just kidding, Daddy."

He gave his daughter an assessing stare. "Okay."

"That would be interesting experience, but I think my life has been… culturally interesting enough."

"You're telling me. Your mother just didn't think when she got married again," he abruptly said. Noticing the frown on Bailey's face, he said, "I shouldn't have said that. They do seem happy together."

"They are. It took some adjusting, but I love my new family." A warm smile graced her face.

Scott stared at Bailey. "I'm glad you do. That's very important to me. And I do adore your little brother and sister."

They walked in silence, observing the exhibits.

"Are you supposed to think with your heart Daddy?" she suddenly asked. "Mom got married because she fell in love with Robert."

"I know that. But love is an unpredictable emotion. Let your mind be your guide and then carefully follow your heart," Scott said thoughtfully. "I think this world wouldn't be so full of broken marriages if people listened to their minds and not just their hearts. That's advice I hope you remember."

"Does that advice apply to anyone I date? No matter if he's black or white or Indian or Brazilian or Asian or whatever?" she asked.

Bailey thought about her two dates with Diante. They'd been to the movies twice, but she felt awkward when she was alone with him and she didn't know why. They communicated better by text or on Facebook. In school, they talked and laughed when they saw each other. But on their dates, face-to-face, she didn't know what to say. Neither did he.

So, when Tequila confronted them at the mall, it was easy to delete Diante's number from her cell phone. Bailey was offended that he would date her and her teammate at the same time. She was mad at herself that she didn't know that he was a man-whore.

Bailey was confused that her total dislike of Matt the ass was changing. It was as if a dimmer light switch was turning in her head—the dark light was getting brighter and brighter. Matt was changing from an asshole into a nice guy. She hoped what she was seeing was the real Matthew Charles.

"Are you trying to tell me something?" her father slowly asked.

"I don't know if I will marry someone white. I don't want you to be shocked if I marry someone from a different race." She stared at her father, searching his face for an answer that wouldn't disappoint her.

Scott fluffed some of the strands of Bailey's blonde hair, looking intently into her blue eyes. "I already know that."

"Oh," she said.

"The advice is the same. I can't guarantee you won't ever have a broken heart. That's something a parent can't guarantee and we certainly would if we could." He sighed. "I hope you make wise choices when it comes to relationships."

They walked around the museum, quietly observing the various art displays.

Bailey broke the silence. "Why did you cheat on Mommy?"

Scott looked into his daughter's curious eyes. "She told you?"

"No, I heard her talking to Grandma. She tried to convince Mommy not to get a divorce."

"I know. Your grandmother likes me a lot. A least she used to."

They walked in silence, before Bailey spoke. "You didn't answer my question."

"No answer will make sense to you at your age. I was wrong. I made a mistake. I think your mother would have forgiven me if I did it only once."

"You cheated more than one time?" she asked, surprise in her voice. She couldn't hide the disapproval on her face.

"I'm not proud of it. I was young and dumb."

Bailey saw sadness and regret in his eyes. "Daddy, I'm kind of shocked. And you really weren't that young."

"You can be old and stupid," admitted Scott. "I was careless and reckless. I've paid dearly for it."

"What?" Bailey asked, a bit confused.

"I lost my family. Don't you think that broke my heart?"

Bailey was quiet a moment, reflecting on the dark period in their lives. "Yes," she simply said.

They walked in silence.

"Why haven't you found anybody yet?" she asked. "Surely you're not still in love with Mommy."

"I don't know. I haven't met anybody special. My mind is probably protecting my heart a little too much," he said. "What about you?"

"What do you mean?"

"Do you like any boy in particular? Like that Matthew kid?"

"Kind of." She shrugged her shoulders. "Actually I'm scared to like him."

"Are you still a ...."

"A what?"

"You know," Scott said, unable to say the word 'virgin.' He paused. "Are you still innocent?"

"What if you don't like the answer?" she challenged.

"Good point," he said. "I withdraw the question."

She strolled to another picture and glanced at an abstract painting. A deliberate sweet smile traveled across her lips. "One hundred percent ...innocent."

"Oh," he said, with a look of relief.

"For now," she added, with raised eyebrows.

Scott hugged his only daughter. "I love you now and whenever it does happen, just let it be with someone special." He shook his head. "I really don't even want to think about that."

"River says I can't graduate high school a virgin."

"River!" He shook his head. "I love River, but she has her own crazy rules," Scott said, chuckling. "You have to make your own rules."

Bailey laughed. "Never thought about it like that. I can make *my* rules."

"Let's go see those Annie Leibovitz photos so I can get you back home," said Scott. "Big game in two days," said Scott.

"I can't believe we're still in the sweet 16," said Bailey. "I thought we would have lost a game by now."

"Win or go home."

"Thanks for the pressure, Daddy."

"Anytime," said Scott.

CHAPTER 38

TEQUILA

"This was your idea," teased Tequila.
"I thought you'd like do something sporty," said Diante.
"I do. And I'm having fun."
"You just like kicking my ass."

Tequila watched Diante carefully position the putt-putt golf ball near the putting spot. He looked at the angle of the shot, picked up the ball and placed it in a different spot. The ball had to travel down a hill, through a castle and over a bridge. The miniature golf course theme was based on fairy tales.

When Diante parked in the golf course's parking lot, Tequila burst into laughter. Diante had never been to the golf course and didn't expect the fairy tale theme.

Diante pretended that he didn't care and registered them to play the entire course. As they walked to the first course, Diante almost knocked over one of the seven dwarfs and screamed when he ran into a fire-breathing dragon that released gushes of hot air. Cool, cocky Diante was not himself.

They had played twelve holes and Tequila was winning. Diante pretended not to care, but he was not very convincing. He was competitive and despised losing.

"This was your idea," teased Tequila.

"I thought you'd like to do something sporty."
"I do. And I'm having fun."
"You just like kicking my ass."
"Yep," she said.
"This is just one game," said Diante. "One game doesn't make you the queen of putt-putt."
"It does in my book," said Tequila, watching Diante's wild swing at the ball. He hit the ball, but it flew high in the sky and they couldn't see where it landed.

At the next hole, Diante gently tapped the miniature golf club against the ball, but it just rolled a few inches away. So, he swung at the ball and it flew in the air, landing somewhere far away on the putt-putt course. It was the last hole.

"You lost," said Tequila, grinning.

Diante threw his golf club on the ground. "You win."

"Sore loser," she said.

After golfing, they went inside and ate pizza and drank Slurpees. They played games in the video arcade.

"I better get home," said Tequila, looking at her watch.

"Are you going to turn into a pumpkin or something?"

"Funny," said Tequila.

"You are funny," said Diante. "Fun to be with."

"Surprised?"

"Let's just say that we're learning more about each other," said Diante.

"Without being awkward," said Tequila.

"Yeah."

"If we make it to the final four my family is coming down," said Tequila.

"That's cool," said Diante. Looking at his watch, he said, "You're right. I gotta get you home."

Thirty minutes later, he turned into Tequila's apartment complex at 11:45 PM.

Diante walked Tequila to her apartment door. He bent over to kiss her, but leaned back when he heard the squeak of the door knob turning.

"Hello Diante," said Tequila's mother. Her voice was stern, eyes unfriendly.

"Hello, Miss Rashonda," said Diante, without looking into her face.

"Call me Rashonda. I'm too young to be called Miss."

"Yes ma'am."

"And don't you dare call me ma'am," said Rashonda. "I'm not an old lady."

"Yes ma'am. I mean okay. I'm just trying to be respectful. What should I call you?"

She looked at him like he was crazy or retarded. "Rashonda, boy! That is my name."

"Okay…Hello Rashonda."

"Well it's about time you took my daughter on a real date."

"We kind of planned…"

"Don't bullshit me," scolded Rashonda.

"I won't."

"I hope you both had a good time." She looked at her daughter.

"I had fun," said Tequila.

Diante flashed a charming grin. "Yes we did. We really did!"

"Why you acting surprised? My Quila is a pretty girl and got some spunk." Rashonda laughed. "Pretty, spunky and funny."

"Yes she is," Diante said.

"You treat my daughter right, you hear me boy. I'm not stupid. Treat her with respect."

'Yes um…Rashonda," Diante said, feeling more and more uncomfortable. "I mean, yes I will."

He smiled at Tequila. "Goodnight. I'll see you at the game."

"Goodnight," Tequila said as she went inside her apartment. Rashonda closed the door and suspiciously looked at her daughter.

"He's just a friend?" asked Rashonda.

Tequila shrugged. "Mom, I don't have time to get serious about a boy."

"And I ain't got time for no babies," warned Rashonda. "You can't fool me. Protect yourself."

"I'm gonna to the WBNA," Tequila confidentially said.

"Keep your eyes on the prize," said Rashonda.

"I am," she said, even though basketball was the last thing on her mind at the moment.

Sitting in Lindsey's large eat-in kitchen with the sun shining through the windows, Tequila was working on algebra homework. She was focused on a linear algebra equation, ignoring the grinding sound from the blender that Lindsey was struggling to operate. The annoying sound stopped, and Tequila looked up to see Lindsey pouring pineapple juice inside the blender.

"What the hell are you making?" asked Tequila.

"I don't know. I call it the luscious Lindsey smoothie," she said, pressing another button that crunched the ice, fruit and juice. "It never tastes exactly the same. Have some."

"I'll pass," said Tequila.

"It's mysterious, but always tastes good," promised Lindsey. She took out two large glasses and poured the concoction inside the glasses. She sipped from one of the glasses and pronounced, "Delicious."

"So you say," said Tequila.

"Try it and see." Lindsey placed a glass in front of Tequila. "You'll like it."

With a skeptical look on her face, Tequila brought the glass to her lips.

"Drink it, girl," insisted Lindsey.

Tequila reluctantly sipped the drink, nodded her head and then took several more sips. "Mmm. It is good."

"I told you!"

"The luscious Lindsey smoothie," said Tequila.

"Yep."

"You should sell it. Make some money from it."

"Yeah, right," scoffed Lindsey. "Got any questions about algebra?"

"I got this," Tequila said confidently. "Check my answers, but I'm pretty sure I got 'em right."

"I'm such a good tutor." Lindsey laughed. "Your cockiness is rubbing off on me."

"I know what I know," said Tequila. "I'm a F-ing good basketball player."

"You're about to win sweet 16. You should be happy," said Lindsey.

"About what?"

"Look how far you've come. Three months ago, you were almost failing your classes and you hated Coach O."

"I hated her when she benched me for my grades, but now I feel better about myself. I'm not as dumb as I thought I was," said Tequila. "I wouldn't be here if it wasn't for Coach O and …you."

"Yeah, you better recognize," said Lindsey.

"Yes, thanks to my cocky tutor," said Tequila. "I have a brain that works."

They sipped on the smoothies.

"Have you heard about Coach Hilton?" asked Lindsey.

"No. What about him?"

"He's being investigated for having sex with one of his students."

"Stop playing!" shrieked Tequila. "Who?"

"I don't know. They're trying to keep it under wraps until after the championship games," said Lindsey.

"But he's the track coach," said Tequila. "He's got nothing to do with basketball."

"They don't want anything in the paper that will be make Riverbrook look bad," said Lindsey. "It's supposed to be a rumor, but my mom thinks it's true and the police are quietly investigating."

"That won't look good."

"You didn't hear it from me."

"Not a word."

"Is your family still coming in from New York?"

"If we make it to the final four." A happy grin crawled across Tequila's face. "I won't believe it until I see them."

"The team is going all the way so your family will be here," said Lindsey. "You know I'll be at the games. All the cheerleaders are going to be there."

"Blondie, you my girl," said Tequila.

"Let me check your homework," Lindsey said, just as Tequila's phone rang.

She saw Diante's name and answered. "What's up?"

"Thinking about you," Diante said. "Where are you?"

"At my tutor's house doing homework," she said.

"Why don't you come by before you go home?"

Tequila was quiet, pondering his request.

"It'll be a pre-victory celebration."

"I'll hit you back and let you know," she said, before ending the call. Tequila noticed the I-know-who-that-was look on Lindsey's face.

"Diante! Diante! Diante!" mocked Lindsey dramatically.

"Thinking about him makes me crazy," said Tequila.

"That's a problem," said Lindsey.

"Maybe," Tequila said with a casual shrug.

"You know how Diante is…a boy that likes a lot of girls."

"You calling him a man-whore?"

Lindsey shrugged. "Just don't want to see you hurt."

"I didn't know I liked him so much until I saw him with Bailey," explained Tequila.

"I get you," said Lindsey.

"We went on a real date. He took me to a miniature golf place. We really had fun together. I know what you're thinking," said Tequila. "But maybe—just maybe—I could be the special one."

"I hope you're right. Let me tell you a story: I had my heart broken before." Lindsey's face turned gloomy. "I thought he was totally in love with me, but then I found out he was screwing a cheerleader." She sipped her smoothie. "Never trust a cheerleader."

"Girl, you are a cheerleader."

"So I know what I'm talking about," she said.

"Are you over him?" Tequila asked.

"I don't think about him until I see him in school," said Lindsey. "Last year, we had three classes together, so I made sure this year not to be in any of his classes. I see him at lunch sometimes. But now I'm with Dillon."

"Are you serious about Dillon?"

"Yeah, for now," said Lindsey.

"So… you know how I feel," said Tequila.

"Yeah, love can be a bitch," said Lindsey.

"I didn't say I was in love with him," said Tequila.

"Neither did I."

CHAPTER 39

CHASE

"*Someone put an offer on our house,*" *Kendall said, tears in her eyes.*
"*Oh my God,*" *said Chase. "I'm so sorry."*
"*I don't want to move,*" *sobbed Kendall.*
"*You're not going to move,*" *predicted Chase. "Something good is going to happen."*

Chase was going through her locker at school, when she heard Kendall's heels clicking against the floor. She looked up and saw Kendall approaching her. From the look on Kendall's face, she knew something was wrong.

"What happened?" Chase asked.

"Someone's buying our house," Kendall said, with a sudden burst of tears rolling down her face.

"Oh no!" said Chase. "I'm so sorry." She wrapped her friend in a warm, comforting embrace.

"I don't want to move," sobbed Kendall.

"You're not going to move," predicted Chase. "Something's going to happen. Your mom is going to get a job. Something will happen so you won't have to move. Just wait and see." She added. "It's going to work out."

As the words came from her mouth, Chase didn't know where the words came from. But then she remembered: it was the something her mother would say, something she'd heard her mother often say to relatives and friends: *it's going to work out.*

Chase hoped she was right. She didn't understand anything about buying houses. She wanted to make Kendall feel better. Chase had to believe that something miraculous would happen to keep her best friend living next door.

She wondered if her new brother was going to end up living with them. His mother was doing fine now, but it was unspoken and understood that her condition might get worse. Chase felt sad and guilty at the same time, because she did not want him to move in with them—no matter what happened.

"You're right," said Kendall. "We have to pray for a miracle."

"Nothing is going to stop us from being friends, right?"

"Right!"

"No matter where you move," said Chase. "We'll talk all the time and hang out."

"Okay."

"You're not going to move to another state, are you?"

"No, Mom wants to stay around here so I can finish high school at Riverbrook."

"So we will still hang out," Chase said.

Kendall closed her locker door. "Are you going to practice?"

"Coach O gave us the night off. She's already worked us to death. She wants us to rest and get mentally ready."

"Cool."

"I gotta practice my shots when I get home."

"Chase, didn't you just say that Coach O gave you the night off," said Kendall.

"Yes."

"So eat, do your homework and go to bed. I know you are tired."

"Gotta do my 100 shots or I won't be able to sleep."

"You're crazy," said Kendall.

Chase shrugged. "Maybe *poco oco* as Selena would say."

"What does that mean?" asked Kendall

"Just a little loco."

"No you are grande loco."

The sound of rippling thunder.

Lightening streaks in the sky.

Rain drops furiously hitting the roof.

That's all it took for Blake to leave her messy bedroom and come into Chase's tidy bedroom.

Chase was almost asleep when she heard Blake slip into the bed beside her. "Scardy cat," she whispered.

Blake said, "So! You're afraid of the bogey man in the closet."

"There's no such thing," Chase said before drifting asleep and falling into the clutches of a dream.

Even though she was physically and mentally exhausted, her mind was spinning with thoughts. Chase could hear a basketball hitting the floor of the court thumping in her head.

The sound took her into a deeper sleep—a sleep where reality and dreams converged. In her dream, she was lost. She couldn't find her family or the basketball team. She was all alone in a strange place. It was dark and unfamiliar.

She was suddenly surrounded by tall trees with basket hoops all over them. They couldn't be real, but some of them had mouths. And the mouths moved. And there were teeth around the basketball hoops. Big, shiny, scary white teeth hanging from the basketball rim. She heard voices—mean, threatening voices.

"You lost, little girl?"

"This isn't a place for a little girl like you."

"Bad things happen to girls like you."

"You could end up like her."

Chase looked up and there was a girl stuck in the middle of a basketball hoop in a tree that seemed to touch the sky. The girl wasn't moving.

"How do I get out of here?" she said.

"You're going to be my dinner," said a tree with big eyes and a wide mouth.

Chase took off running. She ran down the dirt road. She didn't know where she was going. She just knew she had to get away from the trees.

She kept running, wiping her tears as she ran.

Out of breath, she stopped. The hoop trees were everywhere. "Daddy! Mommy! Help me!" she screamed.

"They're not here," said a little bush.

Chase looked around and couldn't figure out where the little voice came from.

She suddenly saw a little bush running towards her. Chase took off running. "Wait," said the bush. "I can help you."

Chase kept running and she heard the little bush running behind her. The bush was fast. When she turned around to see where the bush was, Chase tripped on the limb of a tree and fell on the ground.

"I'm gonna get you," said a tree in the middle of the road.

The little bush said. "Keep running. You will see an orange road. Get on the road and you'll be safe. The trees can't fit on that road."

Confused and scared, Chase didn't know what to do.

"Hurry! It's not that far. Follow the orange road. It will take you where you need to go. Don't turn around or you won't make it."

Chase got up, wiped the tears from her face and ran as fast as she ever ran in her life. She saw orange bricks ahead. She was tempted to turn around to see if the bush was behind her and to see if the trees were still there. Somehow, she remembered her Coach telling her not to look behind when running on the court, so she let her senses guide her.

She looked straight ahead. And kept running—faster and faster and faster. Suddenly she was on an orange brick road. She stopped for a second and just kept running on the orange brick road.

She had no idea where was going on.

And then she heard someone calling her name.

"Chase, Chase, wake up."

Chase opened her eyes and was relieved to see her bedroom. Everything was familiar—the pictures on the walls, the comforter on her bed, the trophies in her bookcase.

"You woke me up Chase," complained Blake. "You were screaming help."

"I had a bad dream. I'm so glad you woke me. I was lost in this forest of trees with basketball hoops and I had to run to an orange brick road."

Blake laughed. "Didn't you watch *The Wizard of Oz* with Grammy the other day?"

"So? They were going to kill me. They were going to eat me alive with their big shiny teeth and put me in their hoops."

"Oh girl, you were dreaming about basketball," said Blake. "You're going crazy."

"It was so scary and real," said Chase. Even though she was awake, she the dream was still ever-present in her mind.

"You are tripping," said Blake. "I'm going back to my room so I can get some sleep." Blake picked up her pillow, just as a boom of thunder seemed to shake the house. "Maybe not," she said, before climbing under the covers with Chase.

'I'm scared to go back to sleep," said Chase.

"Dream about the flying monkeys," said Blake.

"That's not funny."

"Don't think about basketball. Think about something else."

"What?"

"Think about me onstage, winning an award and everyone clapping for me. That always puts me to sleep," said Blake.

DARIAN-BALL-BLOG: NUMBER 15

We won sweet 16.

Sweet 16. Sounds like something sweet and wonderful like a sweet 16 birthday party.

There's nothing sweet about ruthless competition.

Imagine the pressure the team felt.

Imagine having to play teams that never lose and beating them for the first time ever.

Imagine if we would have had to play Swanson again. We almost did. But the team that played them before us beat them. They whipped their ass the way we did.

Karma got you Swanson.

The last team we had to play was against a team from Augusta—the team everyone said was going to win Sweet 16. We had never played them before. They have a national reputation, winning ninety-five percent of games they played—even teams from other states. We were the underdog. But our girls played like they were top dogs! We ate them like they were dog food.

That's because Coach O had a plan.

They expected us to meow like pussycats, but we growled like hungry panthers.

Chase dribbled down the court so fast that no one could catch her—they were eating her dust.

Marley was stealing balls like taking candy from a baby.

Tequila was making shots like the net was bowing down to her.

Selena and Bailey scored three points with their eyes closed (just kidding!)

None of the starters were in the third quarter. We had a 25-point lead and Coach O put in the other players who I think are extremely good.

Heaven and Jay-Nay-A showed their super bad skills.

Maybe we won because the other team started with their B team game expecting us to lose. We brought our A game and we beat them!

Riverbrook won sweet 16 and felt the glory of the moment. What a beautiful moment. A YOLO moment (shouting out to rapper Drake: You only live once.

But it's not over.

Now the road to the state championship gets more brutal and deadly in the world of basketball.

Elite eight is next.

Again—win or go home.

More pressure girls. But you've come this far…keep reaching for the stars. W-I-N-N-I-N-G!

Comments

Girlbball: They won the sweet 16.
Mindyourbiz: Say it again: they won sweet 16
Aleyhoop: I didn't believe they could do it. But they did. I bow down.
Basketqueen: Their basketball swag is the swag-swag.
Coolnerd: I'm still hoping that blue eyes will go out with me. I'm her number one fan.
Realguy: I'll take the red head. She's sassy and she knows what to do.
Watchyourback: Don't stop winning girls. Get it! Get it!
Lovegames: Sports is so unpredictable. Never know what's gonna happen until the buzzer ends the game.
Yeahitsme: No one would have predicted that our loser team would take the Sweet 16. YOLO Riverbrook girls!
Fromwayback: We used to be losers. We are winners again. Doesn't it feel good?
Mindyourbiz: March madness. Love it!
Sportsqueen: Basketball madness!
Gamewatcher: I love every minute of every game. Even when my heart feels like it's gonna stop.
Lovehighsh: From underdog to top dog!
Ibelieve: Don't forget their super alien powers. Supergirls!
Iknowsports: The madness continues…

THE STARTERS

Madplayer:. We been winning games like mad.
Justagame: Yeah, I can feel it….their spirit and determination.
BBswag: Can you feel it?
Irockyoudon't: They got the heat!
Fanfever: They are unbelievable. Coach O is a miracle worker.
Thinkyoucanplay: They played against teams that are beasts.
Hategirlsbb: They bring the heat while flying higher than the sun. They got my respect!

CHAPTER 40

SELENA

"We're going to a bowling party," she said.
　"That's cool. You'll have fun," Miguel said.
　"I'm not a happy bowler," she said."
　"I'll teach you. Going to teach you a lot of things," he said. *"Un día."*

Selena got off the school bus with her sister Maria and brother Paco. They weaved their way through the crowd of kids and then went separate ways to their lockers. They had ten minutes to get to class. Selena approached her locker and saw the number 22 on her locker door.

This was the third day there was a random number on her locker. She didn't know why or who put the number on her locker. She thought it was a meaningless number.

Today, the number wasn't random: it was her uniform number.

But she didn't who put it there or why.

At first she was curious.

Now she was irritated.

She called Miguel's cell phone, but she knew he wasn't going to have time to come to her locker because his class was on the other side of the school. She had to be careful using her cell phone, because administrators were on the look-out for inappropriate cell use.

If she got caught using her phone at the wrong times, she could get in-school suspension or Saturday school.

"Miguel, it happened again. Someone put a number on my locker."

"That is strange. What's the number?"

"22."

As soon as she said it, he recognized it. "That's your uniform number."

"I know."

"But you said that it started with 35," said Miguel.

"Yeah, but I don't know what it means."

"Maybe it's a countdown to a basketball game."

"We're playing in the elite eight. It's going to be over before 35 days."

"If I find out who's doing this to you, they won't like what I'm going to do," said Miguel with a trace of anger.

"I don't like this Miguel. I don't have a good feeling," said Selena.

"I'll come see you after second period. We'll figure it out and stop it."

"You are the prettiest girl in the school," Miguel said, talking to Selena on their cell phones. She was sitting on some boxes in the supply closet in the back of her family's restaurant.

"Gracias," Selena blushed. "How was your day in school?"

"Couldn't focus on school," said Miguel. "Couldn't stop thinking about you."

"I have the same problem, sometimes. I think about you in Spanish," said Selena.

"Yo me pregunto lo que mi Selena bonito hace," he said.

"I wonder what my handsome – guapo – Miguel is doing," she said, repeating what he said in English.

"What are you doing right now?"

"Talking to you," she giggled. "Chico tonto."

"I know chica tonta," he said, "silly girl. "What your Papá got you doing?"

"Nothing right now. I was so happy when he came to my game, Miguel." She repeated "so happy" in Spanish, "Ssí que feliz. And when Mama came to my last game I didn't believe it was really her."

"She is so proud of you."

"I know. Mama believes in dreams like the stars in the sky. Papa doesn't see the stars," she said.

"One day he might change the way his mind works," said Miguel. "He's in America."

"Maybe."

"Has Hector's scary friends been around?" asked Miguel.

"No, I can tell they're bad. Into bad things. Hector has been gone since then."

"He left?"

"Nobody knows where he is. Juan told him not to come back."

"Juan's a good big brother."

"I love him a lot," she said.

"Familia."

"Miguel, I want to find out who put those numbers on my locker," said Selena.

"I'm going to get my friends to watch the hallway in the morning so we can find out what's going on," said Miguel.

"Gracias."

"I'm not letting anything happen to you," said Miguel.

"I have mucho homework," Selena said. "Test tomorrow."

"Want to go to movie on Friday?" asked Miguel.

"Wish I could. Basketball team is having a celebración for going to the elite eight," said Selena. "Coach says it's grande, mucho grande. I don't understand all the stuff she talks about sometimes, so I keep quiet."

"Mi novia," he said, "it is mucho grande. Like being in the play-offs in baseball."

She felt butterflies in her stomach when Miguel said, mi novia, which means my sweetheart in English. "I'm just so happy," she said. "Muy feliz."

"You are really good in basketball. You don't even know how good you are," he said.

"Maybe not, but you know you are a great basketball player," she teased.

"I'm the very best," he said, laughing.

"Mucho cocky," she said.

"Sí, I've been playing since I was five," he said. "What are you doing to celebrate?"

"We're going to a bowling party," she said.

"That's cool. You'll have fun," Miguel said.

"I bowl gutter balls."

He laughed. "I'll teach you one day. I'm going to teach you a lot of things," he said. "Un día."

Selena wondered what things he planned to teach her about, but she would find out one day. "Un día," she said. "Depends on what it is…you plan to teach me."

"Things that make you happy," Miguel said, and then repeated in Spanish: "Las cosas que hacen usted feliz."

"I have to go," Selena said.

"I'll call you to say good-night," Miguel promised.

Selena sauntered inside the dark bowling alley, glowing with laser lights. It didn't take long to spot her teammates gathered around two side-by-side bowling lanes.

"Hola chicas!" she said, greeting everyone who was there.

"Hola Selena," Chase said.

"Hola, hola," Tequila said.

"Get your shoes," said Marley. "We're going to get started."

"Everybody's not here," Selena said, observing that several players were missing.

"We've reserved several lanes, so we'll just play as people get here," said Coach Olivia. "Be right back. I'm going to get my shoes."

"Can I get the lane with the bumpers so I don't throw gutter bowls?" Selena asked.

"No way," Bailey said sitting next to Matthew Charles.

"I can bowl," said Matthew Charles.

"So can I," said Bailey.

"Selena, you must be kidding about bumpers," said Chase.

"I'm not a happy bowler," said Selena.

"Oh, you suck," teased Zoey.

Selena giggled. "Yes, that's the word."

"I suck too," said Heaven.

"What? You admit to not being good at something?" said Marley.

"Nobody's good at everything," said Zoey.

"Speak for yourself," said Ja-Nay-A.

"Whatever!" said Heaven.

"I'm going to get my shoes," said Selena.

"It's just you?" teased Tequila. "Where's everybody? Your fifty brothers and sisters."

"I love my family. Adoro mi familia," she said, "but it's just me today."

"Where is Miguel?" asked Marley. "Your hottie boyfriend."

"Sí, he is my caliente boyfriend. He's coming to get me later," admitted Selena.

"You are a cute couple," commented Chase.

"Watch out for those other girls," said Layne.

"The Miguettes," said Zoey.

"He got a lot of girls chasing him," said Heaven.

"I know. I can't worry about them," she said. "Or I would go loco."

"You are already loco," said Tequila.

"No, Selena is chica feliz, our happy girl," said Marley.

"That's me," Selena admitted, grinning.

Coach Olivia approached the group, holding a pair of bowling shoes. "Ready to celebrate?"

"Yes, we are," said Layne. "This is going to be fun."

"I have a confession," said Coach O. "I'm a terrible bowler."

"I suck too," said Selena.

"Well, I didn't exactly say I sucked," said Coach Olivia, raising an eyebrow as if offended. "But we're going to have fun!"

"Mucho fun!" said Selena.

"Because we are going to the elite eight," shouted Coach O. "And then final four."

"Then we rock the state championship," screamed Layne, standing in a chair.

"If you fall on your ass," said Zoey. "I will laugh my ass off."

Some of the girls laughed.

"I hope we can really do it," said Chase. "I've been having crazy dreams."

"We have come this far," said Rachel.

"Yes, we're going to kick ass," Coach O said, not caring about her no-cursing rule. "Elite eight is an honor. I'm proud of you, girls!"

"Elite eight. Best of the best," said Tequila.

"Yes, you are," said Diante. "The best."

Tequila's heart dove into the middle of her stomach. She looked up and saw Diante standing next to year. "What are you doing here? I didn't invite you."

"I invited myself," Diante said, holding a pair of bowling shoes in his hands.

"It's real simple," said Tequila. "I'm going to beat you."

DARIAN-BALL-BLOG: NUMBER 16

Aren't you proud of our girls' basketball team? We're going to the elite eight. That means eight of the best teams in the state. Riverbrook is one of the eight.

History in the making. Our girls are not faking. Coach O is not joking.
They are taking it: not losing, winning. No ceilings. Touching the sky.
Fiercer competition.
Fireball games.
Second–by–-second action.
Heart-pounding excitement.
We need super powers to win. Alien powers. And we got them.
We can do this, girls. We got this far, right?
We have to use those super baller powers to win the elite eight.
Yes the competition is fierce; the teams will-kill-to-win.
But we are fiercer, mightier, and stronger.
We are bringing the heat. 2000 degrees of basketball power.
We are already on victory fire.

DARIAN-BALL-BLOG: NUMBER 17

You didn't expect to hear from me so soon. Game just ended. Why wait? We won!

We won the elite eight.

Maybe it was fate.

Either way we are going to state.

Coach O said expect the unexpected.

Done. She delivered.

What is there to confess?

Our players are the best.

We are going to win.

We will be state champions!

Riverbrook rules this basketball season.

For all the right reasons.

What else is there to say?

CHAPTER 41

MARLEY

"Don't say that word. We can't use the L word around Coach O."
"What word?" asked Tianna, the PantherTV reporter.
"L-O-S-E," said Zoey, spelling it out. "It's like a curse word."
"Bad as the F word," said Layne. "Coach O doesn't allow us to say it."
"Ever!" said Marley. "Never ever!"

"This is Tianna Dressler: your roaming PantherTV reporter on the prowl. I'm outside of the girls' basketball locker room where they've been practicing for the championship games. Right now, we're going to interview some of our players. This is an unusual event because we are going to the final four for the first time in forever!" Tianna screamed: "Woop! Woop! We are on the way to becoming state champions. It's a big-big thing and guess what? We're going to interview all the players on the team."

Dressed in a black shirt, ankle-high boots and a colorful flowing shirt, Tianna motioned for the cameraman to turn the camera towards Marley. "Before we get started, this is John, our camera guy. Isn't he adorable?"

Marley looked at the almost seven-foot tall, white guy with thick red hair and a scruffy beard. "Yes, an adorable giant!"

John laughed.

"Too bad you don't play basketball," said Marley.

"I'm too clumsy. Can't catch a ball. Can't run. I'm no athlete," said John. "You girls would just laugh at me."

Marley giggled.

Tianna asked Marley. "Ready?"

"Not exactly dressed for an interview," she said, wearing her practice uniform. "I'll be right back." Marley went into the locker room, removed the pony tail holder and quickly brushed her hair so that it hung loosely around her face and shoulders. She put on some cinnamon-brown lipstick before leaving the locker room.

She walked over to Tiana. "Ready!"

"You're hot!" said John.

"Focus, John. We're interviewing her," said Tianna.

"Oh, right," said John.

"On," Tianna signaled to John who pressed the video camera's button to the 'on' position.

"This is Marley Woods. Our Marley, Marley, Marley," said Tianna with a giggle. "She's a starter on the girls' basketball team."

"Hi everybody," Marley said with a charming smile.

"I know you are excited to be going to state," said Tianna. "And my journalism teacher would say that's not a question."

"Well, here's my answer: Pumped, pumped, pumped! The whole school has turned into panther mania. Everybody is rooting for us like they do the boys team," said Marley.

"It's about freaking time," screamed Layne in the background. The camera man captured a shot of Layne and then zoomed back to Marley.

"We are finally getting our props. So I'm feeling it. Loving it," said Marley. "Ready to win!"

"Coach O came to our school, waved a magic wand and turned the team into winners," said Tianna.

"Hey," said Layne, as the camera man pointed the camera at her. "Some of the blog readers say we've turn into aliens," said Layne. "Maybe I have an extra heart that I don't know about."

Tianna and the camera man laughed. "Good one," said Tianna.

The camera man zoomed from Layne to Marley. "What did Coach O do differently?" asked Tianna.

"Coach O changed everything. The way we work out. Our plays. Our strategies and she's very motivating. She was like a charge of positive energy," said Marley.

"Sounds like you really respect Coach Remmington," said Tianna.

"Yes. She picked me to be a starter," said Marley with a cocky smile. "So I liked her from the beginning."

"I heard not everyone liked who she picked to be starters. Is that right?" asked Tianna.

"Some of girls were upset," said Marley.

"She didn't pick me to be starter," said Layne, in the background. "I thought about killing Marley, but then I realized I would go to jail. So I decided to let her live."

With a lopsided grin, Marley turned to Layne. "Thank you for your generosity."

"Layne come stand by Marley," said Tianna, and signaled to John to point the camera at Layne. "What was that, Layne?" asked Tianna.

"I was so kidding. The coach picked the right starters. I wasn't mad even at the beginning of the season. Some of the other players were furious," said Layne, as Zoey came from around the corner.

"Were you mad you weren't a starter?" Tianna asked Zoey, signaling the cameraman to film Marley, Layne and Zoey standing together.

"Nope. I really wasn't expecting to be starter. I know what I'm good at," said Zoey.

"Yep," said Layne.

"Yeah, it's like theatre, everybody got a part to play," said Zoey, the camera tightening on her face. "We all played our parts so now we are going to state championship!" Zoey tossed her arms in the air. "We go from being the school that super sucks to a school that blows teams out. Unexpected, right?"

"Everyone at school is so happy," said Tianna. "Even if you guys lose, we are still going to celebrate the team going to the state."

Zoey's face turned bright red. "Don't say that word. We can't use the L word around Coach O."

"What L word?" asked Tianna, motioning to John to tighten the camera's zoom on Marley, Zoey, and Layne.

"L-O-S-E," said Zoey, spelling it out. "It's a bad word. Like a curse word."

"Bad as the F word," said Layne. "Coach O doesn't allow us to say it."

"Ever!" said Marley. "Never ever!"

"You say the L word and I'm not talking about a girl liking a girl. I'm talking about *not* winning," explained Layne. "Say it in front of Coach O and you will be running around the gym for an hour."

"She don't play," said Tianna.

"That word is band from our lips."

"It's eliminated from my mind, from my subconscious," said Marley.

"So, we are going to state to win!" said Layne.

"W-I-N!" said Zoey, she said, eyeing the cameraman.

"Now we know why y'all been winning." said Tianna.

"Yeah, we're going to keep on winning," said Marley.

Zoey moved over to the cameraman. She slowly slid her hand down his long arm, a sly smile on her face. "You and I can celebrate our victory alone."

The camera man just nodded his head. His face turned red. He didn't know what to say.

"I promise we'll have fun," Zoey said, stroking the cameraman's cheek.

"Don't make him drop the camera," said Layne.

"Yeah, Zoey!" Marley screeched. "He's filming us."

"She doesn't care," said Layne.

"John cut," said Tianna, signaling the cameraman to turn off the camera. "That is going to be so edited," Tianna said to Zoey.

While sitting in the food court at the Lenox Mall, Cooper sat back and watched the shoppers. He loved watching people at different places—whether it was Target, Macy's, the grocery story, the airport, Tiffany's or Ethan Allen. He was good at observing a person and figuring out something about their life—as least a part of it. Not just the expensively-dressed person who shopped at upscale stores or the wealthy person who had a personal driver or the struggling single mom who was stretching her money to buy dinner for a week. Sometimes he could figure out: what a person did for a living, what kind of car they drove, where they lived, relationship status or other interesting things about a person.

Watching people was a game that he often played with Marley. He always told her: "You learn more about people from their actions and interactions with people." He was observing an interracial couple—the man was older and white, and the woman was young, black and very attractive. Cooper could hear some of their conversation, but was interrupted when Marley came to the table, toting bags, looking at her phone and not even watching where she was walking.

"Hi, Daddy," she said.

"Hey, baby," he said.

Marley noticed the couple that Cooper had been watching. "She's a gold digger," she whispered.

Cooper laughed. "How much of my gold did you spend?"

"Good one Daddy," she said.

She showed him a bag from Victoria Secret. "Some pajamas for the sleepover."

"Marley, you have a drawer full of pajamas that you've never worn."

"I had to get something for this occasion. The state championship! It's a historic event in my life."

"Cut the drama. What else did you get?" he asked peeking inside the Victoria secret's bag.

"Nothing," she said a little too quickly.

Cooper saw what was in bag. "Thongs!"

"Let's not talk about that Daddy," she said.

Sighing, Cooper shook his head.

"I also got a little overnight bag to take to the sleepover. Have to bring extra clothes when we go celebrating."

"That's a Coach bag?" he asked.

Marley hesitated. "Yes sir," she said.

"Don't sir me," he said. "You only 'sir' me when you want something or you're sorry about something."

"I got something fun. Something for all the girls."

"Fun?"

"It's really cool," she said. "I got panther tattoos for the team. They're temporary of course, but I think it's cool. It will show that we are a united team."

"I like it," said Cooper. "Text your coach and make sure it's cool with her."

She smiled sweetly. "I already did."

"Now I have a surprise," said Cooper.

"Yay! I love surprises!"

"Hi, Marley," a voice said from behind her.

Marley turned around. "Aunt Martina! What are you doing here?"

"Guess my little genius," said Aunt Martina.

"You came to see me play!"

"Yes, baby!"

"I can't believe it! Thank you," Marley said wrapping her arms around Aunt Martina. She felt the softness of the mink fur coat her aunt was wearing.

"I'm so happy you're here. You have no idea how important this is to our team. Our school hasn't gone this far in over fifteen years."

"Cooper told me," said Aunt Martina. "I'm proud of you. I know your phenomenal skills are why they made it so far."

"I'm one of the reasons why," said Marley, extending her index finger to reflect the number one. "We are a team."

"Humility. That's a change," said Aunt Martina.

"Marley, one more surprise," said Cooper.

"What? Who?" screeched Marley.

"Me," said a squeaky, familiar voice from a short distance.

"Aunt Laurel," said Marley, running to her and almost knocking her aunt to the floor. "I can't believe you're here." She gave her aunt a tight hug. Laurel was tall and thin, light-brown with freckles spread around her small face. Her reddish-brown hair was pulled back into a loose ponytail.

"I'm here, Marley. I came to support you," said Aunt Laurel.

Marley looked around to see if her cousins and uncle were with Aunt Laurel. "Where are the kids?"

"They're at home."

Marley frowned. "You never leave them."

"On special occasions I do. This is a special occasion. Your uncle will watch them and take good care of them. I go back on Sunday," said Aunt Laurel. "That's as long as I can be away from my babies."

"Thank you so much!" said Marley.

"You're welcome," said Aunt Laurel.

Tears welled in Marley's eyes. "The team is staying at a hotel the night before the game."

"We know. We're staying at the hotel too," said Aunt Martina. "We're staying at your house tonight and tomorrow."

"Then we're all going to be at the hotel the night before the game," said Cooper.

"This is going to be so much fun. I have to tell E," she said, grabbing her cell phone. "A lot of Daddy's family is going to be there. Whoop! Whoop! I will have my family rooting for me."

She sent a text message to Egypt. After hitting the send button on her phone, Marley's face suddenly changed. The glow of excitement instantly disappeared.

"Oh no! No, no, no!" said Marley. "I'm so slow and so freaking stupid."

"What are you talking about?" asked Cooper.

Marley slowly looked at their faces.

After several minutes passed, she softly asked, "Is Franchesca coming?" Her tone simmered with anger and disappointment.

They were all quiet.

Marley looked at their faces and knew the answer.

"I'm sorry baby, she's not going to make it," said Aunt Martina in a calm voice.

"The game is on Saturday," Marley said. "There is no court on Saturday."

"Your mom has to prepare for a deposition on Monday," explained Aunt Martina.

"Something like that," Aunt Laurel said with undisguised disapproval in her voice.

Marley grabbed her shopping bags. "I don't care. I don't care. I don't care," rushed out of Marley's mouth. "I can't," she said, fighting back tears. "If I get emotional I won't play well."

"That's right," said Cooper. "You have to zone her or any distractions out of your mind when you're playing."

"I've become very good at that," said Marley. "I zone Franchesca out a lot. All the time!"

Marley plastered a smile on her face. "Sometimes she doesn't exist."

Cooper, Martina and Laurel exchanged uncomfortable looks.

"Calm down," Aunt Laurel said, tenderness in her voice. She hugged Marley, whispering comforting words in her ear.

"Okay," Marley said, wiping the tears from her face.

"Let's have a good time together. You have to find the good even when things are bad," said Aunt Laurel.

Marley nodded her head, regaining her composure.

"It's not often that we're together like this," said Aunt Laurel.

"You're right, Aunt Laurel. I can't remember the last time you were in Atlanta," said Marley. "And you're going to be here almost a week! Yay!"

"So, let's have some fun," Aunt Laurel said.

"Okay," Marley whispered.

"Let's get ready for your victory," said Aunt Martina. "Thongs and all."

Marley laughed.

"That's right," said Aunt Laurel. "We are going to have a good time!"

Both aunts hugged Marley. The warmth of their embrace and support was an adrenaline shot of love that slowly brought a genuine smile to Marley's face and melted her tears away.

CHAPTER 42

BAILEY

Will You Go to the Prom with me?
Will You Do the Romp-Romp with me?
Will you put on a sexy dress?
Will you let me touch your breast?

"Will you go to the prom with me?" Bailey read that same question all day long—different times, different places.

She read three text messages from three different numbers, but with the same question. She called the numbers and no one answered.

A poster board with *"Bailey, will you go to the prom with me?"* was taped on her locker door. There was another poster on the door in two of her classes.

When she went to practice, she saw another poster on her locker door in the girls' basketball locker room.

So, she was teased all day long.

"It's that private school boy," said Layne, when the girls were in the locker room getting dressed for practice.

"His name is Matt," said Bailey.

"He *is* cute," said Layne.

"Sure is," said Zoey. "If you don't go with him, I'll go with him."

"Watch Zoey," said Layne. "She's a man-stealer."

"She calls him Matt the ass," said Marley.

"How do you know?" asked Bailey.

"Girl, you know there are no secrets around here," said Heaven.

"Why do you call him that?" asked Chase.

"When I first met him he acted like a jerk. He was saying all this racist stuff about different races and people. I thought he was a jerk."

"He didn't know your Mama was married to a black man?" asked Ja-Nay-A.

"No, but it didn't matter. I didn't like what he said about other races."

"He comes to all your games," said Chase.

"A lot of games," said Zoey. "Is he obsessed?"

"No. He just wanted to change my opinion of him," explained Bailey.

"He's not all bad. He's friends with your best friend," said Heaven.

"Stay out of my business," said Bailey.

"We're in it now," said Marley, teasing Bailey. "He brings flowers to your games."

"Yeah I know. He's not as bad as he was at first. I've gotten to know him," Bailey said, her voice softening. "My opinion of him has changed…a lot."

"So he's not acting like an ass," said Layne.

"No, and at first I thought he was just pretending…"

"To be an ass?" asked Zoey.

"Pretending *not* to be an ass," said Bailey.

Confused, Chase said, "Huh?"

"I mean I thought he was pretending to be cool and open-minded just so that I would like him."

"So you figured out he's not pretending to be an ass," said Layne.

Bailey was quiet. "No, I don't think he's pretending. He's not like some of his snobby private school friends."

"All private school kids aren't the same," said Layne. "I went to private school."

"Me too," said Zoey. "I'm normal."

"Not really," said Rachel.

"Yeah Zoey, you think you are," teased Marley.

"So do you like Matt?" asked Chase.

"I don't know," said Bailey.

"Girl, you know you like him," said Zoey. "Don't make it complicated."

"You don't have to like someone to go to the prom with him," said Marley.

"I know," said Bailey.

"So what you gonna do?" asked Heaven.

They were interrupted by the professional trainer, hired specifically to prepare them for the state playoffs. "Ladies, it's time."

"It's time," said Bailey, mocking the trainer.

"Time to give that boy an answer," said Heaven.

"I don't even know if it's really him. There's no name on the signs."

"Don't play yourself," said Marley. "You know it's him."

"You're tripping," said Heaven.

"It could be that boy…um David," said Zoey. "He follows you around like a puppy."

"He's a geek," said Bailey.

"You're sort of a geek," said Zoey. "No offense."

Bailey rolled her eyes at Zoey.

"Geeks fall in love," said Rachel.

"He's too scared to say hi," said Bailey. "When I catch him looking at me, he grabs himself like he's going to pee on himself."

"Eeew," said Rachel.

"Maybe that's why he's putting up signs," said Chase. "He's too scared to talk to you."

"It's not him," said Layne.

"It could be the boy in the blog who talks about your pretty blue eyes," said Selena.

"Or the one who talks about aliens," said Kaylee.

"Ewww," said Rachel.

"He's creepy and weird and…"

"We might not ever see you again. He'll take you to another planet," said Zoey.

"When I find out who it is, I will tell you all of you." Bailey raised her voice. "Since you're all in my business."

"Swimming in it, girl," said Marley. "Doing backstrokes in it."

After two hours of extensive workouts with the special trainer, the girls stumbled into the locker room. The workouts were advanced basketball exercises and drills typically done by college teams. The girls were exhausted. Very few words were spoken in the locker room. Not even complaints of exhaustion, starvation or sleep deprivation.

They all felt the same way—they just wanted to go home, eat and sleep.

Bailey was the first to leave. "See y'all in the morning."

She walked to her car and the first thing she noticed was the colorful writing on the back of her jeep. Same question: *Will you go to the prom with me?*

Bailey looked around the parking lot for a familiar car or face. She looked for a strange car or strange face.

She had a creepy feeling that she was being watched. So, she got in her car, locked the doors and drove off.

At the moment, she didn't want to think about the prom. It was next month. She had a more pressing question on her mind: Homework or bed?

Ten minutes later, Bailey pulled into her driveway. She decided that she was too tired for homework. She was going to shower, go to bed and get up early to do homework.

But, then the question that was haunting her all day still haunted her. She couldn't escape it if she wanted to: there was a huge poster on the outside of the garage door with the same question.

It was time to find out who was her prom stalker.

Bailey opened the garage door and drove inside. She called River, but the call went straight to voice mail.

She gathered her belongings and was ready to get out of the car when her phone rang.

The number was unfamiliar. But she answered it anyway.

She heard a loud song, with a familiar voice singing a horrible song. There was only one verse and one lyric.

After the person stopped singing, they hung up.

But then the song started again. This time it was live.

It was Matt singing off-tune and loud:

Will you go to the prom with me?
Will you do the Romp-Romp with me?
Will you put on a sexy dress?
Will you let me touch your breast?

Bailey laughed so hard, she couldn't stop laughing. She was laughing so hard, she couldn't even get out of the car.

"Going to the prom makes you laugh?" asked Matt. "Or going to the prom with me makes you laugh?"

Bailey laughed for what seemed like an eternity to Matt. She couldn't stop laughing.

So Matt laughed with her, not knowing if she was laughing at him or with him.

Matt's hands were on the edge of the driver's side door, laughter erupting from his mouth. Slowly and eventually, their laughter stopped. He didn't know whether to ask her again—she might start laughing again.

When she appeared calm and in control, he seriously asked, "Bailey, will you go to the prom with me?"

"I would love to go to the prom with you," she said, with a short giggle.

"Okay," Matt said.

"Okay," Bailey said.

After a few minutes, Bailey explained, "I was laughing because your singing was so awful." She giggled a little. "I've never heard you sing and it was just unexpected and hilarious."

"I just wanted to make you laugh. I was hoping you would laugh after harassing you all day." he said.

"And embarrassing me," she said.

"Just wanted to get your attention," said Matt.

"Mission accomplished," she said, getting out of the car and closing the door. "You went through a lot of trouble to put up those signs."

"That was actually fun," said Matt. "Are your silly giggles gone?"

"Yes," she said, with an impish grin.

Standing face-to-face with her, and staring into her eyes, he asked, "Just to be sure, you said you will go to the prom with me?"

"Yes! Matt the ass…now Matt Charles, I will go to the prom with you."

"Cool," he said. "How are you?"

"It was a long practice." She released a long weary sigh. "I'm so tired, Matt. Practice was brutal."

Matt wrapped his arms around her and hugged her for several minutes. He kissed her on the cheek and the forehead. "I understand."

Bailey closed her eyes and relaxed in his embrace. She felt something unusual, something unfamiliar. It was her heart. Even though her body was weak and tired, her heart was beating faster and faster.

Bailey was coming out of the cafeteria when she heard her name. She turned and saw the reporter Tianna and John the giant cameraman from PantherTV. She knew that they were interviewing the team and tried to avoid them. But at the moment, the PantherTV crew were unavoidable. The reporter Tianna stuck a microphone in front of Bailey's face.

"Ready for Saturday?" asked Tianna.

Bailey didn't respond right away. "Yeah, I'm ready. We're all ready. Coach O is making sure of that."

"You know the whole school is rooting for you."

"Yes, I've seen the signs everywhere. We appreciate the support."

"Which is your favorite sign?" Tianna asked, referring to the signs with different messages: Take the State; Riverbrook Rules GA; Riverbrook Got the Hook; We Came to Win; We Rock the State; Hi and Bye; You Droll, We Rule; and other victory-declaring signs.

"Um, I like…. Riverbrook Got the Hook," Bailey said.

"Let's get serious for a moment," said Tianna. "Is it true that you didn't want to be starter?"

Bailey shrugged her shoulders. "I didn't think Coach O was going to pick me. I was shocked at first."

"How do you feel about it now?"

"Honored." With a wide grin, she said, "I like my position. I like being a starter."

"We can tell. You play hard and handle that ball, girl."

"Oops," laughed Tianna. "Edit, John. I'm not supposed to say, 'girl.'"

She looked back at Bailey. "You can really handle the ball."

"Thanks!" said Bailey. "We practice a lot."

"Hey Kaylee," said Tianna, flagging Kaylee from the crowd of onlookers. "Come over here so we can interview you for the story."

Tianna tugged on John's arms. "Make sure you get Kaylee in the shot."

Kaylee reluctantly walked over to Tianna.

Tianna looked at the camera and then Kaylee. "This is Kaylee from the basketball team. She's a very good player or she wouldn't be on the team, right? Coach O only picked winners."

Looking uncomfortable in the glare of the camera, Kaylee said, "Yes."

"All the girls on the team really love basketball. Is that how you feel too?"

"Yeah, but I also like the…

"Violin," interrupted Tianna.

Kaylee nodded.

"Are you going to bring your violin on the court?" Tianna asked, directing John to focus the camera on Kaylee's face.

"What?" Kaylee asked, confused.

"Just joking. I heard that you play the violin like a professional violinist."

"I've been playing the violin since I was three," said Kaylee.

"You got mad violin skills and mad hoop skills," said Tianna.

"I guess so," said Kaylee.

"We may not see you playing the violin, but we see you playing basketball," said Tianna. "Dribble, dribble, swish, score."

"Isn't that what I'm supposed to do?"

Everyone laughed.

"Kaylee is one hundred percent reliable," said Bailey. "She does exactly what Coach O tells her to do and sometimes she comes up with some interesting plays," said Bailey.

"I try to help," said Kaylee.

"She says some of her ideas are from being in orchestra," said Bailey.

"Orchestra helps in a weird way. Instruments have different sounds and play different notes. But when we follow the notes there's harmony." Kaylee shook her head. "We gotta be a team…in harmony."

River sat on the bottom of Bailey's bed. She was wearing a camouflage army jacket, black skirt with green tights and a pair of high-top black sneakers. She was scrolling through her laptop, showing Bailey random pictures of prom dresses.

Bailey glanced at a couple of the pictures. She fell back against her pillows, near the bed's headboard. "My body is so sore from practice."

"Poor thing," said River.

"I don't want to think about the prom right now."

"I thought you were going to two proms—Matt's prom and your prom."

Bailey shrugged. "I can wear the same dress."

"No you won't! I might do something like that, but that's not you."

"Whatever, River! It's a month from now and I can't think about the prom right now. I still can't believe Matt did what he did."

"With my help," said River.

"I know you were behind most of it," said Bailey. "Matt wouldn't come into my school and put up so many signs. He had to have help from someone bold and crazy like you."

"You said yes."

"I was pressured." Bailey dramatically put her hands around her head. "All those signs. I was brainwashed."

"Well… call him up and tell him you changed your mind."

"Stop messing with me River. I have other things to think about."

"Like your date with him."

Bailey got up from her bed and threw a pillow at River.

"We went to the movies. So typical," said Bailey as she walked over to her pillow-padded window seat and stretched out, leaning her back against the side wall.

"No comment," said River.

"Then he took me to some place at Kennesaw Mountain and we stared at the stars in the sky." Bailey smiled. "He actually named some of the stars."

"That's lame," said River.

"I thought it was cool."

"Did he kiss you?" River asked, walking over to the window seat.

"None of your business."

"It's me. If you don't tell me I will ask him. Then I'll put signs all over your school."

"I don't know why I stay friends with you. Yes, he kissed me. He was very sweet. Not aggressive or pushy."

River sat inside the window seat, in her usual position, face-to-face with Bailey. "He's just waiting for you to get comfortable."

Bailey scrunched her face. "So he can attack me?"

"That's not his style. He's smoother than that."

"I guess that's good," said Bailey.

"Graduation is only three months away. You can still lose your virginity by then."

"River, I'm not thinking about that right now."

"Ok, you got basketball on the brain."

"You don't get it?"

"Duh! You're going to state championship. I'm going to be there screaming your name like crazy maniac."

"Of course you will."

"I got a whole crew coming to root for you."

"Awww!" Bailey said.

"Hell yeah!" said River, pushing against Bailey's shoulder.

"I'm scared," said Bailey. "I can't mess up. I can't make one mistake."

"You won't. You've been playing without fear. Gotta stay fearless. That's how I get through a performance. I kick fear in the ass," said River.

"Okay," said Bailey.

"You have a bunch of people coming to the game. Your mom and her family are going to be there. Your dad and his family. Of course I'm going to be there making more noise than anybody."

"I know."

"Too bad we can't bring our instruments in." She twisted her lips. "Maybe we can sneak in a guitar."

"I don't want to know anything about it," said Bailey, giggling.

"Might surprise you!"

"The whole team is staying at the hotel."

"You told me," said River.

"My mom and brother and sister are staying at the hotel, too. They don't want to chance being late."

"I get it."

"Matt has been so supportive. Sometimes I don't believe he's the same dude I met at your party."

"Yep, you're going to lose it before graduation," said River.

DARIAN-BALL-BLOG: NUMBER 18

Countdown time: Tuesday, Wednesday, Thursday, Friday, Saturday

The state championship is five days away.

Yes, I said this before, but I will say it again.

We are going to win.

We are going to be champions.

We are going to take state.

We are going to fly.

Ain't we Riverbrook High?

CHAPTER 43

TEQUILA

"Quila is crying," said Tevon, his voice filled with concern.

Tequila smacked Tevon on the head. "You are such a tattle tale."

"You don't have to tell everything," said Rashonda, wiping away her tears.

"I'm sorry, Mama," said Tevon. "I didn't mean to make you cry, too."

Tequila was near the cafeteria door when she heard her name. She turned and saw Tianna Dressler the reporter and John the camera man from PantherTV just a few steps away.

"Oh shit," Tequila muttered.

"Panther on the prowl!" said Tianna, the PantherTV reporter.

"Oh yes. It's time."

"Bite me," said Tequila.

"Come on Tequila, you know you love the spotlight," said Tianna.

Tequila eyed Tianna's fancy-for-school dress and knee-high boots. "You rocking that outfit."

"Thanks," said Tianna. "So you ready for the interview?"

"Just let me put on some lipstick," said Tequila, taking a tube of red lipstick from her purse and applying the lipstick on her lips.

The camera man watched Tequila. "You look hot!"

"I know," she said, dressed in jeans and a low-cut sweater. "If you got, flaunt it, right Tianna?"

"You know it!"

"Ready?" Tianna asked Tequila.

"Yes!"

"Let's move away from the cafeteria. It's too noisy," said Tianna, while walking around the corner. Tequila and John followed her. "Okay, John," Tianna said to the camera man. "On."

John pointed the camera at Tequila and Tianna.

"So are you ready for the championship game?" asked Tianna.

"I've been ready. I was ready even when were losing last year," said Tequila.

"Our record is 15-5. Last year it was…unmentionable," said Tianna.

"You're right. Don't mention it."

"What's the difference from last year to this year?"

"Me, of course," bragged Tequila.

Tianna laughed.

"I'm a beast. I get teased for acting like Kobe Bryant on the court."

"You do kind of act like Kobe," said John. "He's the best player in the…"

Tianna frowned at the cameraman. "Be quiet, John. You're not supposed to be talking. You know that."

"Sorry," stumbled out of his mouth.

Tianna motioned for John to point the camera at Tequila. "So it's Tequila and the team?"

"No. I was joking."

Tequila motioned for John to zoom on Tequila's face. "I know it takes a team to win. Coach O taught us that," said Tequila. "She's the best coach in the world. She's why we are going to state."

Ja-Nay-A jumped in front of the camera. "You better give all of us credit, miss wanna-be-Kobe. "I hustle on the court and so does Elise."

"Ja-Nay-A, don't go anywhere. Elise, come over here by the camera," directed Tianna. "We're interviewing all the players on the team."

Elise reluctantly walked over. When the camera panned to her face, she forced her lips to form a smile. "Hi," she said awkwardly.

"Congratulations on going to state. Your family must be excited," said Tianna.

"We're all excited," said Elise.

"Is it true that your mother played basketball when she went to high school here at Riverbrook?" asked Tianna.

"Embarrassing, but true," said Elise with a half-proud smile.

"Yes. She was a power forward."

"I know she's proud of you," said Tianna.

A real smile slipped on Elise's face. "Yes."

"I've seen your family at the games. They really root for you," said Tianna. "They all have signs with your name on it."

"Yes."

"Say something other than yes," said Ja-Nay-A. "Does the camera scare you that much?"

"I'm happy we're going to state and I want us to win," said Elise.

Tianna turned toward Ja-Nay-A. "So, Ja-Nay-A, you scored a lot of points this year. What do you…"

"Are you shocked? Did you doubt me?"

"I'm congratulating you," said Tianna.

"I got real skills. I've been playing basketball since I was in the fourth grade," said Ja-Nay-A. "Coach O knows I can be a terror on the court."

"Good luck, girls! We can't wait to celebrate our victory," said Tianna.

"Victory for the taking," said Ja-Nay-A, making a V with her two fingers.

"Victory," said Elise.

"Come on, Elise. We can't sound lame," said Ja-Nay-A. "Get in here with us Tequila."

Tequila moved next to Elise and Ja-Nay-A.

John focused his camera for a close-up shot when Tequila Elise and Ja-Nay-A formed a V with their fingers. They screamed "Victory!"

"Do you think they're really coming?" Tequila asked her mother as they drove out of the rental car parking lot.

Rashonda shook her head. "I rented this van so we would have room to drive everybody around. They've sent us text messages on the bus. I've taken off work to hang out with them. Why are you still so worried?"

"You're a big worry wart," said Tevon.

"Shut up, big head," said Tequila. "You know how they are. They hate leaving New York. They thought we were crazy to move to Atlanta and swore we wouldn't last down here."

"We proved them wrong, didn't we?" Rashonda said. "We've been here for three years and we doing fine."

"I like it here," said Tevon. "I'm not scared anymore."

"I still miss Brooklyn," said Tequila. "They're so lame here."

Rashonda sighed. "Stop complaining. We're here. Make the best of it."

"That's what you always say," said Tequila.

"That's what you need to do," said Rashonda.

"Right," said Tequila.

"You're doing great in school. Your grades are better than they've ever been your whole life. You have a coach who believes in you," said Rashonda. "Be grateful."

"I miss everyone…."

"Me too."

"I miss Rasheed," said Tequila.

"I miss your brother every single day. Every freaking day," Rashonda said with deep sadness in her voice. "I know he would be proud of you. He'd be proud of us."

Unexpected tears dropped down Tequila's face. Her feelings about Rasheed were still surface level, not buried deep enough to escape the wave of sadness that washed through her soul when she heard his name.

"Quila is crying," said Tevon, his voice filled with concern.

Tequila smacked Tevon on the head. "You are such a tattle tale."

"You don't have to tell everything," said Rashonda, wiping her tears away.

"I'm sorry, Mama," said Tevon softly. "I didn't mean to make you cry too. I have to take care of my girls."

"My girls," Rashonda said, with a half-smile. "Tevon, I just remembered Rasheed smiling…his silly grin."

"That make you cry?" asked Tevon.

"One day, you'll understand," said Rashonda. "It makes me sad to think he's gone…forever, but I won't forget him. I try to think happy thoughts about him even when I think sad thoughts."

"Oh," said Tevon.

"Would you smile if I told you Tequila has a boyfriend? She smiles when she sees Diante."

"Tevon," said Tequila, gritting her teeth. "I'm going to get you…"

"I know about him. I have my suspicions about that boy," said Rashonda. "Don't you be stupid."

Offended, Tequila said, "I'm not stupid."

"I should believe you like we believe Aunt Dee when she says she ain't doing crack, right?"

"I'm not going to get…you know. I want to keep playing basketball."

"My ears hear you," said Rashonda.

Tequila didn't answer. She couldn't fool her mother.

THE STARTERS

They listened to an 'old school' radio station playing songs from the 80's and 90's while driving to downtown Atlanta. Rashonda blasted a Mary J. Blige song. She sang each and every word. Tequila joined in. The closer they got to downtown Atlanta, the more excited they became. As soon as Rashonda pulled into the Greyhound bus station, Tevon spotted his aunts and cousins. "There they are! There they are!"

A few hours later, Rashonda's two sisters, two nieces and nephew sat in their living room. They were eating lasagna, chicken wings, bread, and salad. The small apartment was crowded with their family and all their belongings.

Smiling at her family, Rashonda screamed, "I'm so glad y'all here!"

"That was the longest, funkiest ride of my life. My first time out of Brooklyn, and it had to be on a filthy, smelly bus," said Beatty, Rashonda's oldest sister.

"You know we love you, girl," said Beatty's daughter, 18-year-old Nikita. "If I wasn't interested in seeing what I done heard about A-T-L, I wouldn't be here."

"I thought you came to see me play basketball," said Tequila.

"I know you got skills," Nikita said.

"I remember how you used to play with the boys," said Aunt Beatty. "You used to kick their asses."

"All the time," said Aunt Beatty's other daughter, Akeisha, 16-years-old.

When Tequila lived in New York, she and Akeisha did everything together except play basketball. Akeisha hated sports.

"Tequila was a tomboy from the day she was born," said Sheria, Rashonda's younger sister. "I used to be the girl basketball player in the family until you came along."

"I got my skills from Rasheed," said Tequila.

"Your daddy used to hoop," said Aunt Beatty.

"I don't remember," said Tequila.

"Until he got on that mess," said Aunt Beatty. "Messed him up real bad."

"Still on it," said Aunt Sheria.

"How do you know?" Tequila asked.

"They never get off," said Beatty.

"Do you ever see him or hear anything about him?" Tequila asked, curiosity written on her face.

No one answered.

"Y'all ain't right. Nobody *ever* answers my questions about my daddy," Tequila said. She looked around the room, waiting for somebody to say something. "I'm waiting. Tell me something."

"You'll be waiting all day, because we don't have anything to tell," said Aunt Sheria. "We need to start working on those signs."

"Yeah cuz, we're going to make big signs with your name," said Akeisha. "Let these Atlanta folks know that we representing Quila from New York."

"I can't believe you are here," Tequila said with an ear-to-ear grin. "Some of the other girls have big families and they come to watch her play. This Hispanic girl, Selena, she cool and all, but she got a big ass family and they are so loud and damn proud of her."

"We gonna be loud," said Aunt Beatty. "We are so proud of you, girl!"

"We gonna be yelling your name so loud that everybody will know who you are," said Akeisha.

"Go Quila," screamed Aunt Beatty. "I'll be shouting: Touch it, steal it, shoot it."

"Swish goes the ball," said Akeisha. "Swish…swish…swish."

"Yeah, it's Quila and the basketball," Aunt Sheria.

"Like Keelah and the bee?" asked Tequila. "That is so whack."

"I can spell the word she says in the movie: p-r-es-t-i-d-ig-t-a-t-i-o-n," said Tevon. "Want to know what it means?"

"No," Tequila and Akeisha said at the same time.

"Well, these people will definitely know who you are," said Aunt Beatty.

"They already know who I am," Tequila said. "We wouldn't be going to the final four if it weren't for me."

"Still cocky Quila," said Aunt Sheria.

Everyone laughed.

"I bet you I can you teach some moves," said Brandon, Sheria's nine-year-old son.

Tequila flicked her hands in the air, whisking away Brandon's comment. "In your dreams, boy."

"The team is staying at a hotel the night before the game," said Rashonda.

"Cool," said Brandon.

"I'm proud of Quila. Her grades are real good," said Rashonda.

"Still boy-happy?" asked Aunt Beatty.

"I ain't got nothing to say about that," said Rashonda.

"Sounds like you got a future down here," said Aunt Beatty.

"And not between your legs," said Sheria, laughing loudly.

"I wish you all could stay for the banquet," said Tequila.

"What's that?" asked Aunt Beatty.

"The end of the season banquet when they give out awards for best players of the season," said Tequila.

"Quila's going to win an award," said Tevon. "I know she is!"

"Aunt Shonda, just promise me that you'll take me to that mall where I can see a celebrity," said Akeisha. "I want to see somebody famous like TI or Usher or Ludacris or Waka Flaka."

"I want to see one of those Real Housewives from Atlanta," said Aunt Beatty.

"We'll go to Lenox Mall and Atlantic Station," Rashonda said. "Can't promise we'll see anybody famous, but that's where they are seen shopping and stuff."

"I'll be shopping at expensive stores when I'm playing in the WNBA," said Tequila. "My fame is on the way."

After watching two movies, everyone was tired and ready to go to bed. Blankets and comforters were spread out on the floor in

Tequila's room, where her female cousins were sleeping. Within a few minutes, her cousins were snoring.

Tequila heard someone creeping outside her door. She got out of bed and cracked open the door. Aunt Beatty was standing there.

"Aunt Beatty," she whispered. "You scared me. Why ain't you sleep?"

"I want to give you something," she whispered. "I don't want anyone else to know about it."

"Money?" Tequila asked, with a hopeful expression.

"No, a letter," said Aunt Beatty.

"From who?"

Aunt Beatty peeked over her shoulder to make sure no one was in the hallway before she handed Tequila a letter. "It's from your father,"

"What?" Tequila's sleepiness instantly evaporated. "A letter from Daddy?"

"Shh! I don't want your Mama to know. She can't forgive him for the things he's done," said Aunt Beatty. "But he can't help who he is."

Tequila usually felt numb about her mysterious father; she pretended not to feel anything about him. She looked at the letter. "He spelled my name wrong. He wrote T-e-k-e-y-l-a. How could he do that?" she asked, hurt and indignant.

"Don't get hung up on small stuff like that," Aunt Beatty tenderly said. "Your coach didn't, did she?"

"Coach O helped me. She made me study and learn." Her voice softened. "I know I'm not stupid anymore." Tequila stared at the letter, the way he wrote in small, capital letters.

"Are you going to read it?" Aunt Beatty asked.

Tequila tried to remember when she last saw her father, vaguely recalling his face. "After the game," she said. "Maybe I'll be ready then."

CHAPTER 44

CHASE

"Everyone came to see me play and they expect to see her," Chase said, pointing to the TV screen, showing Chase playing in the 6th grade.
"Her? You mean you?" Michael asked.
"I mean her. I was little and fast and good."
"You're an even better player."
"Against giants?"

Chase came out of the gym, her face dripping with sweat, holding a bottle of Gatorade. She didn't see the PantherTV crew while walking around the corner to the locker room.

"It's your turn, Chase," said Tianna, the reporter for PantherTV.

"You already filmed me," said Chase.

"That was at practice. We got shots of the whole team," said Tianna. "We're talking to all the girls on your team about the state championship."

"Oh, okay," Chase said, standing outside the door to the girls' basketball locker room.

"We got it on film that you are the fastest girl in practice. Marley's a close second but you win almost every time."

"Sometimes I slow up so they don't hate me."

"I just have to ask you a few questions," said Tianna.

"Okay." She wiped the sweat from her brow and self-consciously brushed her hair with her hands. She sipped some of her Gatorade. "This is my after work out look. Not very cute."

"Doesn't matter," said Tianna.

"Okay."

"So, the final four is three days away, how are you feeling?"

"We practiced early this morning and after school so I wasn't very happy about getting to school at six in the morning." Suddenly, Chase flashed a bright smile." But we don't have practice tomorrow. "Yay!"

"You know the school is rooting for the team."

"I love seeing the signs everywhere. Everyone is so pumped. It just keeps us so pumped up like we're really going to win."

"What are you doing different in practice?" asked Tianna.

"Running suicides is normal. But we have a pro trainer that's making us do different drills. He's really good," explained Chase. "He's teaching us some new things. Coach O is getting us ready to play like we're going to the Olympics."

"So do you think you're going to win?" asked Tianna.

"Yes, we're going to win. I have to say it! But that's what's exciting about sports, you never know what's going to happen in a game."

"She's right," said Heaven, putting her arms around Chase. "This is our baby baller."

"I won't be a freshman next year." Chase turned away from the camera and looked at Heaven. "So maybe they'll finally stop me calling baby baller."

"Maybe," said Heaven. "I just can't wait to win state! It will feel like Heaven! That's my name by the way."

"Like I don't know who you are girl," said Tianna. "We go way back to middle school."

Tianna signaled the cameraman to spotlight Heaven. She pointed the microphone at Heaven. "We hear that one of the players on the team you're playing against has been signed to a division one college. How does that make you feel?"

"I ain't scared," said Heaven. "We're not scared, right Chase?"

"Right," said Chase.

"Ready to win no matter who's on the court?" said Tianna.

"Hell, yeah," said Heaven. "We are the panthers, right? We score and win."

"We run the court," said Chase.

"Heaven, I noticed that you hardly ever smile when you're playing," said Tianna.

"Cause when I hit the court I'm in the zone. I don't have time to smile. I play defense mostly but when I get that ball in my hand, I'm going to score. That's what I'm going to do on Saturday."

"We'll be watching," said Tianna, signaling John to turn off the camera.

Michael Anderson knocked on Chase's door. "I have something for you."

Chase was sitting on the floor of her room, watching DVDs of her basketball games. Evan usually filmed the games. She rarely watched them: when the game was over, it was over. She didn't like to see herself playing, not even extraordinary basketball shots, phenomenal moves or running faster than lightening. She actually felt embarrassed to watch herself play. Her family often would show the recorded games to relatives and friends. After a while, Evan would just tape the games, label it with the date and team played, and file the DVD in the family room bookcase.

So, when Michael came into the bedroom and saw Chase watching one of her basketball games from two or three years ago, he was surprised.

"Hi, Daddy," Chase said, without looking away from the television.

"I bought you some cheesecake. It's the last piece."

"Thanks, Daddy," she said.

"There are a million people in the house and it was about to disappear into someone's mouth."

"A million people," she said, laughing at his playful exaggeration.

"Let me see: my brother and his two kids, my cousin and his daughter. Your mom's two sisters and kids. That's a million people. And we rented a van so we can get around."

"My room is going to be a wreck when all the girl cousins take over my room," complained Chase.

"Just two are staying in your room and three are staying in Blake's room."

"Blake's a slob and she doesn't care," said Chase. "They better not mess up my room."

"Don't worry about your room. They're here because of you. To see you play in the final four. They took time out of their schedules and traveled all the way here for you," said Chase's father.

Big tear drops suddenly plopped down Chase's face.

Michael put the cheesecake on her desk and sat on the floor beside her.

"What's wrong, sweetheart?" asked Michael.

"Look at me playing," she said, her eyes focused on the TV screen, showing footage of Chase running down the court like she had wheels for feet.

Michael watched the game: Chase was shooting a free throw shot and made both of them. Chase was in the sixth grade.

"Great shot!"

"Everyone came to see me play and they expect to see her," she said, pointing to the TV.

"Her? You mean you?"

"I mean *her.*" She pointed at the TV screen. "I was little and fast and good."

"You're still very good."

"But if I don't play better than her," she said, pointing to herself on the screen, "then I will be disappointing the millions of people in this house who came to see her."

"First, stop saying her when it's you. Second, you are older, have more skills and you're a better, stronger and smarter player."

"Daddy, do you know how many people are going to be at that game on Saturday? Important people like agents and scouts," said Chase. "I'll be playing against girls who are giants and have contracts already. I don't want to let the team down. What if I mess up?"

Michael rubbed his hand through his daughter's hair. "You're not going to mess up."

"You don't know that."

"I know that you are highly-skilled and highly-motivated. And when you get on the court, something clicks inside of you that turns you into basketball beast," her father said in a comforting voice. "I don't know where it comes from, Chase. You have it. It's a gift. It will be there tomorrow."

Letting the tears flow, Chase sobbed for a minute or two. "I don't want to disappoint my cousins and aunts and uncles. Even people from church are coming," said Chase.

"They are coming to support and encourage you. That's it. They will love and care about you no matter what happens."

Michael wiped the tears from her eyes.

"I'm proud of you pumpkin. I will always be proud of you."

"No matter what happens?" asked Chase.

"No matter what happens. You are my daughter and you are a talented basketball player. One game isn't going to take that away from you," said Michael. "You are my daughter. My little girl. I love you no matter."

Neither spoke for several minutes.

"Daddy, I feel guilty that I'm not happy about the Jamal situation."

Michal sighed. "I know... and I understand."

Chase stared into her father's eyes. "You're not mad at me for wanting him to go away?"

"I'm not the least bit mad. But this is not the time to think about Jamal. Totally get him out of your mind. Concentrate on the game. It's two days away."

"Okay."

Michael smiled at her. "You get to stay at that fancy hotel. That's pretty cool."

"Very cool," said Chase. "And then there's the banquet in two weeks."

"After the game, we're all going site seeing and shopping and just have fun together. It will be kind of like a family reunion."

Chase smiled. "I love family reunions."

Michael reached up from the desk and picked up the cheesecake. He sliced a piece with a fork, and then fed it to Chase. She chewed it and smiled. "Delicious!"

Just as he feed her another piece, Blake came in the room.

"You big baby!" screeched Blake. "You got Daddy in here feeding you food."

"Be quiet!" said Chase. "It's none of your business."

"Wait until I tell Mom. And Nicki, Lauren, Taylor, Tanessa, and Ellie will laugh at you."

"Blake, don't be a big mouth," said Michael in a calm voice.

Blake looked closer at Chase's face. She saw the tear stains on her cheeks. She looked at the TV screen: Chase playing in middle school.

She patted Chase's head. "Goodness, must I be the one to tell you that you are a superstar. I will let you be the superstar of the family on Saturday okay? Just Saturday."

Michael laughed along with his daughters.

"I don't need your permission to run the court," said Chase. "I love the game. I love playing basketball. And I love winning."

"Whatever, Chase. But you get to be the star on Saturday only. After that, I'm taking my crown back."

Chase laughed. "Thank you your highness."

"You're welcome, baby baller."

"You're the baby in the family!" screamed Chase.

CHAPTER 45

SELENA

Selena hopped in the front passenger seat of the van. As soon as she saw Juan's face she knew something was wrong. "¿Qué sucedió? What's the matter?" she asked.

"It's Papá," Juan said.

"Papá? Is he sick or in the hospital?" Selena asked.

"I'm ready! I'm ready," Selena said to Tianna, the PantherTV reporter who was standing outside of Selena's class.

"I was waiting for you," said Tianna. "Hey John, come over here so we can interview Selena."

"Rachel is in your class too, right?" asked Tianna.

"She should be here any sec," said Selena.

"John, zoom the camera on Selena's face," directed Tianna.

John pointed the camera, pressed the on button and captured Tianna and Selena in a frame.

Tianna said, "I've asked almost everyone on the team if they are ready for the game and they all say…"

"Yes, we're ready to win," said Selena with a wide smile that showcased her deep dimples.

"What's going to be different about Saturday's game?" Tianna asked.

"Everyone from everywhere is going to be there. They're going to be watching us like hawks," said Selena.

Tianna motioned for Rachel to join them. "Hey Rachel," said Tianna. "What do you think?" She directed John to point the camera at Selena and Rachel.

Rachel nervously looked into the camera's lens. "It's going to be tremendous pressure. We have to be calculating. Every move we make is going to count," said Rachel.

"The pressure will be on big-time," said Tianna.

"Yes, but we can handle pressure," said Selena. "We handled it in the sweet 16 games and the elite eight."

"Yeah, we have nerves of steel," said Rachel sarcastically. "I'm nervous before the beginning of every game."

"We're used to the pressure by now, right Rach?" said Selena. "Our nerves disappear as soon as we hit the court."

"Yeah, our nerves just magically go away," said Rachel. "Kind of like that blog reader who says we're aliens because we win."

Tianna laughed. "Some people will write anything."

"We know," said Selena. "But it doesn't matter because Coach O has a plan for everything. And she keeps up pumped up with quotes."

"Oh yeah? What's one of her quotes?" asked Tianna.

"She has so many," said Rachel. "Here's one: *Losers quit when they're tired. Winners quit when they've won.*"

"Riverbrook has come a long, long way. We're already winners," said Tianna.

"Ganadores," said Selena. "That's Spanish for winners."

"We look forward to Riverbrook winning state. The whole school," said Tianna. "Good luck!"

Practices for the final four were more intense than Selena ever experienced. Selena stayed after school for three-hour practices. She thought the other practices we're difficult, but Coach O had the team doing college-level drills and intense conditioning with a trainer.

Selena ran her last lap, feeling like she was going to faint. She collapsed on the floor, waiting to catch her breath and watching the other girls finish their laps. When everyone dropped to the floor or stumbled over to the benches, gasping for air she was relieved. Practice was finally over.

Coach Remmington looked at them, a wicked smile on her face.
"This isn't fun coach," said Tequila, breathing rapidly.
"Yeah, this miserable," said Zoey.
"Mucho exhausting," said Selena.
"Mucho, mucho," said Chase.
"I'm smiling because you're ready. You're ready for Saturday."
All the girls cheered—a tired cheer of relief.
"We won't have practice tomorrow. You can rest," said Coach O, with another wicked smile.
"Yeah!" the girls cheered with more enthusiasm.
"Rest your bodies and I'll see you Friday night," said Coach O. "Check in is at 6."

Selena sat outside the front of the school, waiting for her brother to pick her up. He was never late because he didn't want her sitting alone outside in the dark. She waved good-bye to everyone as they were leaving.

"You need a ride?" asked Marley, from the inside of her father's car.

"Juan should be here any minute."

"We'll wait," said Cooper, parking the car in front of the school, rap music blasting from the speakers.

Five minutes later, Selena's brother arrived in the Barney-colored purple van.

"See ya," Marley," Selena said, smiling.

"Bye," Marley waved, as her father sped out of the parking lot.

Selena hopped in the front passenger seat of the van. As soon as she saw Juan's face she knew something was wrong. "¿Qué sucedió? What's the matter?" she asked, a nervous feeling in the pit of her stomach.

"It's Papá," Juan said.

"Papá? Is he sick or in the hospital?" Selena asked.

"He's been taken!"

Selena drew her brows together, confusion on her face. "I don't understand."

"The immigration people came and took him. They might send him back to Mexico," Juan explained.

"No, el hermano. No Papá," Selena said, tears streaming down her face. "They can't take Papá away from us. My heart will stop," she said. "I will die if they do."

"Calm down, chicko."

"What are we going to do?" Selena sobbed.

"I don't know," Juan said. "I don't know yet."

"My game is in two days. I'm supposed to check in the hotel tomorrow at 6."

"I know."

"What am I going to do?" she asked.

"I don't know," said Juan.

Neither spoke for a few minutes.

"What would Papá want me to do?"

"He told me to keep the restaurant open. To keep doing what we do."

"So I should do normal stuff?"

"Yes."

"I'm going to call Coach O. She might be able to help Papá. She knows important people."

"You trust her?" asked Juan.

"Yes."

DARIAN-BALL-BLOG: NUMBER 19

Tomorrow is D-Day. Let's say V-Day for Victory.

Yes, tomorrow is the final four. We have to win two games.

Winning the first game means we get to play the second game.

Winning the second game means we will be C H A M P I O N S.

CHAPTER 46

"Coach O. We're been waiting for you so we can watch the DVD," said Chase.
"I don't want to see it," said Heaven. "I look a hot mess."
"I look fabulous," said Marley.
"I could watch it 1,000 times," said Tequila.
"My hair was redder than a Santa Claus suit," said Zoey.

The hotel elevator doors opened. Coach Olivia Remmington smiled at the last passenger on the elevator before getting out. She followed the directional signs to the room where her team was staying and turned left. She walked down the hallway and never had to pay attention to the numbers on the doors. She heard the girls—their voices louder and louder the closer she came to their room.

For a few minutes, she stood at the door and listened.
Voices.
Laughter.
Screams.
Giggles.
"Look at Marley."
"Tequila always got something cocky to say."
"The whole floor can probably hear Ja-Nay-A's big mouth."
"Heaven your mouth is bigger than mine."
"Remember when Rachel never said a word. Now she says a couple of paragraphs."
Snickers.

Shrieks.

"Bailey smiles a lot now. I think it has something to do with her private school boyfriend."

"You only have two months to give it up before you graduate."

"Shut up!"

Laughter.

The song "We run the court" was playing loudly.

"That's my joint. This one has the dub mix. Turn it up!"

After listening for a few more minutes, Coach Olivia knocked on the door.

Shellie Anderson opened the door. "Hey Coach O," she said screaming over the music.

Coach O walked inside the hotel room and observed the girls dancing around. Some saw her and waved. "Are you going to be okay by yourself with the girls?" asked Coach O.

"Bailey's mom is here in the hotel on stand-by," said Shellie. "But I'm fine. They're just boisterous."

"As usual," said Coach O.

"I spiked the punch," joked Shellie.

Coach O laughed. "Success is the best high."

"Would you like something to drink?"

"No thanks," said Coach O.

The girls gathered around the coach. Some of the girls gave Coach O hugs and high fives. Other girls greeted her with "hi, hey, what's up" or whatever greeting came from their lips.

"Coach O. We're been waiting for you so we can see the DVD the school made for us," said Chase.

"Want to watch it with us?" asked Shellie.

"Of course," said Coach O.

"Girls, we're going to watch the DVD the school made for us," announced Shellie.

"Okay," said Marley. "Kill the music, Heaven."

Heaven turned off the music.

"Can we show you our tattoos?" asked Marley.

The girls gathered around and showed Coach O their left arms with a panther's sleek body. The black panther's mouth was open, teeth showing like he was growling.

"This is so sick," said Zoey, smiling and rubbing her arm.

"Love it," said Layne.

"Shows we got team spirit," said Elise.

"My mom doesn't like tattoos, but she let me do it this time," said Chase.

"I can't wait to show my mom," said Rachel. "She's going to have a heart attack."

"Okay, okay," Coach O. "I think the tattoos are cool for the game tomorrow. I am not an advocate of tattoos, but that's my personal decision." Coach O slipped off her jacket, and angled the left side of her body to show the exact same tattoo.

"No you didn't," said Tequila. "Coach O is gangster."

"Oh yeah!" said the girls.

"It's a team thing," said Coach O. "Now let's watch the DVD."

"I don't want to see the interviews of us again," said Heaven. "I look a hot mess."

"I look good," said Marley.

"I could watch it 1,000 times," said Tequila.

"My hair is redder than Santa Claus's coat," said Zoey.

"It looks crayon red," said Layne.

Everyone laughed.

"Ready?" Chase asked as the girls found somewhere to sit: on the floor, sofa, or chair.

Coach O sat on the end of the sofa in the living room area of the three bedroom suite, next to Shellie.

"Hit it, girl," said Ja-Nay-A.

Chase pressed the on button and Riverbrook High School appeared on the screen in large letters with a blank panther under the school's name. A montage of shots: the girls' games, the team practicing, fans screaming, Coach O yelling, the scoreboard, the cheerleaders cheering, fans singing, the panther mascot dancing, fans dancing, kids chanting, different people singing the national anthem. Mixed in were shots of the team: getting on the bus, at practice, sitting near or listening to the coach. The interviews of the entire team by Tianna Dressler for PantherTV were mixed in with the video presentation. The different interviews with the girls brought roars of laughter from everyone on the team.

There was a series of brief comments from Riverbrook students, teachers and administrators. The comments were inspiring, encouraging, funny, proud, motivating. The DVD showed a picture of the girls' team, and then a tight shot of a banner that said 'Congratulations' and lots of signatures.

The DVD ended with the boys' varsity team singing the school's anthem.

The girls laughed when the DVD was playing, but when it ended, no one spoke a word.

The reality of tomorrow seized their thoughts.

The game was in fourteen hours.

Playing in the state championship was no longer a possibility.

It was a reality.

A next-day reality.

"Tomorrow is it," said Coach O, breaking the silence. "Game day. I know you're excited."

"Yes!" they all said.

"Scared…nervous?" asked Coach O.

Slowly each girl admitted to feeling anxious about tomorrow.

"I'm so proud of you girls. Very, very proud!" said Coach O. "I have a confession." She paused for a long moment. "I didn't think we would make it this far," she softly said.

"Really?" said Tequila.

"We weren't allowed to say the L word," said Heaven. "L O S E. I still can't say it."

"Don't," Coach O firmly said.

The girls looked at each other with bewildered expressions.

"I don't understand," said Chase.

"You didn't believe in us?" asked Marley.

"Well, I guess we proved you wrong!" said Ja-Nay-A with an indignant attitude.

"Listen girls. Please don't misunderstand me," said Coach O. "I believe in you. I picked each one of you for a different reason. I saw your individual skills and potential to be a team." She looked around at their serious faces. "I wasn't sure if *you* believed in…*you*."

She didn't speak for a few minutes. "To use my words I said 'expect the unexpected' and you gave me the unexpected and more."

"We did?" asked Elise.

"Some of you played last year and your record was horrible. The school hadn't won in years. So I wasn't sure if I could transform the team, the way you think as a team, and the way you think as individuals. I wasn't sure I could I make you think like winners in one season."

"That's why you picked some of us," said Tequila. "So our cockiness…I mean confidence could rub off."

"You made us remember all those quotes," said Chase.

"Because I wanted to change the way you think about yourself and your team. I already knew you were talented and athletic. Some of you don't know you truly talented you are. And some of you are still discovering your best skills."

"Brilliant and amazing," said Shellie. "Thank you for a great season."

"This was the best season ever," said Ja-Nay-A.

"I never thought I would play basketball and not be afraid the whole time I'm on the court," admitted Rachel.

"I know I'm a better player," said Elise.

"Everyone is better. You've grown as players and as young ladies," said Coach O. "Don't be afraid of tomorrow. Look at how far you've come. There is nothing to fear. When you get on the floor, get in the zone. Stay in the zone. Be the zone."

"Okay, Coach O," said Kaylee.

"No matter what happens tomorrow, you are the best players I've ever worked with," said Coach O.

"Coach O, you know we love you. I mean for real, for real," said Ja-Nay-A.

"We respect you," said Chase.

"Admire you," said Heaven.

"You made us work hard. I hated when you made me go to a tutor. I was so mad. But now I don't mind," said Tequila. "You helped me become a better player and a better student." She laughed and said, "I know I have a brain."

"You are awesome, dude," said Zoey.

"I like that our team is so diverse," said Layne. "I know my parents can't wait for me to get back to soccer, but I love hanging out with all my girls."

"Don't forget the drama," said Heaven. "It's been interesting sometimes."

Bailey laughed. "Real interesting."

"I've never been around so many different people except in class," said Kaylee. "It's been fun. We got to know each other and learn about different worlds."

"Thank you, girls. I think it was a good experience for all of us," said Coach O. "We all learned something and I just don't mean basketball." She paused. "I have something to give you girls. I have a card for each one of you."

"A card," said Tequila with disappointment.

"Yes a boring card. I want you to read it before you go to sleep. Here's the thing. Don't show the card to anyone else."

"Coach, you know how hard that's going to be!" complained Zoey.

"Expect the unexpected," said Heaven.

A half-smile appeared on Coach O's face. "Yes. But that's the deal. Don't show it to anyone else. Not even your mother."

"That means you Chase," said Marley.

Chase rolled her eyes. "I know."

"It's my personal note of inspiration. It's between me and each of you individually. Not to be shared."

"That's very sweet and thoughtful, Olivia," said Shellie.

The girls gathered around Coach O. She hugged each girl and handed them a card with their name written in fancy script.

The girls stayed near the coach as she gave out the cards. They closed in for a group hug. Some of the girls said, "We love you."

"Thank you, girls and," said Coach O, "I love you too."

"Lights out at ten. No music. No cell phones. No computers. No iPads. Nothing to distract you from thinking: 'I'm a winner. I'm a winner.' That should be your last thought before you go to sleep."

"They have to turn in their phones and stuff by 9:30. I will keep it in a locked drawer. Don't worry. They will be in bed by ten," said Shellie. "Breakfast will be delivered to the room at 6:45 and we'll leave for the van at 8."

"Good night, everyone," Coach O said, before heading to the door.

The girls didn't notice Coach O's eyes mist with tears. But Shellie Anderson saw them.

CHAPTER 47

FINAL FOUR PLAYOFFS

"Riverbrook scored the first basket made by Marley Woods," the announcer said.

"Now Cherrywood has scored for a tie," said the gritty-voiced announcer.

"Not even one minute into the game and it's a thriller."

Three games are held at the final four playoffs. Two separate games are held; two teams play each other to determine which two teams win and advance to the state championship game. The winners of the previous two games will then play against each other—the third game—the championship game.

Held at the Peachtree Civic Center, the venue was packed with different teams, friends, family, and fans from all over the state of Georgia, including coaches, college scouts, and media outlets.

At the beginning of the season, the Riverbrook team did not expect to make it to the final four playoffs.

But they were there—ready to go all the way to victory.

Nor did they expect to have such a large crowd of Riverbrook fans to watch them play. The number of Riverbrook fans proudly decked in the school's colors—red and black—dominated the civic center. They were proud and loud, ready and rowdy to cheer for Riverbrook's girls' varsity basketball game.

The Starters

Coach Olivia said very little in the locker room. She gave the girls a pep talk in the van on the way to the civic center. She reviewed strategies and plays, and expressed her heartfelt feelings for them. "I'm so proud of you, young ladies. You've come a long way and you've worked hard. You've done what I needed you to do. So, on the court today perform your..."

"Best always and all the time," the team simultaneously said, and then burst into laughter.

Twenty minutes later, the Riverbrook varsity girls' basketball team entered the floor through their designated entrance, dressed in their red and black uniforms with coordinated sneakers. They stood side-by-side showing off their panther tattoos before forming a circle and reciting their pre-game mantra and ending with a high-energy stomp and dance.

Riverbrook fans screamed like fans of a professional basketball team. They waved signs and chanted: "Riverbrook! Riverbrook! Riverbrook!"

The girls took their spots on the bench. A deep male voice announced that the game would begin with the presentation of both teams' starters.

"For Riverbrook High, the starters are:
Chase Anderson.
Marley Woods.
Bailey White.
Selena Sanchez, and
Tequila Paxton."

Each starter stood up as their names were called, smiling and waving as the crowd applauded. They ran down the row of two lines formed by team members standing directly opposite each other. The starters ran onto the court to the sound of cheering fans and cheer leaders.

The starters for the opposing team, Cherrywood High, were announced. Five minutes later, both sets of starters were on the floor positioned for the game tip-off.

The buzzer sounded.

Game on.

Riverbrook scored two points within the first thirty seconds of the game. It was an exciting, unpredictable game with both teams taking turns with alternating leads of only two or three points ahead of each other.

The starters demonstrated why they were the starters. They dribbled, rebounded, scored and played fierce, fundamental basketball with aggressive moves. Inspired by the presence of her family, Tequila played with her usual style of street ball and confidence but with a higher degree of showmanship. She toned down her aggressive moves after getting two fouls, but was an unstoppable force on the court. Chase was stealing balls, scoring lay-ups, and out running players. Bailey didn't play nervous like she did at the beginning of the year; she played with fierceness. Marley displayed her basketball intelligence—anticipating and out thinking the other team.

Even though Coach O had given Selena the option not to play, Selena refused to sit on the bench. She and her family were extremely worried about her father, but the Sanchez family stood up through the entire game, screaming Selena's name. There were moments when Selena was distracted; the thought of her father being deported would make her mind go blank. Coach Olivia would sense that Selena had lost her focus and would send in Ja-Nay-A or Heaven. Seeing her family and noticing Miguel holding up a sign with her name, buoyed Selena's spirits and jolted her confidence to keep playing.

During the game, Coach O substituted some of the starters with Ja-Nay-A, Heaven, Zoey, and Layne but not for long. The game was too intense, the score was too close.

With five seconds on the clock in the last quarter, Riverbrook was winning by two points. The opposing team had the ball and made an amazing, phenomenal play: a player passed the ball all the way to the other side of court, with missile-like speed. The girl who caught the ball, was positioned on the right wing of the basket for a three-pointer. She shot the ball. The ball dropped through the basket just as the buzzer sounded.

Riverbrook lost by one point.

A buzzer-beating win.

DARIAN-BALL-BLOG: NUMBER 20

Our girls' basketball team made it all the way to the state championship. Last year we only won two games, but this year we won 15 games and competed in the regional championships. We advanced to the Sweet Sixteen and won the Elite Eight to make it to the state championship level. How freaking awesome!

Congratulations to every player on the team! I bow down to Coach O because I showed her no respect at the beginning of the season. I saw with my own eyes how much she cares about her players and winning. Notice I said players first and then winning. I still don't understand why a basketball professional with her credentials would waste her time at our high school, but she has made a huge….huge…huge difference. It showed from the moment she arrived. Maybe she's doing the 'give back to the community' thing, but whatever her reason, I appreciate it. I'm going to say, we all appreciate Coach Remmington.

Yeah, I didn't start the blog talking about the fact that we lost by one point. But we haven't been to the final four in forever and we came so freaking close to winning that I don't even care that we didn't win. There's always next year. So, I'm putting all the schools in the state of Georgia on notice: Riverbrook is THE team to watch, respect and fear. I've heard two of our seniors might even get basketball scholarships!

The starters brought the heat. Tequila was definitely in her basketball zone and Selena (even with her personal drama that I won't put on blast) was delivering 3-pointers like it was nothing. Chase was a gazelle, speeding past players and stealing balls. Bailey is always consistent—a quiet force that can't be ignored. Marley just outsmarts the other players with unpredictable moves. And the rest of the team was on fire: it was in their eyes and every move they made. We applaud you: Layne, Zoey, Heaven, Ja-Nay-A, Kaylee, Rachel, and Elise We had the game on lock—if it wasn't for that buzzer beater three-pointer.

We made history today. We are going all the way next year!

Comments

allyMM: One second and your whole world can change. Amazing and scary.

Mindyourbiz: Much love Riverbrook girls!

Basketqueen: We will take it to the bank next year. I'm putting money on it!

Lovehighsh: The stands were packed with Riverbrook fans. We definitely represented. It was unbelievable. It was exciting! It was thrilling!

Hategirlsbb: I swear I my heart stopped when the three pointer dropped through the net on the buzzer. That was so unfair. I couldn't believe my eyes. I even cried!

Ibelieve: Alien madness. They will be back!

Ilovesports: We love you, Selena. Hope everything works out for your family.

Highlikeplanes: The girls played like pros. Coach O is a force to be reckoned with.

Inthezone: I'm sure talent scouts were peeping our girls. Spotlight on Riverbrook.

BallBasket: Darian, who are you? How do you know so much? Are you going to reveal your identity?

Dribblebb: Yeah, you know too much. Are you one of the players playing us?

Basketballs: Don't matter. I just love seeing those girls hoop. They are real ballers. They bring the heat—blazing heat!

EPILOGUE

The Riverbrook girls' end-of-the-year basketball banquet was held at an upscale dining restaurant in a private room. It was a major celebration and the girls were allowed to invite family, relatives and friends. Different groups and individuals who supported the team were also invited: school administrators, the cheerleaders, PantherTV crew, Riverbrook News, media outlets and other groups.

The twelve girls dressed up for the occasion as if they were going to a party. The private room was decorated with basketball-themed accessories, but with a touch of elegance. The girls gathered at a separate table specifically designated for the team. Their family and friends sat at different tables throughout the private room. Printed programs were on every table, highlighting the events for the evening.

Marley Woods arrived with her father and his latest girlfriend Angela, along with Egypt, Uncle Kenneth, and Aunt Lydia. They found an empty table, and Marley chatted with them for a few minutes before going over to the designated team table.

Marley hugged her teammates. They were all excited to be at the banquet, eager to find out who was going to receive awards. They complimented each other on their new outfits, which they all admitted to buying especially for the banquet.

Near the back of the room, a video screen showed pictures of the season. There were over two hundred shots from the games with

THE STARTERS

comments and highlights of the season. The girls watched the slide show, remembering the good and bad moments from the season.

With the arrival of all the players, the hostesses directed the team to a long banquet table—showcasing a delicious display of different types of foods. The basketball team—the stars of the evening—lined up at the buffet table first, fixing their plates, and then returning to their table. Next: parents, family members, friends and guests stood in line, prepared their plates and took seats at the tables scattered around the restaurant's private dining area.

When everyone was seated at their tables, Coach Olivia Remmington stood in the middle of the room, holding a microphone. She was fashionably-dressed in a beautiful black dress and high black heels.

"Welcome, welcome everyone to our basketball banquet." She smiled, surveying the room full of people. "I'm so glad all of you could come and share in this joyous occasion. We are here to celebrate these beautiful young ladies and their amazing athletic abilities and this victorious season."

There was a big round of applause.

"This has indeed been an incredible year. I'd like to thank the parents for their outstanding support. Parents are fundamental to our success and I humbly thank you for the privilege of working with your wonderful daughters and...for allowing me to coach in my own—sometimes controversial—style."

The parents stood up and acknowledged Coach Olivia with a thunderous applause.

"We've had some interesting things transpire during the season and you parents have been extraordinarily understanding and encouraging. I said 'expect the unexpected and the unexpected and unpredictable really happened," she said.

Everyone stood up and clapped.

"I'd like to take this time to acknowledge the presence of our athletic director and the principal. Your support for my "new jack style"—as some people has called my coaching approach—has empowered me and paved the way for our wonderful journey.

Everyone applauded again.

"By now, you're probably tired of hearing my voice. So, I'll let you enjoy your meals and then we'll present the awards." She laughed, and then said, "I know you're looking forward to our final event. We're going to dance to the electric slide and the wobble." She glanced at the girls table. "Yeah, I know about the wobble."

The girls laughed.

"Everyone has to dance, even if you've never done it before. Even you Henry Nickels," Coach Olivia said, referring to the athletic director who looked rhythm less and clumsy. "Enjoy your dinner. Be talking to you soon."

"This looks delicious," Cooper said to his girlfriend-of-the-month, a beautiful, light-skinned woman named Angela Johnson. Egypt took a bite of the pasta and said, "Yummy." They started discussing the basketball season when Franchesca approached their table.

"Hello, Cooper," Franchesca said.

He glanced at his ex-wife. "Hi." Nodding to the woman next to him, he said, "This is Angela, and this is Franchesca, my ex-wife."

The women exchanged polite "hellos."

"Hi, Egypt, how are you?" Franchesca asked.

"I'm good. Just enjoying myself. The food is to die for," gushed Egypt.

"How have you been, Kenneth?" Franchesca said to Egypt's father.

"Living and surviving," answered Kenneth.

She made eye contact with Lydia. "Still enjoying being a principal?"

"Loving every minute of it," Lydia said. "I hear you're doing well."

"You know me," Franchesca said. "I stay ahead of the game." She redirected her gaze to Cooper. "I thought I would give you a heads up, Cooper," she said, placing an envelope on the table.

Cooper looked at her suspiciously before opening the envelope. Within ten seconds of reading the first page, he jumped up from his seat, his eyes filled with rage. He saw Marley looking at them from across the room, and regained his composure. He slowly sat down, and forced a smile on his face. "I will fight you on this!"

"Of course, you will," Franchesca said. "And…you will lose."

"All of a sudden you want custody of Marley and you think you're going to win?" he asked, shocked by her audacity.

"I'm a lawyer, baby."

"You forgot that you chose partial custody," said Cooper. "You did not want full custody when she was only seven-years-old. It's not going to happen now."

"I need to get to know my daughter," Franchesca said, with a twinge of regret in her voice.

"You didn't come to her championship game. It was her most important game of the season. How could you not be there? Other families flew or drove hundreds of miles. Tequila's family took a twenty-one hour bus trip to see her play. What's your excuse?"

"It's not my fault they can't afford to fly," she said. "I had to take care of business. I don't have to explain myself to you."

"Marley does not want to live with you," he said. "You won't win this."

"Yes I will," she said, with a heavy dose of confidence.

Cooper stood up. Hostility and rage was on his face. "You better not say anything to her today."

She raised an eyebrow. "Don't tell me what to tell my daughter."

"She's having fun. Leave her alone!" he insisted.

Kenneth stood up next to Cooper, trying to calm his brother down.

"Please Franchesca," said Lydia. "Let Marley have fun. This is a special night for her."

Cooper looked over at Marley and realized that she was watching them. He took a deep, calming breath, but his eyes were glowing with anger….cesspools of anger.

Franchesca noticed that Marley kept looking at them. When they made eye contact, Marley accidentally dropped her plate. A waitress immediately came to assist her.

"Okay, I won't say anything to her today," said Franchesca.

Cooper tapped Egypt's shoulder. "Don't you say anything, either! Let Marley enjoy the banquet."

"Okay, Uncle Coop," Egypt said, struggling to hold back her tears. She knew Marley was going to be devastated.

Lydia said, "We mean it, Egypt. Don't say a word about this to Marley."

"Yes ma'am," Egypt said, feeling sad for her cousin.

"Just to let you know," Franchesca said. "I will fight for her."

"You will lose!" Cooper said, his voice louder than he intended.

Franchesca walked away from Cooper's table and sat down with Sterling. They were sitting with Bailey's family; she wouldn't have chosen to sit with them, especially near two small children. But Sterling had struck up a conversation with Bailey's stepfather Robert.

When she returned they were discussing immigration laws. Confused by the seriousness of the topic, Franchesca asked, "What's going on? Why such a heavy conversation at a basketball banquet?"

"Selena's father was taken into custody by immigration," said Jennifer.

"I know that's difficult for her and her family," said Franchesca.

"Very difficult," said Jennifer.

"And complicated," said Franchesca. She was hesitant to express her unsympathetic views on immigration.

"The coach is getting an attorney who specializes in immigration law. She has some good connections," Robert explained. "I'm glad she's willing to help Selena."

"They're going to need a very high-powered attorney with experience and success handling cases like this," explained Franchesca. "I know some attorneys who specialize in immigration law that can help."

"Selena is devastated. It's amazing that was she able to play so well in the championship game even though her world is crashing around her," said Jennifer.

"That has to be devastating," agreed Franchesca. Hearing Coach Olivia's voice, Franchesca was relieved to have something different to talk about.

"It's time for the awards," said Coach Olivia standing in the middle of the room, holding a microphone near her mouth. "I'm not going to talk long. I think you'd rather socialize with each other." She looked over at the girls, and observed them nodding their heads in agreement.

"The Best Offense award goes to Tequila Paxton," said Coach Olivia. "She's cocky as can be, but she brings street skills to the court in a way that I respect. She rebounds her own rebounds. She had the most shots. Another player was very close."

Everyone clapped as Tequila walked over to receive her award. She hugged the coach. "I knew I was going to win this award," she said with a goofy grin. "Thank you, Coach O."

"You're welcome."

"Coach O, can I say something?" asked Tequila.

"Yes ...be mindful of your words."

Tequila giggled. "I just want to thank you for making me study and get better grades. I'll be straight honest. I was mad as hell...Hades when you benched me and made me get a tutor... but I understand why you did and I thank you. And where's my girl Lindsey?"

Lindsey stood up, her table occupied by other cheerleaders.

"Thanks for being the best damn tutor on the planet."

The cheerleaders stood up and did a mini-cheer for the basketball team.

Everyone clapped when the cheerleaders were done.

"Please, I need to say something else," said Tequila.

"Okay, it's the players' night," said Coach O. "But keep it brief."

"I want to thank my mom Rashonda Paxton," said Tequila. "My mom always says she's my number one fan. I really appreciate her support. But I haven't made it easy for her. She's wanted me to take school seriously and I never did. I know I drove her crazy. But she stayed on my butt even when I was hard-headed brat. But I have good grades Mama for the first time in my life," said Tequila. "Thank you, Mama."

Tequila ran over to the table and gave her mother a hug; both had tears in their eyes.

"Come back over here," Coach Olivia said. "I want all the winners together."

As Tequila walked back over to the center of the room, Coach Olivia said, "That was beautiful Tequila."

"You're welcome," said Tequila. "Can we move on?" Coach O asked, smiling with misty eyes.

Tequila shook her head.

"So, let's get to the next award. The best defensive player goes to... the youngest player on the team."

"Yeah!" Chase screamed, along with her sister Blake.

"That's my little sis!" said Evan.

"Defense, defense," said Grammy.

Chase walked up to the coach. "She's the baby baller on our team, but she's a fierce little player," said Coach O. "She rarely lets a player run past her and she never gives up. I love her spirit."

"Thank you," Chase said, giving Coach O a warm hug.

"You're welcome," said Coach O.

"I also thank my family for their support and my teammates for accepting me even though I'm just a freshman," said Chase.

"Don't go anywhere girls," she said to Tequila and Chase. "All award winners, please stay up here until we're done."

"My coach's award goes to...Marley Woods. She's got what I call extraordinary basketball IQ," said Coach O. "Marley is smart as a whip and she applies it to her playing style and takes basketball moves to another level."

"Yes! Yes!" said Marley, as she walked over to Coach O. "Thank you, coach." She took the award and hugged the coach and other team mates who had received awards.

"The MVP award goes to Bailey White. She didn't think she belonged on the team, but she proved to be a valuable asset. She's there when and where you need her to be," said Coach O.

Bailey walked over to Coach O. "Thank you Coach O for believing in me," she said as tears started coming down her face. "I was scared to be on the team. I thought the other players were going to hate me. But I knew it was an honor for you to select me. So I had to do my very best to meet your expectations and," she laughed, "do the unexpected."

Bailey gave Coach O a long, warm hug.

"I have another award," said Coach Olivia. "The most improved player award. It goes to Heaven. You didn't think I didn't see you, but I did. You have the heart of a player and the soul of an athlete."

Heaven jumped up from her seat. She ran over to the coach, almost knocking her down. "Sorry," she said. "I just wasn't expecting this," she said. "Thank you so much. You know I was so mad at first, but I learned a lot. I'm a better player," said Heaven. "Thank for believing in me and seeing my potential."

"I have to acknowledge our team managers: Adrina Montgomery who goes by Rina and Poppy Parsons," said Coach Olivia. "They provide behind the scenes support that helps the team concentrate on their skills."

The girls lined up as parents took group pictures and individual pictures of the players who received awards.

"Before we end the evening, I want to acknowledge the seniors who are graduating," said Coach O. "I'll begin with Bailey White. She's didn't think she was good enough to be a starter. But I knew with some pushing she would believe in herself the way I do. Her confidence grew in every game. She knows she's a baller. Come up here, girl."

Bailey walked over to the coach and they embraced.

"Thank you for a wonderful season. Let's congratulate Bailey on her acceptance to the University of North Carolina. She was awarded an academic scholarship for a 4.3 GPA and partial athletic scholarship. She hasn't decided whether she wants to play basketball in college."

"Layne, please join us," said Coach Olivia, motioning Layne to the middle of the room. "Layne Evansville is also a senior. She has a 3.5 GPA and hasn't decided what school she's going to. She has several soccer scholarships to consider," said Coach O. "Layne is an excellent fundamental basketball player, but I think she's going to end up on a soccer field."

Layne stood beside Coach O. "Thanks coach. I had a great year and I learned so much. You are the best."

"Soccer, Layne, how could you choose soccer over basketball?" asked Coach O.

"I've been playing since I was four," said Layne.

"I'm just kidding," said Coach O. "I played overseas and I learned to really enjoy the game and have friends who play. So if you're going to play soccer…be the best soccer player you can be."

"We have another soccer traitor. Little Miss Red-Head. Zoey Burkhart. She's a knee-kicking soccer player."

Zoey joined the girls "Just stay out of my way," she said, causing an eruption of laughter.

"Thanks Coach O for a wonderful season and for broadening my horizons about different races and cultures."

"Thank you, Zoey," said Coach O, surprise in her voice.

"I know everyone thinks I'm a wild girl, but I have my serious moments," Zoey said. "Believe it or not, I want to be a psychologist."

Some of the girls at the table giggled.

"Do you know how many crazy people are in the world? I'm going to have thousands of clients," she said, laughing.

"Zoey always makes us laugh," said Coach O. "Thank you for being an important member of the team and helping us go to the final four."

"Our next senior is Ja-Nay-A Banks. Come join us," she said to Ja-Nay-A. "I must admit, we've had an interesting relationship. Ja-Nay-A is extremely passionate about basketball. I'm pleased to announce that Ja-Nay-A has accepted an athletic scholarship to Peach College, where she will major in education."

Ja-Nay-A joined the group of seniors. "Coach, thanks for everything. We've come a long way, but I really appreciate everything you've done for me," said Ja-Nay-A.

"You're welcome," said Coach O. "I admire your determination."

"I know I shocked everyone when I didn't stack the team with seniors. That's the norm, right? I have a vision far beyond this year. My goal is to groom a team of phenomenal basketball players," she said. "Now, let's congratulate our seniors and wish them well on the next phase of their lives."

Bailey, Layne, Zoey and Ja-Nay-A stood together as everyone clapped for them, and smiled for the cameras for the Kodak-moments.

"Two more things, next year is a new season," Coach Remmington said. "No one's spot is guaranteed." She saw the surprised reactions on the players' and parents' faces. "So practice hard this summer," she encouraged.

"I would also like to introduce you to my daughter," she said, motioning to a pretty, tall girl who was sitting near the back. "This is my daughter Alina. She's been living in Germany, but she may be coming to Riverbrook next year."

"Hello everyone," Alina said, shyly.

"I've been reading Darian's Blog, like everyone else," said Coach Remmington. "No one seems to know who she is. It really doesn't matter—she gave us more exposure. I do know my girls are not aliens as someone commented in the blog."

Everyone laughed.

"We had an outstanding season and next year will be even better! We'll give the blogger new and more interesting stuff to write about. Whoever that person is!"

Everyone in the room stood up, clapping and screaming: "Riverbrook! Riverbrook! Riverbrook!"

When everyone sat back down, Coach Remmington signaled to the DJ to start playing music. "Now for dessert and dancing."

Chase went to the dessert table and placed several brownies on a plate. She returned to the table where her family and friends were sitting, along with Kendall and Ms. Regina. She put the plate of brownies in the middle of the table. "This is for everyone who wants a brownie."

"We should be getting you the brownies," said Michael. "Congratulations on winning your award, baby." He hugged her tightly. "You still are the little girl on those DVDS, just better," Michael whispered, bringing a smile to Chase's face.

"I'm proud of you," said Shellie.

"I knew you would win," said Grammy.

"Congratulations," said Ms. Regina.

"You know what I'm happiest about?" Chase said.

"You're not going to Disney," said Evan. "Only on TV."

"Kendall doesn't have to move!" Chase announced, her eyes radiating more excitement than when she received the award.

Kendall stood up in the chair and screamed, "I'm not moving."

"Regina, I'm so happy for you," said Shellie.

"Believe it or not, I just found out today and I didn't want to talk about it right now. This is Chase's moment."

"I'm so glad," said Shellie, smiling with delight. "Congratulations, girl." Shellie looked at Kendall. "You girls are going to be crazy."

"Regina, that's got to be a big weight off your shoulders," said Michael.

Chase bit into a second brownie. "Just color me happy!"

"If you don't stop watching that movie," said Blake. "It is so corny!"

"I like the movie too," said Kendall. "You just don't get it."

"Whatever!" said Blake.

"We love *Pretty Woman*," said Grammy. "Don't we, Chasey? We watch it all the time."

"Grammy's favorite part is when Julia Roberts sings that song by Prince in the bathtub."

Grammy closed her eyes and started singing, "*I just want your extra time and your ...kiss*," and then she made kissing sounds with her lips.

The Anderson family shook their heads, cracking up at the same time.

"Sorry you didn't win arrepentido, chica bonita," Miguel said to Selena, while standing near the dessert table.

"I'm not sad," said Selena. "I was just happy to be on the team. Not everyone can win an award. "El comprendo."

"That's a good attitude," Miguel said.

She flashed a grin. "There's always next year."

"You always see the sun even in the dark," said Miguel.

"I can't find the sun without Papá," said Selena. "Mi familia está preocupado."

"I know everyone is worried," said Miguel. "We still look for the sun."

"Sí," said Selena. "Coach O is going to help us. I trust her. She knows a super good lawyer who's not going to charge us."

"Your Papá will be home and everything will be okay."

Selena nodded. "That would make me so happy."

"Let's be happy for now. Enjoy the party, okay?"

"Sí," she said, as Miguel kissed her on the cheek.

Bailey walked over to her family's table. She was greeted by hugs and kisses. Her father, mother and stepfather all said, "Congratulations," at the same time. It wasn't planned and everyone laughed.

Bobby, Jr. said, "You are a winner."

"Thank you," she said.

"Mommy, I didn't say that other word. I didn't say wussy," said Bobby, Jr.

Jennifer covered her mouth, not wanting her son to see her laugh.

"Don't say that word," Robert firmly said "Not ever."

"Okay, Daddy."

Darby tugged on Bailey's arm, so she picked her up. Darby said, "Wussy," in a very loud voice.

"She can't pronounce my name, but she can say something like that," said Bailey. "If River was here, she'd be on the floor laughing."

Jennifer, Scott and Robert laughed.

"If they can laugh, I can laugh," said Matthew Charles.

Bailey laughed. "Why not?"

"Congratulations on your award, baby," said Matthew. He kissed Bailey on the cheek. "MVP. That's a big award."

"Thank you," said Bailey.

Matthew stroked her cheek and whispered in Bailey's ear: "You are so sexy."

Darby pushed Matthew's hand away from Bailey's face.

"I'll take her," said Jennifer, as Bailey handed her little sister to her mother.

"I'm afraid to hug you in front of your family," said Matthew.

Scott cleared his throat.

"I'd like to take her to the prom with your permission, sir," said Matthew.

"You can," said Scott. "And that's all I say for now."

"I was just talking to your Mom and her boyfriend," said Lindsey.

"Ugh, I can't stand Cedric so I'm not talking about him today." Congratulations on your award," said Lindsey. "I think it's really OUR award." "In your dreams," said Tequila. "Thanks for coming to the banquet."

"Girl, thanks for making me cry, getting all sentimental," said Lindsey. "I was about to say: girl you from New York stop all that blabbering."

"You are too crazy," teased Tequila. "You know how to do the electric slide?"

"Yes!" Lindsey said.

"They're going to be playing it in a little while. Coach O wants us all to dance."

"Well, let's party," said Lindsey.

"My mother is looking forward to it. She loves the electric slide." said Tequila. "We won't be able to get her off the dance floor."

Tequila went over to the table where her mother sat with Cedric and Tevon. They had already congratulated Tequila on winning the Best Offense award, and were eating some of the desserts: coconut cake, chocolate fudge cake, and brownies. Tevon was biting into a brownie while searching through Tequila's purse. "Hey!" She grabbed it from him. "Don't look at my stuff."

Tequila checked the inside zippered pocket to see if her father's letter was still there. It was in a separate envelope she had put it in. She wasn't ready to open it. Not yet. Not when she was enjoying the glory of a successful basketball season.

"Never go in a woman's purse," Cedric said.

Tequila glared at Cedric, even though she agreed with what her mother's lusting-eyes boyfriend said. She was afraid that Tevon was going to find the letter that she took out of the zippered compartment of the purse every night. She stared at the letter, the unfamiliar handwriting. She had the letter for almost two weeks, but still was afraid to open it. At that moment, she decided to stop carrying the letter around until she was ready to read it. She planned to tuck it under her mattress, until she found the nerve to read the words of her father—a stranger.

"I knew you were going to win," said Diante, he said, hugging her. "Congratulations!"

"Thank you," she said.

"We'll have to do some celebrating," said Diante, as they walked away from the table.

"I heard the miniature golf place is open until 2 in the morning," said Tequila.

"I could probably beat you too," said Tevon. They looked down; neither knew he was standing there.

"Get out of my business," said Tequila.

"I'll tell Mommy about the kisses."

Marley went over to her Dad's table. She had noticed the exchange between her mother and father. "What were you and Franchesca talking about?" she asked.

"Nothing for you to think about," Cooper said, refusing to ruin Marley's moment of happiness.

Surveying the faces around the table, Marley was unconvinced. "Are you sure?"

"I'm sure," said Aunt Lydia.

Marley flashed an inquisitive stare at her cousin Egypt. "You'll tell me what's going on, right E?"

Egypt shook her head, remembering the promise she'd made to her uncle and mother. Besides, she really didn't want to upset Marley tonight, and she would eventually find out anyway. She knew that the battle for Marley would be ugly. As much as she admired Franchesca's career success, Egypt hoped that this was one case she would lose. Even though Marley missed her mother and they had a love-hate relationship, Marley was happier living with her father. Egypt knew it, so did everyone else—everyone except Franchesca.

"I'm very proud of you. You still got A's and you won an award." Cooper hugged her tightly. "I love you, baby."

"Love you too, Daddy," She looked over at Coach O's table. "Are you surprised that Coach O has a daughter and she's never mentioned her before?"

"A little," said Cooper. "But people have complicated lives."

A cynical—not joyous—laugh escaped from Marley's lips. "Like us," she Marley, reflecting on their chaotic, complicated lives.

"Yeah, girl," said Egypt.

"So you think her daughter plays basketball?" Marley asked.

"She's got the height. She's almost six feet," said Egypt.

"Who knows?" Cooper asked.

"We'll find out next season," said Marley.

"I heard she plays," said Quinton.

"Hey, I didn't know you were here," said Marley.

"Slipped in when the awards were given. Congratulations Marley, Marley, Marley," said Quinton. "Not surprised."

Cooper laughed. "I might have to watch out for Quinton. Not everyone calls her Marley, Marley, Marley."

Quinton smiled. "M is going to be my girl."

"You got to check with me first," said Cooper.

"I know Mr. Cooper," said Quinton. "There are going to be rules."

"You got to follow my rules."

"For Marley, I will," said Quinton.

Coach Olivia announced that the DJ was going to play the 'electric slide.' "Everybody report to the dance floor," said Coach O. "We will be playing the electric side and other songs. "I'm taking my heels off because it's time to party."

Some the girls removed their shoes. People started moved to the dance area.

"And the girls probably want to do the South Dallas Swag," said Coach O. "So DJ get ready to play that too."

The girls all laughed.

"She's got a funny side," said Cooper.

"Come on E," said Marley. "Let's show them how to do this dance."

-- TO BE CONTINUED --

THE STARTERS

BOOK 2: UNLEASHED
COMING 2013

ROBIN ALLEN

THE STARTERS

BOOK 2: UNLEASHED PREVIEW

DARIAN-BALL-BLOG

School has been out for just three weeks than and already there is a rumor that Coach Olivia Remmington isn't coming back. I don't know if it's true, but I've heard it from several sources. I sound like a journalist. Guess what? That's what I want to do after college.

Someone said that the school was getting applications from basketball coaches from other schools. I'm not sure what that really means.

I don't know why Coach O would leave after accomplishing so much. Maybe it's personal…like she's getting married or something. I do know that if Coach O doesn't come back we are going to be in big trouble. Some of best girls have graduated, so probably half the team will be gone. I'm guessing that Marley, Tequila Chase, Kaylee, Rachel, Selena, Elise and Heaven will be back. (I heard that Heaven might be moving over the summer.) They are great players, but we didn't start winning until Coach O was running the basketball team.

I heard another rumor. Since we almost won the state championship, girls from other schools are moving into the school district so they can play with Coach Olivia. Other schools know we got real talent and lots of attention and that means coaches and scouts will be checking us out.

If Coach Olivia doesn't come back, the girls' basketball team won't be the same. They'll suck again. I don't believe another coach would have her magic touch. Last basketball season was so exciting and fun. I don't want to go back to being a loser team. I want another winning season. I know the school does too!

I hope it's just a rumor. A rumor that's a nest of lies. Lies, lies, lies.

THE STARTERS
BOOK 1: UNEXPECTED
READER BOOK CLUB

Get a group of friends together to talk about **The Starters – Book 1: Unexpected.** Discussion questions are listed below. Feel free to add other questions to the list. Talk about other subjects in the book and in your personal lives. Share stories and have fun!

Check out the Reader Book Club: www.thestartersbook.com

DISCUSSION QUESTIONS

1. Who was your favorite character? Why?
2. Who was your least favorite character? Why?
3. What character(s) made you laugh?
4. Did you like Coach Olivia? Why or why not?
5. Do you know someone similar to a character or characters in the book?
6. What was your favorite scene?
7. Do you play sports in school? Do you like or dislike your coach?
8. What did the players learn about themselves from being on a team?
9. What did you think about the starters' relationships with their families?
   - Bailey
   - Marley
   - Selena
   - Chase
   - Tequila
10. Do you think it's difficult to meet academic requirements while playing sports in school?
11. Who do you think changed the most during the season?
12. Do you think the blogger is one of the players? Who do you think is the blogger?

13. Have you ever been jealous of a friend or team mate?
14. What are your plans after high school?
15. Add your own questions. Talk about other issues in the book

Made in the USA
Middletown, DE
03 December 2014